PETER ROBINSON

CARELESS LOVE

McCLELLAND & STEWART

Library and Archives Canada Cataloguing in Publication
is available upon request

ISBN: 978-0-7710-7277-2
ebook ISBN: 978-0-7710-7278-9

Jacket design by Kelly Hill
Jacket art © Lyn Randle / Trevillion Images

Typeset in Plantin Light
Printed and bound in Canada

McClelland & Stewart,
a division of Penguin Random House Canada Limited,
a Penguin Random House Company
www.penguinrandomhouse.ca

1   2   3   4   5   22   21   20   19   18

Penguin
Random House
McCLELLAND & STEWART

To Sheila

"Come all you fair and tender maids
That flourish in your prime.
Beware, beware, keep your garden fair.
Let no man steal your thyme.
Let no man steal your thyme."

"The Sprig of Thyme" (traditional)

I

Broad ribbons of fog lingered in the valley bottom as Detective Superintendent Alan Banks drove the unmarked police car slowly along Belderfell Pass, cursing the fact that his beloved Porsche was in the garage for its MOT. Fortunately, visibility was good on the winding road, about halfway up the steep fell side. Though it was only three o'clock in the afternoon, it was already starting to get dark as the sun sank below the hills to the west.

'Here they are,' said DS Winsome Jackman as they came around a bend and saw a patrol car stopped by a metallic blue Megane, reducing the two lanes to one.

Banks brought the car to a halt by the tapes, and he and Winsome got out, flashing their warrant cards. One of the uniformed officers was talking to a woman beside the Megane, while his partner kept an eye on the road in order to warn any oncoming traffic to slow down.

All three looked twice at Winsome. Not only because she was beautiful, which she was, but because it wasn't often you saw a six-foot-tall black woman on Belderfell Pass. Or anywhere else in the Eastvale area, for that matter. As usual, Winsome took it in her stride, edging to the sideline and taking out her notebook and pen.

Tucked away in a lay-by cut into the hillside, half hidden by shrubbery, was a damaged Ford Focus, the result of a minor crash. Nobody had been seriously injured, but the car was a write-off, its radiator grille crushed, bonnet buckled and the engine hanging half out of one side. Given the remote location and the weather conditions over the previous week, the attending officer must have known it would take some time to get the wreck towed to a garage, so he had placed a yellow POLICE AWARE sign in the front windscreen. That made it clear to passers-by that the police already knew about the accident and would get around to dealing with it in their own time.

'What have we got?' asked Banks, eyeing the Focus.

'She's in there,' said the patrol officer, pointing. The woman beside him was leaning back against the Megane's bonnet. Her arms were folded tight and she looked upset.

The Focus stood in the lay-by facing in the wrong direction. Banks edged around to the driver's seat and glanced through the window. A young woman was behind the wheel, eyes wide open, staring straight ahead. It didn't take a police doctor to tell him that she was dead.

Banks slipped on his latex gloves and opened the car door. The metal squealed. He bent to examine the body. Blonde hair trailed over her shoulders and a ragged fringe and hoop earrings framed a heart-shaped face that must have been quite beautiful in life. She was wearing muted pink lipstick, blue eyeshadow and a fashionable black, strapless dress, the kind of item a young woman might wear for a special night out, a dinner at a fine restaurant, say, or an evening at the theatre. She also wore strappy sandals, high-heeled, but not to the point that would cause problems of balance, and some costume jewellery. Her hands were folded on her lap, a charm bracelet on her right wrist and a watch on the other. The seat belt wasn't fastened, and there was no handbag or coat anywhere to be seen inside the car. Her skin was pale and smooth. As far as Banks could tell, there was no physical evidence of any mistreatment of the body. No bruises, cuts or traces of blood. Also nothing to offer any clues as to her identity. He checked the glove compartment and found some petrol receipts, nicotine gum and a screwdriver.

Banks turned back to the constable. 'Any idea of the circumstances of the accident, PC . . .?'

'Knowles, sir. Barry Knowles.'

'Well, Barry, what can you tell us?'

Knowles gestured to his partner. 'What do you want to know? Ted and me were at the original scene.'

'You'd better start at the beginning. All I know so far is that this Focus was involved in an accident here last weekend.'

'That's right.' Knowles checked his notes. 'Friday night, it was. Incident called in from Trevor Vernon's mobile at ten thirty-seven p.m. That's the owner, sir. There was a bit of patchy fog and Mr Vernon ran into a white van on a tight bend. They were lucky to get away with only cuts and bruises. If one of them had gone over the edge . . . well . . . ' He gestured down at the valley bottom and swallowed.

Banks remembered arriving at a scene not far from here by helicopter when a van full of dead farm animals had gone over the side. Being close to the spot again brought back the horrific images of that day, not least of which was the sight of an improbable combination of man, steering wheel and engine block that more resembled a horror-film scene imagined by H.R. Giger than it did a human being. 'Go on,' he said.

'It was all above board,' PC Knowles went on. 'Neither of the drivers had been drinking. The bloke in the van, John Kelly, was a builder going home late from a job. He admitted he was in a bit of a hurry but denied exceeding the speed limit. The other two, Mr and Mrs Vernon, were on their way back from a play at the Georgian Theatre in Richmond. Mr Vernon said they'd each consumed a glass of wine during the interval, and our tests showed the driver was not over the legal limit.'

'A builder? Working until after ten thirty on a Friday night? I suppose miracles might happen, but . . .'

PC Knowles shrugged. 'It's what he told us, sir. He gave us the address of the property he was working on, too.'

'OK,' said Banks. 'What happened to them all?'

'Eastvale General. Just cuts and bruises. Shock, of course. Treated and released. Kelly's van was still roadworthy, so he drove himself home afterwards, but the Focus . . . well, you can see for yourself. It can take a few days to make the arrangements with the garage. Vernon made a bit of fuss, going on about it being Kelly's fault and all for driving too fast, but we put it down to shock.'

'How long were you here?'

'It was after twelve when we put the sign in the window of the Focus and left,' said Knowles. He checked his notebook again. 'Twelve-o-nine a.m.'

'And what about the girl?'

PC Knowles paled. 'Don't know, sir. Our dispatcher got a call this morning. The lady here, Mrs Brody. She talked about an abandoned car, and Sergeant Harris was just about to tell her that we already knew about it, that's why we had the POLICE AWARE sign in the window, but she said there was a dead girl in the car. There was certainly no girl here when we attended the scene of the accident on Friday night. Dead or alive.'

Banks smiled. 'I should imagine not, PC Knowles, or you would have made a note of it, I'm sure.'

Knowles reddened and shuffled his feet. 'Yes, sir.'

'Did you examine the boot?'

'No, sir. I mean, we . . .'

'It's all right. Was the car left unlocked?'

'Yes, sir. I tried to lock it, but the key wouldn't work. Too much damage to the doors.'

'Do either of you recognise the girl?'

'No,' said PC Knowles. 'Never seen her before.'

Banks turned to Mrs Brody, who was as tall as Winsome and just as statuesque, with short curly brown hair. Handsome rather than beautiful, Banks thought, in her early forties, casually dressed in black slacks, buttoned blouse and a padded zip-up jacket, wedding band on the third finger of her left hand. 'Mrs Brody?'

'Kirsten, please.' She leaned forward and stretched out her hand. Banks shook it. Winsome came back from examining the car to stand beside them, notebook and pen in her hand.

'You found the body?' Banks asked Kirsten Brody.

Kirsten Brody touched her throat. 'Yes. It was a terrible shock. It's the first time I've ever seen a dead person outside of a funeral home. I was just so glad I managed to get a signal for the mobile up here.' She had a lilting Scottish accent. Edinburgh, Banks guessed. Morningside, most likely.

'It can be a bit hit and miss around these parts,' Banks allowed. 'Did you recognise her from anywhere?'

'No. I've never seen her before.'

'Did you touch the body?'

'Lord, no.'

'How did you know she was dead?'

'Well, I don't suppose I did, really. Not technically. But she wasn't moving. Her eyes were open. And she was so pale. I don't, I just . . . There was nothing I could have done. I didn't open the door. I tapped gently on the window, but you can see . . .'

'Yes.' Banks paused for a moment to let Kirsten Brody collect herself, then asked, 'What made you stop in the first place? I mean, I assume you saw the POLICE AWARE sign?'

'Yes. I see them often enough on out-of-the-way roads like this. I work for the National Parks, so I do quite a lot of country driving. I don't know what it was, really. It was more like a feeling. Perhaps a shadow that shouldn't have been there, maybe a draught blowing a lock of her hair, some sort of movement? I really don't know what it was that made me stop. I can't explain it. I just felt there was something *wrong* about it.'

'And what did you do then?'

'Well, I pulled in as close to the side of the road as I could and went to have a look. There was no other traffic around. I remember the stillness when I got out of the car. The silence. Then, when I saw her, I got scared. I thought how foolish I was being. I mean, what if someone had done something to her? What if that someone was still around?'

'Did you see any other cars?'

'None. No one passed me while I was waiting, and I hadn't seen one single car on my whole drive along the pass.'

'Did you see anyone around or notice anything odd? A sound? Movement? A smell?'

'No. Nobody. Nothing. I know it sounds silly, but I didn't feel right leaving her. I knew she was dead, or I thought she was, but ... I don't know ... It just wouldn't have seemed right. I calmed myself down and called the police. They said they'd send a car up immediately and to stay where I was.'

'What did you do in the meantime?'

'I sat in the car and waited. I called my husband. He was expecting me back.'

'OK,' said Banks. 'I think that's all for now. We'll get you away from here. You can make a statement at the police station in Eastvale, if that's all right? Maybe with a nice cup of sweet strong tea? Just follow the patrol car.' Banks gestured to Knowles, who got back into their car, leaving his partner to keep the scene secure.

Kirsten Brody nodded and smiled briefly.

After he had watched them drive away, Banks had another look at the body then turned to Winsome. 'We'd better get Dr Burns up here,' he said. 'Make that the full CSI team. Peter

Darby, too. We'll need photos and video. And I'll need Peter to prepare a suitable image of her in time for the TV's local evening news. We'll get prints, DNA and dental records, but they can all take time, and I doubt she's in the system. We need to know who she is. God knows what we've got on our hands here. We don't know whether she died in the car or was dead before she got there, but one thing I am pretty sure of is that she didn't get here under her own steam.'

Trevor and Nancy Vernon lived in a Georgian-style semi-detached house just off Market Street, in the same part of Eastvale where Banks used to live with Sandra, Tracy and Brian, years ago when he first moved up north. The area hadn't changed much since he had moved to Newhope Cottage after the divorce. Still the same bay windows, doors panelled with frosted glass, net curtains, well-tended gardens with trim lawns. And across Market Street were the same shops: the newsagent's where Banks had picked up his morning *Guardian* on his way to work, a reliable butcher and greengrocer, a hairdresser Sandra had never liked, a bakery that made wonderful baguettes, and a betting shop Banks had used only on those rare occasions when he had a flutter, such as the Grand National and the Derby. There was also the dentist's surgery on the corner, which had featured in his previous major case, and a pub called the Nag's Head a bit further along. Banks had only been in there once during the time he had lived in the neighbourhood, and he found he would rather walk into town to somewhere with better beer, quieter music and a more convivial atmosphere.

Banks rang the doorbell and soon saw a blurred figure moving beyond the frosted glass. The man who answered had a puzzled and slightly annoyed expression on his face. He was about forty, wearing a grey V-neck jumper over a white shirt and muted tie. His hair was thinning at the front, and he was running to fat around the middle.

'Mr Vernon?' Banks asked.

'Yes, that's me. I'm afraid whatever it is, it's not convenient at the moment. I don't negotiate financial transactions of any kind on the doorstep.'

'Very wise, sir, if I may say so. And I can't say I blame you.' Banks showed his warrant card. Winsome did likewise.

'Police? What's all this— Oh, it must be about the car. Of course. You've got it sorted? Sorry, do come in.'

They followed him into the hallway. A number of coats hung on pegs, and Vernon added Banks's and Winsome's to the row.

'What is it, Daddy?' asked a girl of about twelve, poking her head around the dining-room door.

'Never you mind,' said Vernon. 'You finish your homework or your mummy will be angry with you.'

The head disappeared.

'Come through here.' Vernon led them into a comfortable but sterile living room. 'I'll just pop back in to tell Nancy what's going on.'

'You might ask your wife to come in here, too,' Banks said. 'We'd like to speak to her as well.'

'Oh, all right. Very well. Please sit down.'

Banks and Winsome looked at one another. Winsome rolled her eyes. Banks glanced at the generic Constable-style land-scape over the electric fireplace, then looked outside. It felt so strange sitting here looking at the street through the gauze curtains and remembering that he had a similar view for so many years – certainly, the houses were mirror images – and probably a similar life. The child, or children, he guessed as he heard the voices from the kitchen, the regularity of mealtimes, the domestic routine. But his life had never been exactly regu-lar or routine. The very nature of his job prevented that, and that was one of the reasons for his expulsion from this Eden to the one where he lived now. Alone.

Vernon came back with Nancy in tow. She was wearing an apron and carrying a tea towel. She was a harried-looking woman, her hair in a mess, but she obviously kept herself in good shape, and her manner proved to be far less grating than that of her husband.

Trevor Vernon rubbed his hands together. 'Right, where were we? Oh, yes. The car. Any progress?'

'Progress?' asked Winsome.

'Yes. That idiot came tearing round the bend like a bloody maniac. And the road conditions were appalling.'

'Well, it *is* Yorkshire, sir,' said Winsome. 'You have to make allowances for the weather.'

Vernon started at her, disbelieving. '*Allowances*? Is that *all* you can say? My wife and I were involved in a serious collision. Through no fault of our own, I might add. We could have died. Nancy here is a witness. And you go on about allowances. I want to know whether you've charged him yet. And what are the possibilities of compensation? Above and beyond the cost of a new car, that is.'

'If you want to bring charges against Mr Kelly, sir, that's your prerogative,' Winsome went on. 'But it's not our department.'

Vernon glanced from one to the other. 'Who's the organ grinder and who's the monkey here?' Then he put his hand to his mouth. 'Good God, that's not what I meant. I mean to . . . I didn't mean any offence. I—'

Banks looked towards Winsome, who simply raised an eyebrow. 'Perhaps if you would just stop blathering for a minute and listen to us,' he went on, 'then you wouldn't put your foot any further down your throat.'

Vernon bridled. 'Yes, of course. I assume you're at least going to have the car moved to my garage for repairs? I can't seem to get anyone there to commit to a pick-up time. That's unless you need to take it in for forensic examination first.'

'Forensic examination?' Winsome echoed. 'Why would we need to do that?'

'To find proof. Evidence. Do you need me to tell you your job?'

'Evidence of what?'

'That it wasn't my fault, of course. There must be something you can find, some scratch or dent that will prove his culpability.'

'I don't think we'll be checking for anything along those lines,' Winsome said. 'But we *will* be taking the car in for forensic examination.'

'But you just said . . . I don't understand. Why? When will I get my car back? When can I get it fixed?'

'We're not a garage,' Winsome said, 'and we're not in the tow-truck business.'

'And from what I've seen,' Banks added, 'the only place that car is headed is the scrapyard.'

'So what am I supposed to do?'

'We'll be in touch when our forensic experts have finished with it,' Winsome said. 'Then you can call your garage and make arrangements.'

'You're telling me now that *I* have to pay to get my own car back after you've taken it away?'

'That's usually how it works, sir,' Winsome said. 'Besides, I think you've got hold of the wrong end of the stick here. There's no evidence of dangerous driving in this case and, as I tried to tell you earlier, we're not Traffic. We're Homicide and Major Crimes.'

Vernon's mouth flapped open. He stared aghast at his wife, who shook her head slowly. 'H-homicide?'

'And Major Crimes,' Winsome added.

'I don't understand. I mean, it *was* an accident. I don't think the other driver *intended* to crash into us. He was just going too fast, wasn't he, love? And nobody died. It wasn't attempted murder or anything like that.'

'We know that,' said Banks. 'As I suggested earlier, perhaps if you were to take your mind off the problem of your car for a moment and listen to what we have to say, we might get somewhere. Winsome.'

First Winsome got the minor details cleared up: that the car did belong to Trevor Vernon, and that he had been involved in an accident with a white van on Belderfell Pass last Friday evening at 10.37.

'Yes,' said Trevor Vernon. 'We were on our way home from Richmond. A rather fine production of *The Importance of Being Earnest* at the Georgian Theatre, as a matter of fact. That's what I thought you were here about, the accident, but I don't understand now why you *are* here.'

'Bear with us a while, and I'll explain,' said Banks. 'Earlier today,' he began, 'we had a call from some patrol officers from the site where your car was left. A woman driving by noticed something she thought was odd and stopped to see what it was.' Banks paused for effect. 'She found a dead girl sitting in the driver's seat.'

The Vernons looked at one another.

'*A dead girl?*' said Nancy.

It didn't come out quite like '*A handbag?*' but it was close enough. Their shock and surprise was certainly genuine, though, Banks thought. Trevor Vernon had turned pale.

'Yes. You didn't have a passenger with you at the time of the accident, did you?'

'Passenger?' echoed Vernon. 'Good Lord, no, of course not. The children were at home with the babysitter. Are you suggesting that we had something to do with this?'

'I'm not suggesting anything yet,' Banks said. 'Just trying to get a few things straight. Though I suppose one could say you definitely did have something to do with what happened. The dead girl was found in *your* car, after all.'

'But that was just a coincidence,' said Vernon. 'It could have been any car, surely?'

'Perhaps. That's something we need to find out.'

'There was certainly no sign of any body in or out of the car when we were taken to Eastvale General,' said Vernon. 'Your men were there. They can verify that.'

Banks nodded. 'Oh, they do. When the car was moved into the lay-by and the notice put in the window by the police officers, there was definitely no body.'

'Well, then? Doesn't that prove it? However she got there, she got there *after* we'd gone.'

'If you do know anything, it would be best to speak now.'

'What do you mean, if we know anything?' said Nancy Vernon. 'How could we know anything?'

'Something could have happened,' said Banks. 'Let's just say, hypothetically, that you hit someone on the road earlier and stopped to help then realised that it was too late, the girl was dead. People get scared in these situations sometimes. They don't always realise that the best course of action is to come to us. They panic. PC Knowles didn't open the boot.' Banks knew the girl hadn't been run over – at least Dr Burns had found no obvious signs of it – but the Vernons weren't to know that, unless they had also seen the body.

'I don't believe this,' said Vernon. 'You think we had a body in the boot all along? This is absurd. Assuming we did what you say, which we certainly did not, why would we want to move a body from the boot of our car to somewhere more open, and how do you think we got back to Belderfell Pass to do all this without a car?'

'All I'm saying,' Banks went on, 'is that people tend to act irrationally in such situations. I just want to know if there's anything you're not telling us.'

'We're not criminals,' said Nancy Vernon in a tremulous voice. 'This is complete madness. We've never hurt anyone in our lives, have we, darling?'

'We certainly have not. And I resent the insinuation.'

'Do you have any enemies, Mr Vernon? Anyone who might want to cause trouble for you?'

'You mean by implicating me in something like this?'

'Yes.'

'Then, no, I'm pretty sure I don't have that kind of enemy. And neither does Nancy. This whole conversation is unreal. I'm a wages clerk, and Nancy works part time at Boots. Our children go to Eastvale Comprehensive. We live a quiet, ordinary life. Things like this don't happen to people like us. We're decent folk.'

Often the worst, in Banks's experience, but he didn't say anything.

Winsome showed them a photograph of the victim that Peter Darby had taken at the scene. Fortunately, she hadn't needed any touching up, just a little help with the lighting. She still looked dead, Banks thought. 'Do you know this girl? Have you ever seen her before?'

They shook their heads.

'Is she the . . . you know . . . the girl in the car?' asked Nancy Vernon.

Winsome nodded.

Nancy touched the photo. 'Poor thing. She seems so young.'

'Yes, she does,' said Banks. He gave Winsome the nod to leave, and they both stood up. 'Sorry to have bothered you at dinner time. And I apologise if some of our questions caused you discomfort. Cases like this are difficult for everyone involved. We may need to talk to you again as the investigation progresses, so please make yourselves available. There's no need to see us out.'

When they were getting back into the car, Winsome said, 'I don't think they had anything to do with it, do you, guv?'

Banks shook his head. 'No,' he said. 'You saw their reaction when I told them about the girl's body. He's an arsehole of the first order, and no doubt has a few enemies, but he's not a killer. Let's get back to the station and see if we get any results from the photo on the evening news.'

It was seven o'clock, shortly after Banks's visit to the Vernons. Kirsten Brody had been and gone without telling him anything more than she had told him before. Peter Darby's crime-scene photo had made it in time for *Look North* and the local ITV news. There was nothing much for Banks to do now but wait and indulge in pointless speculation. He was standing at his office window in the dark looking down on the Christmas lights that glowed and twinkled in the market square. Rebecca Clarke's viola sonata played in the background.

Kirsten Brody could have put the body in the car herself before reporting it, Banks thought. She was up there alone at the scene for long enough. But why do that, then call the police to report it? No. It didn't make sense, and it wouldn't until they found out more about the victim's life. And death. The girl's body had been transported to the mortuary in the basement of Eastvale General Infirmary, Dr Burns having pronounced death at the scene, possibly due to asphyxiation on her own vomit, he had said, which pointed to some sort of drug overdose, either accidental or deliberate. They would have to wait until the post-mortem to be certain.

Dr Burns wasn't sure about time or place of death, putting it at two or perhaps three days earlier, which meant Saturday or Sunday, quite a window of opportunity. Banks hoped Dr Glendenning might be able to narrow it down a bit more when he got her on the table. The weather had been poor until Monday, so very few people would have used Belderfell Pass. The locals certainly knew how treacherous the winding, unfenced road could be even in the best of conditions.

But for Kristen Brody's 'feeling', the body might well have remained where it was until Trevor Vernon stopped waiting for the police to do it and arranged for the garage to come to take his car away. If someone had placed the girl in the car, or dropped her off there to die, he or she must have known that her body would be discovered before too long. There were far better places nearby to hide a body than in a damaged car with a POLICE AWARE sign in its window, especially if you didn't want anyone to find it for a long time. As yet, nobody had reported a young woman missing. If she had got there herself, then how? She couldn't have walked, especially dressed the way she was; she was too far from anywhere for that. Someone must have given her a lift and either dropped her off or dumped her.

The telephone snapped Banks out of his stream of thought.

'I think I know the identity of the girl whose photo they showed on the news tonight,' the caller said. 'I just can't believe she's dead.'

'You knew her?'

'Adrienne Munro,' repeated the caller. 'That's her name.'

'Was she a friend of yours?'

'Not a friend. A student. I'm a lecturer at Eastvale College. Biology. Adrienne was one of my students. One of the brightest. I can't quite believe what I just saw.'

A student. That perhaps explained why nobody had reported her missing yet. She could have been in a hall of residence, or lived alone in one of the many flats and bedsits that thronged the college area. 'Could you please come by the infirmary and confirm that identification, Mr . . .?'

'Stoller. Luke Stoller. Would I have to look at her?'

'We can arrange for video identification. We'll still have to go to the family for formal identification, of course, but you could really help us out here. We'd hardly want to upset the poor girl's parents if we're not sure it's their daughter.'

'No. Of course not. I can see that. Naturally, I'll come. I don't know why I'm being so squeamish. I teach biology, after all. I've dissected a frog or two in my time. It's just . . . someone you know. Especially someone so vital, so young. Christ, Adrienne was only nineteen. Just starting her second year.'

'Was she studying biology?'

'Agricultural sciences. Biology was one of her required components.'

'Maybe we can talk to you about her later, once we know a bit more about what's going on? For the moment, though, the identification would be a huge first step.'

'I can meet you in reception at the infirmary in about fifteen or twenty minutes, if that's all right?'

'Excellent.' Banks hung up the phone and went down to the squad room to find Winsome. She should have no trouble tracking down Adrienne Munro's address, and that of her parents.

Luke Stoller identified the body as that of Adrienne Munro, and Winsome came up with the necessary addresses. While Banks and Winsome waited for Adrienne's parents to be driven down from Stockton to make a formal identification, they obtained a key from her landlord and walked down the tree-lined street of tall Victorian houses to number 27, where Adrienne Munro had a bedsit on the second floor. The bare branches stood in stark silhouette against the streetlights and above them, the clear crisp night was full of stars. Inside the building, it was warm, the stair carpet was clean and relatively new and the walls of the staircase and landings were decorated with tasteful reproductions of old masters. A smell of curry permeated the building, but that was to be expected in any student digs. Curry was cheap to make, and takeaways were plentiful.

As bedsits go, Adrienne's was fairly spacious, though the roof did slope at quite an angle over the bed itself. You'd bang your head when you got up in the night if you weren't careful, Banks thought, realising he was now at the age when he had to get up in the night far more often than he did as a student.

They put on their gloves and began the search.

The room came with an en suite, which consisted of a tiny walk-in shower, toilet and sink. There was barely room for towels on the narrow rack and flimsy shelves. Still, it was better than a toilet and bathroom down the hall, shared with the rest of the house. The medicine cabinet revealed nothing but a toothbrush, toothpaste, deodorant, nail clippers, a shaver, paracetamol and various cosmetics. There was no sign of prescription drugs, no contraceptive pills or devices, either in the bathroom or in any of Adrienne's bedside drawers. Nor were there any obvious signs of vomit in the sink, toilet or bathtub.

The room itself was tidy, the bed made, dishes lying on the draining board next to the sink. Banks ran his finger over one of the plates. Quite dry. It felt like a cosy home away from home, with a certain warmth about it and an aura of being someone's safe and special place or refuge. Above the small desk was a shelf of books, mostly textbooks on animal welfare and behaviour and wildlife conservation, along with a few paperbacks by Philippa Gregory, Antonia Fraser and Bernard Cornwell, showing a predilection for historical fiction. The ubiquitous *Game of Thrones* set of paperbacks was there, too, and it appeared to have been read. There was even an illustrated copy of *Black Beauty*, which also looked well thumbed, probably a relic from her childhood.

One drawer held a passport, issued in March of the previous year, a bank statement showing a balance of £2,342 – perhaps the residue of her student loan – and Adrienne's birth certificate, National Health card, student rail pass and other pieces of official paper. There was no sign of a driving licence. Another held a small amount of costume jewellery. Banks handed it all to Winsome, who bagged everything for later examination. All seemed in order, and it didn't appear as if anything untoward had taken place in Adrienne's bedsit, but the whole place would still require a thorough forensic search by a CSI team. For now, Banks thought, it would do no harm for him to get a little ahead of the game. On the desk sat a laptop and a mobile phone, which he asked Winsome to bag.

'It's probably one of those smartphones that needs a fingerprint,' he said.

'We can do that at the mortuary.'

Banks looked at Winsome. 'Yes, I suppose we can. It just feels sort of . . . I don't know. Creepy. Like those movies where the baddies cut off someone's finger to get access to the vault.'

Winsome smiled. 'We don't have to cut her finger off, guv. And if you don't mind my saying so, you seem to watch some terrible movies.'

'I suppose I do. Anyway, we'll hand the phone over to the techies and see if we can get a print-out of her emails and texts by tomorrow, along with a list of her phone calls and contacts.'

The walls were painted cheerful colours, mostly yellow and orange, which Banks found a bit OTT, being more into muted blues and greens. Several posters were tacked up here and there; instead of pop stars or actors they featured *National Geographic* pictures showing a variety of wild animals – lions, leopards, elephants – along with a star chart and a reproduction of Breughel's *The Fall of Icarus*. There were also posters advertising a recent *Tosca* at Covent Garden, Simon Rattle conducting Mahler's 7th at the Barbican and Nicola Benedetti with her violin poised for a performance at the Royal Festival Hall. No Harry Styles or Justin Bieber. A serious young woman, then, or so it seemed.

Adrienne owned a Dali Katch Bluetooth speaker, a pair of expensive Bowers & Wilkins headphones and an Astell &

Kern AK70 portable music player. All expensive gadgets. Banks whistled between his teeth and picked up the AK70. He had considered buying one himself after Apple cruelly discontinued the iPod Classic. He scanned the contents. There were a few pop bands and singers he had never heard of, except for Radiohead and Parquet Courts, but the bulk of her music was classical: Beethoven, Brahms, Schubert, Bach, Tchaikovsky, Mozart, a few Verdi and Puccini operas, even violin works by some contemporary composers like Ligeti, Tavener and John Adams. He was impressed. A violin rested in its case on the armchair, a selection of sheet music beside it on a music stand: Fauré's 'Après un rêve' and the 'Meditation' from Massenet's *Thaïs*. A competent violinist, then, as well as an agricultural sciences student. Adrienne Munro became more interesting the more he found out about her.

The small wardrobe was filled with clothes, including distressed jeans, fashionable blazers and assorted tops as well as more formal skirts and dresses, like the one she had been wearing when they found her. They were all good quality, though not top designer labels. She also owned a row of fashionable shoes, from sandals and trainers to court shoes, high heels, strappy sandals, like the ones she had been wearing, and leather and suede ankle boots. It wasn't hard to see where any spare cash Adrienne Munro might have had went. Clothes and gadgets. But how much spare cash did a student have these days? Did she have a part-time job? Rich parents? Banks didn't think so.

Banks also wondered whether Adrienne had a boyfriend. Though most women balked at the idea that they dressed for anyone other than themselves, he nevertheless regarded Adrienne's wardrobe as one at least as calculated to impress men as to please herself. But there was no evidence of a boyfriend in her bedsit. No stray socks, extra toothbrush or condoms.

Nor was there any evidence of drug use. And there wasn't any booze at all.

'It certainly doesn't look as if she died here,' Winsome said. 'Though I'm not sure how we'd tell.'

'If she did,' said Banks, 'she didn't lie down on the bed to do it, and it's hardly something you'd do sitting or standing, is it? Don't you think it's odd that there are no signs of a handbag or a purse, either here or in the car?'

'Yes, I do,' said Winsome. 'I was going to mention that at the scene. Most girls her age wouldn't go anywhere without a lipstick, money or credit cards, and keys. And a mobile, of course.'

'That's what I thought. But she left that here. Why? And where's the rest of her personal stuff?'

'I suppose if someone's intent on committing suicide, they don't necessarily think the way they would normally,' she said. 'I mean, the way most of us do. Anyway, I'll ask around.'

'Just another mystery to add to the list.' Banks took a final look around the bedsit and saw nothing he had missed on first glance. He checked his watch and touched Winsome's shoulder. 'Come on, we'd better call the control room and get some CSIs out here asap. And someone to preserve the scene until they get here. We should head back to the infirmary now. The Munros will be arriving soon, and we owe it to them to be there to meet them.'

It was after ten o'clock when Banks got home to Newhope Cottage, having dropped off Adrienne's phone and laptop with IT for analysis first thing in the morning. Adrienne's parents had been too distraught to talk when they came in to identify the body, so he had arranged to drive up to Stockton and interview them the following day. He remembered how, in the cold, dreary mortuary, Mr Munro had tearfully identified his daughter's body because his wife had been too upset to look at her. Winsome had offered them the services of a local doctor, accommodation in town and counselling, but they had insisted on returning to the family home, the only place they thought they would feel 'right'. At least they had agreed to phone Mrs Munro's mother, who lived in Middlesbrough, and she had said she would be waiting in the house with a pot of tea brewing when they got back.

The postman hadn't called at the cottage before Banks had left for work that morning, but there was nothing of interest waiting for him on the mat behind the door. He had ordered no CDs recently, having gone much more digital in his listening, exploring the world of lossless downloads, and he even got his copy of *Gramophone* directly on his iPad. Though he liked the ability to browse the archive, he missed turning the pages, the feel of a real magazine in his hands, and thought he might change his subscription to include the print version. He thought of Adrienne's Astell & Kern and, once again, thought it might well be worth buying one. Streaming was all well and good when you had a Wi-Fi signal, but he liked to listen in the car, and on headphones while he walked, and he was running out of space on his Classic. He could use his smartphone, he supposed, but he associated that too closely with work.

He had eaten only a ham and tomato sandwich from the police station canteen that day, so after turning up the thermostat a notch, he went through to the kitchen and found some aged cheddar and Rustique Camembert in the fridge. The crackers in his cupboard were a bit stale and tended to bend rather than snap, so he binned them. The cheese would be just fine by itself. Or rather, it would be fine with a glass of wine.

He turned on the TV on its ledge above the breakfast nook to watch the news, but quickly turned it off again. The world news had been depressing throughout most of his life, but this past two or three years, it had seemed even more so, with the parade of creepy and dangerous clowns that British and American politics had become, the nuclear threat growing and Russia up to her old habits.

Banks went through to the entertainment room and selected a CD of Chet Baker live in London, recorded in 1983. Baker was supposed to be well past his prime then, ruined by drugs, and not many years away from his mysterious demise after a fall from a high window in Amsterdam. But Banks thought it an excellent concert, and Baker was in terrific form. Music playing, he took his cheese and wine through to the conservatory.

Outside the windows, the long hump of Tetchley Fell loomed black and forbidding in the distance against the night sky, where a half moon shone among the bright constellations. Banks could recognise only Orion, with its hunter's belt pointing towards Sirius, and the dim glow of the nebula in the bottom half. It was about the only constellation he had ever been able to recognise apart from the Plough, despite a boyhood obsession with astronomy that had lasted at least a couple of school terms. His telescope had lasted about as long as his microscope.

When he switched on the shaded lamp by his wicker chair, its reflection swallowed the view. Banks turned on the small fan heater, as it got especially cold in the conservatory on winter nights.

No matter what, he knew he was lucky to live where he did and vowed they'd have to carry him out feet first. Though he could do without the terrible winter storms that brought the county to a standstill, nowhere else could he imagine enjoying all the seasons as much as he did, from the turning leaves of autumn to the first fogs of November, the December frost, then the snowdrops and bluebells of early spring and the hot still days of summer when bees droned among the fuchsias, and tits and finches flitted around the garden all day, then the swallows and swifts took to the skies in early evening. Most of the birds remained throughout the winter, except the swallows and swifts, which flew off to South Africa. But there were plenty of robins, blackbirds and great tits. He had even seen a tawny owl sitting on the fence at the bottom of his garden early one morning the previous week, just as the light was growing. It was probably the closest he had ever seen an owl and the experience had made him feel strangely light-hearted all day.

Banks wasn't even lonely most of the time – it had been over twenty years since he had split up with Sandra – but there were days when he ached for a companion, a lover, someone to share it all with. Time was running out for such things, he realised, and there was nothing more pathetic than an old man in a desperate search for young love. Better remain by himself than become a figure of fun or vilification.

He had come close to relationships a few times, most recently with Jenny Fuller, an old friend, almost lover, returned from overseas. But time and distance had changed them both, and it wasn't to be. Jenny had made it clear that while she still wanted to remain friends, she had no interest in picking up from where they had left off so many years ago.

Linda Palmer, a poet he had met through one of his cases, had intrigued and attracted him enough to make him think that something more might develop between them, but there was distance about her, a strong aura of *noli me tangere*, which he attributed mostly to the circumstances that had brought them together in the first place – an investigation into her historical rape at the age of fourteen by a high-profile celebrity. Maybe she just didn't fancy him, and that was all there was to it.

Penny Cartwright, the folk singer, clearly wasn't interested, either, and she would never let him forget that he had treated her as a murder suspect in one of his first cases in Eastvale.

They got along well enough. Banks admired her talent, went to listen to her sing in the Dog and Gun whenever he could, but he had given up any hope of more.

And then there was Annie Cabbot.

Banks and Annie had both been lonely of late, Annie since she had split up with her last boyfriend, Nick Fleming. And it had been a few years, Banks realised, since he and his last lover Oriana had parted company. There were moments when he and Annie had almost consoled one another, but something always held them back. Whether it was fear of rejection or fear of success, neither seemed quite sure. Maybe it was the way times had changed, the way the rules that forbade abuse of power in the workplace sometimes also destroyed the possibility of love. Any relationship Banks and Annie had had in the past, they had entered into of their own free will. Mutual. Consensual. But that seemed irrelevant these days. In certain moments, Banks wondered if all this would hold them back for ever. They still flirted occasionally, and he sometimes wished it was more than that. God knew, he still had feelings for her.

But tonight he was happy with his wine and cheese and Chet Baker playing his trumpet. He settled back in the cushion of his wicker chair and mulled over the day.

He was still troubled about the dead girl, Adrienne Munro. It never went away, even after all these years, that feeling that grabbed and twisted his gut every time the victim was a young girl. He felt it every time he saw Linda Palmer, even though she was close to his own age now. He had to admit that he had no idea exactly what Adrienne was a victim *of* yet, but she was certainly dead, and that was upsetting enough.

As he did so often in these cases, Banks thought of his own daughter Tracy when she was Adrienne's age, so full of hope and a sense of immortality. She had gone through a difficult period later, including an almost fatal relationship with a serious bad boy, but she had come out at the other end a stronger person with a clearer sense of where she wanted to go and how to get there. Now she was working on her doctorate in history not far away in Newcastle, teaching part time. She had a flat, a steady boyfriend, of whom Banks almost approved, and all was well for the moment. He thought of phoning her but decided it was too late. He would call her tomorrow.

Brian, his son, was away on tour with his band The Blue Lamps most of the time, endlessly on the road or in the recording studio. Fame didn't seem to have changed him much, from what Banks had seen, though it hadn't given him much of a chance to meet someone special and put down roots anywhere. He had once confessed to Banks, after a glass of wine too many, that he was often lonely on the road, that groupies weren't really his scene and the rock-and-roll life wasn't all it was cracked up to be, especially when you were in your early thirties.

Adrienne Munro, sitting in that car, staring straight ahead with her dead eyes, had got to Banks even more than some of the more obvious victims of violence he came across in his job. So far, he had nothing but questions.

A lot depended on Dr Glendenning's post-mortem results, but as far as Banks was concerned, no matter what conclusion the doctor came to, there was a villain out there who needed catching and putting away. Even if Adrienne Munro had died from a self-administered overdose of drugs, then someone had supplied her with those drugs, and someone or something had pushed her towards the edge, and over. Even if she had died of a heart attack or a cerebral haemorrhage, someone had moved her body to the abandoned Focus, perhaps without first checking to make sure that she was dead. Why anyone had done that remained a mystery. It could have been a tasteless joke, putting her in a car marked POLICE AWARE.

Or perhaps a well-wisher had wanted her to be found quickly, but hadn't wanted to become entangled in an investigation into her death? Well, he would see about that. The unwritten rule on dealing with suspicious deaths was that it was better to err on the side of suspicion and put in place scene preservation and crime management procedures unnecessarily than fail to do so, only to discover later that the original suspicions were correct.

The Chet Baker CD had finished, and Banks's glass was empty. He wandered into the kitchen and refilled it, then went into the entertainment room again, where he programmed the system to play 'Après un rêve' from the hoard of music on his computer. He had a vocal version by Véronique Gens, but he chose the violin version by Nicola Benedetti, whose poster Adrienne had on her wall. He added her *Thaïs* 'Méditation' to the mini playlist, too, and stuck on Vaughan Williams's 'The Lark Ascending' and Arvo Pärt's 'Spiegel im Spiegel' just because he liked them so much. Those four pieces, along with another glass of claret, should see him to bed, he thought, though he doubted he would enjoy a deep and dreamless sleep. They were few and far between these days.

2

While Banks was attending the post-mortem of Adrienne Munro and Winsome was following up on the forensic results from the Belderfell Pass crime scene the following morning, DI Annie Cabot and DC Geraldine Masterson were at the scene of another suspicious death.

Annie and Gerry parked next to the patrol car in the tourist car park at Tetchley Moor and struggled against the wind as they made their way through the twisted heather and gorse roots towards the stunned group of ramblers. Had last week's mist still been shrouding the moors, it would have been easy to mistake them for an ancient druids' stone circle, Annie thought, but a sharp wind had finally arrived, especially on the heights, and it dispersed the low-lying cloud and drizzle that had been plaguing the Dales for weeks, replacing it with significantly lower temperatures. Now the sun shone bright and the sky was robin's egg blue, with only the merest hint of white gossamer clouds twisting in spirals like DNA high above.

The wind moaned and whined and Annie's winter coat flapped around her legs. Gerry's long red hair whipped around her face, however much she tried to hold it back. When they got closer to the group, Annie recognised one or two of the faces from folk nights at the Dog and Gun she had attended with Banks.

Police Constable Ernie Garrett, who had been first officer on the scene, was standing guard over the gully, hands clasped

over his groin like a footballer in the wall waiting for the free
kick. Annie and Gerry approached, watched closely by the
stationary walkers. One of the members held a handkerchief
to her mouth, pale with shock.

When Annie leaned over the edge, she saw why. It looked as
if the man had lost his way in the mist and fallen down the
chasm, perhaps tripping over one of the heather or gorse roots
that snaked all around the moors. He lay on his back, and his
neck was twisted at an awkward angle. Annie guessed that the
fall had probably broken it. There was also a fair amount of
blood, which appeared to have come from where the back of
the man's head had hit a sharp stone. That he was dead was
obvious enough, even to the layman. Small animals had clearly
been nibbling at him, too, leaving marks on the exposed flesh
of his face, ears and hands.

But there was another feature odd enough to snare Annie's
interest: the man was wearing an expensive slate grey suit,
white shirt, striped tie and black brogues. Hardly the latest
trend in walking gear, and certainly not the kind of clothing
anyone in his right mind would have worn for a hike on
Tetchley Moor at any time of the year.

But then, Annie thought, nobody in his right mind would
have been walking in *any* sort of gear on Tetchley Moor over
the past week or so.

Nobody, that is, except for the dead man in the grey suit.

Drinks in the Unicorn after a post-mortem was fast becoming
a tradition. The pub was conveniently located opposite
Eastvale General Infirmary, and it was usually quiet enough
that he could hear himself think and have a private
conversation.

Banks hadn't seen any reason why he should inflict
Adrienne's post-mortem on Winsome, so he had texted her
and asked her to walk down from the station to meet him

afterwards. While he waited, he read again through the report the IT specialist had handed him after their brief chat that morning. They were still working on Adrienne's laptop, and probably would be for some time, but they had been through the mobile without having recourse to go to her corpse for a fingerprint, and they were finished with it. He had her phone records before him.

The emails all seemed innocuous enough, mostly to or from family and friends, as far as Banks could gather. There was no evidence of cyber stalking, sexting, bullying or the myriad other offences social media had made it easier to commit. Adrienne also received a lot of automatic notifications of forthcoming classical concerts in the area along with regular newsletters from the Sage, Wigmore Hall and other music venues.

As far as apps were concerned, Adrienne had subscribed to the streaming and downloading services Idagio and Qobuz, and most of the downloaded music on her phone was classical. She had also bought an app for live screenings of the Berlin Philharmonic concerts which, Banks knew, cost around €150 a year. It was something Banks had thought about subscribing to himself, but felt that he wasn't at home often enough to enjoy the luxury of the live broadcasts. Maybe he'd do it anyway. They all appeared in the archive eventually, and he could watch them at his leisure. The lure of seeing Patricia Kopatchinskaja dancing barefoot around Simon Rattle as she played the Ligeti violin concerto was almost too hard to resist.

Adrienne also had both Facebook and Twitter accounts, along with Instagram, Snapchat and WhatsApp, but there was nothing unusual about their content: a few photos of her and her college friends acting silly or formally dressed at a ball or wedding, wearing funny hats at a birthday party, holiday photos from a pal in Spain, along with Twitter feeds from her favourite classical musicians and scientific thinkers. There was certainly nothing risqué, no nude images, or even sexy poses. Nor did she have Tinder or any more sinister dating apps. It would all have to be sifted through in detail, of course, along with the contents of her laptop. There might be a clue to what happened to her among all the detritus of her private life. There usually was. There is no privacy for the dead.

The pub was almost empty, as usual. The landlord didn't serve food, which discouraged the tourist trade, so the place survived on a clientele of serious drinkers and hospital shift workers, and sometimes the one was inseparable from the other. Truant pupils from Eastvale Comprehensive School down the road sneaked in now and then, and the Unicorn was well known as the pub where many an underage drinker had his or her first alcoholic drink.

The Unicorn certainly wasn't the Queen's Arms, being a rather shabby and rundown Victorian street corner pub, but at least it served a decent pint of Timothy Taylor's, which was what Banks was drinking. As he sat in his corner and shivered, he also realised that another technique the landlord used to drive prospective customers away was keeping the heat turned low.

Winsome arrived and came over with her Britvic orange, keeping her fleece jacket on. She wasn't drinking alcohol at all these days – not that she ever had drunk much – and Banks wondered whether that had any connection with her marrying Terry Gilchrist last March. If Winsome had an announcement to make, he was sure she would make it in her own time. Marriage seemed so far to have agreed with her. It had given her more confidence and encouraged her to speak her mind more freely. Before, she had often kept her own counsel, and Banks had had to coax ideas out of her, but now she tended to say what was on her mind. She had also lost much of her prudish aura and sometimes surprised him with a bawdy comment or even, God forbid, by swearing. Terry, the ex-soldier's, influence, no doubt.

'Anything on the mobile, guv?' she asked as she sat down beside him at the corner table. It had been there so long it was still scarred with cigarette burns from the days when smoking was permitted in pubs.

'Not as far as I can tell,' said Banks. 'Just the usual personal and college stuff. Nothing stands out. We'll get the phone number from her call log and contacts checked.'

'So what's the doc's verdict?'

'That it seems very much as if Adrienne took enough sleeping pills to kill her.' Banks remembered vividly the moment when Dr Glendenning had opened Adrienne Munro's stomach. He took a gulp of beer to stem the rise of bile at the memory. The whole thing, her pale, beautiful, naked body on the stainless-steel slab, seemed a travesty of what her life should have been. On the one hand, she was nothing but an empty shell with no more personality or allure than a life-size doll, but on the other, she should have been pulsing with vitality and hopes and dreams and music. He thought of the beautiful melody of 'Après un rêve'. 'But, as it happens,' he told Winsome, 'she did a Jimi Hendrix before the sleeping pills could kill her, as Dr Burns suspected at the scene. Choked on her own vomit, too drugged to wake up. Jazz Singh is going to get to work on the toxicology.'

Winsome pulled a face. 'What a horrible way to go,' she said. 'Though I suppose she would have been unaware of what was happening.'

'Yes. And it could hardly have been an accident. She took a far larger dose than anyone might take for recreational purposes. And on an empty stomach.'

'Suicide, then?'

'Looks that way. Or she just didn't understand what powerful stuff she was playing with.' Banks shook his head slowly. 'Where was she, and what did she see or experience that scared her so much she killed herself?'

'We don't know that she did it because she was scared, guv,' said Winsome.

'No, you're right. She may have been depressed or unhinged.'

'There was no vomit in the car, was there?'

'No. Meaning?'

'Maybe someone cleaned her up.'

'Good point. We'll bear it in mind.'

'Anything else of interest?' Winsome asked. 'Body art, birthmarks, distinguishing features?'

'No tats or piercings. Small birthmark high on her right arm.'

'Maybe someone could have forced her to take the pills?'

'I suppose so. But that's pushing it a bit, isn't it? Besides, the doc went over every inch of her skin, and he found nothing suspicious. Not a bruise, not a needle mark, nothing. In addition, he couldn't find any of the physical or medical problems that might have pushed Adrienne towards taking her own life. She wasn't pregnant, was in general good health, no eating disorders, no signs of a heart attack, aneurysm, incurable cancer, debilitating nervous system disease, cerebral haemorrhage, stroke, seizure or anything like that. As far as mental-health problems go, we just don't know yet. Or whether she had any problems with her love life.'

'Every girl her age has some problems, guv, believe me,' said Winsome. 'Even if they're not immediately apparent.'

Banks gave her a sharp glance. 'Aren't we the cynical one?'

'Not cynical, just realistic. Put it down to experience. Late teens can be a tough time for girls.'

Banks nodded. 'Sorry. You're right, of course. Boys, too, if I remember correctly. I had no idea where my life was heading at that age, what I wanted to do. I was in business college, but I spent most of my time hanging around with the art and music students, going to rock festivals. I certainly never saw a police career in my future. But Adrienne had everything going for her – looks, education, brains, the lot.'

'There's always something. Even when it appears good from the outside. The things we think are so wonderful are often superficial.'

'So you think she reached some sort of crisis point?'

'Just that it's possible, that's all.'

'What do you think would suddenly drive an otherwise normal girl like Adrienne Munro to commit suicide, if that's what happened?'

Winsome shrugged. 'Love? Loss of love? Clinical depression? Despair? Loss of faith? I don't know, guv. We don't even know that it was sudden.'

'What do you mean? That something was happening to her that she couldn't live with any more? Something ongoing?'

'Possibly.'

'Like what? Rape? Sexual abuse?'

'But there's no evidence of anything like that, is there?' said Winsome.

'Not in the post-mortem, no. No rape, anyway. Or physical abuse. But if it happened some time ago, and she was keeping it all inside, not confiding in anyone or seeing a counsellor . . . Who knows? It's just another thing to consider when we're questioning her friends. The doc says Adrienne wasn't a virgin, but there were no signs of recent sexual activity or rough sex of any kind. And no signs of sexually transmitted disease. What about blackmail? That can be harder to pin down.'

'But what could she possibly have been blackmailed over?' Winsome asked.

'Who knows? Maybe it was because of something she did.'

'Somebody must know what happened.'

'Well, the only way we'll find out is by digging deeper into her life,' said Banks. 'By talking to people who knew her. What about your inquiries? Any forensics on the car?'

'Just what you'd expect,' said Winsome. 'Plenty of finger-prints, inside and out. None of them on file. And none were the deceased's. Hair. Coffee stains. Fast-food wrappers. Still no sign of any of Adrienne's possessions.'

'So she was in the car but she didn't touch it?'

'So it appears. If she'd opened the door herself, we'd have found her prints somewhere. She wasn't wearing gloves. And if someone had wiped it down, the other prints would be gone, too.'

'The doc also says the pills were washed down with alcohol, whisky by the smell of it, and you say forensics didn't find anything interesting around the car. I assume that includes an empty whisky bottle?'

'Right,' said Winsome. 'There was no sign of a bottle or any trace of alcohol. But someone could have removed them. Could Dr Glendenning tell whether she died in the car or before she got there?'

'She didn't die in the car. He says there was no way she could have walked the ten miles from her bedsit to Belderfell Pass, but I think we already knew that. He also said that, according to the post-mortem lividity, it seems very much as if Adrienne died elsewhere and her body was moved. She was sitting up when we found her, but the lividity showed she'd been lying on her back for a while after death. At least, that was where some of the blood had settled after her heart stopped beating. But the evidence is contradictory.' The problem was, Dr Glendenning had pointed out, that livor mortis, or hypostasis, begins twenty to thirty minutes after death, but the purplish red discolouration is not observable by the human eye until about two hours later. It increases over the next three to six hours and it reaches its maximum in eight to twelve hours. 'He thinks she may have been moved quite soon after death, not left lying down long enough for livor mortis to take place completely, and the rest of the time she was in a sitting position. As he can't accurately pinpoint time of death, given the amount of time that's gone by, it's a bit of a quandary.'

'There was no trace of another vehicle at the scene.'

'We'll check with the taxi companies, but it's looking very much as if someone took her there. Maybe someone she knew. The way it appears is that she died somewhere else, lying down, then maybe an hour or two later someone drove her to Belderfell and dumped her in the Ford Focus. All we need to know now is who and from where.'

'Maybe an ex-boyfriend?' Winsome suggested. 'I mean, if they'd been having problems and she killed herself because of him, perhaps even at his house or flat, then he wouldn't want to get involved, but he'd probably feel guilty enough to want her body found quickly.'

'We'll certainly be talking to any boyfriends. Past and present.'

'I still can't get over what a curious place it is for someone to dump a body,' Winsome said. 'I suppose it's possible that she committed suicide in a place that was very inconvenient for someone, so they had to move her. We know she didn't do it in her bedsit.'

'We know it doesn't seem like she did,' Banks said. 'The CSIs might find traces of drugs or vomit someone thought they'd cleaned up.' Banks paused. 'The doc also said something about Adrienne possibly having been in water some time before or after death. Apparently, there were traces of certain substances on her skin.'

'There was no water in her lungs though?'

'No. She didn't drown.'

'A bath, perhaps?'

'Possibly. But there's no bath in her bedsit, remember. Just a walk-in shower.'

'Would that be enough to produce the effect Dr Glendenning noticed?'

'I don't know. He wouldn't commit himself as to how or where, just to the indication of her having been in water. She could have just taken a shower before she went out, for example.'

'Dumping her where she was found would certainly guarantee she'd be discovered fairly quickly, so whatever the reason, it can't have been to hide the body. More to put it in plain view. And POLICE AWARE? I mean, was that meant to be some sort of sick joke?'

'What do you mean?'

'Was it some kind of message from a killer? You know, rubbing it in our faces, like saying, "Be aware of this, then." What are we supposed to be aware of? That Adrienne committed suicide? Of something she did? Is her death an example of something we're aware of and ignoring, supposed to be doing something about? I mean, why tell us that?'

'You've got a point there,' Banks admitted. 'Maybe it *is* supposed to mean something and we haven't figured it out yet. I don't know. Maybe we're just reading too much into it, grasping at shadows. But we'll keep it in mind.'

Winsome glanced at her watch and knocked back the remainder of her orange juice. 'Come on, guv, sup up. Time to go and visit the parents. Maybe they'll be able to enlighten us.'

There had been no other vehicles parked in the moors car park from which Annie and Gerry had just walked except the walking club's minivan and the police patrol car, and Annie doubted very much that the dead man had walked all the way from Eastvale, or even Helmthorpe. The surface of the car park was tarmac, and if any other cars had pulled up there recently, no traces would remain, especially after the weekend's rain and today's wind. Unless, of course, the driver/killer had flicked a cigarette end out of his window, which had become caught in the weeds and would lead to an immediate DNA match. Dream on, Annie told herself. That only happened on television and in books. Besides, not even killers smoke these days.

Annie gestured towards the body. 'Anyone recognise him?' she asked, conscious that her words were almost ripped away from her lips by the wind before she uttered them.

The members of the walking club mumbled and turned away or shook their heads.

There wasn't much else to do but question the walkers one by one as they all waited for the mountain rescue team to lift the body out of the gully. That would not be done, of course, until Peter Darby had arrived and extensively photographed and videoed the scene, then Dr Burns would have to pronounce death before the body was released to the coroner.

The preliminary questioning of the walkers didn't take long, so as she waited, Annie took a few snaps of her own with her smartphone. It wouldn't be long before Peter Darby was made redundant, she thought sadly. These days it seemed anyone could be a photographer, even a crime-scene photographer.

When the experts started to dribble in, Annie arranged for the walkers to be escorted out of the wind and back to their minivan by the uniformed officers. In the relative comfort of the nearest police station, in Helmthorpe, they could give their official statements and leave their names and addresses.

As Annie stood at the edge of the moors and watched the green van drive away, she looked at the valley spread out below her. She could pick out Banks's isolated cottage easily enough, just a couple of miles to the north, next to the terraced falls of Gratly Beck, and below that the square tower of Helmthorpe church, with its odd turret attached. Beyond lay the meandering River Swain, then slowly, the dale side rose on the other side, a patchwork of drystone walls marking fields where sheep grazed, all the way to the sheer limestone curve of Crow Scar, like a grinning skeleton in the winter light.

Annie fastened her coat high around her neck and made her way back to the scene.

Peter Darby did his work, even going so far as to scramble down the gully from a nearby access point to get pictures he claimed he couldn't get with his telephoto lens. The drop was only about fifteen or twenty feet, Annie reckoned, but certainly enough to break a man's neck and crack open his skull if he fell at the wrong angle. On the other hand, it would have been quite possible for someone to survive the fall with only a broken leg and lie there screaming for help until some came, or until he died of exposure.

When Peter Darby had finished, Annie gave the signal for the rescue team, who had been fixing up their winches and slings, to bring the body up to the surface, which they did quickly and smoothly in as fine a coordinated and choreographed operation as Annie had ever witnessed.

Now the body lay on a stretcher at their feet, ready for Dr Burns's examination before being shipped to the mortuary. The man was of average height, Annie noted, and definitely overweight, though somewhat short of obese. He was in his mid-sixties, with thinning grey hair, a grey Van Dyck beard, wrinkles and a few liver spots on his wrists and the backs of his hands.

Dr Burns knelt before the broken figure, touching the skin here and there, checking front and back, taking the body temperature, making calculations and recording observations on his notepad. After a while, he stood up with some difficulty and massaged his knees.

'Getting old,' he said, with a fleeting grin.

'Aren't we all?' Annie agreed.

'You two speak for yourselves,' Gerry chipped in.

Annie rolled her eyes. 'Ah, yes, the mere child.'

Gerry gave her a look. 'Well . . .' she said. 'Don't count me in as a member of your old fogeys' club. Not yet.'

Annie smiled and turned to Dr Burns. 'So, what have you got for us, old fogey?'

'Not a lot, I'm afraid. Probably not much more than you could see for yourself. Neck's broken at C five.'

'Would that cause paralysis?'

'More than likely. There certainly wasn't much chance of his crawling out of there once he'd gone in.'

'Is that what killed him?'

Dr Burns shook his head. 'No. I'd say it was the blow to the back of the head, and the blood loss it caused.'

'From the fall?'

'Almost certainly. No doubt in his post-mortem Dr Glendenning will be able to match the wound more closely with the rock it hit, but the impact certainly fractured the skull, and it would have caused definite brain damage and severe bleeding, as you can see for yourself.'

'He bled out?'

'More or less.'

'Would he have been conscious?'

'Unlikely. Not for long, at any rate.'

'Thank heaven for small mercies,' said Annie with a shudder, imagining what it must be like being trapped all alone at the bottom of a gully where no one was likely to venture for some time, with a broken neck, paralysed, aware of your life's blood leaking away. 'Now for the question you hate most of all.'

'Time of death?'

'That's the one.'

'Going by body temperature, rigor and the extent of damage done by the local fauna, I'd say at least three days, no longer than four. That's allowing for the low temperatures we've had since the storm last week. Probably sometime last weekend, in fact. But don't quote me on that.'

'So what happened?' Annie asked, mostly of herself. 'He wanders up here in his Burton's best, for whatever reason, trips over a heather root, tumbles down the gully, breaks his neck and smashes his skull and dies.'

'Something like that,' the doctor agreed. 'From what I could see, the blood has gathered where you expect it to be if he fell and died in the position he was found in. When Dr Glendenning gets him stripped off on the table, he should be able to give you an even better idea whether your man died here or was transported from elsewhere and dumped, but I'd say it happened here. Dr Glendenning will also be able to tell you whether a stroke or a heart attack or drug overdose was involved. But unless you want me to strip him right down here and now and open him up, I've told you all I can for the moment.'

'No, that's OK,' said Annie. 'Best leave it for the post-mortem.' She paused and pushed some strands of hair behind her ears. The wind soon whipped them out again. 'But it doesn't make much sense, does it?' she asked. 'Where did he wander from? Why? Was he drunk? How did he get here? Where's his car? He surely can't have walked here, can he?'

Banks lived in Gratly, and he had a fine view of Tetchley Fell from the back of his cottage. Though Annie knew that he liked walking and thought himself reasonably fit for someone who wasn't an exercise fanatic, she also knew that he had never so much as thought of attempting the two-mile walk up to the moors. Like most people, including the walking club, if he fancied a ramble on the moors he would have driven and used the car park.

'That I can't tell you,' said Dr Burns. 'But I will agree that he's not in the sort of shape to be doing much climbing and walking.'

Annie put on the latex gloves she had carried from the car and knelt by the body. 'Let's at least see if we can find out who he was without disturbing things too much.'

Deftly, Annie searched through the dead man's pockets. All she found was a fob of keys in his side jacket pocket, which she held up for Gerry to see. Then she turned to the men from the coroner's van who were standing by with a gurney. 'All right, lads,' she said. 'He's all yours now.'

Stockton-on-Tees was only about an hour's drive from Eastvale, though the traffic around the Scotch Corner road-works on the A1 added at least another ten minutes on that particular afternoon. The problem was, as Banks understood it, that the workers kept digging up more Roman ruins as they widened the road, and therefore had to bring in more teams of archaeologists, thus slowing progress. Whatever the reason, the 50 mph zone seemed to go on for ever. Banks took the Darlington exit, then carried on along the A66 heading east.

Much of the manufacturing Stockton had been known for was in decline these days, and as a result, there were some tremendously depressed and depressing areas, which often rubbed shoulders with more affluent neighbourhoods. Banks wouldn't have called the terraced street where Adrienne's parents lived either affluent or depressed. It was part of a slightly shopworn early sixties council estate. Each house had a small unfenced garden, but there were no garages or drive-ways. The road was filled with parked cars, and none of them were Beemers or Mercs.

Mrs Munro, wearing jeans and a navy jumper, recognised Banks and Winsome from the previous evening and invited them in. She was an attractive woman in her early forties, with wavy fair hair, long legs and a waspish waist, but today her eyes were red-rimmed with grief, and there was a pile of used tissues on the low coffee table between the sofa and the electric fire. The wallpaper was a simple striped pattern, the furniture IKEA, from TV stand to small bookcase, which was mostly filled with souvenirs from Greek and Spanish holidays: figures in peasant dress, a bulbous empty wine bottle, a plastic model of the Acropolis.

'Excuse the mess,' Mrs Munro said, immediately grabbing a handful of tissues and taking them into the kitchen to put in the bin. 'I don't know whether I'm coming or going. Jim's just having a lie down upstairs. He didn't get a wink of sleep last night, poor lamb. I'll get him if you want.'

'No need yet, Mrs Munro,' said Banks. 'Let him sleep. We can talk to him some other time if we need to.'

'Brenda, please.'

Banks and Winsome sat on the sofa. 'Brenda, then,' said Banks.

'Can I get you both a cup of tea or something?'

'No, thank you,' said Banks.

But Brenda Munro was already on her feet. 'It's no trouble,' she said and disappeared back into the kitchen.

'She seems jumpy,' Winsome mouthed, when Brenda had left the room.

Banks nodded. 'Still in shock, probably.' As far back as he could remember, people seemed nervous when the police came to call, and Brenda Munro had just lost her daughter. Banks felt more than a little guilty for intruding on her grief so soon, especially with so little evidence other than a vague sense of something being out of kilter.

When Brenda came back with the tea and cups on a tray, Banks said, 'We're really sorry to be bothering you at a time like this, but there are one or two questions you might be able to answer for us. As yet, we know very little about Adrienne or her life.'

Brenda clasped her hands on her lap and wrung them together, an unused tissue tearing between them. 'What can I tell you? She was just a normal girl. Maybe a bit shy and quiet. I'm her mother. I loved her very much. We both did.'

'Did you get along well?'

'As well as any mother gets along with her teenage daughter.' She shook her head slowly. 'I like to think we were close.' Her eyes filled up and she reached for a tissue. 'I'm sorry.'

'It's all right,' said Banks, leaving a brief pause for Brenda Munro to compose herself. 'We all have secrets. She was nineteen, is that right?'

Brenda sniffled. 'Yes, just starting her second year at Eastvale College.'

'Any brothers or sisters?'

'Mari. She's married. They live in Berwick. She's on her way down right now. She'll be devastated.'

'Close, were they?'

'Like twins, though Mari's three years older than Adrienne.'

Banks remembered the chatty emails to and from Mari on Adrienne's mobile. 'Did Adrienne confide in her big sister?'

'She did when she was younger, but they don't see one another quite so often, not now Mari has baby Nadine and Adrienne has her studies. Had.' She shook her head slowly. 'I can't believe I'll have to get used to saying that.'

Banks saw Winsome make a note and guessed she was jotting a reminder to have a chat with Mari. 'Did Adrienne always want to study agriculture?'

'Yes. She was crazy about animals and the countryside, and she was one of those keen environmentalists. Vegetarian and everything. We can't have any pets because Jim's allergic to just about everything that moves, except people, but she had a part-time job at an animal shelter in Darlington, for the RSPCA, like, taking care of mistreated pets and so on, and she'd watch just about any documentary on animals and environmental issues that came on. David Attenborough, all that sort of thing.'

'Is that why she chose Eastvale College, the agricultural connection?'

'Yes. Partly. It has an excellent reputation. And Adrienne loved the Dales. I think it was reading all those James Herriot books when she was a little girl. They inspired her. And she was very bright. She got good A level results. She had her heart set on Eastvale, and she wouldn't hear of going anywhere else.'

'What about the music? We noticed a violin and some music in her bedsit.'

'She started learning at school. She was very talented musically. Everyone said so. We were able to afford violin lessons for her for a while. We even harboured dreams of her going to a music academy or somewhere a few years ago. But it's not a career, is it, music? More of a hobby, really. She just loved that classical stuff. We couldn't afford to keep up the lessons, but she played in a youth orchestra. At least she did until she started university. She had a good singing voice, too. She used to sing in a choir.'

'Why did she give it up?'

'Too busy, she said. Too big a course load. But she told us she still practised the violin when she had a few spare moments. Kept her hand in, like.'

'Was she a party girl? Nights on the town, that sort of thing?'

Brenda managed a weak smile. 'Like I said, Adrienne was a normal teenager. A bit shy, but she liked being with her mates. I'm sure they all liked to get dressed up and go out for drinks and dances. I know they went to Leeds clubbing from time to time. But she wasn't a binge drinker or anything, and I have a really hard time believing she took drugs. She was a hard worker, and she loved her studies.' Brenda Munro paused. 'What happened to her?' she asked. 'Nobody ever did tell us what happened. Why she died. The newspaper said that it was an overdose of drugs. I just can't believe it.'

Under his breath, Banks cursed the local newspaper for running the story half-cocked, and Adrian Moss, the police media liaison officer, for letting them get away with it. The papers were already headlining the story, 'The Girl in the Car'.

'I'm afraid it looks very much as if she died of an overdose of sleeping tablets,' Banks said, sparing her the gruesome details of the asphyxiation. 'I'm sorry if anyone gave you the impression it was a drug-related death. I mean, I know that sleeping tablets are drugs, but Adrienne wasn't involved in any illicit drug activity as far as we know.'

Brenda put her hand to her mouth. 'Sleeping tablets! But where would she get something like that? Why on earth would she want them? What happened?'

'That's something we were wondering, too. Do you know if she ever had a prescription for anything like that, had any problems sleeping?'

'Never. Not that I knew of. Even though she'd moved away, she was still on Dr Farrow's list. He's our local GP. You can ask him, if you like, but I'm sure she wasn't taking anything like that. Where could she have got them from?'

'That's something we'd very much like to know, Mrs Munro,' said Winsome.

'Sleeping tablets,' Brenda Munro repeated quietly, as if to herself. 'That means she took them herself, doesn't it? That she committed suicide?'

'We don't know what happened,' said Banks. 'Just that the doctor found that she had taken enough to be unable to wake up.'

'Suicide. Our Adrienne. No.'

'Had Adrienne been depressed or anything lately?' Banks pressed on. 'Any weight loss, eating problems, anything like that?'

'No,' said Brenda. 'She wasn't anorexic or bulimic, if that's what you mean. She never had any eating problems in her life.

And she wasn't depressed. That's why what you're suggesting is such a shock.'

'Were there any traumatic events in her life that might have weighed on her mind?'

'None that I can think of,' said Mrs Munro. 'Not as far as we know.'

'*Would* you have known?'

'I think so,' said Brenda.

'Sometimes people can hide these things very well.'

'Oh, I know that. But no. Our Adrienne was never the life and soul of the party. If people talked to her she'd chat back happy as anything, but she wasn't good at making approaches. She could be withdrawn occasionally, too. And she did get stressed out sometimes. But I think I'd have known if something was really bothering her, yes. I like to think she would have told me.'

'Did she ever talk to you about any problems she might have had?'

'No. I mean, nothing serious. She was a bit strapped for cash in her first year, and we tried to help her as best we could, but it's hard. And uni's so expensive these days. You know what young girls are like, with their clothes, make-up, music and what have you.'

Banks smiled. He remembered Tracy when she was that age. Clothes mad, he used to call her. But university life was a lot less expensive then. He also remembered Adrienne's wardrobe, the mix of casual student wear, and the more formal, expensive outfits. 'Did Adrienne take out student loans?'

'Yes. They all have to, don't they? It seems a terrible thing to me, starting out your working life so deep in debt, but I suppose most people do, one way or another, with mortgages, hire purchase and the like. And all these money marts you see on the high streets these days. Jim and I have never been able

to afford to buy our own home. The first year was very difficult for us all, but Adrienne did really well, and she got a
scholarship this year. It didn't cover everything, of course, but
it's made her life a lot easier. And not only hers, but ours, too.
Not that we minded helping her, you understand, but you can
only stretch what you have so far.'

'Which scholarship was this?'

'I don't know what it was called. Just something you get if
you do well.'

'She won it, like a prize?'

Brenda frowned. 'I think so. You'd have to ask the people at
the university. We don't know the details. All we know is that
it was a godsend.'

'How much was it?'

'I don't know that, either.'

'When was the last time you saw Adrienne?'

'When she went back to Eastvale to start the second year.
She'd got a bedsit and was very excited for us to see it, so Jim
drove us all down and we made a day of it. We went to see the
castle, had a nice pub lunch in the market square.'

'And how was she? Was there anything on her mind at the
start of this academic year? Are you sure you didn't notice any
subtle changes in her behaviour or mood?'

'No, nothing. She was fine. Same as she'd been over the
summer holidays. Like I say, she was excited about her bedsit.
She'd been in halls her first year and didn't really like it. She
was supposed to be coming home for Christmas.' Brenda
reached for a tissue and wiped her eyes. 'Sorry.'

'Did you talk to her recently?'

'Only on the phone.'

'Did she phone this week?'

'Not since the weekend. Saturday morning was the last time
we heard from her.'

'What did you talk about?'

'Not much. You know. The sort of things you do talk about. College, Mari and baby Nadine, her work, that sort of thing.'

'How did she sound?'

'Fine. Maybe a bit distracted.'

'Distracted?'

'Yes. You know, as if she had something on her mind.'

'Did she give you any idea what it might be?'

'I just thought it might be her studies.'

'How was she doing at college?' Winsome asked.

'Oh, Adrienne always played herself down rather than up,' Brenda answered. 'She was never one to blow her own trumpet. She'd tell us she thought she was doing all right, and then when she came out with a star or distinction or whatever, she'd be surprised. Obviously, there must have been something bothering her, but whatever it was, she didn't tell us.'

'Children don't always confide in their parents,' said Banks. 'I know I didn't always, and I doubt you did, either.'

'No,' said Brenda, clutching her tissue. 'Her friends from college might know more. She spent more time with them than she did with us.'

'What about boyfriends?'

'No,' said Brenda. 'She had someone in her first year. Nice lad. She brought him up for tea once or twice.'

'What happened?'

'I don't think anything much happened. They saw each over the summer a few times then they just sort of drifted apart, like you do. Adrienne told me she wanted to concentrate on her studies this year. She didn't have time for boyfriends.'

'What was his name? Do you remember?'

'Colin. Colin Fairfax.'

'Was he in the same department as Adrienne?'

'I don't really know . . . I don't think so. I think he was studying languages. French, German and so on.'

'Did Adrienne still keep her job at the animal shelter after she was awarded the scholarship?'

'Oh, yes. But that was never really for the money – they hardly paid more than a pittance – it was just to help the poor animals, and to be with them. She'd have done it for nothing. And it was only on weekends.'

'Would you happen to have a recent photograph of her we could borrow? It may help us when we're talking to people.'

Brenda Munro walked over to the rows of framed photographs on a table beside the TV set and picked one out. 'This was taken just last year,' she said, as she took the photograph from its frame. It showed Adrienne leaning against a farm gate with Crow Scar in the background. She was wearing jeans and trainers, and her blonde hair didn't hang quite as far over her shoulders as it had when she died. But she was clearly an attractive young woman with a shy smile. Banks thanked Mrs Munro and slipped it in his briefcase.

'We'll take good care of it,' he said.

'Don't worry too much,' said Brenda. 'Jim can always print another copy. I'm sorry he's not up yet.'

'Never mind. We'll leave you be for now,' Banks said. 'Thanks for your time. And let me say again how sorry I am about Adrienne.'

'You'll find out who did it, won't you?' Brenda said, grasping his arm.

Banks extricated himself gently. 'We don't know that anyone has done anything to anyone yet,' he said, 'but you can take my word for it, we'll do our best to find out what happened.'

Brenda nodded.

Banks gave Winsome a quick glance and she put away her notebook. They said their goodbyes, offered more condolences, then left.

'Anything in it, guv, the father not appearing?' Winsome asked as they drove along the A66.

'I doubt it,' said Banks. 'Bloody exhausted, I should imagine. We'll talk to him later.'

Wherever they went next, he thought, it would have to be tomorrow. When he looked at his watch, he realised he'd just about have time to get home, phone Tracy, then shower and change before Annie stopped by to pick him up and drive him over to Ray and Zelda's for dinner.

3

As Banks's Porsche needed a little work and wouldn't be ready until the following afternoon, Annie picked him up at Newhope Cottage at seven o'clock, as arranged, and they drove down the hill though Helmthorpe, across the bridge over the River Swain and about halfway up the opposite dale side to the village of Beckerby. Ray and Zelda's cottage stood on the northernmost edge of the village, separated from the far end of the High Street by a field of grazing sheep on one side and wooded area on the other. Banks could actually see the place from Gratly Beck, just outside his front door.

As she drove, Annie slipped a CD in her car stereo and suddenly she was singing along with Neil Diamond's 'Sweet Caroline'.

'What the bloody hell's this?' asked Banks.

Annie turned in her seat and grinned at him. 'Payback,' she said.

Ray had bought the cottage in summer, mostly for the view and the quality of light, which were hardly in evidence on that late November night. On a clear day, Banks knew, he could see as far east as Eastvale and as far west as the Swainshead viaduct. But the old place had needed a lot of work. All autumn, Ray had been travelling to and from Cornwall, where he had been living in an artists' colony since Annie was born, in order to oversee the various builders, carpenters, plumbers and electricians and make sure everything was exactly the way he wanted it. Finally, just two weeks ago, he had declared it fit for habitation and had driven up with the last of his belongings.

And Zelda.

'So we've got two suspicious deaths,' Annie said, drumming her fingers on the steering wheel in time with the music. 'Probably not so far apart in timing, though we've no idea who died first. And both bodies were found formally dressed in improbable locations without any visible means of getting there. Oh, and neither was carrying any of the usual personal possessions or identification. Interesting.'

'Indeed,' said Banks. 'A three-pipe problem, perhaps?'

'Do you think they could be connected?'

'Normally I'm suspicious of coincidences, but we've got a long way to go yet before we start to speculate about anything like that. You and Gerry keep working on your mystery man, and Winsome and I will carry on investigating what happened to Adrienne Munro. We'll have regular meetings to pool information. And don't forget, in neither case do we have any evidence of foul play.'

'You're saying they could have been accidents?'

'I'm saying that Adrienne Munro could have committed suicide, and your man could have fallen down the gully in the bad weather.'

Banks settled back in his seat and felt some of the weight of his cares slip away as they approached the village of Beckerby. It had been a difficult day, and he knew he would never get rid of the images of the dead Adrienne Munro lying there on the post-mortem suite slab, that it would join the other exhibits in his own personal chamber of horrors, and would parade before him unbidden in those dark nights of the soul that seemed to come more often these days.

He made an effort to put the business as far out of his mind as he could. Neil Diamond singing 'Girl, You'll Be a Woman Soon' provided some distraction, however unwelcome. He was looking forward to a fine dinner, decent wine and, best of all, entertaining conversation. It would be good to get to know Zelda better. He realised he didn't really know very much about her at all.

The music would be a treat, too, better than what he was listening to now. Ray was an old sixties guy, like Banks himself, only he had never expanded his horizons to include classical music and jazz, so tonight it was going to be the real thing all the way.

Annie drew to a halt outside the low-roofed cottage – Ray's only complaint was that it was a bit small after the spread he had enjoyed in Cornwall for so many years – and they both stood still and took in the silence punctuated only by the occasional late bird call and whistling wind for a few moments before knocking at the door. Despite the chill, it was another clear evening, the sky studded with stars and the half-moon shining bright.

Ray Cabbot opened it and ushered them into the hall. Annie gave her father a hug and Ray and Banks shook hands.

'Drinkies, anyone?'

'G&T, please,' said Banks.

'Not for me,' said Annie, slipping off her coat. 'Designated driver.'

Ray hung it up for her beside Banks's. 'You can always stop over.'

'I don't plan on getting pissed. Besides, I have to drop Alan off at home.'

Ray scratched his head. 'Well, golly gee, we've only got one small spare bedroom but you're both welcome to it,' he said with a big grin.

Annie thumped his arm. 'Stop it, you'll embarrass me.'

'Embarrass? You? If pigs could fly.'

Annie grinned at him. 'I'll have a glass of wine with dinner later and that will be my limit.' She rubbed her hands together. 'A bit brisk out there.'

'Go through to the living room,' said Ray. 'The fire's lit. Zelda's just doing some last-minute fiddling with dinner.'

The room was lit by dozens of candles on the low tables, mantelpiece, everywhere, and a log fire crackling in the hearth. The paintings on the walls appeared ghostly in the candle-light. Ray's studio was upstairs, Banks knew, in what would have been a large front bedroom, facing the stunning south-ern view and catching plenty of light.

Ray bent over the cocktail cabinet to mix Banks's drink and handed it to him. Banks could smell something delicious cooking in the kitchen – a stew of some sort flavoured with herbs and spices. The new Neil Young CD was playing. Well, not so new. Banks remembered reading in *MOJO* that *Hitchhiker* was recorded in 1976 and not released until years later. Neil was in the middle of a haunting acoustic version of 'Powderfinger' that Banks thought almost as good as the elec-tric version on *Live Rust*.

And it probably wasn't a CD. He remembered that Ray was a vinyl freak, and if *Hitchhiker* was available on vinyl, that would be the version he bought. Banks had let his own exten-sive collection slip away over the years. He had moved the boxes of LPs up to Eastvale from London when he first came up to work there in the mid-eighties. It was after that when he bought a CD player and made the switch. He sold a few of his records to the used vinyl shops that had started springing up, but then he lost the rest of his collection in a fire, when a villain set fire to Newhope Cottage with Banks in it, drugged on the sofa.

Banks accepted his gin and tonic and took a gulp. It was strong.

The door opened and Zelda made her entry, wearing figure-hugging jeans and a white knitted cashmere jumper. She was tall and slender, long-legged and small-breasted. Willowy, perhaps, but not a blonde. Her wavy black hair tumbled over her shoulders and framed an oval face. She had exquisite cheekbones, and there was something distinctly Eurasian about her eyes and flawless complexion. The only jarring feature was a slightly crooked nose, which had clearly been broken once. But as so often with such imperfections, it merely managed to enhance her beauty. Most of all, it was her eyes that drew Banks in. Dark and beguiling, they spoke of a sadness beyond words. All in all, Banks thought, she was probably one of the most beautiful women he had ever seen.

Ray and Zelda certainly made an odd couple, and not only because of the age difference. They were actually a refreshing rebuke to those who took issue with older men and younger women. While Zelda was only thirty, she had an aura of having lived about her, and the wisdom and experience of a much older person – she was what one of Banks's previous girlfriends would have called an 'old soul' – and while Ray was over seventy, his soul was young, and everything about him sang of sprightliness, creativity, youthful energy and enthusiasm.

Zelda sat casually, leaning back in the armchair, long legs crossed, and lit a cigarette. 'Alan. Annie. It is so good to see you.' Her slightly accented English merely added to her exotic persona. Zelda came from somewhere in Eastern Europe. Banks vaguely remembered Ray mentioning a small town in Moldova, the name of which was hard to pronounce, along with a past shrouded in mystery and tragedy that had only been vaguely hinted at thus far. 'How are my two favourite detectives?'

'Looking forward to dinner,' said Banks.

'Hah. It will be dreadful. Raymond insisted on adding too much chilli pepper. It will burn your tongue right off.' Zelda was the only person Banks knew who called Ray 'Raymond'.

'He definitely does have a liking for spicy food,' Banks said.

'Always did,' Annie muttered.

'Don't be so soft,' Ray said, joining them. 'It'll be delicious. Just wait and taste.' He raised his glass. 'To crime.'

Banks and Annie exchanged a glance, then shrugged and joined in the toast.

Banks had noticed on the only other occasion they had all met that Zelda and Annie had tended to circle one another, as if they couldn't quite make up their minds how to relate. They were friendly on the surface. There was certainly no open animosity, perhaps none at all, just a hint of jealousy on Annie's part, as a woman might feel when she meets someone younger and more beautiful than herself. Annie was also naturally protective of her father.

Though Zelda and Ray had lived together in Cornwall for over a year, they had only been up in Yorkshire for a short time, and neither Banks nor Annie had got to know her well. Ray was the kind who liked to spring surprises, and though he had mentioned Zelda from time to time, he hadn't explained the full extent of their relationship.

Like Ray, Zelda was an artist. She painted occasionally, but mostly she worked at pottery, jewellery and sculpture, which she intended to sell at local craft fairs and folk festivals. She also had some sort of mysterious job that required her to spend a few days in London every now and then. When they had first met, she had given Banks a small carved wooden object she had made that felt alive and seemed to twist and curve gently in his hand when he held it. She said it was meant to calm people down, like worry beads and rubbing pebbles, and he looked as if he needed calming down. He did, too. And it worked. He used it at work quite often.

Zelda finished her cigarette and went into the kitchen to 'rescue' dinner, as she put it. Ray changed the record. Banks strained to listen for a moment to the music, unsure of what it was, then he said, 'Donovan? "Legend of a Girl Child Linda". You skipped the first track on the album.'

'Yeah, "Sunshine Superman" was always a bit too hippy-dippy for me. A bit too flowers in your hair.'

Banks laughed. 'And this isn't?'

'Nah. This is nice. The mono version, of course.'

Annie rolled her eyes. 'Of course.'

But it was 'nice', Banks had to agree, the soft, slightly sibilant voice, a haunting melody, and sparse orchestral backing – here a few strings, there a touch of woodwinds – seemed to emphasise the song's ethereal quality. He hadn't listened to it for years. Donovan had always been the poor man's Dylan until this album, Banks remembered, where he set out to forge his own medieval troubadour brand of folk and jazz.

Five minutes later, Zelda called them into the dining room, which shared the back of the cottage with the kitchen itself. There were candles already lit all over the place, creating an intimate and relaxing atmosphere in the small space, casting shadows on the walls. Ray served plates of what he called a sort of Moroccan-cum-Mexican beef bourguignon, complete with button mushrooms and pearl onions, served with roasted root vegetables and basmati rice. Whatever it was, it was delicious, Banks thought as he took his first taste, and not too hot at all. Ray had opened a bottle of burgundy earlier, and it went well with the food. Annie took only a small glass.

There were paintings and sketches in various stages of completion all over the place, even in the kitchen, propped against the wall, or hanging on it, including a series of beautiful charcoal nude studies of Zelda. She caught Banks trying not to look at one of them and gave him an enigmatic smile.

Conversation wandered from compliments on the food and how nice the cottage was to more personal matters, and the subject of first meetings came up.

Zelda peered over her glass at Annie and asked, 'How did you and Alan meet? Over a dead body? Something romantic like that?'

Annie seemed thrown for a moment. She glanced at Banks, who simply gestured for her to go on and tell the story.

'Well, sort of,' she said, with her eyes still on Banks. 'As a matter of fact, it was a skeleton. A very old skeleton. It had been buried since the war.'

Zelda clapped her hands. 'I knew it would be romantic,' she said.

Annie frowned at the interruption. 'We were on a bridge,' she went on. 'I was already at the scene and Alan was trying to get to it. I stopped him. I didn't know who he was, and he . . . well, let's just put it this way, he wasn't exactly dressed like a detective chief inspector.'

'And you call jeans, sunglasses and red wellies suitable attire for a detective sergeant?' Banks countered.

'It was muddy,' Annie said. 'Anyway,' she went on, 'we almost had a fight on the bridge, like Robin Hood and Little John.'

'I know that story,' said Zelda, laughing.

'And you?' Banks asked.

Zelda beamed at Ray. 'You tell it, my love. Your English is so much better than mine.'

'Don't be ridiculous. You're one of the most articulate people I know. Nevertheless . . .' Ray swigged some burgundy and smacked his lips. 'It was a John and Yoko moment,' he said. 'You might not know this, but the lovely Zelda here was a pavement artist in London when we met. An excellent pavement artist,' he added. 'What she couldn't do with a piece of coloured chalk . . . Though I must say she dressed far more like a tomboy than she does today. Her hair was short and shaggy, she wore a man's shirt and baggy jeans. Red wellies would have been a real treat.'

Banks imagined it was a sort of protective colouration, the way some women wear wedding rings at work so their colleagues don't make assumptions that they are available.

'Anyway,' Ray went on, 'she was doing the *Annunciation*. You know it? The da Vinci?'

Banks and Annie nodded.

'Well, something about the way the Angel Gabriel's robe fell just didn't seem right to me, so I took a piece of cloth, bent over, rubbed it out and put in my own correction.'

'I'd have belted you one,' said Annie.

Zelda seemed surprised. 'Then I suppose you are not made for John and Yoko moments, Annie. More Robin Hood and Little John for you?'

'What did you do?' Banks asked Zelda. He had noticed Annie's expression darken and wanted to deflect the conversation.

'Do? I didn't do anything. I just stood there with my mouth open. I was too angry to do anything.'

Ray looked at her. 'Angry? But you said—'

Zelda smiled. 'That was later. My anger passed. Very quickly. I saw, of course, that you were a genius and that you knew exactly the way to depict the creases of robes in chalk, and I fell immediately madly deeply and truly in love with you right there and then, on the spot. Is that right? Will that do?'

'It'll do,' said Ray. Banks could have sworn he was blushing. 'Everybody finished?'

They had. Banks noticed how clean Zelda's plate was; not a scrap of food nor a blob of sauce remained to smear its pristine surface. It was as if it hadn't been used at all. Ray collected all the plates and put them in the dishwasher, then he disappeared into the living room and turned the record over. Banks heard the strains of 'Season of the Witch'.

Zelda lit a cigarette. Banks felt the craving, after all those years, ripple through him, but it passed quickly. Ray brought out a runny French Brie, a well-aged Colston Basset Stilton and a nutty Manchego and served them with water crackers, grapes, figs and dried apricots. He poured more wine, claret this time.

'Sainsbury's best, don't you know,' he said in a posh accent, winking at Banks. 'And maybe we'll have a drop of port, too, later. Us gentlemen, that is. Send the ladies to the drawing room to practise their accomplishments, what ho? I've got a couple of nice Cubans hidden away for a special occasion. Cigars, that is.'

Annie elbowed him. 'Behave.'

Ray just laughed and moved to pour her some more wine.

Annie put her hand over the top of her glass before he could manage it.

They settled back to enjoy the cheese and wine, then Ray cleared his throat and said, 'There's something we've been meaning to bring up with you two. We just haven't been quite sure how or when to do it, what with one thing and another. It was a matter of waiting for the right time. And Zelda said we shouldn't get your hopes up too much.'

Banks and Annie exchanged glances and both spoke at once, 'Yes?'

Ray turned to Annie. 'Do you remember that time when you visited me in Cornwall, and you asked me if I knew anything about a man who had taken advantage of you?' he asked. Then he turned to Banks. 'And set fire to your cottage, Alan, almost killing you? An art forger. You gave me a photograph of him taken in a pub somewhere. You thought I might have come across him somewhere in the art world.'

Banks felt his skin crawl at the memory. He remembered the one photograph they had, which Annie had snapped with her mobile during their early days.

'I remember,' Annie said.

'Phil Keane,' said Banks. 'Not a forger, exactly. He was the one who got into the archives and forged the provenances for the fake paintings.'

'Yes.'

'But that was years ago. We've had a few trusted colleagues on the Met and various other forces keeping their eyes and ears open, but so far, not a sausage. Phil Keane is long gone. The last sighting we had was in America, Philadelphia, but the follow-up drew a blank. Why mention him now?'

'Raymond described this man to me when we were talking about remembering faces one evening last week,' said Zelda. 'Then he showed me the photograph Annie gave him. I recognised him.'

'You ... what?' Banks couldn't believe what he was hearing.

'I recognised the man. But not from the art world.'

'Where had you seen him before?'

'His photograph was in a file I saw at work. They wanted to know if I had ever seen him before. If I knew who he was.'

'Had you? Did you?'

'No.'

'What sort of work is it you do?' Banks asked.

Zelda glanced at Ray, who gave her a brief nod. She lit another cigarette before continuing. 'I can't tell you very much, but I work part of the time for an international organisation that tracks and prosecutes sex-traffickers.'

'Phil Keane is involved in sex-trafficking?'

Zelda held Banks's gaze and nodded. 'I think he must be. They didn't tell me his name. They just showed me the photograph. But after what Raymond has told me, and what you have just said, your Phil Keane must be a documents man. He knows how to get access to archives, to change the past, and he knows how to find new identities, how to get the correct certificates and fake papers. That is all I know about him. He must be someone who provides documents and false backgrounds for some of the people I encounter in my work.'

'Who are these people?'

'The people we monitor and hunt – the bosses, couriers, fixers, runners, even the girls – they sometimes need believable new histories and convincing papers, "legends", as the spy writers call them, or provenance, as it is in the art world. Also, because the people who commit these crimes belong to criminal gangs, they often operate in more than one area of criminal enterprise. Documents have become an important part of their existence and survival. As I understand it, your man's skill is definitely transferrable.'

'When did they show you this photograph?'

'Two weeks ago. Maybe three.'

'Could you tell where it was taken?'

'It was in London. On the embankment. I recognised a fragment of Tower Bridge in the background. He was with another man. A man I did recognise. He was a very bad person. A big man in one of the trafficking gangs. Evil. He likes to hurt the girls, you know what I mean?'

'Do you know where Keane is now?'

'No. I am sorry. I never did know. I've never met him, only seen the photograph, but I am sure it is him. I'm sorry I . . . that was what we meant about not wanting to get your hopes up. It is just a little thing. Raymond said I should tell you. I did not want to disappoint you.'

'You haven't seen or heard of him since you saw the photograph?'

'No. Only that once, in the file my supervisor showed me, someone they wanted me to identify. I had never seen him before, but I remembered the photograph when Raymond showed me the one you gave him. It is him. I do not forget faces. Not even when the hair is changed. And the people he works for are not the kind to let anyone like him walk away. As long as he behaves himself, he will be too valuable for them to kill him. If what you say is right, he has a rare talent. These people move around very much and recruit new people. Many are wanted by the police and need new identities. It is all the more important now with Brexit. The borders will change, became more difficult. It will be harder to move the girls around.'

'And you know the people he works for? What exactly is it you do?'

'I told you. I look at pictures, give names to faces. My work is much like your work. I know many different kinds of people. I see many pictures when I help. I can ask questions, keep my eyes open.'

'No,' said Banks. 'No, Zelda. I'm sorry. I'm very grateful you told us and everything, but it's far too dangerous. I don't know how you got involved in it, but I've been on the fringes of that world, the sex-trafficking, and I know how violent it can be. Keane's just as bad. I'm sure he fits in fine.'

'Dangerous? How is this dangerous? Mostly I work in an office in London looking at photographs or videos. Surveillance and police mugshots. That is all. I do nothing dangerous. Nobody sees me except the people I work with.'

'But surely your organisation, whatever it is, has access to facial recognition software?'

'Of course,' said Zelda. 'But for that they need a database. I am there to help them build that database. Some of the faces I know are already in the system, but many are not. Your man Keane was not.'

'Why you? I mean why are you doing this work?'

'You think it's not a job for a woman?'

'That's not what I meant,' Banks said. 'It's very specialist work.'

'Zelda is a super-recogniser,' Ray explained. 'She never forgets a face. I noticed when we met that the faces of Mary and Gabriel from the *Annunciation* she was drawing on the pavement were spot on, as far as I could tell, and she didn't use a crib or any kind of visual reference. It was amazing. She's been tested and everything, at Cambridge no less, and she's way up there. It's quite a rare gift.'

'Gift?' said Zelda. 'Sometimes I wonder.'

'Can you tell us the name of your supervisor? Put us in contact with him?'

'I'm sorry, but I cannot do that. He would never forgive me. Much of his work depends on secrecy. Much of the department's existence depends on secrecy. I have probably said too much already, but I want to help. I can look into it for you myself.'

'If anything happened to you I'd never forgive myself.'

'You're pissing against the wind, mate,' said Ray. 'I've never met a more stubborn woman than Zelda. Let her help you. She won't take no for an answer. Believe me.'

Zelda nodded. 'That is true. I will simply observe while I do what I do anyway. Perhaps ask some questions of the right people. I cannot promise anything, but I might be able to find out if this man is still in the country. Even where he is and what he is doing. If he is still called Keane or if he has a new name.'

Banks leaned back and glanced at Annie. He could see the hungry look in her eyes. Felt it in his own. It was a tempting offer, too tempting to resist. This man had tried to kill him, had burned down his home, and he would have succeeded if it hadn't been for Annie and Winsome. Keane had taken Annie in so thoroughly that she hadn't been able to trust herself in a relationship with a man ever since. 'It seems that we can't stop her, doesn't it?' Banks said. Then he turned to Zelda again. 'But I don't like it. Don't take any risks. And be careful.'

Zelda tilted her head sideways, a ghost of a smile playing on her lips. 'Always,' she said. 'Oh, have some more wine, Alan. Tell me what music you have been listening to. Raymond is such a philistine.' She waved her hand at the music in general. 'This is all right, but where is Bach, Beethoven, Brahms and Mozart?'

She was signalling the end of the conversation, a change in topic. Donovan had finished some time ago. Now Bridget St John was singing 'Ask Me No Questions'.

Banks smiled. 'Zelda, you can come and listen to my Bach cantatas anytime you like.'

Zelda laughed.

'Watch it, mate,' said Ray, smiling.

Annie rolled her eyes. 'Give me Barry Manilow any day.'

So they talked about music, about Bruckner and Mahler, Zelda's favourites, and Verdi and Maria Callas. Then they went on to poetry. Zelda seemed to know a lot about the Russians: Pushkin, Akhmatova, Tsvetaeva, Pasternak. Poets whose work Banks knew very little about. Akhmatova was her favourite, she said. Banks still felt unsettled at the mention of Phil Keane, but there was a spark of excitement that they might finally bring him to justice. He was worried about Zelda, though, mostly because he was ignorant about what she actually did and how good she was at it. Surely it couldn't be as easy or as straightforward as she made out?

Still, it had started now, and there was nothing he could do except hope to hell that nothing bad happened to her because of it. No matter what she and Ray had said, if anything did happen, he would never forgive himself, and he didn't think Ray would forgive him, either, for all his talk. He helped himself to a wedge of Stilton and watched Zelda pour more wine and tease Annie for not drinking any. The candles flickered in a draught from the back door. Banks felt himself shiver. Ray went to put on some more music, but even Quicksilver Messenger Service doing 'Mona' couldn't dispel the mood brought on by Zelda's story, and he found himself wondering about her motives for her work and these faces she never forgot. Where had she seen them in the first place?

'Are you sure you won't stay and have a snifter?' Ray asked as they stood at the door. 'I've got a very nice Armagnac.'

'No, Ray,' said Annie. 'I told you. I'm driving. And we've got a busy day at work tomorrow.'

'Ah, yes. Criminals to catch. The offer of the spare room is still open. Even just for one. Alan?'

'It's tempting, Ray,' said Banks, 'but I'd better be off, too. Thanks for . . . well, for a very interesting evening.'

Zelda gave him a peck on the cheek and Annie hugged Ray.

'Goodnight, Dad,' she said firmly, letting go, then grasped Banks's arm and half-dragged him towards the car as he continued saying his own goodbyes.

'Maybe that wasn't such a bad idea Ray had,' he said. 'About staying.'

'Oh, just be quiet and put your seat belt on. Honestly,' Annie said as she set off along the village High Street. 'Will he never grow up? For crying out loud, she's young enough to be his granddaughter. And you and Ray behave like a couple of little kids.'

'Nevertheless,' said Banks, 'they seem to make a nice couple. And they seem happy together. What can be so wrong with that?'

Annie shot him a piercing glance as she set off too fast along the High Street. 'You would say that. That's a typical male response. I'll bet she has you all eating out of her hand. It's practically bloody paedophilia.'

'Come off it, Annie. Zelda's thirty. She's a grown-up. Old enough to make her choices. And at least she has the chance to do that now. And it sounds as if she does important work.' He paused. 'Don't be so hard on her. And slow down. The roads might be icy.'

The glance Annie gave him was icier than any road. 'A beautiful damsel,' she went on. 'And bloody Mata Hari to boot. Who could resist?'

'That's a cruel thing to say, Annie. And it's not fair.'

'I notice you didn't waste any time before you started flirting with her.'

'What do you mean?'

'"You can come and listen to my Bach cantatas anytime you like, Zelda",' Annie mocked.

Banks laughed. 'What's wrong with that? I meant it innocently enough.'

'*Men.*' Annie put her foot down as they left the village for the dark unfenced road down the dale side. Banks hung on for dear life.

Fortunately, it wasn't a long journey. Annie screeched to a halt outside Newhope Cottage, spraying gravel in all directions. The place was in darkness, but when Banks clicked his key ring, a light came on over the porch.

'Want to come in for a coffee or something?' he asked.

'No, thanks.'

'Come on, Annie. Don't sulk. We've got a lot to talk about.'

'Have we? I don't think so.'

'Phil Keane.'

'It probably won't come to anything. Besides, that business is all in the past. It happened, and it's over and done with.'

'Maybe for you.'

'He was *my* mistake.'

'He cost us both a lot.'

Annie leaned across him and opened the passenger door. 'Are you going to get out now or what?'

Banks sighed and got out of the car. As he bent to thank Annie for the lift and say goodnight, she shot off in another spray of gravel and left him standing there alone in the glow of the porch light.

4

The meeting in the boardroom that Thursday morning was attended by the only four detectives remaining on the Eastvale Regional Homicide and Major Crimes squad: Detective Superintendent Alan Banks, DI Annie Cabbot, DS Winsome Jackman and DC Geraldine Masterson. Their fifth member, DC Doug Wilson, had recently left the force to pursue a teaching career. Due to budget restrictions, no replacement had yet been found for him, and Area Commander/Chief Superintendent Catherine Gervaise had warned Banks not to hold his breath waiting for one.

A few images of the victims and a number of points raised by the investigations so far graced the whiteboard, but it didn't amount to very much. Winsome had talked to both Kirsten Brody and the van driver John Kelly again, and it was now clear that nobody involved in the accident on Belderfell Pass or the discovery of the body had placed Adrienne Munro behind the wheel of the abandoned Ford Focus. The problem of how she had got there remained.

Banks finished his coffee, stood up and started the proceedings. 'Basically, we've got two suspicious deaths,' he began. 'Let's start with Adrienne Munro, aged nineteen. The way it appears is that Adrienne died from an overdose of sleeping pills, or to be more accurate, died from asphyxiating on her own vomit while unconscious from an overdose of sleeping pills.' He waved Wednesday's morning paper in the air. 'Though thanks to some shoddy reporting, everyone thinks she died a drug addict's death, probably with a needle sticking out of her arm. Jazz Singh is working on the toxicology to determine exactly what composition and brand of sleeping tablets were used. There was no physical evidence that they were forced on Adrienne in any way. The other death, a male in his mid-sixties, appears to be due to injuries sustained from a fall into a gully on Tetchley Moor.

'Adrienne clearly had to have been taken – most likely driven – to the abandoned car she was found in after her death. The unidentified male appears to have wandered into a gully and died from the fall. But Tetchley Moor is pretty remote, so we need to know how he got there in the first place and what he was doing there dressed the way he was on such a night. It's not impossible that someone could have pushed or tossed him over the edge of the gully. Or perhaps he was being chased.

'In neither case do we have any evidence of injuries inflicted on the victim by another person, which means that both deaths could be accidental, or the result of suicide. What we do have is evidence of the involvement of another person or persons *after* death, or possibly even, for a short time, before death occurred. It's a bit of a conundrum, to say the least.

'As regards timing, the best I can gather from studying Dr Glendenning's post-mortem results and Dr Burns's crime-scene examinations is that the victims could have died at the same time, within a day of one another, or as long as two days apart. When pushed, the doctor told me that it was likely Adrienne Munro died first. Either way, we're looking at last weekend, Friday night after midnight at the earliest, and Monday at the latest. Adrienne Munro's parents last spoke with her on Saturday morning, and all they said was that she seemed a bit distracted, perhaps by her university workload.

'We don't know the identity of the deceased male yet, and needless to say that's slowing us down. Animal activity has made arriving at a suitable image with which to go public difficult, but we have both our photographer Peter Darby and our occasional sketch artist Ray Cabbot working on it. Once we've identified him, we can work on finding out when and where he was last seen. He was wearing an expensive made-to-measure Hugo Boss suit and handmade leather brogues, so he was probably fairly wealthy. We hope for some results soon. In the meantime, we keep our eyes and ears open for any missing persons' reports. Who knows, maybe he's a Russian spy. Another Sergei Skripal. Maybe they're both Russian spies. But somewhere, someone must be wondering where he is. Any more progress with this, Gerry?'

Gerry Masterson shook her head. 'Nothing, sir. No missing persons of that description, no matching fingerprints in the system. Ray and Peter hope to have something for us before close of play today. I've spoken with Adrian Moss at media liaison, and he assures us he'll get it on tonight's news. Until then, there's not much more we can do. We're guessing that the man lived locally, or at least not too far away, so we've got some of the beat constables and PCSOs asking around the nearby villages.'

'Getting anywhere with the keys in his pocket?'

'No, sir. Just common or garden house keys. A couple of Yales, deadlock, a few smaller ones that could belong to cupboards or sheds. I doubt they'll tell us anything more until we find a house to match them.'

'The key ring itself?'

'Generic. No initials or "a present from Benidorm" sort of stuff.'

'Pity.'

'We could use a bit more help with the door-to-door enquiries, sir. Can't we draft in a few foot soldiers?'

Banks nodded. 'I've put in for a couple more PCSOs. And if we find we're dealing with homicide, then I'll have to go on my knees to headquarters and beg for office staff. For the moment, we'll work both cases out of here. What did Dr Glendenning have to say about the body on the moor?'

'No evidence of a struggle,' Annie Cabbot said. 'It was much the same as Dr Burns told us at the scene. All the evidence points to the fact that he died where we found him, two or perhaps three days earlier. On further examination, we found nothing more in his pockets to help us uncover his identity, and there were no distinguishing marks on his body. There are still too many unanswered questions. What if someone did push him down that gully? A gentle push would have done it, and wouldn't necessarily have left any traces. We've no way of knowing who else might have been up there at the time, no footprints or handy threads of fabric caught on the heather.'

'Any signs of a boyfriend in the Munro case?' Gerry asked. 'Or someone she'd rejected recently, upset in some way?'

'There was someone she was seeing last year, and we'll be talking to him,' said Banks. 'But no one at the moment. Not according to her mother.'

'Perhaps her parents didn't know?' said Gerry. 'My parents certainly didn't know about all my boyfriends.'

Annie looked at her. '*All?*'

Gerry blushed. 'Never you mind, guv. What I'm saying is that parents don't necessarily know everything. When it comes right down to it, they don't know very much at all.'

Banks thought about his own adolescence and how little his parents knew about what he got up to. It had been the same with his own children too. 'True enough,' he said. 'I suggest that first we find out what we can from Adrienne's teachers and friends at the college. Winsome and I will head down there later this morning. We've got results on some of the phone numbers from her mobile. Nothing suspect so far, except perhaps the ex-boyfriend her parents mentioned to us.

Colin Fairfax. They were supposed to have split up last year, but there are a number of calls from him since then. He may have been pestering her or stalking her. The last call made from her phone was on Saturday morning. The parents. That checks out. Annie, I'd like you and Gerry to keep on trying to find out the identity of the male. Put a bit of pressure on Peter and Ray. And keep in touch with Adrian Moss, too. He might be a bit of a pain in the arse, but he does have the contacts and the occasional good idea when it comes to media liaisons.' Banks picked up his folders and empty coffee cup as the detectives drifted out of the boardroom.

Annie got his attention in the corridor.

'Got time for a coffee? My treat.'

'Fine,' said Banks.

The Golden Grill had morphed into a Costa almost overnight, or so it seemed, and by mid-morning on a Thursday it was full of shivering shoppers taking a break. Banks ordered simple black coffee and a lemon poppy seed muffin, while Annie went for a latte and a giant chocolate chip cookie, and they made their way through the prams and shopping bags that cluttered the aisles and managed to find a table for two at the back, next to the toilets. The sound of children overdosed with sugar, and of babies crying for attention, made it unlikely that anyone would overhear their conversation.

Before Banks could open his mouth, Annie touched his forearm and said, 'I want to apologise for last night. I was out of line.'

Banks nodded. 'Maybe I was insensitive. I hadn't realised how difficult it must be for you seeing Ray and Zelda together.'

'No need to be patronising, Alan. I've said I was out of line. I've apologised. And, by the way, you *were* flirting with Zelda.' She paused and took a bite of her cookie without taking her eyes off him.

'She's a remarkable woman. Ray's a lucky fellow.'

'There you are. That's exactly what another bloke *would* say. I'm trying to apologise here, not start another argument.'

'All right, all right.' Banks tested his coffee. It was still too hot.

'It's just so sudden, that's all,' Annie said. 'And startling. I mean, I've been used to Ray having girlfriends over the years. Of course I have. I was just a kid when my mother died, and when I look back, Ray wasn't so old. He had his needs, as they say. And they all treated me respectfully.'

'It's quite a shock when you realise how young your parents were at certain key moments of your life. Somehow, they always seemed so much older than you.'

'That's because they were, you daft pillock.'

Banks laughed. 'You know what I mean.'

Annie smiled, cradling her latte in both hands. 'Yeah, I suppose I do. My mother always seems young. In my memories. In my dreams. But she never got old, so I suppose that makes sense.'

'You still dream about her?'

Annie nodded. 'Sometimes.'

'What's so different about this time, about Zelda?'

'I don't know what it is. Partly because they're here, of course, and not in Cornwall. Also maybe it's because it so obviously is the "real thing" this time, whatever that is. For Ray, at any rate. And maybe it's because I'm getting old, and I don't have anything like that myself, or anyone in my life, for that matter. I could analyse myself till the cows come home and still not find an answer. Maybe *I'd* like to be adored. I mean, I couldn't even keep Nick bloody Fleming, and he's not exactly the catch of the day.'

'Simple jealousy?'

'Jealousy's rarely simple.'

'It's still a dog-in-the-manger attitude.'

'Sort of. Maybe. I don't know. Watching them just put me in a bad mood, that's all. Not being able to drink didn't help much, either.'

'Next time we'll take a taxi.'

'Lord knows what I'd say or do if I got pissed with them.'

Banks laughed again. 'Maybe it wouldn't be as bad as you think.'

Annie gave him a sideways glance and cockeyed smile. 'Ever the optimist.'

'Do you really hate Zelda?'

'I think I do, yes.'

'Why?'

'Because she's young and beautiful and she's going to break my father's heart.'

'You can't know that. What makes you say that?'

'Come on, Alan. Open your eyes. You can't tell me a beautiful woman like Zelda is going to stay with Ray on a permanent basis. She'll be off with the first handsome pizza delivery man who comes along, and guess who'll be left to clean up the mess.'

'I wouldn't be too sure about that, Annie. And I think it's a harsh thing to say.'

'I'm talking about *my* feelings now. Aren't I allowed to talk about my feelings?'

'Calm down. I didn't say that.'

'You certainly implied it.'

Banks paused and sipped some coffee. Just right. The espresso machine hissed and gurgled in the background. 'For what it's worth,' Banks said, 'I think they've got a chance. No, hear me out. I don't know why, but there's a powerful chemistry about them, and that may be what makes you feel the way you do. Maybe Zelda needs a father figure. What's so bad about that? I get the impression that she's had some tough experiences in her life. In fact, I think she was probably trafficked herself. It would be one way of explaining how she first saw those faces her organisation wants her to recognise again. Remember, she recognised the man with Keane and said he was evil, that he liked to hurt the girls. If that's so, can you imagine what her experiences must have made her feel about men, about sex?'

'Yuck. I don't even want to think about their sex life. Besides, how do you know what her life was like? You're only guessing.'

'Perhaps. But maybe she feels safe with Ray. Have you thought about that? That's all I'm saying.'

'Whatever that means.'

'It means he's a good man, Annie, a kind man, a gentle man. Maybe that's what she sees in him. Maybe that's what she needs. Maybe that's why she loves him. Not all women are hung up on six-packs and pecs.'

'You're so bloody naive sometimes, Alan Banks. Most of us *aren't* really interested in six-packs or pecs at all. We're far more interested in the person inside than in the packaging. That's why you men can let yourselves go, eat what you want, get fat and grow man breasts and still end up in the sack with a stunner like Zelda. Look at you. What about that Italian babe you had, Ophelia, or whatever her name was, and the lovely Sonia? They were both young enough to be your daughters.'

'Surely you're not saying I'm fat or have man breasts?' Banks said. 'And besides, it's Oriana and Sophia.'

Annie stared at him open-mouthed for a moment, then she burst out laughing. One or two people at the nearby table gave her funny looks. 'No, Alan,' she said. 'That wasn't my point at all. As a matter of fact, you're in pretty good shape for a bloke your age. No tits at all.'

'Now you're talking.' Banks paused. 'Anyway, I'm sorry. Sorry you feel that way. If you ever want to talk about it again . . .'

'I'll know where not to go. Just joking. Strangely enough, I do feel a bit better, thanks. At least you've given me a good laugh.'

'Give them a chance.'

'Promise you'll help clean up the mess if she bolts? A shoulder to cry on?'

'Promise. I like Ray. I'll be there for him. I consider him a good friend.'

Annie nodded. 'I know you do. You and your bloody sixties music.'

Banks shrugged. 'I feel sorry for you, having to grow up in the eighties.'

'It wasn't so bad. At least we had Michael Jackson. Anyway, what are we going to do about Phil Keane? Do you believe that, too? Little Miss Super-brain?'

'Super-recogniser,' said Banks. 'I've heard of that. Again, why would she lie? And it makes sense. Keane would hardly go back to his routines in the art world after what happened. He's probably persona non grata in every art institution in Europe. His skill was in altering the past and forging official documents, making them appear real, as if they've been around for years. He's like the Donald Pleasence character in *The Great Escape*, only he's not going blind. He's also a psychopath. What better line of work for him?'

'I suppose you're right. Should we have a chat with Charlie, then?'

Charlie Fox was their contact on the Met. He was a specialist who dealt in art fraud and theft, consulting with the various squads both at home and around the continent when they needed his expertise. 'We should,' said Banks. 'But I don't think he'll be able to help us.'

'Why not?'

'Think about it. Keane has moved on. What's the odds he no longer has anything to do with the art world? What's the odds he hasn't changed his name?'

'People make mistakes. You know that as well as I do, Alan. Criminals sometimes make the most basic mistakes because they can't give up a certain routine or line of operation. They have habits, like everyone else, and habits are often unconscious.'

'True. Modus operandi. But Keane is smart, remember. And he tried to kill a police officer. Me. He'd know it makes sense to move on, adapt his skills to another criminal venture. It sounds like this is it.'

'Can't we contact the people Zelda works with ourselves?'

'It doesn't appear as if she's likely to help us with that. You heard her. I suppose we can't really blame her. It's obviously a relationship that nobody wants broadcasting. We could go through other channels, I suppose. Dirty Dick Burgess, for a start. But I don't want to bring trouble or danger down on Zelda.'

'God forbid.'

'Annie!'

'Sorry. So where do we go next? Do we just wait for Super Zelda to come up with something?'

'There's not much else we can do,' said Banks. He glanced at his watch. 'In the meantime, I'd better go and pick up my car from the garage, or they'll be charging me parking for it.'

Winsome knew the campus of Eastvale College fairly well. A couple of cases over the years had taken her there, and she found the racial mix of the area most refreshing after the almost total whiteness of the rest of town, and of the Dales in general. Not that she felt uncomfortable with where she lived or what she did, just that she felt a bit more at home when she walked down a street crowded with young Asian, Chinese and black students as well as white ones. Besides, she liked the tree-lined streets of tall Victorian houses, divided into student flats, with the steep front steps and iron railings and brightly coloured doors, the outside stairs leading down to basement bedsits, the aromas of curry, Thai and Chinese spices that infused the air. It was another world. You could almost imagine yourself in a thriving city rather than a quiet country town.

But that feeling lasted only as far as the campus itself. Its buildings were spread over a large area, mostly ugly and functional squat concrete and glass blocks with fields and woods beyond. There were a few listed buildings, remnants of the original agricultural college, but mostly it was an architectural mess. Winsome paused and consulted her map, then headed for the science buildings, which formed a quadrangle with a central square of grass surrounded by benches. When the weather was fine enough, Winsome knew, students would sit out there chatting or working on essays. They would stretch out on the grass, the young lovers side by side. But not in November.

Professor Luke Stoller had agreed to talk to her about Adrienne Munro in his office. She entered the building through the double glass doors, and a security guard at a semi-circular reception desk told her where the office was on the first floor. The steps were concrete, the rough walls lined with cork boards on which were pinned ads for concerts, 'ladies' night' at The Cellar Club, any lecture changes or cancellations, departmental communications and the meetings of the various clubs and societies. There seemed to be so much going on, Winsome almost wished she were a student again. Almost. The problem was that if she went back these days, she would leave not only with a degree but with the albatross of debt around her neck for many years to come. The Munros were right: it was no way to start a working life.

Professor Stoller answered her knock with a chirpy 'Come in' and stood up to shake Winsome's hand as she entered. He was a paunchy man in his early fifties, she guessed, curly grey hair and matching beard. Even his suit was grey. His tie was the only colourful thing about him, and that looked as if a drunken student had done the Technicolor yawn all over it. He wore it loose at the top, the way Banks always did whenever he had to wear a tie. The bookcases were stuffed with textbooks, and piles of papers sat on top of his filing cabinets and desk, but though the office was cluttered, it was tidy. A large poster showing the human circulation system hung on his wall.

'Please excuse the mess,' Stoller said. 'Work tends to pile up.'

'I know the feeling,' said Winsome, sitting down in the hard-back chair.

'It's about Adrienne, isn't it?'

'Yes. When did you last see her?'

'Wednesday, just over a week ago, when she came for her weekly tutorial.' He shook his head slowly. 'This is a terrible business. I simply can't take it all in yet.'

'It came as a shock?'

'A huge one.'

'Did you know Adrienne well?'

'As well as one gets to know a student. We met in tutorials, of course, and I also supervised some of her lab work.'

'Was she a good student?'

'Excellent. She was very intelligent. Quiet and thoughtful. Adrienne took her work seriously. She wasn't flighty or lazy, like some of her classmates. She was a hard worker. She was usually on time with her projects, and her examination results last year were exemplary. She had a clear, logical mind. Not only was she good academically, but she had a real feel for the work. She would have made an excellent agricultural scientist.'

'Not a farmer, then?'

'Good heavens, no. Whatever gave you that impression?'

'Agricultural sciences.'

'A bit misleading, I'm afraid. It's a catch-all discipline, but we're not a training school for farmers. The students study methods of farming, true enough, but we tend to see the larger picture: crop management, land use and efficiency, environmental issues, food needs, animal husbandry. It's a very broad field, including courses in statistics and earth sciences, climate, geology and geography, even a bit of chemistry, and biology, which is my area of speciality. Inter-disciplinary, if you like.'

'And Adrienne?'

'Adrienne was especially interested in conservation and wildlife issues, responsible land use, growth cycles, environmental factors such as climate change, alternative energy sources, GMOs, that sort of thing.'

'GMOs?'

'Sorry. Genetically modified organisms. Adrienne wasn't sure whether she was for them or against.'

'Where would she have been likely to end up working after she'd finished?'

'A government department? Or a consortium? Perhaps even one of the many private consulting firms.' He smiled. 'Who knows, she might even have ended up teaching somewhere like this. What she really wanted to do was to go to Africa and work in farming, energy and land use. She was very forward-looking. She always said there's no practical reason at all for anyone in today's world to be starving. And she's right, of course.'

'If it weren't for politics,' Winsome said.

'Yes.'

'Would you say Adrienne was a conscientious student?'

'Yes, I'd say she was.'

'What do you think went wrong? Was something eating away at her?'

Stoller shook his head slowly. 'I can't for the life of me think what it was. The newspaper seemed to imply that she was a drug-taker, which I found hard to believe, but you said on the phone that she committed suicide?'

'I said it appeared that she took an overdose of sleeping pills. Had she been depressed lately, upset about anything?'

'Not to my knowledge. Her work . . .'

'Yes?'

'Well, this year her work wasn't quite up to the standards she set herself in her first year, but that's not uncommon in second-year students. They all seem to hit a patch where other things seem more important than university work. I suppose it means they've finally settled in. Besides, it's early days yet. Start-of-term struggle.'

'What other things?'

'Who knows? Almost anything can get in the way, really. Social life. Boyfriends. Shopping.'

'Did Adrienne have a boyfriend?'

'Not that I knew of. But then, I wouldn't be in the best position to know. It's not a good idea to discuss such private matters with students, as I'm sure you're aware.'

Winsome nodded. 'The times we live in. But was she still doing well enough academically?'

'Oh, yes. So far. She just missed a few lectures, a couple of tutorials, was late with an essay once. Seemed distracted in lectures. That sort of thing. In most students you wouldn't even notice, it's par for the course, but with Adrienne . . . well, I suppose she'd set herself too high a standard last year.'

'Do you think the course work was too hard for her? Did it lead to stress?'

'There's always a certain amount of stress involved if you want to do a good job, but I'd say Adrienne could handle it. I can't imagine it being too hard for her.'

'Do you know if she had something else on her mind, what it was that might have been distracting her?'

'No. If she did have any serious problems, she didn't tell me about them.'

'Was she worried about anything? Anxious?'

'On occasion, I thought so. Like I said, distracted, distant, as if her mind were elsewhere.'

'But you've no idea about what? You've no idea where?'

'No. Sorry. Maybe it was money. A lot of the students have money problems these days.'

'What about the scholarship?'

Stoller frowned. 'What scholarship?'

'According to her parents, Adrienne was awarded a scholarship at the beginning of this year.'

'First I've heard of it.'

'Would you be likely to know?'

'There are all kinds of scholarships around. I can't say I always pay as much attention as I should to departmental memos and the like, even if they sent me one. I can't say it surprises me though. As I said, she was a bright student.' He paused. 'But I like to think she would have told me about something like that. If she'd been her old self she would have been excited, and I'm sure she would have told me.'

'Could being free of money worries have affected her work?'

'In what way?'

'I don't know. Made her feel she had to give more in return? Or the opposite – feel that she could kick back and relax a bit. Have fun. She'd have more money to go drinking or clubbing, shopping, do other things. Things that might distract her from her studies.'

'I suppose it's a possibility. But, as I said, I know nothing of this scholarship, or what she did in her own time. You'll have to check with the bursar's office about the money.'

'Do you know of anyone Adrienne might have confided in?'

'Neela, perhaps. Neela Mitchell. They were very close. Best friends.'

It was one of the names Winsome had already picked up from the phone calls and emails. 'Do you know her address?'

'Yes. She was in the same tutorial group as Adrienne. I needed her details in case I had to get in touch.' Stoller walked over to his filing cabinet and pulled out a folder. 'Should I be giving you this information?' he said. 'I mean, isn't there some sort of confidentiality rule?'

'Professor Stoller,' said Winsome, 'a suspicious death usually trumps confidentiality, but if you insist, I can go and get a court order.'

'No, no. I'm sorry. I wasn't meaning to be difficult. I gave your colleague Adrienne's address. I just don't want to get into trouble.'

'Believe me, you'd be in much more trouble if you *didn't* tell me what I want to know. Besides, we have this Neela's phone number and email address already. You'll just be saving me a little time. If you wouldn't mind, sir?'

'You said "suspicious death",' Stoller said. 'I thought she'd committed suicide? Are you saying now that you suspect foul play, that someone might have done this to her? Do you think Adrienne was *murdered*?'

'I'm not suggesting anything of the kind, and I'd be very grateful if you wouldn't go around repeating that to anyone else. Suspicious means there are unanswered questions, that's all. We like to dot our i's and cross our t's, just like you academics.'

Stoller gave her Neela Mitchell's address. 'I don't know if she's still there, though,' he said. 'She was very upset when she heard the news about Adrienne. She came to see me, and I recommended counselling. We have an excellent centre here on campus. She may even have gone home to her parents.'

'I'll take it from here, sir, don't worry. Thanks for the address.'

Stoller nodded, sat down again and rearranged the papers on his desk. At least he wasn't playing the busy card, trying to get rid of her, Winsome noticed, the way a lot of professionals tend to do with the police. 'Do you happen to know if Adrienne was on any prescription medication? Was she taking anti-depressants, tranquillisers, sleeping pills, anything like that?'

'Good Lord, I don't think so. I doubt it. Not Adrienne.'

'Drugs?'

'I never saw any signs.'

'Would you have recognised them if you had?'

'We've had seminars on the problem of drugs on campus, so I know a few of the things to watch out for. I saw none of them in Adrienne's case. At worst, she was sometimes over-tired in a morning, but I just assumed she'd been up working late. Otherwise she always seemed perfectly normal to me.'

'Did she go clubbing, that sort of thing?'

'Again, I wouldn't know. At a guess, I'd say she did about as much and no less than most of the girls, which wasn't excessive. Dances, pub nights, that sort of thing. Young people need to have fun as well as work, DS Jackman.'

'I know that, sir. It wasn't so long ago.'

'I . . . I . . . didn't mean . . . Which university, if you don't mind my asking?'

Winsome smiled. 'Not at all. Birmingham. And I studied psychology and criminology. So you saw no signs of excessive clubbing, drug-taking or binge-drinking, just Adrienne being tired occasionally from a late night's working?'

'As far as I know. I mean, I assumed it was work, but she may have been out dancing late. Where's the harm in that?'

'There isn't any, as far as I can see. Is there a doctor or a student clinic on campus?'

'Yes. A very good health centre. But they won't tell you anything, of course. I know doctors are bound by confidentiality.'

'Oh, they'll tell me,' Winsome said. 'That sort of thing only happens on television.'

'But patient confidentiality—'

'Is all very well and good, sir. While the patient is alive. I'm afraid that all bets are off now.'

Stoller hung his head. 'Of course.'

'Ever heard of a Colin Fairfax?'

Stoller's brow furrowed. 'No. I can't say as I have.'

'He wasn't a student?'

'Certainly not in this department, or I'd remember.'

'Is there anything else you can tell me about Adrienne? Anyone else I should talk to?'

'Neela would know far more about her other friends and her social life in general.'

'I'll talk to her. Thank you very much for your time, Professor. You've been most helpful.'

'I have? It's a pleasure. I . . . I mean . . . I'm only too glad to help. Poor Adrienne.'

Winsome scribbled a few more notes in her book, but all it really amounted to was that Adrienne had seemed a bit more tired and distant than usual this year, but that her work hadn't suffered seriously yet because of it. That and the mysterious scholarship. She hoped Neela Mitchell would have a bit more useful information to tell her. Or Colin Fairfax, when they tracked him down.

For now, it was time to get back to the squad room and do a bit of work on the computer. The rest could wait until tomorrow morning.

5

'Laurence Edward Hadfield,' said Gerry as she and Annie hurried down to the police garage to sign out a car. 'The cleaning lady's waiting for us there. Her name is Adele Balter. She's fifty-three years old, been cleaning for him for going on ten years now. Here, I pulled a picture of Hadfield from LinkedIn.' Gerry passed her a thin file folder and Annie paused to examine it. An Internet image of Hadfield sat next to her father's interpretation of Peter Darby's crime-scene photograph. 'Doesn't it look like the same person?'

Annie agreed that it did.

Gerry drove, heading east out of town on the main dale road, and Annie relaxed in the passenger seat. It was Friday morning, and she was planning to attend an ex-colleague's surprise fortieth birthday party in Ripon that evening. It promised to be quite a blowout, but with any luck, she would have a couple of days to recover. Weekends were notoriously slow in investigations, and unless there was an urgency or some sort of time factor involved in the case, most detectives tended to do what everyone did and take the weekend off. Either that or catch up with the paperwork.

'Hadfield's sixty-six years old,' Gerry went on, from memory. 'A banker by profession. Runs a private investment bank in the City. Or ran. He's semi-retired, or whatever you call it when people like him hand most of the work over to others. He's had his little hideaway in North Yorkshire for twenty years. It's called Rivendell. He spends most of his time up there these days, but he still keeps a flat in Mayfair. Got his OBE eight years ago. Reputed to be extremely wealthy. No number, I'm afraid.'

'Well, you certainly don't get poor running a private investment bank,' Annie commented.

'Might make a few enemies as well,' Gerry said.

'Now, now. You know what the super said. Let's not go seeing a murder where there's no evidence of one. We don't even know if he's our man yet for certain.'

'But it is all pretty dodgy, you must admit, guv. Reported missing around the same time we find an unidentified body of a male in his sixties dressed in an expensive business suit.'

'Dodgy, yes. Murder, no. Not yet.'

Soon they had left the last housing estate behind and passed an area of allotments, dotted with ramshackle garden sheds, where in summer men worked their little strips of earth with their sleeves rolled up, or sat having a smoke and a chat beside the vegetable patch. Today, the allotments were deserted and bleak even in the winter sunlight. Ahead of them stretched The Leas, where the valley bottom widened and flattened and the river meandered through meadows made unseasonably green by the recent rains. Beyond, on the opposite side of the dale, they could see Lyndgarth high on the valley side, beside the ruins of Devraulx Abbey.

'Well connected, by all accounts,' Gerry went on. 'Politicians, financiers, managing directors, that crowd. Even a rock star and a footballer or two. Liked mixing with celebrities, apparently. Generous with his charitable donations. Oxfam, Save the Children, War Child and so on. Or at least he was until the scandals hit.'

'Any form?'

'None. Brought up in front of the Financial Conduct Authority once. Suspicion of insider trading, I believe. Never got beyond a preliminary investigation. No charges. That's it.'

Gerry turned left at Fortford, by the Roman fort unearthed on the hill beside the village green, which still had its ancient stocks planted firmly at its centre. They had found a body there not so long ago, she remembered, and far worse had happened at St Mary's, about half a mile out of the village, the previous winter. As they passed the church, Annie shuddered at the memory of the scene of the mass murder, bodies dead and wounded lying about the ancient country churchyard. Today it looked like any other innocent country church on a sunny day, except for the heaps of flowers by the lychgate. There were always flowers beside the lychgate now.

'What about his family background?'

Annie flipped a page in her folder. 'Parents deceased. Twin sisters, three years younger than him. Wife died three years ago after a long struggle with cancer.'

'Children?'

'Uh-huh. Two. Son Ronald, age thirty-eight, following in father's footsteps. Also works in the City. Lives in Hampstead with wife Olivia and two boys Rufus and Roderick, aged eight and ten. Poor sods,' said Annie.

'I know. I felt terrible when I lost my grandfather, even though we weren't all that close.'

'I mean their names. All the R's. Wonder Olivia didn't have to change hers to Regan or something.'

'Oh, right. Yes. Well, with names like that they'd probably fit right in at Eton.'

'Eton? Really.'

'Oh, yes.'

Annie turned and flashed her a grin. 'You said two children. Who's the other?'

'Daughter named Poppy.'

'Good Lord.'

'She's the black sheep of the family,' Gerry went on. 'No

banking for her. Went through a variety of jobs, played in a garage band for a while, tried acting but didn't make the grade. There's rumours of a couple of soft porn shoots. Hooked up with a bad-boy rocker, Nate Maddock – Mad Dog, they called him. Usual exploits. Drugs. Wrecked hotel rooms. Assault. Weapons charges.'

'Weapons?'

'Liked his guns, apparently, did Mad Dog.'

'Liked?'

'He's dead. Two years back.'

'Don't tell me. Drug overdose?'

'How on earth did you guess that?'

Annie looked over at Gerry and saw that she was grinning. 'So what's she up to these days, our Poppy?'

'Nothing much. Gets an allowance from Daddy, makes the society pages occasionally, usually for getting photographed in some nightclub or other without her knickers. I get the impression she's a sort of walking wardrobe malfunction. Got a supermodel for a girlfriend now. The latest accessory. All the rage. Nobody you'll have heard of.'

'Sounds like a barrel of laughs. I take it both offspring live in London?'

'That's right. I've already put a call through to the locals to get in touch with Ronald, see if he knows anything of his father's whereabouts.'

'And Poppy?'

'Erm . . . well, according to Adele Balter, Poppy's here already.'

Annie's eyes widened. 'Is she, indeed? Well, how interesting.'

'I can't say Adele sounded too thrilled about it.'

Gerry drove on through the deep channel of the pass to the next dale south, taking an unfenced road to the south-west, not far from where she lived in Harkside. She then wound through some woods to the edge of the reservoir, easternmost in a chain of three, where Laurence Edward Hadfield's house stood high on the northern bank. It was an ideal location, she thought, pulling up on the tarmac drive beside the house, which was hidden from the road by the woods, and faced south over the water to the rolling Pennine hills beyond. It was also far enough away from where his body was found that the officers making door-to-door enquiries hadn't reached the area yet.

'Well, here we are,' she said, parking behind a shabby green Hyundai, in front of which a red sports car was parked diagonally. 'Looks like Poppy got here before the char.'

Perhaps mansion would be a better word than house to describe the place, Annie thought. Laurence Edward Hadfield had to be a wealthy man indeed. Instead of the usual Victorian gothic pile or Elizabethan extravaganza, this was an art deco construction with a large rounded front covering all three floors. Some of the windows resembled large portholes. Built of reinforced concrete, most likely, the whole place was clad in white stucco and looked a bit like an iced cake. It had two wings, one extending from each side, also round-edged, and a separate, more functional double garage. The house was far too large for one person and could have doubled as an apartment building, Annie thought, housing a whole village of Syrian refugees.

They got out. Annie sniffed the air. It was fresh and cold. She could hear the reservoir, stirred by the wind, lapping against the bank below. Diamonds danced on the water's surface. She heard the click of a door opening round the corner. 'Right,' she said to Gerry. 'Gird your loins and let's go and see how the other half live.'

'Thanks for coming, Ray,' Banks said after they had given their orders in the Black Bull in Lyndgarth. 'And thanks for your efforts with Peter on the sketch.' It was Friday lunchtime, and the pub was almost full, mostly with off-season tourists, who had parked their cars all over the village green. Banks was happy to have his familiar Porsche back, though it was looking distinctly old these days. Still, he'd never be able to afford a new one, so he would hang on to it until it fell apart.

'You didn't have to offer to buy me lunch to get me to meet you,' Ray said.

Banks smiled. 'My pleasure.' He raised his pint. 'Cheers.'

'Cheers.'

They both sipped some Black Sheep bitter, then Banks smacked his lips and said, 'Thanks for dinner the other night, Ray. It was great. Zelda's a fine cook.'

Ray's eyes narrowed. 'You know I made most of that meal?'

Banks laughed. 'I complimented you often enough about your cooking when you were staying with me. This time, you can pass on my compliments to Zelda.'

'It'll go to her head.'

'Better than it going to yours.'

Ray grunted. 'So what is it you want to see me about? You want to argue Cipollina over Garcia or Kaukonen?'

'No contest,' Banks said. 'Jerry wins hands down every time. But thanks for the Quicksilver. I enjoyed that. And the Donovan and Bridget St John. Haven't listened to them in ages.'

'I got the impression that my wayward daughter wasn't too impressed by the music. Or the evening.'

'Annie's musical tastes run the gamut of A to B. That's Abba to Beyoncé. I've given up on her as far as that's concerned. She puts her hands over her ears if you play Dylan. As for the other stuff, give her time, Ray.'

'Of course. But what is it? Doesn't she want me to be happy? Surely she can't be feeling it's disrespectful to her mother after all these years?'

'I don't think it's that, no. As I said, just give her time.'

'Zelda was upset, you know, after you'd gone. She wants Annie to like her.'

'So was Annie,' said Banks. 'With her it usually comes out as anger. Though I think she was more angry with herself than anyone else. Except me, maybe. Anyway, that's not what I wanted to talk to you about.'

Their lunches arrived, two giant Yorkshire puddings filled with roast beef, vegetables and onion gravy. Perhaps not the healthiest meal around, but one of the tastiest, especially with a good pint to wash it down. The sounds of conversation and laughter rose and fell around them. Beyond the window, on the edge of the green, a group of ramblers with sticks and all the right Gore-Tex winter gear stood listening to someone giving them instructions.

'So, what is it?' Ray asked, after a bite of Yorkshire pudding and a swig of beer.

'What we suggested to Zelda the other night, about trying to locate Phil Keane, or whatever his name is now.'

'Oh, that.'

'I've been thinking about it, and I'd like you to tell her to stop, not to do it.'

'You think she'll listen to me?'

'Make her listen, Ray. The man's poison. He tried to kill me. Nearly succeeded. He'd have killed Annie, too.'

'I know that. But you obviously don't know Zelda. Once she gets her teeth into something she never lets go.'

'I can understand that when it comes to the work she's doing against the traffickers. But this isn't her fight. And it's too dangerous. Tell her to hand what information she has over to us, and we'll pursue it through the proper channels.'

'I don't think Zelda trusts the proper channels. Besides, it's not as if she's going out on the streets to search for him herself.

All she ever does is look at pictures. And she's made it part of her fight now. She'll ask around, that's all.'

'From what little you and Zelda told us the other night, Ray, I think you're taking a pretty naive view of what Zelda does when she goes off on her little work trips.'

Ray put his knife and fork down. 'What do you mean by that? What do you know about it?'

'Doesn't it worry you, her going off like that for days at a time?'

'Oh, that. I gave up being possessive and jealous years ago. Especially as far as women are concerned. It only brings you grief. Besides, Zelda's a free spirit. She can do what she wants. I'm just happy she seems to want to spend some time with me.'

'Noble sentiments, Ray, and very sixties, love the one you're with and all that, but that's not what I meant. I know something about the kind of people she works for. They're ruthless. They wouldn't hesitate to put Zelda in harm's way if it meant netting a big catch. And those are the good guys.'

'That's rubbish. She just sits in a room and studies pictures.'

'That might be what she wants you to believe, but it must be more dangerous than that. She cares about you, Ray. She doesn't want you to worry about her. Why do you think she does it?'

'Because she feels she owes it to the victims. I don't know all the details of her background, but I know she lost someone close to her to those people.'

'I'm not quibbling with the work she does – that's admirable – I'm just trying to set you right about the true nature of the kind of people who employ her. Don't be so trusting about their motives. Or their methods. Not to mention the criminals they chase. What I *am* saying is that you have to try to persuade her not to go off half-cocked against someone like Phil Keane, not to let anyone know she's interested. He's a psychopath,

Ray, a cold, clever psychopath with no qualms about killing anyone who gets in his way. And he's manipulative. He draws people in. He could sell ice cream to Eskimos, as they say. He forged the provenance of some very pricey works of art, including a Turner, for crying out loud. That meant getting access to the archives, getting influential and important people in the art world to trust him. And it takes nerve.'

Ray picked up his fork again. 'What are you suggesting I do, then?'

'Talk to her. Or let me talk to her. I'll try again to persuade her to put me in touch with her supervisor. There's nothing wrong with a little cooperation.'

'I could try,' Ray said slowly.

'Because the moment she becomes even a blip on Keane's radar, she's in danger. You, too, for that matter.'

Ray sighed and played with his food, then turned back to Banks. 'I'm not a fool, Alan. I'm well aware that Zelda might have been a victim herself, forced into it, and it's easier for her to make up a story about someone close to her being trafficked than it is to tell me the truth. But for whatever reason, she hasn't talked to me about her past, and I don't want to push her. The balance is fragile enough as it is. What I do know is that she lived much of her life before we met in danger and fear. She was a child in Eastern Europe in the late eighties and early nineties, and that must have been bad enough. She let slip once that she's an orphan, too. She's told me some of it, but not all. OK, so maybe she does want to protect me from the hard truth. She has dark moods, and she disappears for hours, days sometimes. Places I can't touch her. Disappears, I mean, in her workshop, or walking the moors, or whatever. It was the same in Cornwall. She's haunted, troubled, and she probably always will be. When I met her just over a year ago she was like some ragamuffin street urchin. I kid you not. She wore baggy clothes. She'd cut her hair short. No make-up. I honestly didn't know at first whether she was a boy or a girl. And do you know, she has the saddest eyes I've ever seen. That lady of the lowlands is no contest. If I tried for a million years I'd never be able to capture that sadness on canvas. When she came back to the colony with me, I gave her her own place. Only a small caravan, but private. She spent a lot of time alone there. It was three months before she came to me one night and climbed into bed beside me. And the night after that she came again, and so on. Just for comfort, you understand. For someone to hold her and make her feel safe. I never put the slightest bit of pressure on her to go any further. That came only in time, slowly. And it came from Zelda. Now here we are, to all extents living together as man and wife. But I know there are parts of her I'll never get close to, aspects of her past that she will never share, perhaps things she has had to do to survive. I've accepted that, or at least got used to it. She doesn't want to cause me pain. She's an incredible woman, Alan. Every day I count my blessings. What we have is enough. It has to be enough.'

'I'm not arguing with you, Ray. I know how special Zelda is, and I can imagine only an inkling of what she's been through if what you say is right. Like I said, I know a little bit about that world. That's why I'm talking to you now. Humour me and ask her to do as I say. I'm sure she's got enough on her plate anyway without chasing after new demons. Think about it. All I want is a contact. Her boss or case handler. I can take it from there. She doesn't need to get involved. Believe it or not, I've got a few contacts of my own.'

'Oh, I believe it.' Ray took another bite of his lunch and looked at Banks as he chewed. His eyes misted over, and finally, he nodded, pointing with his fork. 'All right,' he said. 'I'll do my best. But I can't promise anything. Do you think I don't know I'm one of the luckiest men on earth? An old codger like me living with a woman like Zelda. And it's real.

She loves me. But do you think I don't worry about losing her? Of course I do. The sixties stuff is mostly just talk. Sure, I get jealous and possessive, but I manage to rationalise the feelings away most of the time. And I know her work might be dangerous, but it comes with the territory, mate. So do the black moods. Do you think I don't worry about her running off with some thirty-year-old stud while I'm down in London at some gallery opening or showing? Or her meeting someone on one of her trips down there? Of course I bloody do. But that comes with the territory, too. And you know what? I'd rather have the territory with all the shit that comes with it than not have the territory at all. That's why I try not to let possessiveness and jealousy rule all my days. Because if I did, I couldn't stand it. So I'll talk to her, OK? But no guarantees. She's her own woman, and I, for one, want to keep it that way.'

'It's all I ask, Ray.'

'Good. OK. We understand one another. Now back to that facile claim you made about Jerry Garcia.'

'It can't be Daddy, it simply *can't* be,' said Poppy Hadfield, handing back the sketch. Annie almost expected her to stamp her little foot, only it wasn't so little. Poppy had stringy blonde hair, bright red lipstick, far too much make-up on her rather horsey face, and the kind of figure most men would call voluptuous but Annie called wobbly. Bracelets jangled on her wrists and chains hung around her neck. There was a ring on every finger, two on some. She wore skin-tight ice-blue jeans artfully torn at the knees and thighs, and a black PUSSY RIOT T-shirt, also torn in a place Annie thought might cause a bit of an uproar at a posh society dinner. She could see what Gerry had meant by describing Poppy as a walking wardrobe malfunction. She was in her early thirties, perhaps a bit too old to be dressed the way she was. But hers was another world.

'Please calm down, Miss Hadfield,' said Annie. 'We don't know anything for certain yet. Only that your father is apparently missing. You've seen the artist's impression. We would like you to come and—'

'Oh, no. I'm not doing that. You can't make me do that. No way. I'm not looking at a DEAD BODY, no matter whose it is. You can get someone else to do that. I need a lie down. Where's my bag, Balter? I need my pills.'

Thinking that pills and a lie down for Poppy might be a good idea for everyone's sanity, Annie suggested she go and do just that while they talked to Adele Balter, who was standing by the sixty-inch flat-screen TV, wringing her hands and staring at the three of them, horrified, with red-rimmed eyes.

After Adele had found the required bag on the floor behind an armchair, Annie signalled Gerry to follow Poppy upstairs and see what she was up to, then she asked Adele Balter to sit down. She sat down on a huge sofa upholstered in some sort of black-and-white striped horsehair material. Annie tried hard to be a vegetarian most of the time, and she didn't really want to know what animal the hair had come from. Maybe a zebra. At any rate, it was enough that it seemed ugly and uncomfortable. She remained standing.

'Are you up to answering a few questions, Miss Balter?'

'I'll try. And it's Mrs Balter. But call me Adele, please. Like the singer.'

'I like her,' said Annie. 'Nice name, too.'

'Well, it's better than Geraldine,' she said, pulling a face. 'That's my first name.'

Annie coughed and put her hand over her mouth to stop herself laughing. She would have to tease Gerry about that. She walked towards the fireplace, intending to keep standing, but found the mantelpiece was far too high to lean on. She felt awkward. In the end, there was nothing for it but sit in a black-and-white armchair. It felt prickly, even through her clothes.

'I'll do it,' Adele said.

'Do what?'

'Identify that body for you. You heard Poppy. She won't do it without going hysterical, and who knows where Mr Ronald is, or whether he can get away?'

'But this could be his father.'

'He's an important man, Mr Ronald. He has obligations. He's away a lot. But I'm sure he'll come as soon as he can.'

Gerry came back down, mouthed the words, 'Prescription Valium' to Annie, then sat in the other chair. The walls were papered in turquoise and white diamonds, which Annie found a dazzling combination. Luckily, a reproduction Bayeux tapestry practically covered one wall, a floor-to-ceiling bookcase another, and the other two were so cluttered with framed watercolour landscapes, seascapes and portraits in oils, that they covered most of it up. Annie certainly didn't envy Adele Balter having to clean the place. Too many hiding places for dust.

'Miss Hadfield is tired and emotional,' Adele said. 'She really is very highly strung. She was already in a bit of a state when I got here. She'll be better after a rest.'

'She was here when you arrived?'

'Yes. She said she drove up last night.'

'Was she expecting her father to be here?'

'Mr Laurence doesn't always tell people when he's coming or going, but Miss Poppy said she had expected him to be here. He knew she was coming up last night, apparently. But he wasn't here. She said she tried his mobile but it went straight to messages. It's in the study there.' She pointed towards the panelled door, which looked about half a mile away. 'I tried it, too, and I heard it ring. Well, they don't ring so much as make funny sounds these days, do they? His goes off like a xylophone or something.'

Annie glanced at Gerry, and they walked over to the study. The room was neat and tidy inside, with bookcases full of

binders and biographies of rich and powerful men throughout history rubbing shoulders with tomes on fly-fishing. A
computer sat on the desk, just a large screen with a wireless
keyboard. Beside it was a thin laptop and a recent model
smartphone. Annie was tempted to pick up the phone, but it
was the rule to hand these things intact to IT, or at least have
a more senior officer, like Banks, present when handling them.
Any messing about with mobiles or computers could damage
or contaminate any evidence that might be on them and
compromise a case. The geek team would have to go through
all Hadfield's files, paper and electronic, anyway, if he was
confirmed to be the unidentified male on the slab in Eastvale
mortuary.

'Was there any particular reason for Miss Hadfield's visit?'

'She just told me she needed to get away to the country for
a while, that she wanted some fresh air and wide open spaces.
She does that sometimes. Turns up at all hours of the day and
night. The city was closing in on her. That's exactly how she
put it. "Closing in on me." Like I said, she's very sensitive.'

'Hmm. I remember that feeling,' said Annie. 'Does Mr
Hadfield go away often?'

'He travels quite a lot. All over the world.'

'Business?'

'Yes. People in his line of work never really retire, do they?'

'But he's here a lot?'

'Oh, yes. Most of the time. He loves it here.'

'Has he been anywhere recently?'

'Not for a month or so.'

'Where did he go then?'

'Cape Town, I think. He goes there quite often. And
Singapore. Zurich. And Hong Kong.'

'Do you know why?'

'He doesn't tell me his reasons for going where he goes. I
assume he has business interests there.'

Annie knew that Hong Kong, Zurich and Singapore were major financial centres, but she wasn't sure about South Africa. Whenever she heard about it on the news, it always seemed to be because of some problem or other. The last time, it was water, or lack of it, in Cape Town, and corrupt politics. But the business travel was perhaps an angle worth investigating. 'Are Poppy and her father close?'

'I'd say so. He adores her. In his eyes, she can do no wrong. She comes up here once every month or so. I've never heard them exchange angry words, if that's what you mean. She's his only daughter.'

'Right. I'm assuming she has a key, the run of the house and all?'

'Oh, yes. Mr Laurence is very generous. Especially with his children and grandchildren.'

'And Ronald?'

'He's not here so often. He's a very busy man.'

'What does he do, exactly?'

'I'm not really sure, but it's something to do with high finance, like his father. I don't really understand that world myself. Stocks and shares and footsies and what have you.'

'Me, neither,' said Annie. 'Do they get on, as far as you know?'

Adele's pause before answering spoke volumes. 'Not quite as well as Mr Laurence and Poppy.'

'I see,' said Annie. 'I understand that Mr Hadfield's wife died three years ago?'

'That's right. Katherine. A terrible tragedy. She was a lovely woman.'

'Cancer, right?'

'Yes. It was slow and painful. Mrs Hadfield was stoic. The end was a blessing.'

'Was she at home or in hospital?'

'Hospital. Just the last week. She took a fast turn for the worse. Until then she stayed at home, which was London then, with full-time nursing care, of course. Mr Laurence was devoted to her. It was only after ... you know ... that he retired and moved up here more or less permanently. Rivendell had just been a weekend escape before.'

'Do you happen to know whether Mr Hadfield has a ... well, I don't suppose girlfriend sounds right, but a female companion, a new partner?'

'A lover?'

'Well, I suppose so.'

Adele Balter stiffened. 'I'm afraid I wouldn't possibly know about things like that. He doesn't confide in me. Even if he did ...'

'Have you ever seen him with someone? Has a woman ever been here in the house when you've arrived at work?'

'No. Never. If there ever was anything, he was very discreet. But I really can't imagine ... no.'

'How often do you clean here?' Annie asked.

'Every week.'

'Always on a Friday?'

'It varies, depending on his movements and my schedule. Usually I do Thursdays, but I had to make a switch this week.'

'And last week?'

'I was here Thursday last week.'

'Was Mr Hadfield in?'

'Yes.'

'Does he usually stay in the house while you work?'

'If he's at home, Mr Laurence usually stays in his study while I do my cleaning work.'

'You don't clean his study, too?'

'No. It's private. I never go in there, not even when he's away.'

'Did you check to see if he was in there this morning?'

'Yes. Of course. I searched the whole house and grounds for him before I called you.'

'Did Poppy help? Hadn't she already looked when she arrived last night.'

'She was . . . well, you know, you saw her. I think she got here very late, after dark. She's scared of the dark.'

'Was there anything strange about Mr Hadfield's behaviour when you last saw him a week ago yesterday?'

'I don't know what you mean.'

'Was he any different from usual?'

'Oh, no. He was the same as normal.'

'Depressed, cheerful, what?'

'Quite cheerful, really. Excited, like, as if he'd made a good business deal or something. He even paid me a little early Christmas bonus.'

'That must have been nice,' Annie said. 'Did he say what he was excited about?'

'No.'

Pity, thought Annie. But then Hadfield would hardly talk to the hired help about his business or his private life. 'Do you know what his plans were for the weekend?'

'No. He never told me things like that.'

'Do you know if he was planning on going away? Taking another trip somewhere? Could that have been why he was excited?'

'I don't know. He didn't say anything about it. It could have been, I suppose, but business trips didn't usually excite him. He hated flying. An occupational hazard, he called it.'

'Did you notice any other signs of disturbance when you got here?'

Adele paused. 'Only . . . well, this. Poppy, you know.' She gestured to the room. 'She's not exactly the tidiest of house guests, if you see what I mean. And as for her own room . . . well . . .'

'Right.' Annie followed her gaze. There were a few empty glasses on the table with bright-red lipstick marks on the rim, one empty bottle of cognac on its side on the carpet, and an ashtray full of cigarette ends, also smeared with lipstick. An expensive suitcase sat on the floor by the bottom of the staircase, contents strewn on the carpet – a suede jacket, jeans, silky underwear, a spilled packet of tampons. 'So you found it just like this?'

'Yes. I haven't had a chance to clear up anything yet.'

'What made you think something was wrong? You said Mr Hadfield goes away a lot. Might he not simply have gone off somewhere without telling you?'

'It was the phone. And the wallet.'

'What wallet?'

'Mr Laurence's wallet. On that table over there.' Adele pointed.

Gerry walked over to the table, picked up the wallet and handed it over to Annie. It was a bulging leather wallet stuffed with ten- and twenty-pound notes, along with several debit, credit and loyalty cards in the name of Laurence Edward Hadfield. The credit cards were almost all platinum, she noticed.

'Mr Laurence would never go anywhere without his mobile and his wallet,' Adele Balter said. 'I mean, they've got everything in them, don't they? Money, contacts, everything. And where *could* he go? His car's still here.'

Annie remembered the house keys that were all she had found in the deceased's suit pockets. She took the key ring from its bag in her briefcase. 'Do you recognise this, Adele?'

'Yes. They're Mr Laurence's house keys.'

'So one of these keys should fit the front door, right?'

'Yes.' Adele pointed. 'That one.'

'Come with me, please.'

The three of them walked over to the front door and Annie tried the key. It fitted. They walked back to the living room. It was beginning to seem more and more likely that Hadfield was their man, unless his keys had found their way into someone else's pocket.

'Is he likely to have gone for a walk or something?'

'Mr Laurence isn't much of a one for exercise. Besides, he wouldn't have been out walking all night, would he, and certainly not in the sort of weather we've been having lately?'

Annie supposed not. Unless he'd fallen in the reservoir and drowned or something and wasn't lying in Eastvale General Infirmary's mortuary. But that was highly unlikely. It was becoming more evident to Annie that Laurence Edward Hadfield was the body on the moors.

'What kind of car does Mr Hadfield drive?' she asked.

'He has an "S" series Mercedes,' she said proudly, as if it were hers. 'A silver one. He's given me a lift in it once or twice when my car was in the garage. It's a lovely motor. Hardly feel you're on wheels.'

'Where is it?'

'It's in the garage. And the car keys and the automatic door opener are on that little table by the door, where he always keeps them. Do you see what I mean? Why would he go out without his wallet or his car? Where would he go?'

'I'll go and check it out,' said Gerry, picking up the car keys and the garage opener from the table.

Annie nodded. Adele Balter was right, she thought. The house was in a very remote spot, and you couldn't really get anywhere without a car. Hadfield certainly couldn't have walked to Tetchley Moor from where he lived; it was over ten miles. Unless someone had dropped by to pick him up. She heard the distant sound of a garage door opening. 'And all this had you worried enough to call us?'

'I saw the picture on TV last night, the one you showed me and Poppy earlier. Only for a second, fleeting, like, and I thought it looked a bit like Mr Laurence, only the nose and mouth were wrong. I suppose when I got here today and saw ... well, that he wasn't anywhere to be found, and Miss Poppy in such a state, like, then I thought back on it, and I realised it *could* be him. That's when I got worried enough to call you. The nose and mouth are wrong, but everything else is right. I can understand if someone had described him to an artist, like, they could have got that wrong easily enough. It's all a bit of a puzzle. I just thought you people would be best to sort something like this out.'

'We're glad you did, Mrs Balter,' said Annie. 'We're going to have to talk to Poppy at more length at some point soon, but in the meantime, we'd like to phone Ronald. Do you have the number?'

'It'll be in Mr Hadfield's contacts book, on the study desk.'

The door opened and Gerry came back in. She glanced at Annie and shook her head. 'Nothing interesting,' she said. 'But the car's there all right. The engine's cold.'

'OK. We'll need to have a look around in Mr Hadfield's study, too,' she said to Adele. 'And we'll see if we can get a couple of constables to have a walk around the reservoir, just in case. We'll get you over to the infirmary. I have to tell you, it's not a pretty sight. There's been some animal activity.'

'I used to be a nurse,' said Adele. 'Don't worry, I'm not squeamish or I wouldn't be offering.'

Banks rang the doorbell and heard it ring faintly inside the house. At first nothing happened, then a small, sad voice came over the intercom. 'I don't really want to talk to anybody now. Please go away.'

Banks glanced at Winsome before leaning forward. 'Neela? Neela Mitchell? It's the police. We'd really like to talk to you about Adrienne. We won't take up much of your time.'

There was another silence, then a buzz and a click. Banks turned the doorknob and the front door opened into a hallway that seemed to be filled with bicycles. They made their way through without injury and climbed the stairs to the second floor, by which time Banks was feeling a bit short of breath. He could feel his heart beating fast and realised he was terribly out of shape. He would have to do something about it. Soon.

When they arrived at the flat, Neela Mitchell was standing in the open doorway clutching a handkerchief. That she had been crying was obvious enough, even before she sniffled and led them inside the bedsit. Hers was about the same size as Adrienne's two streets away, but the house was slightly more rundown, and it didn't seem as if there was an en-suite bathroom.

Neela was a small, large-breasted girl, which made her seem slightly top-heavy, and she was wearing a baggy sweater and black tracksuit bottoms with a white stripe down the sides. She had wavy hennaed hair, a round face with light brown skin, and she wore wire-framed glasses. From her name and features, Banks guessed that her mother was Indian or Pakistani and her father British. Behind the lenses, her reddened eyes appeared slightly enlarged. She seemed so young and vulnerable that Banks felt his heart go out to her. She had just lost her best friend. But he had to be objective; it wouldn't do to take anything or anyone at face value. The room smelled fresh, as if Neela had just given it a shot of lemon air freshener. Banks noticed a crushed cigarette butt in an ashtray on the windowsill and realised she probably had. Smokers were feeling guiltier and guiltier these days.

The bedsit felt crowded with three of them in it. There was a sink and hot plate in a little alcove, and Neela offered to make tea, but they declined.

'We don't want to put you to any trouble,' Winsome said. 'Professor Stoller at the college said you were Adrienne's best friend, that we should talk to you.'

Neela nodded. 'Yes,' she said. 'I'm sorry I was so rude over the intercom, but I just didn't feel like talking to anyone.'

'We'll be as quick and painless as we can,' said Banks.

'It's all right. I'd like to help if I can. I just can't understand any of this, what happened to her. It doesn't make sense. The papers mentioned she was in a car or something, had an over-dose of drugs. That wasn't like Adrienne. She didn't take drugs.'

Banks and Winsome exchanged a glance. Again, the incom-petence of the local paper was warping people's perceptions of what had happened. Banks thought he might have to have a sharp word with Adrian Moss. Not that Moss wrote the rubbish, himself, but he was supposed to be their media liai-son officer.

'It wasn't what you'd call a drug overdose,' Winsome explained. 'I mean, nobody's saying she was a regular drug user. The doctors think she died of an overdose of sleeping pills.'

Neela's eyes opened wide. 'Sleeping pills? Adrienne? You mean, like, accidentally?'

'We don't know for certain,' said Winsome, glancing at Banks. 'But at the moment, we don't think it could have been an accident.'

'You mean she . . . she took them *herself*? On purpose?'

Winsome nodded. 'That's the thinking. I'm sorry.'

Neela shook her head violently. 'No way. I don't believe it.'

'Why not?'

'Because she wasn't the kind of person who'd do something like that. Kill herself. Not Adrienne. She loved life. She was saving up to go on safari in Africa after her finals the year after next. She wanted to go to a game park, climb Mount

Kilimanjaro, see the big five and all the rest and then get a job with VSO. She would never kill herself before doing that. It was her dream.'

'People can change, you know, Neela,' Banks said.

Neela shook her head vigorously. 'No. Not Adrienne. Not without my knowing.'

'Do you know if Adrienne had any problems lately, anything weighing heavily on her mind?'

'No. Not as far as I could tell. Nothing that serious. Oh, sometimes she'd been feeling a bit down lately, you know, but that happens to all of us. She had her moods. And she could get sulky.'

'Did you ask her what was wrong, why she felt down?'

'I might say, "What's wrong?" or something like that, you know, but she'd just shrug and say, "Oh, nothing" and flash that little smile of hers. I don't know what it is you want me to say, but there was really nothing odd or unusual about Adrienne lately. Or different. Maybe her moods were a bit more frequent or lasted longer sometimes, and she was more subdued than last year, but basically she was still Adrienne. She hadn't undergone a personality change or anything.'

'Was she seeing anyone, a counsellor, therapist or psychiatrist? Someone like that?'

'No. Why would she?'

'If she was troubled by something, depressed or anxious.'

'But she wasn't. Like I said, she got a bit blue sometimes, like the rest of us. And maybe she'd been a bit distracted recently, off in her own world, but I didn't realise it was a such bad place that she was in.'

'Distracted by what?' Banks asked.

Neela looked at him as if assessing whether to answer or not. 'I don't know if there was anything in particular,' she said. 'Certainly there was nothing she told me about. All I mean is that I hadn't seen as much of her as I used to. She'd been stopping in more on her own, said she had to work. She became a bit sort of withdrawn, maybe less enthusiastic about going out and having fun and doing stuff. She seemed a bit anxious, nervous, you know. I suppose distracted isn't quite the right word. But not depressed or suicidal. Once or twice she seemed sort of frightened. No, that's not really right. More apprehensive.'

'About what?'

'I don't know. Nothing in particular.'

'Perhaps she really did have to work?'

Neela nodded. 'We both did. It's a hard year academically and exams are notoriously tough. You worry about things like that. It's a big cause of stress. But they're a long way off. Like I said, it was nothing, really. She had her moods. We all do.' Neela sniffed again and blew her nose.

'Do you know if she was taking any prescription medications?'

'Not that she ever told me about. I mean, it's something that might have come up, you know, if she had been. We talked about all kinds of stuff. Or we used to. But she didn't have any problems with her health. She went to the gym twice a week and worked out. She went swimming most mornings. We both did.'

'When did you see her last?'

'Just before last weekend. Friday morning. We went swimming.'

'And after that?'

'No.'

'Is that unusual?'

'A bit, I suppose. But it was only the day before yesterday I heard . . . you know . . . about what happened. That was only Wednesday. She hadn't turned up for our tutorial with Professor Stoller.'

'Weren't you worried?'

'No. We didn't live in each other's pockets. Not seeing her from Friday to Wednesday wasn't a big deal.'

'What about weekends?'

'I never saw her much then, anyway. She worked at that animal shelter and usually stopped over with friends in Darlington.'

'Do you know their names?'

'No. They weren't uni people. Just people she knew from the shelter, like.'

'Did you talk on the phone often?' Banks asked.

'We mostly texted. But not so much lately. She seemed to have lost interest.'

'Was Adrienne very attached to her mobile?'

'Well, she used to use it a lot. I mean, we all do. Facebook and Twitter and Instagram and Spotify, or whatever classical streaming service she used, but she wasn't a slave to it. Me, neither. We used Snapchat and WhatsApp mostly to keep in touch, send selfies and stuff, but again, not so much this term.'

'Would she go out without it?'

'Not usually, no.'

'Was she forgetful? Might she leave it behind in her flat when she went out somewhere?'

'Are you saying that she didn't have her mobile with her when you found her?'

'It was in her bedsit.'

Neela shook her head. 'That's odd. Even though she seemed a bit off it lately, I don't think she would normally leave home without it. I mean, would you?'

'Do you know if she ever used Internet dating? Tinder, that sort of thing?'

'Not as far as I know, she didn't.'

'You said earlier that Adrienne didn't take drugs. Are you sure about that?'

Neela looked down at her hands clasped in her lap.

'Neela, it would be best if you told us everything,' Banks said.

'All right. She took E now and then. We all did. OK?'

'All?'

Neela nodded. 'But only now and then. Nothing bad ever happened. It's not like she was addicted or it was dangerous or anything. Besides, you said she died of an overdose of sleeping pills. E isn't a sleeping pill. Adrienne said it took her out of herself a bit, made it a bit easier for her to socialise.'

'When did you get this E? Where?'

Neela paused before answering, 'At The Cellar Club.'

'Who from?'

'Just someone who hung out there. Not a student.'

'I saw The Cellar Club mentioned on a poster on my way to see Professor Stoller,' said Winsome.

A few nightclubs had sprung up around the college campus since the expansion, most of them simply back rooms of pubs fitted with a loud sound system and a few flashing coloured lights. But The Cellar Club was far more sophisticated. It consisted of a large cellar that used to belong to an old carpet sales centre and warehouse, now an arcade of student boutiques and used bookshops. Like the famous Cavern of old, it was dark and dank, with arches and walls of stone and brickwork plastered with concert posters. Though Banks had never been there on a busy warm night, he imagined sweat dripping down the walls as the strobe lights flashed and the beat pounded away mercilessly. But he *had* been there. They advertised raves. Not the old-style raves or the more recent illegal parties, where hundreds of people, alerted by phone or social media at the last minute, congregated and orgied all night in abandoned warehouses, but just dances that went on really late. The fire brigade had been out there once or twice on overcrowding issues. And The Cellar Club was a known magnet for drug dealers and users. Since its expansion, Eastvale College had become a target for dealers from Leeds and Manchester.

'Why The Cellar Club?' Banks asked.

Neela shrugged. 'It's the coolest place near campus. And the DJ is really wicked.'

'As in a DJ who plays records?' Banks asked.

'What? No, like, a real DJ.'

Banks assumed that she meant one of those idiots who spins records backwards and talks all the time. 'And you and Adrienne used to go to these dances and take E?'

Neela nodded. 'Sometimes. Not always. And not for a while. Mostly it was last year. There was a whole gang of us.'

'All girls?'

'No. Mixed. But we were all just, like, friends. Nobody was going out together or anything.'

'Just E? Any other drugs? Cocaine, speed, downers? I happen to know you can buy just about anything at The Cellar Club, Neela. You probably also know that Eastvale has a grow-ing drug problem these days, and the college especially. Places like The Cellar Club.'

Neela looked horrified. 'No. Nothing *serious* like that. Honest. Just a little E. And only now and then.'

'I know that E might seem safe,' Banks said, 'but it has caused problems with some people who've used it.'

'That's just dehydration, though, isn't it? We always make sure we drink gallons of water.'

'There can be other problems,' Banks went on, aware he was sounding like a boring old fogey. 'Contaminated pills. Depression. Heart disease. When was the last time you went to The Cellar Club?'

'About a month ago. Just after the start of term.'

'Did Adrienne take E on that occasion?'

'No. None of us did.'

'OK. Let's move on. Did Adrienne have a boyfriend?'

'Not this term.'

Adrienne's parents had said the same, but Banks was more inclined to believe her best friend. 'You sound very sure about that, Neela.'

'I am. She didn't have time, working at the shelter on weekends and keeping up with her term work during the week. Then there was her music. She thought it was important to keep practising her violin, even though she didn't have enough time for the orchestra any more. She told me she wasn't planning on dating anyone this year, and as far as I know she didn't. Besides, she would have told me.'

'Usually when any of my best friends got boyfriends,' said Winsome, 'I saw a lot less of them. You say you saw less of Adrienne. Might that not be why?'

'No. Not in this case. I would have known. Besides, she told me she didn't have or want a boyfriend. Why would she lie?'

Good point, Banks thought. Though if the boyfriend were someone who might elicit Neela's disapproval, Adrienne might keep it to herself. On the other hand, they say that young love puts a spring in your step, and best friends notice things like that.

'And last year?'

'Colin Fairfax.'

It was the boyfriend Adrienne's parents had mentioned. The 'nice lad' she took home for tea.

'What happened between them? Did they have a row?'

'Dunno. Don't think so.'

'There was no big split up, no fight or falling out?'

'Not as far as I know.'

'Was it because of someone else? Because Adrienne took up with another boy, or Colin with another girl?'

'I don't think so.'

'Did Adrienne cry on your shoulder? Was she upset about the break-up?'

'I'm sure she was upset, but she wasn't the type to cry on anyone's shoulder. We shared lots of stuff like best mates do, but she could be secretive, could Adrienne, and sometimes she kept her feelings bottled up.'

'Is Colin Fairfax still around?'

'Yes. We bump into him every now and then.'

'At The Cellar Club?'

'Not so much there. Just around campus. The coffee shop, the pub.'

'And did he and Adrienne get along all right?'

'They were fine. Just, like, old friends. But he wasn't part of the gang. Mostly we hung around with Jessica, Cameron, Chloe and Callum and the rest.'

'Can you give us the full names, Neela?'

Neela did so and Winsome wrote them down.

'There was Mia, too, at first,' Neela said, 'but she dropped out. I'm sorry I don't know her second name.'

'When did she drop out?'

'Quite early. I remember she was around at the start of term, that was the twenty-fifth of September, but she'd gone by mid-October at the latest.'

'Why did she leave? Where did she go?'

'Dunno. I didn't know her very well. I guess she decided Eastvale College just wasn't for her.'

'And Colin Fairfax wasn't part of the gang?'

'No. Like I said, we just saw him occasionally, to say hello to.'

'What's he studying?'

'Modern languages.'

'Is there any chance he might have been stalking Adrienne? You know, pestering her to get back with him or anything like that. Is that what might have made her distracted, on edge? Frightened or apprehensive, even?'

Neela shook her head. 'She certainly didn't say anything like that to me, and I'm sure she would have done if there was a problem like that. Anyway, Colin's not particularly scary.'

'So you never noticed him hanging around when he wasn't wanted, that sort of thing?'

'No. Like I said, we just saw him in the coffee shop or the library sometimes.'

'OK, Neela,' said Winsome. 'Have there been any wannabe boyfriends since Colin Fairfax? Anyone Adrienne was interested in, or who was interested in her?'

Neela made a snorting sound. 'There was always someone interested in Adrienne. You should have seen her. She was so pretty. Boys fell all over themselves to buy her drinks and stuff.'

'But she didn't single out anyone in particular for her affections?'

'No. She wasn't interested. Just wanted to save up and go to Africa. That was her dream. We always did stuff as a group, like. Not pairing off in couples.'

It was what a lot of young people today did who didn't want commitment or unwanted attentions, Banks knew. 'What about money?' he asked.

'What about it?'

'Was it a problem for her?'

'Money's always a problem. It's very expensive to go to university.'

'But surely the scholarship must have helped?' said Winsome.

Neela frowned. 'Scholarship? What scholarship?'

'The one she got this year. The one that paid her fees and allowed her to avoid taking out student loans.'

Neela shook her head. 'I know nothing about any scholarship.'

'She never told you?'

'No. But come to think of it, she *was* a bit more flush this year. She didn't go on about money problems as much as she did last year. Never asked to borrow any. She even paid me some back. I thought maybe she'd got a raise at the shelter as well as working extra hours there, but they don't really do things like that, do they, not in jobs like that? Mostly they expect you to volunteer because you love animals. Adrienne would have done it for nothing. As it was, they barely paid her the minimum wage.'

'Did she work there more hours this year?' Banks asked.

'Yes. Most of the weekend. All of it, sometimes.'

'And you know nothing about any scholarship?'

'No. And it's not the sort of thing she'd keep secret. I mean, she wouldn't have any reason not to tell me, would she? She'd have been over the moon.' Neela laughed. 'She'd probably have taken us all out for a slap-up meal and bought us a bottle of champagne. That's what Adrienne was like.'

Banks could think of a couple of reasons Adrienne might not have mentioned her good fortune. Perhaps she had wanted to keep the money to herself, add it to her Africa fund, or perhaps its origins were connected with the drug trade. If she really was as generous as Neela thought, then perhaps she *would* have treated her friends. So why didn't she? It was odd that Adrienne hadn't told her best friend about the scholarship. He remembered how excited Tracy was when she got a postgraduate scholarship in Newcastle. She couldn't wait to tell everyone.

'Can you think of any reason at all why Adrienne might have committed suicide?' Banks asked finally.

Neela was silent for a few moments, her lower lip quivering, tears in her eyes. Then she said, 'No.' The tears spilled over and she started to sob, burying her face in her hands. 'I should have known, shouldn't I? I should have seen it coming. I was supposed to be her best friend, and I let her down. Why would she do something like that? She was beautiful, she was a sweet person, she was clever, she had everything going for her.' Neela looked up at Banks, imploring through wet, reddened eyes. 'Why?'

6

It was quite clear when Poppy wobbled down the stairs that she had taken more than the recommended dose of Valium, perhaps even washed it down with vodka or brandy. Nevertheless, she seemed used to being perpetually stoned, and she carried it off well. Annie and Gerry certainly didn't plan on babysitting her until her brother showed up, but they did want to talk to her. Which left them in a bit of a conundrum. They also needed to take Adele Balter to Eastvale mortuary to identify the body as soon as possible. The key fitted the door, which was a start, but only if and when they had a positive identification of the body could they really set an investigation in motion. But they didn't dare leave Poppy alone in the house. The way things were going, it could be a crime scene and as such would need to be preserved. They certainly couldn't have the Hadfield offspring walking around the place willy-nilly. Neither Poppy nor Ronald would be too pleased to hear that, Annie thought, but too bad.

In the end, Adele agreed to drive Gerry to the infirmary and then back to the police station to make a formal statement, and Annie would use the car she had signed out of the police garage. She certainly didn't want Poppy driving, the state she was in, however nice her sports car was.

Gerry had come up with a simple solution to the Poppy problem earlier, which was to get her out of the house, somewhere neutral, and ask her the questions they wanted answered. Annie knew a country pub by the side of the middle reservoir and, though it was risky taking Poppy on licensed premises, it would certainly offer the most peaceful and soothing prospect for a chat. Then, depending on Adele Balter's identification, Annie would already have Poppy out of the house and would simply have to prevent her from going back inside. Well, perhaps it wouldn't be exactly *simple*, but a couple of burly uniformed constables guarding the scene should be able to see to it. On the other hand, with Poppy Hadfield, she was beginning to realise, you could never be quite sure.

The lounge bar wasn't especially crowded just after lunch, when Annie and Poppy arrived. It was a pleasant enough space, with plush red covers on the chairs and banquettes and a number of hunting scenes on the walls. Keeping Poppy in view, Annie went to the bar and bought two Diet Cokes then took them back to the table.

Poppy took a sip of her drink and pulled a face. 'What the fuck is this?' she said, then proceeded to pour it on the floor.

So much for the soothing effects of Valium. Annie looked around in horror, but nobody had seen them. She managed to grab the glass from Poppy before it had been completely emptied. Luckily most of the Coke had gone under the table, where it was more or less hidden from view.

'Stop being so fucking childish,' she said, then managed to hold her anger in check and said, 'I can get you a tea or coffee, if you'd prefer.'

'What I'd like is a fucking gin and tonic, love. A double.'

'Sorry. No can do.'

'What do you mean, "no can do"?' She did a passable imitation of Annie's clenched tone.

'I mean exactly what I say,' Annie said. 'And if you give me any more lip, I'll have the handcuffs on you and drive you down to the station before you can say crack cocaine.'

Poppy snorted. 'What planet have you been on? Nobody does crack any more.'

Annie reached for her handcuffs. 'We'll see what a night in the cells does for your temperament.'

'All right, all right.' Poppy said. 'Enough with the hard-arsed act. I've seen *Scott & Bailey*.'

'Where have you been? Nobody watches *Scott & Bailey* any more.'

Poppy scowled, then giggled. 'Well, aren't you the witty one? Tell me, are you gay?'

Annie just glared at her and drank some Coke.

'OK. I promise to be good.'

'I want you to understand the seriousness of the situation,' Annie said. 'Your father may well be dead. We'll find out when Gerry phones me from the mortuary. We don't know how he ended up that way, but you might be able to help us.'

'Me, how? I told you, I just got here last night and he wasn't around. I haven't seen him for at least three weeks.'

'So what did you do when you got here?'

'I went to bed.'

'After doing major damage to a bottle of cognac first, it appears.'

'What's that got to do with you? Why should you care what I drink?'

'I care about the state of mind you're in, and from where I'm sitting, it doesn't look good.'

'Well, fuck you. You don't look so hot yourself. Besides, the bottle was already half empty.'

'Oh, goody. That makes it so much better.'

'You're a real sarky bitch, do you know that?'

'So I've been told on occasion.'

Annie's phone rang like a sixties police car. Poppy laughed. 'That was quick,' Annie said, when Gerry spoke. 'So what's the verdict?'

'Adele identified the body as that of Laurence Edward Hadfield. We're just about to head up to the station to take her statement. I thought you'd want to know as soon as possible.'

'Thanks,' said Annie. 'Appreciate it.'

'How's Poppy?'

'Don't ask.'

'That bad?'

'I'll talk to you later. Bye.'

'Bye.'

Annie put her phone away and turned to Poppy. 'I'm sorry, but I've got some really bad news for you. That was my partner, Gerry. Adele Balter has just identified the body we found as that of your father.'

Poppy stared at her in silence for a moment, then she burst into tears.

After his lunch with Ray, Banks returned to his office on Friday afternoon and closed the door. Winsome would probably be back soon with the fruits of her morning's labours, but in the meantime, Banks had paperwork to catch up with. As he did so, he listened to the Grateful Dead's *Cornell 5/8/77* concert.

Mostly the paperwork was a matter of signing memos to say he'd read them, then putting them back in their envelopes and posting them in the internal mail system again. Boring work, but the music helped. Garcia's solo on 'Scarlet Begonias' was a joy to hear. In fact, any version of 'Scarlet Begonias' was guaranteed to lift Banks's mood, no matter what menial task he was doing at the time.

Winsome knocked and entered during 'Morning Dew', an old favourite, and he reluctantly turned down the volume. Rather than have her sit across from him at the large work desk, they adjourned to the low glass coffee table and low-slung tube chairs. Winsome got out her notebook.

'Busy day?' Banks asked.

'But fruitful, guv. Very fruitful.'

'I'm all ears.'

'First and easiest stop was the bursar's office. No scholarship.'

'You mean she lied to her parents?'

'Well, I suppose she had to explain why she wasn't hitting them up for money somehow. It wouldn't make any difference to Luke Stoller, or to Neela.'

'I suppose not. So where did the money come from?'

'Your guess is as good as mine. Apparently she paid her fees directly out of her bank account. I've put a request in for her banking records for the last two years, but you know what they're like. They take their time.'

'OK, keep at them. Find out who deposited the money, and how. Cheque, electronic transfer, cash? So . . . she paid her own fees. Anything else?'

'Well, that's about it from the bursar. Next, I paid a visit to the student health centre.'

'And?'

'Nothing. They were a bit tougher, but luckily one of the nurses there is Jamaican, and she comes from a village not so far from me, so she was quite happy to tell me that Adrienne Munro had not availed herself of their services in either her first or her second year, except for a minor ear infection last February, for which the doctor prescribed a course of antibiotics. That was all. She balked at the mere suggestion they would hand out sleeping pills to students. They're quite aware of problems with teen and student suicides and what have you. I must say, it seemed to me you'd have to have the signature of the Surgeon General to get a bloody Valium out of that lot, let alone a sleeping pill.'

Banks laughed. 'Well, I suppose it's good to know they're in control of the situation. It doesn't do us much good, though, does it? We still don't know where the pills came from.'

'Students usually manage to find drugs when they want them.'

'I suppose so,' Banks agreed.

'I talked to Steph Dobyns from the drugs squad. They don't know about anyone selling sleeping pills at The Cellar Club or any other of the student hangouts. Seems the market's still mostly for E, a little coke and the occasional amphetamine. They want to stay awake, not fall asleep.'

'Another blank.'

'I made one more visit.'

'Where to?'

'Darlington. The animal welfare shelter.'

'There's a good chance that a place like that would stock some sort of animal tranquillisers, isn't there? Jazz Singh is still working to identify exactly what pills Adrienne took.'

'Apparently, they don't,' Winsome said. 'They leave that sort of stuff to the vets. What's interesting, though, is that no one there has seen Adrienne since summer.'

'What? You mean she hasn't been working weekends there?'

'That's right, guv. It surprised everyone because she loved her job, loved working with the animals. Was very good at it, too, so everyone told me.'

'Did she just quit?'

'Didn't turn up. Not a word.'

'When?'

'Second week of term. She'd put a bit of time in over the summer and seemed set on carrying on with weekends like before, but . . .'

'Now that is definitely strange. Everyone believed that's where she spent her weekends. Her parents. Neela.'

'I know. She's been lying to them all. I talked to the girl Paula, the friend she sometimes stayed with in Darlington on weekends. She hasn't seen or heard from Adrienne for weeks.'

'So what was she doing?'

'We don't know. I also checked with Steph, and DI MacDonald over at criminal intelligence. They've got nothing on Adrienne Munro or any of her friends as far as drugs are concerned. Remember those names Neela mentioned?'

'I remember,' said Banks.

'I managed to get a few more details out of the bursar's office. They're Jessica Mercer, Cameron Macrae, Chloe Sharma and Callum O'Brien. I ran them through the system. None of them have as much as a traffic offence or drunk and disorderly against them. And Steph says she knows quite a few of the Eastvale students do E, but this lot doesn't come up in any of their more serious drug offence intelligence.'

'So nothing?'

'Clean records all. Including Colin Fairfax.'

'Didn't Neela mention someone called Mia?'

'She did. But there's no trace of a Mia anywhere in the college records.'

'Odd. Maybe it was a nickname? Or perhaps she wasn't a student? You do get a few townies hanging about now and then.'

'And sometimes it's the townies who bring in the drugs,' said Winsome.

'Well,' said Banks, 'we seem to be developing a bit of a narrative here. A bright, attractive young woman dumps her "nice" boyfriend for no apparent reason, lies about a non-existent scholarship and a weekend job, even to her best friend, has mood changes, seems a bit anxious, distracted, even apprehensive, isn't doing so well at her course work, doesn't hang out with her friends like before. There's something we're missing here. The question is, what's it all adding up to?'

'Drugs,' said Winsome. 'Neela admitted that they did E once in a while, but it could have become more serious than that. For Adrienne, at any rate. It's not a great stretch from that to maybe selling some E. Other stuff, too. We know there's a drug problem at the college, and we know the big city gangs use kids as mules to get the stuff into rural areas.'

'Check out this mysterious Mia a bit more. Perhaps she's the connection, the catalyst, setting up a pipeline then disappearing into the background. See if you can find out anything about her.'

Winsome nodded. 'Will do, guv.'

'What about the ex-boyfriend, Colin Fairfax? You said he's clean, too, right?'

'As a whistle. I did a more in-depth check on him. No form. Good student. Fine cricketer, too, apparently. He's in the modern languages department. Last lecture is two to three this afternoon. After that, he can usually be found in the student pub.'

Banks glanced at his watch. 'What are we waiting for, then?'

'I suppose I was just trying to pretend to myself that it wasn't Daddy,' said Poppy, dabbing at her eyes. 'That he was really all right, you know. I don't care what you think of me, maybe I am a total fuck-up, but I did love him.' She put the handkerchief to her eyes again, now smeared black with mascara. When Annie realised the genuineness of her grief, she relented and went back to the bar and bought her a double gin and tonic along with another Diet Coke for herself. One or two people were staring at them now, but Annie ignored them. Poppy took a swig then set the drink down, gave Annie a ghost of a smile and whispered, 'Thank you.'

Annie also found herself feeling sorry for Poppy because she was clearly going to have to deal with her father's death on her own. Ronald Hadfield turned out to be unavailable. According to his personal assistant, he was in Tokyo for a series of important business meetings and wouldn't be back until after the weekend. The PA said she would attempt to

contact him about his father, but even if he dropped everything right now, it would still take some time to arrange flights
and get back. Then there was the time difference. 'Tell me
about your father,' Annie said.

'I told you. I loved Daddy. I suppose I was his favourite,
"daddy's girl", though I never tried to seek his approval. Quite
the opposite, really. It was Ronald who was desperate to
impress and please him, but it never got him very far. Daddy
was a complex person.'

'Didn't he and Ronald get along?'

Poppy shook her head. 'Too alike. Peas in a pod. Fractious.
I suppose that's how I'd describe their relationship.'

'And yours?'

She widened her eyes. 'With Ronald? He's a stuffy old bore
as far as I'm concerned. And a cold fish, to boot.'

'What did your father do, exactly? I know he was in finance,
but in what way?'

Poppy shook her head. 'I really have no idea. That world is
beyond me. Don't you know I'm just a good-time girl? I'm
thick. I hardly got any more "O" levels than Princess Diana.
As long as the money keeps coming in, I don't ask where it's
from, I just spend it. Daddy did deals, facilitated things for
people. Offers bribes and loans for all I know. I never asked
him and he never said. Why?'

'The circumstances of his death are a little unusual, to say
the least.'

'Are you saying he was murdered?'

'No. There's no evidence of that. But there are a lot of questions to be answered.'

'You think it could have had something to do with his
work?'

'Possibly something to do with the world he worked in. It's
easy to make enemies when you're handling huge amounts of
money. Easy to upset the wrong people.'

'Oh, I'm sure Daddy pissed off the odd CEO or two.' Poppy went back to her drink. She seemed much calmer now, even lucid, and far less likely to need to create a scene.

'Did you visit him up here often?'

'Now and then, when I felt the need to get away for a few days.'

'Did you ever see him with anyone?'

'What do you mean? Like a woman? A girlfriend?'

'Maybe.'

'No. Never. Not since Mummy died. I'm sure he must have had some female company, but if he did he was very discreet about it.'

'Other friends?'

'He had people around occasionally. Other businessmen. Local bigwigs. But he'd usually advise me not to come if he was going to be busy networking. They were all such bores.'

'Oh? I thought you just dropped in when the spirit moved you?'

Poppy snorted. 'You must have been listening to Balter. She thinks I'm the devil incarnate, or some female version of it.'

'So you don't just drop by whenever you feel like it?'

'I always check with Daddy first. If he's going away or going to be busy, I put off my visit. I wouldn't want to drop in and find him . . . you know . . . with someone. There are plenty of places I can go when I want a break from the city.'

'But I thought you arrived at all times of the day and night whenever you needed to get away?'

'Balter again. I like driving at night. I'm afraid of the dark. It helps to be doing something like driving up the M1 with a lot of other cars around and the music playing loud.'

'I see. And that's what you did last night?'

'Yes.'

'When did you last speak to your father?'

'I rang him on Friday and asked if I might come up for the weekend. He told me he was busy, but it would be OK to come midweek.'

'Was that unusual?'

'Not at all.'

'Did he say what he was going to be busy with over the weekend?'

'No. Like I said, he never explained his business to me, and I never questioned him about it.'

'Were you here the weekend before?'

'No. I went to Brighton. Well, just outside. A country house party. Lady Barton. You wouldn't know her.'

Poppy excused herself to 'powder her nose'. Annie stared at a hunting scene and felt sorry for the fox. Poppy came back. Her expression was set, lips downturned at the edges, eyes still watery. She sniffled occasionally, and Annie couldn't tell whether it was due to a quick snort of coke or grief. Probably a bit of both.

'What time did you arrive last night?'

'I don't know. I don't wear a watch. Time's a nuisance.'

'Tell me about it.'

Poppy squinted at her. 'You're weird, you are.'

'So I'm told. Guess what time you arrived.'

'Maybe two, three in the morning. I know I was tired, too tired to unpack.'

'Did you expect your father to be awake at that time?'

'Not really. But he knew I was coming. I assumed he'd be home.'

'So you were worried when you arrived and found him absent?'

'Not at first. Like I said, I was tired. He didn't usually wait up for me. I thought he was probably in bed asleep. I tried to keep quiet, so as not to disturb him. I had a few drinks, just to take the edge off, like. Next thing I knew it was the following morning and Balter was knocking at the bedroom door.'

'You were worried then?'

'Yes, when he wasn't anywhere to be found. I'd tried to phone him on his mobile earlier, when I first woke up. He never goes anywhere without it. But it went straight to voicemail.'

'It was in his study. Didn't you hear it ring?'

'No. I was in bed when I called. It's a long way.' She put her fingers in her ears. 'Besides, my hearing's not great at the best of times. Too many loud rock concerts. Tinnitus. I didn't hear anything until Balter started banging on the door.'

'You were once connected with Nate Maddock, right?'

'I'd rather not talk about that period of my life. Besides, it's not relevant to my father's death.'

'And now you're connected with a supermodel?'

'That's rubbish,' Poppy snorted. 'Just the fucking tabloids wanking themselves off as usual. Gretchen's just a drinking buddy. I'm unattached at the moment, and not looking for anyone, either. Man or woman.' She slugged back the rest of the gin. 'I want to go home.'

'London?'

'No. Rivendell.'

'Was your father a *Lord of the Rings* fan?'

'Do you know, I think he was a bit of a hippy back in the day, before he got bitten by the money bug. He still listens to Pink Floyd and King Crimson.'

Not unlike Banks and Ray, Annie thought. They stood up and walked towards the car. 'What are your plans now?' Annie asked.

Poppy shook her head. 'Not a clue. I suppose I might as well hang about up here until . . . well, you know . . . the funeral and all that.'

'It could be some time until the funeral, depending on what we uncover.'

'I told you, I don't fucking know.'

They went out and got in the car. Annie started it up.

Poppy stretched herself out in the passenger seat and yawned. 'No doubt my arsehole brother will be arriving this evening. I'm not sure I could stand being in the same house as him for very long, so maybe I'll just go back down south, anyway. Why? Am I not supposed to leave town?'

'Just stay in touch, that's all,' said Annie. 'There may be developments very soon, and I may have to talk to you again.'

'Yeah. Sure. Fine.' Poppy dug around in her bag and found a pair of sunglasses. She put them on, rested her head back on the car seat and feigned sleep. Annie tapped her fingers on the wheel as she drove, wondering how she could break it gently to Poppy that she couldn't return to Rivendell to spend the night now that they knew the suspicious death was that of her father. That the house was a crime scene, at least technically. Even letting her inside to repack her bag under supervision was pushing it at this point, but Annie reckoned she could balance that against showing consideration for the victim's daughter and give her a few minutes to pick up her pills and tampons.

The girl behind the bar pointed out Colin Fairfax, who sat alone hunched over a laptop at a booth in the student pub, a pint beside him. It was a dim, cavernous place, full of little nooks and alcoves, along with open areas with large tables, all done in dark wood. The music wasn't too loud to prohibit conversation. Banks thought it was Vampire Weekend, but he couldn't be certain; he didn't know their music well enough.

He edged into the booth next to Fairfax, showing his warrant card, and Winsome took a chair opposite them. Fairfax glanced from one to the other and closed his laptop.

'Adrienne?' he said.

Banks nodded, then glanced at his glass. 'Can I buy you another drink?'

Fairfax shrugged. 'Why not?'

Banks went back to the bar.

'Man, this really does my head in,' Fairfax said when Banks put the pint down in front of him.

'In what way?' Winsome asked.

'Adrienne. I loved her.'

'But she didn't love you?'

'I guess not. I don't know where her mind was these days. I don't even know if she cared for me or not. She just wasn't herself at all.'

Winsome took out her notebook and made a few jottings.

'Let's start at the beginning,' Banks said.

Fairfax was a skinny youth in jeans and a T-shirt, with a wispy goatee beard, a few spots and spiky fair hair. Nothing to write home about, Banks thought. But there was no accounting for taste. Everyone had said he was a decent kid.

'The beginning?'

'When you and Adrienne first met.'

'It was at a party early in our first year. November, I think. Just over a year ago. She was a wall-hugger. You know, just leaned back against the wall with her drink in her hand watching everyone. She found it hard to approach people. Shy. So I went over to her and we hit it off right away. After that we went out together all year and part of the summer.'

'Only part?'

'We both had to work to save up. I was at home in Doncaster working nights at a frozen food factory. Adrienne was back living with her parents in Stockton and working at the animal shelter in Darlington. It was hard for either of us to get time off, so we didn't see a lot of each other during the summer. I went up once, for her birthday. I'd bought her a charm for her bracelet. Cost me an arm and a leg, but I knew she liked them. I didn't want to just put it in the post, you know. I wanted to see her open it. See the expression on her face. So I took the train up.'

'And?'

He smiled wistfully. 'It was worth it.'

'And after that?'

'We went to Glasto and the Green Man festival. It rained all the time, but we didn't care.'

'And since then?'

'We went out a couple of times right at the beginning of the year, but she seemed a bit cool. I'd ask her what was wrong, but she wouldn't say. A few days later she told me it had been fun, but she couldn't see me any more.'

'Colin,' Banks said, 'I want you to think carefully about this. Did you get the impression that something might have happened to Adrienne over the summer to cause her to become deeply upset or depressed?'

'Like what?'

'Some traumatic event. Was she assaulted, robbed, raped?'

'No!'

'How do you know? It might have been something she didn't want anyone to know about, something she hid away, buried deep.'

'If you put it like that, I suppose anything's possible, but if there *was* something like that, I had absolutely no sense of it. I mean, things weren't *that* different. She wasn't *that* different. She just dumped me, that's all.'

'How did you feel about that?'

'How do you think I felt? Devastated. I was gutted.'

'What reason did she give?'

A group of laughing students came in and took a table some distance away.

Fairfax remained quiet for a few moments until the hubbub died down. He was soft spoken, Banks noticed. 'She didn't. She just said that she wanted to concentrate on her work. I suggested we maybe just see less of each other, but she said that wouldn't work and it would be easier in the long run to stop altogether. I asked her if there was someone else, but she assured me there wasn't.'

'Did you believe her?'

'Not at first, but later, I think I did. I mean, if I saw her at all, she was with the usual crowd. Neela, Cameron, Chloe and the rest. Never just with one special guy or anything.' He paused for a moment.

'Thought of something?' Banks prompted him.

'There was this girl. Mia. That was right at the beginning of term, when things were starting to go wonky with me and Adrienne. I must admit, I was a bit worried there for a while.'

'What do you mean?'

'They were hanging out together so much. I mean, it wasn't that I thought Adrienne was gay or anything, not that there would be anything wrong with that, but it just gave me a funny feeling, like it was some club I couldn't join. They seemed really intense. They always made me feel left out.'

'I assume,' Banks said, 'that you were being politically correct just then, and there would be something very much wrong with Adrienne being gay if you were in love with her?'

'Well, yeah, but you know what I mean. She wasn't. OK?'

'So what about Mia?'

'I just got a bad vibe from her, that's all. She didn't like me, and Adrienne behaved different when she was with her, as if I was, like, on the outside and they had some little private thing going. I was worried she was having some sort of adverse influence on Adrienne.'

'How? What for?'

'I don't know. Like manipulating her or something. Adrienne was easily led, that's all. I suppose Mia was sort of charismatic.'

'Where did you think she was leading Adrienne?'

'I don't know. Nowhere. There wasn't anything in particular. It was just a feeling. It was my imagination, my jealousy, my fears. Haven't you ever had anything like that happen, man, when you imagine all kinds of awful things happening to someone you love? It really distorts your vision.'

Banks knew what he meant. He remembered nights sitting up staring out of the window if his girlfriend was late coming home, imagining all kinds of terrible things that might have happened to her, from falling into the hands of a serial killer to sleeping with another man, though admittedly, the second of these would have been far more terrible for him than for her. He assumed it was a pretty normal form of insecurity. 'How long did this go on?' he asked.

'Dunno. Couple of weeks, maybe, into October. Then Mia just seemed to disappear from the scene. Adrienne told me she'd dropped out. No explanation. Nobody even knew what department she was in.'

'How was Adrienne after Mia left?'

'She was fine at first. I mean, that was when I knew, you know, that there was nothing in it, my fears and so on, that it wasn't a lesbian thing. Adrienne wasn't upset or heartbroken or anything. Maybe just a bit more distant. I saw less and less of her. But that was happening anyway. She seemed to be a bit weird. I don't know. Just not her usual self.'

'Do you think they could still have been seeing one another?'

'No. I don't think so. I mean, I never saw hide nor hair of Mia again.'

'What if Adrienne wanted to keep their meetings secret?'

'I suppose she could have been doing that if she wanted, but why?'

'Did you ever suspect that drugs were an issue with Adrienne and Mia?'

'Not at first. Adrienne was so anti-drug. But I must admit it crossed my mind later, when she seemed a bit out of it sometimes.'

'Out of it?'

'You know, not really following conversations, not respond-
ing to texts or emails, as if her mind was always somewhere
else.'

'Any idea where that might have been?'

Fairfax shook his head. 'Sorry, no. I still find it really hard
to believe it was drugs, but . . . well . . . it's an obvious option,
isn't it? People change.'

Vampire Weekend, or whoever it was, gave way to The
Killers.

'Colin,' said Winsome, 'we've been investigating Adrienne's
mobile use, and it seems you called her quite often.'

'Yeah. So what?'

'Well, you'd split up. Why were you still pestering her?'

'Who says I was pestering her?'

'There's quite a lot of calls. Were you stalking her, Colin?'

'No way. She liked me to call. If you check it out you'll see
she called me sometimes, too. It wasn't all one way. She still
liked to talk about stuff we had in common, like movies and
music and stuff. And environmental issues, anti-fracking
demos and so on. We were both interested in politics, Jez and
all that. Hope for the future, for the many, that was something
we still shared.'

'Jez?' said Banks.

'You know. Jeremy. Jeremy Corbyn.'

'Oh, Jeremy Corbyn. Yes, I know who you mean. I just don't
understand the link.'

'You wouldn't understand. You're too old. Adrienne and I
were both members of the Marxist Society. We talked about
politics a lot. How to change the world. Get rid of inequality
and starvation and all the other evils.'

Maybe Banks was too old for Jeremy Corbyn. He had
believed in all the man's policies when he was sixteen, but that
belief had faded by the time he reached thirty. Though he still
considered himself to be part of the liberal left, perhaps he

had become more cynical over the years, more conservative, even. As far as Corbyn himself was concerned, Banks detected a whiff of the demagogue, the steely glint of Stalinism in his eye, and he didn't like that at all. Not that any of the alternatives seemed much more acceptable.

'And how did this make you feel, this telephone relationship?' he asked.

'I enjoyed it. I mean, it wasn't as good as being with her, but I suppose I felt there was always a chance, like, as long as we were still communicating, still on the same wavelength, that we might get back together as long as we stayed friends and had lots in common. That whatever it was that was bothering her would go away and she'd see the light. But they made me sad, too, the phone calls. Like, I always felt really lonely and a bit down after our conversations.'

'But you were happy to remain just friends?' Winsome asked.

'Yeah. We talked. It's just that I didn't see her so often, and I felt like a bit of an afterthought. Why are you asking me all these questions? First the papers implied it was a drug overdose, then they said it was suicide. I have to say, I can't imagine her doing that. She was such an alive, positive person most of the time. I just can't see her killing herself. But you know more about the circumstances than I do, and you've no reason to lie about it. So why? Tell me. Why did she do it?'

'We don't know,' Winsome said. 'That's why we're talking to her friends, to try and make sense out of all this.'

'Well, I'm sorry but I can't help you. I would if I could, honest.' Fairfax paused again for a moment. 'Is there a chance that she *didn't* take her own life, like it was an accident, or somebody did it to her?'

'Do you know of anyone who might have done something like that to her?'

'No. But there could be another explanation, couldn't there? Other than suicide, I mean.'

'There could be,' Banks conceded. 'When did you last talk to her?'

'If you have her mobile you'll know. It was last week. Wednesday or Thursday. She called me.'

'Did she sound any different from usual?'

'No.'

'What did you talk about? It was a short conversation.'

'We were supposed to go to a demo on the weekend. She rang to tell me she couldn't make it.'

'Did she say why?'

'No.'

'How did she sound.'

'Same as usual.'

'Does POLICE AWARE mean anything to you?'

'It's that yellow sign you stick in broken-down cars when you leave them on country roads, isn't it?'

'That's right.'

'Then I don't understand the question. What else should it mean? Why should it mean anything other than what it says?'

'That's what I'm asking you. Does it mean anything else? Does it have any special significance for you? Or for Adrienne?'

'Well, no, I guess. I can't say as I've ever thought about it, and Adrienne certainly never mentioned it. Why?'

'Have you ever had a prescription for sleeping pills?'

'You must be joking.'

'Not at all.'

'Then, no. I've never had any trouble sleeping. And I don't like taking pills, not even paracetamol. Before you even go there, I don't do drugs.'

'Nobody says you do, Colin.'

'But it always comes up, doesn't it? Student. Ergo, must be drugs somewhere.'

'Are there?'

'No.'

'What about E?'

'Never tried it.'

'Adrienne took it at The Cellar Club with her friends.'

'Maybe she did. But I wasn't a part of that crowd. And I don't like The Cellar Club.'

'Does it surprise you that Adrienne took drugs?' Winsome asked.

'Maybe she did E occasionally with her mates. But she wasn't a druggie.'

'Let's just go back to this Mia for a minute,' Banks said. 'Can you tell us what she looked like?'

'Mia? She was about the same height as Adrienne, around five six, very attractive, with an olive complexion and brown eyes. It was weird, though. I mean, you could tell she had a great figure, but she dressed it down, if you know what I mean. Dressed to cover it up. I never saw her in a skirt or a dress or anything, just jeans and baggy sweatshirts and stuff. And her hair was messy, like she didn't bother with it much.'

'Long or short?'

'Medium really.' He touched his shoulders. 'Reddish brown and sort of wavy.'

'You say she had an olive complexion. Was she Asian, or black?'

'Neither. Not that dark. Just sort of Mediterranean, you know? Or South American. But she wasn't foreign. I mean, she was English. I think she came from somewhere down south. Winchester, if I remember right. Somewhere with a cathedral, anyway.'

That really helped a lot, Banks thought. 'How old was she?'

'About my age, I'd guess. Twenty or so.'

'So you did talk to her?'

'Once or twice. She just wasn't very friendly towards me. Not forthcoming. A bit monosyllabic.'

'And you've no idea what became of her?'

'None at all. It was like she just disappeared into thin air.'

Winsome put her notebook away and she and Banks stood up.

'Thanks for your time, Colin,' said Banks. 'We're sorry about Adrienne, but believe me, we're doing our best to find out what happened to her. Here's my card. If you think of anything that might be relevant, however minor it may seem, please let us know.'

Colin took the card. 'Thanks, man,' he said. 'Yeah, I will.'

7

The church bells were ringing. Clanging was more like it – real *Hunchback of Notre Dame* clanging – as if they were just across the street. Which they were. Annie remembered that she was staying at Carrie and Don's house in the close and it was Saturday morning. Must be a wedding. She opened one gummy eye and saw that she was in a child's room – Tabitha's, obviously – with Disney princesses and fairy-tale castles dotted all over the pink wallpaper. Under the window sat piles of stuffed animals and a glass-fronted bookcase ran the gamut from Beatrix to Harry Potter. When Annie grasped the duvet to pull it over her head, she saw that it was covered with appliqué robins and wrens. A stuffed owl stared at her from pride of place on the dresser.

Annie's head was pounding and her mouth was dry. Sure signs of a hangover. She spotted the glass of water on the bedside table and downed half of it in one. That felt better. Then she fumbled in her handbag for the handy pack of Panadol Extra Advance she always carried with her, took three and washed them down with the rest of the water. She then rested her head back on the pillow and took stock.

At least she was alone. That was a good start. She didn't think she had done anything terrible or outrageous last night, though she did remember a bloke chatting her up until his wife saw what was going on and intervened. Rather rudely, Annie thought. Then there was the handsome crime writer. She might even have kissed him and given him her phone number, but that was all. Afterwards, it was slim pickings as most of the partygoers drifted off home. In the end there was just Annie and her friends talking about old times. Hence the hangover. Still, she thought, stirring and throwing off the duvet, she'd had a good girly time with her friends Carrie, Pat, Natalie and Fran, none of whom she'd seen for a while. It was Carrie's party, and she and Don had shipped the kids off to Grandma's for the night. Most of the guests had been connected with local bookshops – The Little Ripon Bookshop, and White Rose, in nearby Thirsk – hence the sprinkling of local writers. The men had simply provided a brief distraction from discussions of Jane Austen and Sara Paretsky.

There had been no police presence other than Annie herself. Carrie had left the force five years ago for a more stress-free life of running a second-hand bookshop. Annie had taken one or two well-meant jibes about police incompetence, corruption and so on, but in general people had either given her a wide berth or accepted her as one of the gang. Which she was. She had known Fran and Natalie, Carrie's best friends for years, even if the booksellers were relatively new to her. It was good to live a part of her life outside the police, she felt.

At least she had been able to put the dysfunctional or deceased Hadfield family out of her mind for the evening. Poppy would probably be proud of her for getting so pissed. And maybe also for that little dance she and Fran and Carrie had done around the Ripon market square at midnight, until the local police constable had told them politely to go home. For a moment, Annie had considered telling him who she was and pulling her rank, but she hadn't. She can't have been that pissed, then, after all, except dancing on cobbles in high heels was hardly the act of a sober person. The last she had heard from Gerry before she left for the party was that both Poppy's alibis held up. She was where she said she was on the weekend of Laurence Hadfield's disappearance. The previous evening, before leaving for Ripon, and after some difficulty and a lot of swearing, along with a bribe of a bottle of VSOP cognac, Annie had stashed Poppy away in a discreet little boutique hotel in Eastvale until she could figure out her next move.

It was freezing in Tabitha's room, so Annie pulled on her last night's clothes as quickly as she could, grabbed her bag, stopped by the bathroom for a quick wash and a spot of make-up, then headed downstairs. She heard voices and found Fran and Natalie leaning on the island in the kitchen, where the coffee-maker was gurgling and emitting its seductive aroma.

Fran smiled. 'Well, look who's up at last.'

Annie pulled a face and glanced at her watch. Only 9.30. 'It's not that late,' she said. 'Them bloody bells would wake up Sleeping Beauty. I didn't do anything really out of line last night, did I? Please tell me I didn't.'

Fran and Natalie laughed. 'Apart from that striptease and the lap dance you gave Steve, you mean? Not at all.'

'Bastards,' said Annie, smiling. 'I think I might remember something like that.' She picked up a mug from the counter, noticing it had a picture of Elvis Presley on it, pulled the coffee pot towards her and poured. The automatic machine hadn't finished its business, and a thin stream of coffee dripped from its basket and sizzled on the hotplate. 'Shit!' Annie quickly put the pot back.

Fran and Natalie laughed again. 'Oh, Annie,' Natalie said. 'What can we do with you?'

'A nice fry-up wouldn't go amiss right now,' Annie answered.

'Thought you were a veggie,' Natalie said.

Annie scowled. 'Yeah, well, but . . . you ever tasted a veggie sausage?'

'You mean the ones without meat? Isn't that what they always used to be like here?'

Fran laughed and pointed. 'There's the bread and there's the toaster. The marmalade's in the top cupboard. And we're back on butter. Apparently it's better for you. Margarine is full of carcinogens or something.'

Annie sipped some coffee then went and put two slices of white bread in the toaster.

'The brown's healthier,' said Fran.

'But how can you tell when it's done?'

They both laughed at that. 'It was a fun night,' Natalie said. 'We mustn't leave it so long again.'

'How's the birthday girl?' Annie asked.

'Carrie? Still asleep,' said Fran. 'Probably enjoying the first lie-in she's had in ages without the kids to wake her.'

'You know she loves them to death.' Annie did, too. She was even godmother to one of them – Melissa, age nine – and when she thought of Carrie's life there were times that she felt she had lost so much by deciding not to have children herself. Not that it was entirely too late – not physically, at any rate, perhaps – but in many ways it was. For a start, she would need a suitable man. Or maybe just an anonymous donor. She scrapped that thought.

The toast popped up. Annie reached for the knife and butter on the side and started spreading. 'Hope Carrie had a good time last night.'

'Oh, she did,' said Fran.

Annie was enjoying her coffee and toast when her mobile made its sixties police car sound. 'Shit!'

'Just leave it,' said Natalie.

'Can't. It might be work.'

'Big case on?'

'Big enough.' Annie found her mobile before it stopped and went into the living room for some privacy. She saw the caller was PC Dave Kingsley, who was supposed to be keeping an eye on Poppy's hotel.

'DI Cabbot?'

'Speaking.' Annie could hear a hubbub in the background. The loud voice sounded like Poppy's, and she guessed the calmer conciliatory one belonged to the desk clerk or manager. She let out a long sigh. 'OK, Constable, what's going on there?'

'There's a bit of a fracas, to be honest, ma'am.'

'I can hear that for myself. What sort of a fracas?'

'It's Miss Hadfield, ma'am. She's creating an awful fuss. Refusing to pay her bill. She was down in the middle of the night shouting the odds, too, but the night manager and the desk clerk sorted things out.'

Annie raised her eyes skywards. 'So what do you want me to do about it now?'

'I think you'd better get over here as soon as you can, ma'am. This time I think she's going to—'

Just then Annie heard a scream of rage and frustration followed by what sounded like a large vase smashing against a wall. The shock waves reverberated through her hungover brain like a kick in the head. The Panadol clearly hadn't taken effect yet, no matter how fast the packet said it acted.

'I'm in Ripon right now,' Annie said. 'Keep a lid on things as best you can. Don't let anyone leave. I'll be there in twenty minutes.'

Annie went to the hall, grabbed her coat, felt for her car keys in the pocket then called out a hasty farewell to Fran and Natalie, who stood in the kitchen doorway looking puzzled. 'Tell Carrie I'm really sorry,' Annie added as she turned the doorknob. 'And wish her a happy birthday again from me. I'll ring later. Got to go.' She paused before closing the door and grinned. 'One day I'll tell you about it.'

'Anna Akhmatova,' said Linda, pushing her empty lunch plate aside. 'She was a strange one. Beautiful, though you'd hardly think it from existing photos. But elegant, aristocratic. Modigliani sketched her, you know. They were lovers for a while. And like all her lovers, he left her. She was always ill. Suffered from TB and heart problems all her life. Not to mention the revolution, the problems of surviving Stalin's Russia and the Second World War. Like all artists in Russia, she had to be so careful what she said, or didn't say. Especially if she committed it to paper. Don't forget, if you fell afoul of the authorities, it wasn't just yourself you put in danger. It was your entire family and circle of friends. Sometimes they would leave you free, so you could suffer the guilt of causing your family's murder. She ended up lonely and sad, with most of her friends and family and lovers and fellow writers dead or on the gulag, but she was celebrated. That was always important to her. That people loved her poetry. She could be very competitive.'

'Do you feel the same way?'

Linda pursed her lips and thought for a moment, swirling her red wine in the glass. 'Competitive? Not so much, no. My life has been very different, of course – for one thing, I have never had to live under a totalitarian regime – and I think the English attitude towards writing poetry is very different from the Russian approach. We're probably more Larkin than Pushkin, on the whole. Oh, I tell myself I don't give a fuck what the critics say, but I'll fume or cry over a bad review like anyone else. I suppose if you do put yourself out there then, you want to be appreciated, celebrated, even, not shat on. But that's not the reason you do it. That's a different sort of compulsion.'

They were having lunch in the Low Moor Inn, a pub Banks had discovered quite by accident in the middle of nowhere, vast stretches of wild inhospitable moorland all around. For some reason, they had taken to frequenting it for their occasional poetry sessions. Today the landscape was shrouded in a grey gauzy haze, with patches of frost still visible on distant stretches.

The pub was squat and sturdy with thick stone walls, a fire-place you could stand up in and watercolours of local scenes all over the rough plastered walls. The dining room was quiet, conversations a gentle rising and falling murmur around them, no music or machines to break the spell. They had finished their discussion of Eliot's 'The Love Song of J. Alfred Prufrock' just before Banks had asked Linda about Akhmatova. Banks had found Eliot's poem fascinating, though he admitted he couldn't really understand it. Linda had said that didn't matter and that he had to get rid of that archaic and irritating habit of wanting to translate poems into rational prose in his mind. He thought he had imagination, but often poetry defeated him; maybe it was because he'd been thinking like a policeman for too many years. Still, he tried, and the effort was rewarding.

'Why are you asking about Akhmatova, by the way?' Linda asked. 'I don't believe I've ever talked about her before.'

'Someone mentioned her to me the other night,' Banks said.
'Why?'

'I'm not sure you should be getting into poetry in translation just yet. Especially Akhmatova.'

'Difficult, is she?'

'Not especially. Not on the surface of it. But there are particular difficulties with just about anything Russian artists produced in the last century.'

'Rather like with anything their politicians produce in this century.'

Linda laughed. 'Well, they do have a complex history.'

Banks nodded. 'I'm a big Shostakovich fan, but half the time I feel lost and stupid when I try to work out the context of his life, the secret meanings of his symphonies and quartets. What Stalin really defined as true socialist realist music

and what he dismissed as "formalism" or unpatriotic bourgeois drivel.'

'I know what you mean. I think you'd have to be Russian to
even attempt an answer to those questions, though Julian
Barnes wrote a fine book about Shostakovich recently.'

'Yes,' said Banks. 'I read it. But it must have been different
for a poet. Music doesn't carry meaning in the same way
words do. It's more subjective, perhaps.'

'True. And it wasn't only criticism of the party that went
against you, it was also embrace of the personal, the romantic. Bourgeois individualism. Anna could sound like a love-
sick schoolgirl, even in her sixties, but there was always some
image, some phrase, metaphor or observation, that would
pull the rug from under you, throw you sideways. Maybe it
would be a cynical comment on her own emotions, or something like that, but it constantly changes and challenges your
perception of what you've just read, puts everything in a
different context.'

'Most poetry does that for me,' Banks said. 'Like most
cases.'

Linda laughed again. 'Maybe that's why so many people try
to avoid poetry at all costs.' She paused to drink some wine. 'I
visited Russia once, you know. Just Moscow and St Petersburg.
I saw all the usual sights: the Kremlin, St Basil's, the Hermitage,
the Nevsky Prospekt, but I remember being struck constantly
whenever I saw elderly people in the streets what some of
them must have lived through. The suffering showed in the
lines of the old women's faces, in the hunched, stiff figures of
the men. And even then, when I was there in the early nineties, there were still long queues for what little was in the
shops. I thought of the famines, the siege of Leningrad,
Stalingrad, the purges, all the depredations visited on that
country – and no, I didn't forget that so much harm was done
by the Russians to themselves, not an invading army, though

it must often have seemed that way. All in the name of Communism. And the terrible things they did to the countries around them – but there's something very . . . I don't know . . . something that really puts you in your place when you visit somewhere like that, with such a weight of history. Now Putin. Have you ever been there?'

'No, but *Doctor Zhivago*'s always been one of my favourite films,' Banks said.

'I could have guessed. Julie Christie. *Men.*'

'That, too. But I was thinking more of Zhivago and his wife's family. In the film. They were from the aristocracy, too. And look what happened. That scene when Zhivago gets back to the family house in Moscow after all he's been through and finds they have to share it with a lot of strangers always scares the hell out of me. I used to have nightmares about getting home and finding my parents gone and families I didn't know living in all the rooms – including mine – and all the way up the stairs.'

'It's a frightening thought.' Linda tapped his arm. 'But you might have to get used to it, the way the housing crisis is going these days. There's plenty of room for a few more families in your cottage.' She glanced out of the window at the broad expanse of wintry moor. 'And who knows? In a few years' time all this may be covered with council estates.'

'Social housing, please,' said Banks. 'It sounds much nicer.'

'Have you read the novel? *Doctor Zhivago.*'

'I'm ashamed to say I haven't.'

'You should.'

'I will. If only there were movie versions of great poems, too.'

Linda laughed. 'Or musicals.'

'Well, there was *Cats*,' Banks said. 'But could you imagine *Prufrock: The Musical?*'

'Or "Ode on a Grecian Urn".'

'"Tintern Abbey".'

'"Elegy Written in a Country Churchyard".'

People turned to look at them laughing.

'Anyway,' Banks said when their laughter died down. 'She sounds like a complicated person, this Akhmatova.'

'I think she was. But fascinating. She certainly fascinated men.'

That made Banks think of Zelda, who had first mentioned Akhmatova to him. He told Linda a bit about their dinner the other night. He didn't feel he could tell her anything about Zelda's government work, but he talked about her sculpture, her excitement at moving up to Yorkshire and her interest in the arts.

'I'd like to meet her,' Linda said when he'd finished.

'I'm sure it could be arranged.'

'I already know Ray Cabbot. The local arts scene is pretty incestuous. But this Zelda is a more recent and exotic arrival.'

'Then consider it a done deal. I'll talk to them. We'll work something out. Dinner or drinks or something.' Banks felt pleased with himself. He had never considered himself a social arranger, but it felt good to think he was putting two people in touch, people he was certain had something in common, and could possibly even become good friends.

'Fantastic.'

'Shall we risk another one or call it a day?'

Linda glanced at her watch. 'Oh, bugger it,' she said. 'Let's have another. You can tell me all about your latest case.'

When Annie arrived at the hotel, a listed building in a discreet backstreet off the market square, she found Poppy in hand-cuffs, bedraggled and penitent, sitting beside her suitcase in the lounge, a burly uniformed constable on either side of her.

She was wearing jeans and knee-high boots, and an afghan jacket over a torn black T-shirt with a picture of Courtney Love sticking her tongue out. Poppy's long blonde hair was greasy and straggly, and it looked as if it hadn't been washed for a while. Though her features were drawn and she had bags under her eyes, she gave off the aura of a little girl lost. A chambermaid was busy clearing up the mess Poppy had made of the reception area, dirt, dead flowers and shattered pottery all over the floor.

Annie took a deep breath. At least the Panadol was working now, and her headache had receded to a dull and distant thumping in time with the beating of her heart.

'What's going on?' she asked PC Kingsley. 'Why is this woman in handcuffs?'

'It was the only way we could restrain her, ma'am,' said Kingsley. 'She was going berserk, smashing things, threatening all sorts of—'

Annie held her hand up. 'OK. Enough. Did she actually assault anyone?'

'Well, no, not exactly, but—'

'Then uncuff her.'

Kingsley swallowed. 'Ma'am?'

'You heard what I said. Uncuff her. This young woman has just lost her father. She's bereaved. Whatever she's done, I'm sure we can put it right.' She glanced around at the reception area. 'It's nothing but cosmetic damage as far as I can see. I'm sure Ms Hadfield will be more than happy to pay for replacements for any objects she broke, and offer compensation for any inconvenience.'

The manager came up wringing his hands. 'But what about the other guests, the trauma, the—'

'I'm sure they'll get over it, Mr . . .?'

'Shadwell. Edgar Shadwell. I'm the night manager. I should have gone home ages ago, when my shift ended, but—'

'Thanks for staying and helping take care of things,' Annie said, showing him her warrant card. Then she gently led him over to a part of the lobby where they couldn't be overheard. 'What exactly did Ms Hadfield do?' she asked.

'It all started about three in the morning. She telephoned the front desk and demanded room service. She wanted a cheeseburger and a bottle of vodka. We don't have twenty-four-hour room service here, so I'm afraid the poor lad on reception had to say no.'

The cognac bribe obviously hadn't lasted long, Annie thought. 'And then?'

'She didn't take it well. She came storming down with her bathrobe half open, yelling at the top of her voice, waking all our guests, scaring the living daylights out of them. That's when I came out of my office to see what was happening. She had a cigarette in her mouth, too, and we're strictly a non-smoking hotel. Tim on the desk explained that we don't have a kitchen on the premises. We use the restaurant next door for all our orders, you see, and they were closed, of course. As for the vodka, well, it was clear that she'd had more than enough already. We did manage to calm her down. Tim gave her a couple of extra minibar vodkas and she went back up to her room. Then it all started again this morning, when she refused to pay. That was when she became . . . well, you can see. Quite abusive. Quite violent.'

'Of course. It's all my fault, Mr Shadwell, and I do hope you'll accept my apology.'

'Your fault? Bu . . . b . . . b . . . but I don't understand. How could it be *your* fault?'

'I had to choose a hotel for Ms Hadfield very quickly, in the wake of her father's sudden death. She couldn't remain in the family home. I thought this place would suit her needs, but I obviously overestimated the hotel and underestimated her needs. I should have chosen one of the larger establishments.'

'I don't think you *overestimated* us, Inspector Cabbot. We do our best to keep our guests happy here at the Swan. We even go out of our way. But there are some things . . . limits . . .'

'Yes, I quite understand. We'll get it all sorted. Would you pass on the bill for the damages to me at Eastvale Police HQ? I'll see that Ms Hadfield gets it and pays it.'

'Of course. But you do understand—'

'I do. But I'm afraid we have to go now. Once again, I apologise.'

Annie went back to Poppy and took her by the arm. Poppy didn't complain or resist, she simply stood and picked up her suitcase with her free hand. 'Where are we going?' she asked.

'I don't know yet,' said Annie between clenched teeth. 'But the first thing is to get you away from here.'

'The sooner the better,' said Poppy, rallying, her voice rising. 'What a dump. I'm considering suing.'

Annie practically shoved her through the front door, annoyed that her mobile rang just as they reached her car down the street. 'Yes?' she answered, a trifle sharply.

'Ooh, are we in a bit of a mood this morning?'

It was Frank Naylor from the search team at the Hadfield house. Annie knew Frank from the occasional departmental booze up. He was one of the good guys. At least he had never tried to grope her in a dark corner at the Christmas party.

'What is it, Frank? I don't have time for this. I'm in a hurry.'

'You sound a bit hoarse. Not getting that cold that's going around, are you?'

'No. What is it, Frank?'

'Ah. You're hungover, aren't you? Tell Uncle Frank the truth.'

'Well, it is only half past ten on a Saturday morning,' Annie said. 'And I do happen to have been up late at a good friend's birthday party last night, so, yes, you might reasonably come to that conclusion. Now what the hell do you want?'

Frank laughed down the line. 'OK. No need to take it out on me. What you do in your own time and all that.'

'Frank!'

'All right, all right. There's been a development here.'

'What sort of development? Where?'

'The Hadfield house. We've found something.'

'What are you doing working weekends?'

'We're spread a bit thin, these days. And there's still a bit of overtime left. Anyway, it's probably better if you come and see it for yourself.'

'Frank, I don't have time for—'

'No, really. It's a bit hard to describe. A piece of jewellery.'

'Are you at the house now?'

'Yes.'

Annie looked at her watch. 'I'm in Eastvale,' she said. 'It shouldn't take me long to get there.' At least the Hadfield house was on her way to her own cottage in Harkside. As soon as she'd dealt with Frank, she'd ship Poppy off to London, go home, have a long shower or bath and maybe just go back to bed. Some hope, the way this day was going.

'Just be careful driving,' Frank said. 'You know how some people are still technically pissed from the night before even the morning after.'

Annie took a deep breath. 'Frank?' she said.

'Yes?'

'Fuck off.'

'There's not much to tell,' Banks said.

'I know you can't give any details away. I've been through it, remember? On the receiving end.'

'I remember,' said Banks. 'But there's still not a lot to tell.'

'I've read the newspaper reports, seen the TV news. It sounds tragic.'

'What's really tragic is that we don't have a lot to go on. No, that's too flippant,' said Banks. 'It *is* tragic. A young girl like Adrienne Munro, cut down in her prime, all her life ahead of her.'

'And you've no idea why?'

Banks shook his head.

'It *is* suicide, isn't it?'

'Even if I knew for certain, I couldn't say. Cause of death is still under investigation.'

'Then there's the other case. Laurence Hadfield. Accidental death, the papers say. Is that yours, too?'

'I'm officially Senior Investigating Officer, though Annie's got the role in reality. It's another puzzle.'

'I know I'm just an overimaginative poet speaking,' Linda said, 'but has it crossed your mind that the two cases might be connected in some way?' When Banks just guzzled some beer and didn't say anything, she went on. 'Unless, of course, you already know they are and you can't tell me?

'No, no. It's not that. I don't believe in coincidences any more than you do. It's one of the first things I thought of, but I've learned over the years not to trust first impressions without evidence. It's just that there's no obvious connection between the victims, no evidence to tie them together, except they both died rather mysteriously within a short time of one another. They moved in very different circles. If I could find something to link them, anything, it would be different.'

'What if there was a point of contact? If something brought the circles to intersect?'

'We think it's possible that Adrienne was involved with drugs in some way, but there's no connection there with Hadfield. At least not yet. It's more likely to be connected with someone at the college.'

'I've heard of Laurence Hadfield,' said Linda. 'I even met him once, briefly. Maybe that's why I'm interested.'

Banks's ears pricked up. 'Met him? Where? When? How?'

'Aha,' Linda teased. 'Now he's interested.'

'If you know anything, you should tell me.'

'It's nothing relevant. Don't get your hopes up. You'll only be disappointed. It's just that Mr Hadfield was a bit of a philanthropist, and his benevolent gestures even extended as far as the arts community. He was involved in setting up a local poetry award, mostly to encourage young people to write poetry. I had the honour of presenting it at a dinner a couple of years ago. We were at the same table. That's all.'

'What did you think of him?'

'I didn't really get the chance to form an impression. He was polite, said all the right things. It was pretty obvious he wasn't really interested in poetry, but that was hardly a surprise.'

'So why not come up with an award for some other field?'

'It's my guess that the other fields weren't doing too badly as far as the Arts Council budget was concerned. He saw a gap, or someone saw it for him. People like Hadfield are constantly searching for ways to unload their money that make them look good in the public eye.'

'Isn't that a bit cynical to say about someone who was so generous?'

Linda snorted. 'For him it was a mere drop in the ocean. For the poet, it was an opportunity to spend a year concentrating on her writing. Have you any idea how much of a godsend that is? I'm sorry if I appear cynical, but I'm afraid philanthropists have often been in the business of whitewashing their business practices, the sources of their wealth, perhaps even seeking atonement, if you like. Basically, they all want to be loved, but they know that what they do makes them unlovable – things like propping up foreign dictatorships or orchestrating coups against moderate governments that might not exactly be marching in time with their financial interests, selling weapons to both sides, or being involved in practices that seriously damage the environment. Not all, of course. Some don't give a damn about public perception or what harm they do, and others are genuinely selfless. But most fall somewhere in the middle.'

'So Laurence Hadfield chose to share some of his good fortune with young, unknown poets. Isn't that a good thing, whatever his motives?'

'Of course it is.'

'I mean, he wasn't trying to impose a programme on them or anything, was he, or using his position to take advantage of . . . well, you know.'

'Yes, I know,' said Linda. 'All those impressionable young girls with their love poetry. But no, I don't think he was. Someone told me he was involved in a lot of charities and good causes, that he donated time as well as money.'

'So did Jimmy Savile.'

Linda glared at him. 'But *he* had ulterior motives. I'm saying I don't think Mr Hadfield did, other than the usual need to be thought well of in the community. Oh, maybe he flirted with the young lasses at the dinner a bit, but it was nothing serious.'

'As far as I know, flirting hasn't been made illegal yet.'

'And you'd know, of course.'

'I can accept that nobody's wholly bad, not even a rapacious venture capitalist. But are you sure he wasn't using his philanthropy to cover up more sinister activities?'

Linda laughed. 'Have you ever wondered how your job warps your perception of the world?'

'Every day. But I try to stay on the straight and narrow.'

'Anyway, on a brief acquaintance, I'd have to say no. I didn't get that impression about Laurence Hadfield. He seemed genuine enough. He came across as fairly well educated, too. I mean, I'm not saying he was a huge poetry fan, but he knew his Keats from his Eliot. Said he mostly read non-fiction, though. Biographies and history. If anything, he seemed a bit bored. Kept looking at his watch. Put his hand over his mouth to stifle a yawn when the winner read her poem.'

'That's hardly unusual at a poetry reading, is it?'

Linda lifted her glass. 'Hey, enough of that, or you'll be wearing this glass of red wine.'

Banks held up his hands. 'I take your point. I take all your points. But Adrienne Munro never won a poetry competition. Never even entered one, as far as I know. She played the violin.'

'Maybe he was involved in sponsoring musical talents, too?'

'It's worth a look,' said Banks. 'Are you after a job or something?'

'With the police? Never. I like the idle life of a poet best.'

'Well, whatever Laurence Hadfield's true motives for his philanthropy, and however he earned his wealth, the mystery remains of what the hell he was doing up on Tetchley Moor wearing a business suit, and how he got there.'

'Well, somebody must have driven him,' said Linda. 'I know I'm not a detective, but I would have thought that much was obvious.'

'I'm sorry,' said Poppy, slouching down as far as she could in the passenger seat of Annie's small car. She looked as if she were trying to shrink or make herself disappear. 'I just couldn't sleep. I mean, it really hit me. About Dad. That I'll never see him again. I didn't mean to lose my temper but they were just so snotty and mean to me.'

'Don't worry about it,' said Annie. 'I'll send you the bill. You OK now?'

Poppy nodded. 'I'm all right.' She gave a wan smile. 'I could do with a drink and a snort, but I'm OK.'

'Valium?'

'Already taken two.'

'We're all set, then. I've got to make a call at your dad's house first. The search team's turned up something they think I should see. I want you on your best behaviour if you're to come in with me. And don't touch a thing. Do you understand?'

'Yes, Mummy.'

'That's enough of that.'

'Then what? If I can't stay there, where am I supposed to go?'

'You might be better off at home.'

'You mean I'm free to go back to London?'

'Yes. It could be a while yet before your father's body is released for burial. There's no point your hanging around up here and wrecking our hotels.'

'You should have seen Mad Dog wreck a hotel room. Gave Keith Moon a run for his money. He once threw a mattress from the sixth floor of a Holiday Inn. Anyway, the rates hotels charge, I think you should be entitled to do a bit of damage.' Poppy smiled at the memory.

Annie had to think for a moment before she realised that Poppy was talking about Nate Maddock, her deceased rock-star boyfriend, and Keith Moon, The Who's late drummer, who had a reputation for smashing up hotel rooms. Even she knew that.

She approached Rivendell on the lane through the woods and saw the CSI and search team vans parked outside, as well as Poppy's red sports car.

'You probably shouldn't be driving,' Annie said. 'Not after the Valium and whatever you had to drink in the middle of the night. Not to mention the cognac.'

'Only a couple of miserable minibar vodkas.'

'Even so.'

'No matter. I don't feel like driving anyway. Too tired. Can I at least leave the car where it is?'

'I don't see why not. I can give you a lift to the station in Northallerton.'

'Station? What do you mean?'

'The train station.'

'A train? You wouldn't catch me dead on one of those bloody things. Can't you drive me home?'

'You must be joking.'

Poppy folded her arms. 'Fine. I'll take a taxi, then.'

Annie swallowed her surprise and parked beside the CSI van. A taxi to London. *How the other half lived.*

'I don't want to go in,' said Poppy. 'Is it all right if I just stay out here in your car until you're finished?'

'As long as you don't wreck anything.'

Poppy looked around the car's interior. 'As if anyone would notice.'

Annie laughed and got out. It wasn't a bad day, now she finally got the chance to sniff the air. A bit cloudy, but not too cold. Annie crunched over the gravel and let herself in the open front door. It was easy to see what Frank had meant about CSIs being thin on the ground. There were only two of them painstakingly checking the large mansion for fingerprints and trace evidence, anything to show how and why Laurence Hadfield had been found dead on Tetchley Moor. There had been nothing up there, so now they had moved on to the house.

Frank Naylor was in the kitchen pouring himself a cup of milky coffee from his vacuum flask. He turned when she walked in. 'Ah, Annie,' he said.

'And no more jibes.'

'Sorry. Sorry. Good time last night?'

Annie smiled. 'Great time, thanks.'

'Good. I'm sorry to drag you away. I suppose it could have waited, but everyone's been stressing just how little there's been to go on so far. I thought you should see this for yourself.' He reached for a plastic evidence bag on the island beside him and passed it to her. 'What do you make of that?'

Annie held up the bag and peered at the object. 'Well, it's pretty obvious,' she said.

'Maybe to you, but not to me. Like I said, it looks like some sort of piece of jewellery.'

'It is. It's a charm.'

'As in charm bracelet?'

'Right. But not just any charm bracelet. It's a charm from Pandora.'

'Is that good? Rare?'

Annie laughed. 'I'm afraid not. Very popular. But it's a hell of a lot better than nothing. For a start, it's not the sort of thing you'd expect a man like Laurence Hadfield to be wearing, that's for sure. Where did you find it?'

'Bathroom. Round the back of the toilet. Any number of ways it could have got there, but most likely someone dropped it and it bounced or rolled and that's where it ended up. They probably didn't even notice.'

Annie examined the charm again. 'Interesting,' she said. 'It's a treble clef, silver encrusted with cubic zirconia.'

'You never cease to amaze me,' said Frank. 'Expert jeweller as well as ace detective. Are you going to be able to find out where it was sold and to whom?'

'I told you, Frank, these things are very popular. You can buy them from lots of places, including online. No, I don't think it's going to lead us to a particular person, but it does tell us one thing we didn't know before.'

'What's that?'

'That Hadfield must have had at least one female friend in the house.'

'A young woman?'

'Not necessarily young. These Pandoras cross a number of age ranges. But that's most likely. And we've no idea how long it's been there, though I'm sure Adele Balter will swear she cleans behind the toilet every time she does for Mr Hadfield. Even so, we'd better get the CSIs to give the rest of the bathroom a good going over. If someone lost a Pandora charm there, then there's always a chance of hair or something down the plughole, stuck to the side of the bathtub, whatever. There may even be a possibility of DNA traces. Can I take it for a moment, Frank? Something I want to check.'

'Course.'

Annie walked back out to her car. Poppy was still in the passenger seat, and when she saw Annie, she guiltily flicked away her cigarette and put up the window. Annie got in beside her and decided to say nothing about the smoking. There was no point treating Poppy like a wayward child the whole time, even though that was exactly how she behaved. Instead, she sat down and showed her the charm. 'Do you recognise this?' she asked.

'What is it?'

'It's a treble clef from a charm bracelet. Pandora. Is it yours?'

Poppy handed it back as if it were contaminated. 'Mine? Mine? What the fuck do you think of me? I wouldn't be seen dead wearing that fucking bling.'

Annie glanced at the bangles on her wrists and the chains around her neck and guessed they were not bling. Or Pandora.

'So it's definitely not yours?'

'Definitely. Never seen it before.'

'Have you any idea whose it might be? It was found in the bathroom here.'

'No idea.'

'A girlfriend of your father's?'

'I doubt that he'd be seen with anyone who wore that sort of thing, either, but there's no accounting for taste. Anyway, I know nothing about the girls he hung out with.'

Annie reached for her phone.

Poppy looked nervous. 'What are you doing?'

'Calling you a taxi. Which part of London did you say you lived in?'

8

Sunday had brought nothing in the way of developments in either case, and it was already lunchtime on Monday. Toxicology on the sleeping pills Adrienne Munro had taken still wasn't ready. Though they were fortunate at Eastvale HQ in having a top-notch Scientific Support Department adjacent to the police station, and their Crime Scene Manager Stefan Nowak worked closely with the Scientific Support Manager Keith Atkinson, they still couldn't make nature move any faster.

Jazz Singh, their DNA, blood and toxicology specialist, had said on Friday that she could identify the kind of sleeping pills Adrienne Munro had been given, but that it might take a while. Knowing the specific brand could provide a useful lead; sleeping tablets of any kind were not that easy to get hold of without a prescription, and DS Steph Dobyns of the drugs squad might be able to trace a supplier or specific batch if she had more detailed information to go on.

Banks had spent a relaxing Sunday catching up with the latest series of *Black Mirror* on Netflix, then taking his wine out to the conservatory to listen to his recent download of Thelonious Monk's *Piano Solo*. As a consequence, he felt refreshed that Monday morning, but he also felt in need of a lead, of something to fire him up before these cases went completely stale on him. It happened that way sometimes. Day after day of little or no progress, and he started not to care, bit by bit he began to shove it to the back of his mind without even realising he was doing it, until he finally ground to a halt.

Banks got up to stretch and looked out over the market square, where the citizens of Eastvale were going about their business, shopping, delivering, chatting with neighbours, a horde of schoolkids piling into Greggs for a pasty or WHSmith for the latest comics. A gang of workmen had cordoned off one area and were hammering away at the cobbles, which seemed to require a lot of maintenance these days. The usual group of elderly ladies was meeting for morning tea in Garfield's Tea Room above the minimart on the corner of Market Street. There were enough patches of blue in the sky to give the appearance of a fine day, even if there was a damp winter chill in the air.

Banks thought he would go over to the Queen's Arms for a portion of Cyril's scampi and chips for lunch, but just as he took his overcoat from the hook behind his door, his phone rang. He supposed he could ignore it, but he wasn't that kind of person. Instead, he hurried over and picked up the receiver.

'Alan?' a familiar voice said.

'Ken? Good to hear from you.' It was DCI Ken Blackstone from the West Yorkshire Homicide and Major Inquiry Team, one of Banks's oldest friends and colleagues.

'Yeah. It's been a while. Sorry.'

'No matter. Busy?'

'It never seems to end.'

'It's been pretty quiet up here until recently,' said Banks.

'I heard about that. That's why I'm calling.'

'Aha. Do tell.'

'I'd rather not talk about it on the phone. Can you get down here?'

'You know me, Ken. I never turn down a chance to visit the big city. Especially when an old mate is buying lunch.'

Blackstone groaned theatrically. 'If that's what it takes. It's twelve o'clock now. Can you get down in an hour?'

'Should be able to.'

'What do you fancy?'

'Whitelock's would suit me. Can you at least give me a hint?'

'Your suspicious deaths. We've got one, too, and we might be able to help one another.'

'I'm on my way.'

Banks hurried down the stairs. Winsome was out working on Adrienne Munro's financial details, so he left a message at the front desk to say where he was going and that he wasn't sure when he would be back, then he nipped out of the back door and into his increasingly ancient-looking Porsche.

Annie had finally got Poppy settled in a taxi on Saturday after coming to a price arrangement with the stunned driver. Poppy had even flashed him a roll of twenties to assure him that she could pay. Though he hummed and hahed and acted like a put-upon, long-suffering oppressed working man, he had nothing to complain about, Annie thought, considering the sum. All he had to do was drive down the M1 and back, and he would be making a nice profit for his day's driving, rather than hanging about on street corners hoping for a fare. Of course, there was Poppy to deal with. She had seemed to be on the verge of sleep when they set off, but Annie knew quite well that she could wake up at any moment and make the five- or six-hour drive feel like an eternity. Especially if the driver tried on his oppressed worker routine.

Once Poppy was gone, Annie had gone straight home from Rivendell and phoned Carrie in Ripon to thank her for the party and accommodation, and apologise for dashing off without saying goodbye. Then she took a long bath, followed by a talent show on TV, a cup of camomile tea and an early night. Sunday morning she spent reading the papers and the rest of the day semi-comatose on the sofa. Now it was Monday and back to work.

Annie felt in a remarkably good mood as she drove along the narrow winding lane to Mossmoor past farmhouses, drystone walls and sheep grazing on the distant hillsides. Perhaps, she thought, it was because Poppy had gone home. Or maybe it was due to her dry Sunday and a Monday-morning lie-in.

Adele Balter lived in an old farm labourer's cottage in the village of Mossmoor, only a few miles east of Annie's place in Harkside, so Annie had decided to head over there before going in to the station, then meet up with Gerry later in Eastvale to plan their strategy. They had already spoken on the phone and Gerry had a list of names from Laurence Hadfield's mobile. The last calls either to or from it had come on the Saturday before last. There were three incoming calls, all from a Dr Anthony Randall: one in the afternoon, lasting seven minutes, then another at 8.02 in the evening, this time for only four minutes, and finally at 11.26, when the call had gone through to Hadfield's voicemail, but the caller hadn't left a message. Gerry had also come up with an address for Dr Randall, in Bramhope, between Leeds and Otley.

It wasn't much to go on, but it would be useful to know what Laurence Hadfield and Dr Anthony Randall had been talking about that Saturday, and why Hadfield hadn't answered that last call. Annie guessed that he must have gone out by then, perhaps to his death, and his phone had been lying on the desk in his study, as it was when Poppy and Adele Balter arrived a few days later.

Annie finally came to the row of tiny old cottages that formed the village high street, along with a post office and general store, parked and went through the gate of the last cottage on the left. Adele, whom she had phoned in advance, opened the door before Annie had the chance to knock. She must have been watching through the net curtains.

There was no Tardis effect in the cottage; it was just as tiny inside as it appeared from without. Adele also kept a very neat and tidy house, which didn't surprise Annie at all. Surfaces sparkled, there wasn't a speck of dust or a cobweb anywhere and the whole place smelled deliciously of fresh baking.

'I've made some scones,' Adele said as she settled Annie on a flower-patterned armchair in front of the fire, where a couple of knotty logs gave off a soothing heat. Annie knew there was no use in protesting when Adele said she would just make a pot of tea and take the scones out of the Aga, so she relaxed in the armchair, admiring the oil painting of York Minster over the fireplace, and enjoyed the heat on her shins.

She heard Adele puttering about in the kitchen, and a while later she came out with a tray. Annie hadn't bothered with breakfast that morning, settling for a pot of coffee, so her stomach rumbled at the sight of the fresh-baked scones, tub of butter and a dish of strawberry jam.

Adele put the tray on the table under the window. 'Please, help yourself,' she said. 'It's not often I get the chance to bake for someone.'

'Well,' said Annie, 'I can guarantee you that this will be much appreciated. I'm starving.'

'Then tuck in.'

Annie did, and when she had filled her plate and her teacup, she returned to the armchair, and to business.

'You said you wanted my opinion on something?' Adele asked.

'Yes.' Annie managed to rest her cup and plate on the floor beside her without spilling anything and took the plastic evidence bag out of her briefcase. She would have to drop it off at the lab for forensic testing later, but it had seemed easier to come and show it to Adele at home rather than have her visit the station.

Adele held up the transparent bag and stared. After a few moments, she asked, 'What is it?'

'You've never seen it before?'

'No.'

'It's a charm for a bracelet.'

'Oh, yes. I know what you mean. We used to have them when I was a little girl. And those ones with your name on. What did they call them?'

Annie nodded. 'Identity bracelets. Anyway, these charm bracelets are popular again.'

'But I don't understand. Why are you showing it to me?'

Annie put the Pandora charm back in her briefcase and managed to balance her scone on her knees and hold the cup in her hand. She took a sip of tea and a bite of buttery, jammy scone. It was delicious. 'You don't recognise it at all?' she asked again when she'd swallowed a mouthful.

'No. I'd remember. Mr Laurence would never wear anything like that.'

'I don't suppose he would,' Annie said with a smile. 'But perhaps a visitor, or a guest might?'

'I wouldn't know about that,' said Adele. 'Nobody ever visited when I was there. Except the postman. Would you like another scone?'

'No. I'm still OK with this. It's delicious.'

'Thank you.'

'You said you clean at Mr Hadfield's once a week, usually on a Thursday. Am I right?'

'That's right.'

'Where do you clean?'

'What do you mean?'

'Well, it's a big house. Three floors. You can't get to every nook and cranny in a day, surely?'

Adele Balter sat up straight in her chair and thrust her shoulders back. 'I defy you to find one spot of dust in that house,' she said.

'I know you're proud of your work,' Annie said, 'and rightly so, but let's be realistic about this.'

'Many of the rooms are never used, especially those up on the third floor. They don't take long, since nothing's been disturbed. Just a quick flick around with the feather duster and a couple of minutes with the vacuum.'

'Fair enough. What about the bathroom?'

'Which one?'

Annie couldn't for the life of her remember how many bathrooms there were. Three, perhaps, she guessed. 'The big one upstairs. With the large hot tub on the platform and the bidet and everything.' She refrained from saying that it was about as big as her entire cottage. Adele's, too.

'That's the main bathroom, the one Mr Laurence uses most of the time, apart from the en suite in his bedroom, of course. But that's just a walk-in shower and WC.'

We should all be so lucky, thought Annie. 'So the big bathroom is the most used?'

'Well, Mr Laurence likes a bath. I know that because he told me. "There's nothing like a good long hot bath to wash away the cares of the world, Mrs B", he said. A shower's useful, of course, especially if you're in a hurry, which he often is, but there's nothing like a bath. Are you sure you won't have another scone? I'll never finish them all myself.'

'No, really. That one did the trick. I'm full.' Annie finished off her tea. Laurence Hadfield was right: there was nothing quite like a hot bubbly bath, a few scented candles, a good book and a glass of wine when you wanted to kick back and shut the world out. 'So you clean that big bathroom every week?'

'Yes. Even if it hasn't been used. Like I said before, Mr Laurence is away quite a lot, so it doesn't get used all that much. But I keep it clean, yes.'

'And the floor and tiles?'

'Of course.'

'There's a narrow gap between the back of the toilet and the skirting board.'

'I'm aware of that.'

'Would you happen to clean around there, too?'

'Of course, I do. You'll never cut the mustard as a cleaner if you don't get to the tough bits everyone else ignores, young lady.'

Annie felt suitably chastised and thought rather guiltily about her own bathroom. Only one, and very small, but it wouldn't sparkle anywhere near as much as the ones blessed with Adele's magic touch. 'And did you clean it the last time you did the house? That would be the Thursday before the weekend Mr Hadfield disappeared, right?'

'Yes. If you say that's when he disappeared. And I most certainly did clean it.'

'So if anything like that charm had been lying around, you'd have found it.'

'Naturally. And it wasn't.'

'Clearly not.' Which meant, if Adele Balter was telling the truth – and Annie believed she was – that the charm had ended up where it was found *after* the last Thursday Adele had cleaned the house. Poppy had disowned it – and Annie had no reason to disbelieve her, either – so whose was it, and how had it got there?

'I know I asked you this before, but it's even more impor- tant now that you give it some more thought. Did you ever notice any signs that Mr Hadfield had female company between your visits?'

'What signs?'

'I don't know. An article of female clothing in the laundry, for example, or a trinket like the one I showed you left on a dressing table. An unusual scent, perfume perhaps, or a stain that couldn't be explained. Maybe a long hair on the pillow or the back of the sofa.' If Hadfield had been having a woman over to the house on a regular basis, then it stood to reason that she had left something behind, however minute a trace.

Adele Balter bristled. 'Nothing of that sort at all. Mr Hadfield was a gentleman, a decent person.'

'I'm not saying he wasn't a perfect gentleman, but surely he must have had ... needs. After all, he'd been a widower for over two years.'

'He adored his poor deceased wife. And even if he had been doing as you suggest, he would certainly not have left any traces for me to discover. He would have made sure nothing remained to upset my sensibilities. He knows I'm very sen—'

'What did you just say, Mrs Balter?'

'Adele, please.'

'Adele. What did you just say?'

'That Mr Hadfield would never leave anything around the house that he thought might shock me.'

'So if he had been seeing a woman, he would have cleaned up after himself?'

'Well, yes. But he hadn't been seeing anyone.'

'Did he?'

'I'm sorry?'

'Did you ever notice any evidence that he'd been tidying up or cleaning up after himself?'

'Once or twice, perhaps.'

'Like what?'

'Sometimes he washed his own bed sheets. He didn't iron them, though. That would have been too much for him. That's how I could tell.'

'He put his own bed sheets in the washing machine?'

'Sometimes. Yes. Why?'

'My question exactly,' Annie said, almost to herself. 'Why?' It wasn't something, in her admittedly limited experience, that men usually did. Unless they had something to hide.

'I assumed it was because he'd spilt something. He had a Teasmade, you know, and he was a devil for his morning cuppa in bed.'

'Right,' said Annie. 'That must be it.' Or not, she thought. 'Did you do any laundry on your last visit?'

'You mean last Friday?'

'Yes.'

'No. I didn't have a chance, what with Poppy creating and me worrying something had happened to Mr Laurence. Then you lot came.'

'OK,' said Annie. 'It's fine.' Hadfield's house was still officially part of a crime scene, though the CSI officers would have left by now. They would have to go back again. If there were any traces of female presence, they would most likely still be there. Annie would get in touch with Frank Naylor and ask him to make sure they took in the bed sheets and pillow cases for forensic examination, which they may not have done, given that Laurence Hadfield's death hadn't been ruled anything but a suspicious accident. The CSIs didn't think they were looking for signs of anyone else in the house.

Annie glanced at her watch and saw it was probably time to head for Eastvale to meet up with Gerry. As a final question, she asked, 'Do you know a Dr Randall? He's a friend of Mr Hadfield's.'

'Yes, of course. They play golf together, and I've heard them chatting on the phone from time to time. They have a club where they sometimes meet as well. For rich folks, like. It's in Leeds, mind you.'

'Do you remember what it's called?'

'Sorry, love. I don't pay a lot of attention to things like that.'

Annie stood up to leave. 'Thank you, Adele. You've been very helpful,' she said. 'But I have to go now.'

'So soon?'

'I'm afraid so.'

'Please. Just wait a moment.'

Adele Balter disappeared into the kitchen and came back a few moments later with a Tupperware container.

'Scones,' she said. 'And a jar of my own special strawberry jam. I told you I'd never be able to finish it all myself. And don't worry about returning the box. Any time will do.'

'I can't possibly . . .' Annie began, and then realised she could, and that in fact it would be polite to do so. 'Thanks very much, Adele,' she said, opening the door.

'And if you ever need a cleaning lady . . .' Adele said. 'Well, I've got a lot more time on my hands now.'

There was a thought. It would take Adele all of ten minutes to clean her bijou palace. 'I'll let you know,' she said.

P.P. Arnold's *The Turning Tide* saw Banks down the A1 to Leeds quickly and pleasantly, especially her version of Van Morrison's 'Brand New Day'. He remembered drooling over P.P. Arnold singing 'The First Cut is the Deepest' and 'Angel of the Morning' on *Top of the Pops* and *Ready, Steady, Go!* when he was a young lad. Over fifty years later, she was making a comeback with an album that had been languishing in the vaults since the late sixties.

Banks marched into Whitelock's only a few minutes late, despite the length of time he had to drive around the multi-storey car park to find an empty slot. He expected to find Ken Blackstone at a copper-topped round table opposite the long bar, but instead the familiar figure, looking more and more like a cross between Philip Larkin and Eric Morecambe, waved from inside the dining area, with a glass of orange juice in front of him. Whitelock's was as crowded and noisy as usual, and Banks had to thread his way through the groups of clerks, students and secretaries in the narrow space between the banquettes and the bar.

'Don't tell me promotion's gone to your head?' Banks said, gesturing towards the orange juice as he sat down.

'No more than it's gone to my bank balance,' said Blackstone. 'No, I've got a team meeting this afternoon. It wouldn't do to go in smelling of booze or Polo mints.'

'I'd be supportive and join you, but I plan on doing a bit of shopping before I head back to work. Plenty of time to walk off a pint.'

'Bastard.'

'And I can't help but notice that you're sitting in the posh section.'

'I thought it would be a bit more private,' Blackstone said, passing a menu over. When the waitress arrived both Banks and Blackstone ordered steak and kidney pie and chips, and Banks asked for a pint of IPA.

'Thanks for coming,' Blackstone said.

'No problem. If there's any chance of a lead in either of the cases we're dealing with at the moment, I'll jump at it.'

'I hope you won't be too disappointed.'

Banks's pint arrived and he took a long swig. Blackstone looked on forlornly.

'How are things, anyway?' Banks asked. 'New job working out?'

Blackstone had recently got a promotion and a place on the West Yorkshire Homicide and Major Inquiry Team. 'It's working out,' he said. 'When you get right down to it, not much changes but the acronyms.'

'Too true,' said Banks. 'Aren't you due for retirement soon?' He knew that Blackstone was a few years younger than he was, but not exactly how many.

'Couple of years.'

'Will you take it?'

Blackstone nodded. 'There aren't a lot of options – unless I get promoted like you did, and I think that's unlikely. As of now, I think I'll go quietly. But we'll see what happens when the time comes. I may not go gentle.'

Their meals arrived. Banks reached for the HP Sauce and shook some dollops on his steak and kidney pie. For a few moments, they devoted themselves to eating, then Blackstone said, 'Shall I start now, or do you want to wait until after?'

'I can listen while I eat,' said Banks. 'I'm curious to know what it is.'

'It's not a pretty tale. Yesterday evening a bloke from a nearby village was walking his dogs in open country just off the A59 between Harrogate and Blubberhouses.'

'Isn't that near Thornfield Reservoir?'

'Further south. And east of Brame Lane. You probably wouldn't know the area. Anyway, he came to an old derelict bothy, and one of the dogs took an unusual interest, so he managed to get the door open – it was almost off its hinges – and take a look inside.'

'And he wished he hadn't?'

Blackstone nodded. 'A girl's body. Our pathologist hasn't carried out the post-mortem yet, but he reckons she'd been there about a week, and death was due to a blow to the back of her head. Hard enough to fracture her skull. It seems like she'd put up a struggle, too. She was wearing a red dress made of some silky material, quite short and low cut, and as far as the doc could tell there were no evident signs of sexual activity. Though she was carrying no identification, no possessions of any kind, it didn't take us long to link her to a missing person's report we just got in on Friday. A second-year history and politics student from the University of Leeds called Sarah Chen. Her father was from Hong Kong and her mother was British, but Sarah was born here, grew up in Derbyshire. Her father died in a car accident two years ago, and her mother's in terminal care for Alzheimer's. No brothers or sisters. Sarah came late, in her mother's early forties.'

'Some lot in life,' said Banks.

'Makes you realise how lucky you are, doesn't it? But by all accounts, Sarah was a gutsy lass. Bright, too. She took things in her stride. Got on with life. Quite a beauty, too.'

'Until . . .'

'Yes. She hadn't been seen since the weekend before last. She went into town shopping with a flatmate from uni a week last Saturday, and that was it. That was when she bought the dress she was wearing.'

'That Saturday keeps on coming up,' said Banks. 'What else did she have with her?'

'Nothing. I mean, she was wearing some cheap jewellery, a pendant, bracelet, that sort of thing. And sexy underwear. Black, lacy.'

'Identifying marks?'

'A dragon tattoo on the inside of her right thigh. Our resident expert tells me it's for the year of the dragon. And a quote tattoo on the back of her left shoulder: "The road of excess leads to the palace of wisdom".'

'William Blake,' said Banks.

Blackstone raised his eyebrows. 'I see your poetry babe must be doing a good job.'

'She's not a "babe", but she is doing a good job. Anyway, people often take the words as licence, or as an excuse, for extreme behaviour, though that wasn't exactly what Blake had in mind.' He paused. 'Though maybe it was. He was an odd one, Blake. One of a kind. Even Linda didn't quite know what to make of him. Anyway, it tells us at least that your girl didn't mind flaunting it a bit, being outrageous, whether she followed Blake's advice or not.'

'From what I could gather she liked people to believe she was more adventurous than she really was.'

'These quote tattoos are a bit of a trend, anyway. I wouldn't read that much into them. Last one I saw was on a girl on the Tesco's checkout. "*L'enfer c'est les autres.*" I asked her what made her choose that particular quotation and she couldn't really say except that it was a good fit. She didn't even know what it meant. I think the tattooist had a book of quotes for people to choose from, and she just liked the look or the sound of it. How was Sarah Chen's state of mind on this shopping expedition you mentioned? Did she give any indication to her friends as to where she was going that night, what she was doing?'

'She just mentioned that she was going to a party. Didn't say where or with whom. Her friend asked about it but couldn't get any more out of her. She didn't think it odd, though, as Sarah often liked to sound a bit mysterious and secretive about what she was doing. Part of giving the impression she was up to all sorts of things, no doubt. Where *does* that quote come from?'

'It's from a play by Jean-Paul Sartre. "Hell is other people".'

'Ah.'

'What made Sarah's friend report her missing after only a week?'

'She was used to Sarah coming and going without notice, but this seemed just a bit too long. She'd missed an important essay deadline and a tutorial. Apparently, that wasn't like her. She liked her fun, but she took her studies seriously. People were asking her friend where she was, if something had happened to her. Sarah liked to keep people guessing, but according to those who knew her, she wasn't in the habit of disappearing for as long as a week.'

'What did you find out from her friends?'

'Nothing much. We asked around. Nobody seemed to know where she was going, if anywhere. According to everyone who knew her, she was a normal student. Conscientious, hard-working, maybe a bit given to depression on occasion, though that's hardly surprising given her home circumstances.'

'Boyfriends?'

'Nobody serious. We talked to two students who'd dated her so far this year, and they both said she could be a bit enigmatic – I think one actually said "inscrutable" – but other than that she was fun to be with, and not in the least interested in commitment. She could hold her end up in most conversations, whether about world affairs or the FA Cup, liked to drink and dance and let her hair down now and then. Apparently, she was no shrinking violet. We assumed she'd run off with a new boyfriend or something, or that there was some family crisis nobody knew about and she was taking care of that. But the staff at the mother's care home hadn't seen her since the week before. We checked out her room, and there were no signs of a struggle, nothing to indicate that she'd been abducted from there.'

'What *did* you find in the room?'

'Nothing of interest. She shared a house with three other students, communal living and eating areas and each with their own bedroom-cum-study. It was just as you'd expect a student's room to be. A bit messy, discarded jeans and T-shirts and stuff scattered about, books, piles of paper and research material. But it was basically well ordered. No sign of handbag or shoulder bag there, either.' Blackstone paused. 'There was another odd thing, too, though.'

'Yes?'

'Her mobile. It was still in her room. It was quite an expensive new model, too. A ten or something. I mean, have you ever known a teenager who doesn't pick up her mobile first thing when she goes out anywhere?'

'Tracy certainly does,' said Banks. 'I can only think of one who didn't, and that's Adrienne Munro.'

'Your dead girl in the car?'

'Yes.'

Banks finished his pie and washed it down with some IPA. The other similarities with the Adrienne Munro case weren't lost on him. She was also a second-year student, dressed for an occasion, found dead in an out-of-the-way spot. Only the way it looked, Adrienne had committed suicide and Sarah Chen had been murdered. The timing was also curious. Nobody Banks or Blackstone had spoken to so far knew exactly when either girl had been seen last, but it appeared that they had disappeared around the same time. The weekend before last. Saturday.

'So apart from the superficial similarities, why am I here?' Banks asked. 'Not that I'm complaining.'

Blackstone smiled. 'I was just coming to that.' He reached for his briefcase, and passed a photograph and a torn-off slip of paper protected by a plastic cover over to Banks. The photograph showed a smiling, beautiful Sarah in full bloom. It was easy to see her different ethnic characteristics, and how they helped form her particular kind of beauty. Blackstone tapped the slip of paper. 'We found this on the desk in her room.'

Written on the slip were a name and a telephone number. The name was Adrienne Munro, but the telephone number wasn't hers.

9

Dr Anthony Randall's house formed quite a contrast to Adele Balter's and Annie's tiny cottages, though it wasn't quite as large and ostentatious as Rivendell. Nor was it built in the art deco style. It was an old detached house of brick and stone with mullioned windows and a slate roof, surrounded by a couple of acres of garden dotted with trees, all enclosed by a moss-covered wall. It was probably a listed building, and perhaps at one time had belonged to the lord of the manor. Dr Randall clearly didn't restrict his duties to NHS work.

Neither Annie nor Gerry had phoned Dr Randall to let him know they were coming. They wanted the element of surprise, so they had to be prepared for his being out. The sight of the BMW parked in the semicircular driveway by the front door seemed to indicate that he was at home, however. Gerry had told Annie that Randall was a cardiothoracic surgeon, not a GP, and that he was sixty-five years old and divorced. The rest they would find out when they talked to him.

They parked the car in the street, opened the heavy wrought-iron gate and walked around the drive. There seemed to be no doorbell, so Annie banged the brass lion's-head door knocker.

A few moments later, the door was opened by a tall, rangy man with a shock of curly grey hair, wearing a V-neck jumper over a white shirt unbuttoned at the throat, and grey trousers with creases sharp enough to cut yourself on. His bushy eyebrows were raised in a questioning arch. Annie and Gerry introduced themselves and flashed their warrant cards. Randall managed to look put out as he gave up his precious time and led them through a cavernous hall into a large sitting room. There was no decorative fireplace, but the room was warm enough without. Most of the furniture seemed antique to Annie, except for the three-piece suite, which was far too comfortable to be old. The doctor offered no refreshments or small talk, but simply sat at the edge of his armchair with his hands clasped on his lap as if he were about to head off somewhere at any moment and said, 'What do you want with me? You'll have to be quick. I don't have much time.'

'Busy surgery?'

'As a matter of fact, it's a private consultation.'

'Ah,' said Annie. 'We'll try to be as quick as we can, then, sir. Have you been following the news?' Annie asked.

'If I had, I wouldn't be asking what you want, I assume. Anyway, I'm afraid not. I've been away at a conference in Malta for the past week.'

Nice for some, Annie thought. Why couldn't the police training college run courses in Malta instead of Hendon? 'Then I'm afraid we have some bad news for you, Dr Randall.'

'It's *Mr*,' said Randall, 'but no matter. What's wrong?'

'Sorry, my mistake. I'm afraid a friend of yours has been found dead. At least we think he was a friend. Laurence Hadfield?'

Randall flopped back in his chair, rather theatrically, Annie thought. 'Larry? Dead? Good Lord. That's a shock, all right.'

'So he was a friend of yours?' Annie asked.

'Yes, indeed, I'd say he was. To the extent that we played golf together frequently and enjoyed a convivial pint in a local hostelry every now and then. Larry also handled some of my investments, though they were rather small fish compared to his usual fare. I can't understand this. As far as I know he was in good health. What on earth happened to him?'

'We don't rightly know yet,' said Annie. 'His body was found at the bottom of a gully on Tetchley Moor last Wednesday, skull fractured and neck broken as if from a fall, but we weren't able to identify him until Friday.'

Randall frowned. 'Bottom of a gully. I don't understand. Was it some sort of accident?'

'It very much *looks* like an accident,' Annie replied.

'But we're not ruling out anything at the moment,' Gerry added, glancing up from her notebook. 'And we've no idea what he was doing there or how he got there. Can you help us at all with that?'

'Me?' Randall shook his head slowly. 'I'm afraid not. It sounds like a tragic accident.'

'The thing is,' Gerry went on, 'Mr Hadfield was wearing a suit and tie, and there was no sign of a car. We were also wondering if you could help us in regard to his movements over the past while?'

Randall ignored Gerry and kept looking at Annie as he spoke. 'As I said, I've been away in Malta. From last Tuesday until this Saturday, as a matter of fact. Valletta. You can check, of course, if you feel it necessary.'

'Thank you,' said Annie, 'but I shouldn't think it will come to that.'

'Just in case, though, sir,' Gerry said, smiling, 'would you give me the name of the conference and the hotel where it was held?'

Randall looked from one to the other, his face reddening slightly. 'Of course,' he said, and gave out the details more slowly than necessary for Gerry to write them down. He was treating her as if she were thick, Annie thought.

'Thank you, sir,' said Gerry.

Randall smirked. 'What is this? Good cop, bad cop?'

'Sir?' said Gerry.

'I don't know what you mean,' Annie said. 'Who's playing bad cop? We're simply doing our job.'

'I didn't mean to be disparaging. It's just that you seem quite polite and friendly, whereas your sidekick over there interrupts with rather rude implications.'

'Sidekick? Implications?' Gerry said. 'What exactly have I implied?'

'That I have something to hide. That I may have to provide an alibi.'

'I assure you it's just routine,' said Gerry.

'Do you?' Annie asked.

'What?'

'Have something to hide. Need an alibi.'

'I've told you where I was.'

'Ah,' said Gerry, 'but we haven't told you when Mr Hadfield died. All we said was he was *found* last Wednesday. I mean, it would be no use you telling us you were in Malta last Tuesday, say, if he was killed last Monday, would it?'

'Was killed?' Randall glanced at Annie again, his eyes narrowing. 'Are you telling me now he was murdered? You said it was an accident.'

'I said it *looks* like an accident, sir. It was you who called it a "tragic accident".'

'In our experience,' Gerry added, 'almost anything can look like an accident.'

'Who's asking you?' Randall shifted in his chair. 'Do I need to call my solicitor?' he asked Annie.

Annie was starting to regard Gerry in a new light. At first, they hadn't got on at all, then they had managed to build a few bridges, but now she was beginning to seem like a natural. They hadn't agreed on a strategy for interviewing Randall, but had planned to play it by ear. That clearly suited Gerry. Annie decided to let things follow the course they were on for the moment rather than trying to placate Randall's ruffled feelings.

'Now, why would you need a solicitor?' she asked. 'You haven't done anything wrong, have you? We certainly haven't charged you with anything.'

'It's just the way this interrogation is going.'

'It's just an interview, sir,' said Gerry. 'Not an interrogation. We're just here to talk to you. There's nothing to be afraid of.'

'I'm not afraid, damn you, I—' Randall took a deep breath and clearly held his anger in check. 'I am not afraid,' he repeated with hushed fury. 'I simply want to avoid being tricked into saying something I would regret.'

'I don't know what you mean,' said Annie. 'Why would you do that? I mean regret saying something. What do you think you have to say that you would regret?'

'Look,' Randall growled, 'can we just get on with it and get it over with? I'm a busy man.'

'Of course, sir,' said Annie, with a pointed glance at Gerry that clearly discomfited Randall even further. 'So far we've gathered that you were a friend of Laurence Hadfield's, that you had financial dealings with him, and that you have been out of the country at a medical conference from Tuesday last week until the Saturday just past. Am I right?'

'A world cardiology conference,' Randall said. 'I was giving a paper.'

'So you're a heart doctor, then?' Gerry commented.

'A cardiothoracic surgeon.'

'Got it.' Gerry made a scribble in her notebook.

Randall pointed to Gerry and said to Annie, 'I don't think she's taking me seriously.'

'Oh, I assure you, she is, sir. It's one of the first rules we learn, to take everyone seriously, especially the professional classes. That way we can avoid misunderstandings later.'

'Later? What misunderstandings?'

'Well, if there is a later,' Annie explained. 'You know. Court. Solicitors. Judges. Stuff like that. The CPS are very strict about us getting all our ducks in a row.'

Randall sighed. 'Can we *please* get this over with?'

'Of course. Hearts to bypass and all that. Won't be a jiffy,' Annie went on. 'The main reason we're here is that you phoned Laurence Hadfield three times on the day we believe he disappeared.' She glanced at Gerry. 'You have the details, don't you, DC Masterson?'

'Yes, ma'am. Three fifty-nine, eight-o-two and eleven twenty-six. All p.m.'

'Can you perhaps tell us why you called Mr Hadfield and what you talked about?'

'I've told you. Larry was a friend. What's so odd about ringing up a friend?'

'On that quiz show, were you, sir?' Gerry said, grinning. 'Needed help with a tricky question?'

Randall ignored her.

'Well, as far as we know,' Annie went on, 'those were the only phone calls Mr Hadfield received that day. Can you remember what you talked about?'

'Not especially. Plans for a round of golf the following day, I think, a new investment opportunity. Something of that sort.'

'The next day would have been Sunday, right?' Annie pressed on.

'It usually comes after Saturday.'

'I don't believe I mentioned that we think Mr Hadfield disappeared on Saturday.'

'You didn't,' said Randall, smirking again. 'But I remember the day I last spoke with him. It was Saturday. A week last Saturday. I'm sure his telephone records will confirm that.'

'Oh, they do,' said Annie. 'They just don't tell us what you talked about. You mentioned golf on Sunday.'

'Yes. We arranged to play. A foursome. We had the round booked at my club.'

'And that would be, sir?' Gerry asked.

'Lyndgarth,' Randall said, in a tone that was clearly meant to impress her.

'Did Mr Hadfield turn up?' asked Annie.

'Well, no, as a matter of fact, he didn't.'

'Did he phone to apologise or explain his absence?'

'No, he didn't.'

'So what did you do?'

'Got another member to make up the foursome.'

'Weren't you worried?'

'Why should I be?'

'Well, you'd talked to your friend three times the day before about a round of golf the following day, and he didn't show up. I mean, I'd be a bit worried, wouldn't you, DC Masterson?'

'I would, ma'am,' said Gerry.

'Did he say he was ill when you talked on Saturday?' Annie pressed on. 'Did he sound depressed or anything?'

'No. Of course not. We're grown men. *Busy* men. Things come up that need urgent attention. Are you now trying to suggest that Larry committed suicide, with all your talk of depression?'

'I don't think so,' said Annie. 'But it's a theory. I was simply wondering if there was anything in his tone or in what he said to you on Saturday that caused you to think he might have a reason for not turning up for a prearranged golf game the following day. That's all.'

'No, there wasn't.'

'Do you know where he was when you phoned him?'

'At home. He said he was working. What does it matter?'

'Did he like playing golf?' Gerry asked.

'Of course he liked playing golf.'

'Did you phone him to ask what was wrong?' Annie asked. 'On Sunday?'

'I . . . er . . . no, I didn't.'

'May I ask why not?

'You may, but I'm afraid I can't really tell you. And I'm not hiding anything. Don't read anything into it. There just wasn't any particular reason. I suppose it never crossed my mind that something might be wrong.'

'Why would it?' Annie agreed. 'If Mr Hadfield was in good health.' She glanced at Gerry, who put her notebook away. 'We should go now, DC Masterson, and leave Mr Randall to his important business.'

Randall didn't accompany them to the door, but Gerry turned around before they left, 'Sorry to do a Columbo on you, sir,' she said, 'but I'm curious about the third time you rang Mr Hadfield. That was at eleven twenty-six on Saturday night, and you got no answer. It seems very late to be calling someone, especially if you can't remember why. Was that normal?'

'Well, I'd hardly say it was abnormal. Not everyone clocks off at five, you know.'

'You didn't think he might have gone to bed?'

'I can't say I thought about it much at all.'

'Bye, Mr Randall,' said Annie, taking Gerry's elbow. 'And thanks for your time. We'll be seeing you.'

Before the bewildered doctor could respond, Annie ushered Gerry out. 'You bloody minx,' she said with a grin as they walked down the drive to the car. 'Like to tell me what you think you were up to back there? Better still. Tell me over a drink. After all, it'll be five when we get back to Eastvale. Clocking-off time.' They laughed as Annie started the car.

Banks hadn't been expecting to spend his afternoon tramping across damp grass, so his choice of footwear could have been better. Fortunately, the ground wasn't too waterlogged, and the paths they occasionally found were either cinder or gravel.

'No chance of any trace evidence surviving out in the open after so long,' said Blackstone. 'The team's done their best, but there's nothing so far. Just a lot of rubbish from inside the bothy to sort through. As you can see, it's not actually that far off the B road, so someone could easily have pulled into a lay-by, dragged Sarah, or chased her to the bothy and killed her, or killed her first and then carried her body there. It's not a busy road, so it could have been done almost anytime, but common sense suggests it was probably after dark. And we think she was killed inside the bothy. The doc says there'd have been quite a lot of blood from a head wound, and that matches what we found there.'

'If she was killed in the bothy,' said Banks, 'then surely there must be prints? His and hers?'

'We're still working on it, but the surfaces are hardly ideal. Rough-hewn stone and rotten old wood.'

'Fair enough.'

The small stone bothy, basically a free shelter for anyone who needed it, stood just off the path and was surrounded by crime-scene tape. The body had been taken away, of course, but a constable stood on guard and a couple of CSI officers were still going over the place, which was just an empty shell with a dirt floor and no windows. You'd have to be pretty desperate for shelter if you were willing to spend a night there, Banks thought. Still, there were dozens of these places all over the north; you saw them on walks and from roads, all in various states of disrepair. They had once been used for storage or shelter by groundsmen or gardeners on the large estates, now divided up into smaller farms. Most of them were uninhabitable, with missing roof slabs, doors or caved-in walls, and this one was no exception.

The area on the floor where the body had lain was marked out, and the CSIs told them to avoid the spots where little flags had been placed. Banks was content to stand in the doorway and look in, not wanting to disturb anything. It smelled of urine and rotten vegetation. What a place to die, he thought, trying to imagine the poor girl's last thoughts and impressions. Had she fought desperately for her life? Had she not even seen the end coming? Had she perhaps been drugged first? Why had she gone to such a place, and with whom? And how did she know Adrienne Munro?

Tired of staring into the gloom and learning nothing, Banks turned back to the path and took a deep breath of fresh air. Blackstone stood with his hands in his pockets, kicking at stones. 'So what do you think?' he asked.

'I think you were right to call me. If it really was the same killer, this gives us two goes at him.'

'I thought you said Adrienne Munro committed suicide?'

'Maybe it was just meant to appear that way. She died from asphyxiation after an overdose of sleeping pills. Maybe that was an accident. It's possible that Sarah Chen was also drugged but didn't die of asphyxiation, that she had to be killed some other way. I don't know, Ken. I've no idea what, or who, we're dealing with. Any connection between this Sarah Chen and drugs?'

'Not according to anyone we talked to, though I know that doesn't necessarily mean much. The drugs squad have no intelligence on her. She wasn't a known dealer, if that's what you're getting at. From what I've heard, I'd guess she might have been a casual user, but not the hard stuff, I don't think. We'll find out more at the PM, of course. I'll also get on to the pathologist about taking special pains over toxicology, considering the Adrienne Munro link.' Blackstone glanced at his watch. 'Why don't you come to the team meeting with me now? You can put your case to our DCS.'

'What? With me smelling of beer?'

'That's all right,' said Blackstone. 'You're from North Yorkshire. They'll be expecting it.'

★   ★   ★

'It wasn't a strategy,' Gerry said over drinks in the Queen's Arms a short while later. 'I just started throwing things in, you know, to see how he'd react, then he really pissed me off.'

'I'm not complaining,' said Annie. 'If I have one criticism of the way you handled yourself it was the use of "ma'am". You know how I feel about that.'

'But it worked, didn't it? It made him feel even more superior, me tugging my forelock to you.'

Annie grinned. 'I suppose so. What first set you off?'

'When he called me your sidekick.'

Annie laughed and drank some beer. Dry days were all very well, but there was nothing like that first pint the day after two in a row. Gerry was on the diet ginger ale, she noticed, which wasn't unusual. The pub was busy with the after-work crowd, and Annie smiled and said hello to a few familiar faces. Cyril was playing one of those interminable playlists that Banks seemed to love so much. Even she recognised 'Will You Still Love Me Tomorrow?' though she had no idea of the name of the group singing it. She quite liked it.

'Actually, it started before that,' Gerry went on, leaning forwards. 'His whole attitude. Right from the start. How important his time was. The "Mr" bit. His tone of voice. The way he looked at me, as if I was something nasty he'd got on the bottom of his shoe.'

'It's been my experience,' Annie said, 'that quite a few doctors are arrogant and controlling megalomaniacs, and surgeons are among the worst. But what do you think? Anything there?'

Gerry tasted some diet ginger ale before answering. 'Well, for a start,' she said, 'I don't believe he was as shocked on hearing about Hadfield's death as he let on.'

'I agree. He knew already.'

Gerry nodded. 'I think so.'

'Then why didn't he say so?'

'That I don't know. But you asked me.'

'OK.' Annie picked up her pint glass. 'Go on.'

'I wanted to test his temper, too, or his restraint. Did you notice how he almost lost it that one time, when I talked down to him, told him he'd nothing to be afraid of?'

'How could I miss it? But what did it mean?'

'Just that he's got a temper and a short rein. If Hadfield was pushed into that gully, there's a man who might have done it.'

'If he'd had a reason.'

'I admit I'm speculating. I'm not even saying I think he did it, or that anything was done. These are my impressions of the man. They could have had a falling out and things got physical. That business about the golf wasn't convincing at all.'

'What about that last phone call?' Annie said. 'It's more than a bit late to be phoning someone under normal circumstances. Even a friend. And Randall didn't leave a message.'

'No,' said Gerry. 'And that's odd, given that they'd had two previous conversations that day. Randall might almost have been expecting Hadfield not to answer. But, then, why call so late in the first place?'

'I don't know what the financial world is like, but could anything so urgent come up that late on a Saturday evening that would prevent Hadfield from answering his phone?'

'A late meeting or something?' Gerry suggested. 'Some sort of business crisis?'

'I suppose so.'

'The financial world is probably still our best bet if we're searching for someone who had a reason to harm Hadfield. I think we need to examine his business dealings more closely.'

'Do you think you can do that?'

'Sure. I can handle it. I've got a few contacts in the fraud squad and white collar crime, and I know my way around the Internet.'

'What about the Pandora charm?' Annie asked.

'Well, I suppose it means there was a woman involved at some point, doesn't it? But let's not make the sort of mistake a man would make and assume that it's impossible a woman had anything to do with the world of high finance.'

'And Randall?'

'We can hardly mount twenty-four seven surveillance on him, can we, but it would be interesting to see what he does now we've made ourselves known to him.'

'I'll have a word with Alan. See if his mate Ken Blackstone from West Yorkshire can help. And I'll see if I can find out any more about that charm.'

'We're in business, then,' said Gerry, raising her glass.

'Indeed we are,' said Annie, clinking.

It was after seven o'clock when Banks got home from Leeds. He had dropped in at the station on his way, found everyone gone and nothing new waiting for him, so he left. Maybe the connection between Adrienne Munro and Sarah Chen – a name and an unknown phone number – was a bit thin, but it wouldn't get any stronger unless they worked at it. Tomorrow they would start to enter everything they had on the two cases into HOLMES, the Home Office Large Major Enquiry System, a computer programme developed to help with case management. It wasn't a substitute for human intelligence, but it kept track of every little bit of information that was entered, and it sometimes came up with connections and inconsistencies that even the most perceptive of detectives missed, especially if the bits of connected information were on statements from two different county forces.

This escalation would mean a meeting with Area Commander Gervaise in the morning, possibly even with ACC McLaughlin. It would also mean begging for a bigger budget and more manpower. All in all, he felt he could do with a quiet evening at home before he took it all on tomorrow.

Picking up the bills and circulars after he had turned on the lights and turned up the heat a notch, Banks dumped the post on the table and walked down the hall to the kitchen. He hadn't had a great deal of time for shopping in Leeds, but one thing he had done was drop in at Marks & Spencer's and buy a ten-quid meal for two – including a bottle of Spanish Tempranillo – which consisted of a main of chilli and coriander chicken escalopes, a side dish of potato croquettes and a melting-middle chocolate pudding for dessert. He'd get two meals out that, at least, maybe three if he exercised a little portion control.

He picked out some chicken and croquettes and put them in the toaster oven to cook. He would see how he felt about the chocolate pudding later. That done, he poured himself a glass of wine and watched the Channel 4 news on the little television above his breakfast nook while he waited. There was nothing new, just war, famine, earthquakes, storms, scandals, trade wars, tariffs, political corruption and murder, as usual. Ken's case got a brief mention, but not Banks's. Another election in Africa had to be done all over again because of fraud. Italy was without a functioning government. Russia was causing trouble again. It was getting so they could write the news a few days ahead and all take a holiday for a while. About the only thing nobody ever got right in England was the bloody weather. Especially in Yorkshire. Maybe there was snow and ice ten miles down the road, but it was a clear night in Gratly, with the stars all brightly laid out on their black velvet cushion of night and a slip of a moon casting a ghostly glow over Tetchley Fell.

Banks ate at the breakfast nook while the news presenter interviewed an economic expert on today's predictions for the country's future. At the end of it, Banks didn't know whether to withdraw all his savings and hide them under his mattress or plough more into his retirement fund. Economics had never been his strongest subject.

As he ate and half watched TV, he thought about the Blake quote Sarah Chen had tattooed on the back of her shoulder: 'The road of excess leads to the palace of wisdom'. Did it? He had heard it said many times before, back in the sixties, but always quoted very much out of context, which was a lengthy poem called *The Marriage of Heaven and Hell*. Opposites intrigued Blake. In the same poem, he had also written, 'Sooner murder an infant in its cradle than nurse unacted desires', which Banks hoped nobody took as literally as some did the excess quote.

His own favourite was 'A dead body revenges not injuries', which was pretty much self-evident and also, in a way, the *raison d'être* for a job like his. It was an interesting poem to read and discuss, but never intended as a manual for living one's life, the way many had taken it in the sixties. Jim Morrison, for example. Then there was Rimbaud with his 'derangement of all the senses', bless him. Add Dalí's melting clock, a Grateful Dead concert and a few doses of LSD and that pretty much defined the era Banks had grown up in.

Things were different now, though. Pundits kept saying that the millennials had different values, and approached life very differently from the previous generation. What had Sarah Chen made of the words she had tattooed on her shoulder? Perhaps nothing, like the Tesco's checkout girl. Or perhaps it was her credo for living. Banks doubted she had taken them literally. Blackstone had said she liked to give people the idea that she was more liberated than she really was, though he also got the impression she was an extroverted personality. So what had she in common with Adrienne Munro, and how had they met, if indeed they had? Adrienne had no tattoos. And according to most people Banks had talked to, she had been rather shy and retiring, perhaps even a bit puritanical, if not entirely virginesque. Still, they say opposites attract. If it wasn't drugs, what was it? Sex? Both were wearing rather fetching and revealing dresses, as if they were off on a night out. But where? And had they been together that night before they died?

Banks finished his meal and put his plate and cutlery in the dishwasher. It wasn't full yet, so he just set it for another rinse cycle.

While in Leeds, he had managed to get to Waterstones and buy an anthology of Russian poetry, and then to HMV, which seemed to have less and less on offer each time he visited, especially in the music section. How he missed the old Classical Record Shop, gone for years now, though he had to admit that one could have far greater choice online. Still, it was a matter of holding the disc, or LP, of having something substantial, like a real book rather than the electronic version. He wasn't a Luddite, but he did believe there was still a lot of value in the old media. There were plenty of deals in the DVD section, now that more people had turned to Netflix and other online sources of movies, and he ended up buying three of his all-time favourites on Blu-ray for twenty quid: *The Guns of Navarone*, *The Bridge on the River Kwai* and *Doctor Zhivago*, none of which he had seen for a long time.

Instead of sitting in the conservatory listening to music that evening, he took his wine into the entertainment room, put on *Doctor Zhivago* and sat facing the large screen TV with the lights out. He remembered first seeing the film years ago with his girlfriend of the time, Emily. They sat on the back row, as usual, and he had his arm around her, which was slowly going numb. He remembered the music, the lushly romantic 'Lara's Theme', smoke from all the cigarettes, including his own, shimmering as it rose and swirled through the projector's light, the girly shampoo smell of Emily's hair as he turned to kiss her, the strawberry taste of her lipstick.

The film had hardly begun when his mobile buzzed, and when he answered it, he heard the familiar voice of Zelda, with her slight Eastern European accent.

'Alan? I am sorry if I have disturbed you. It is not too late, is it?'

'No. Not at all. As a matter of fact, I just this minute started watching *Doctor Zhivago*.'

Banks thought he heard Zelda laugh. 'I hope you don't take it too seriously as a lesson in history.'

'I'll try not to. What can I do for you?'

'I am going to London tomorrow. They called earlier. I thought we should talk first.'

'Good idea.'

'May I come to your office tomorrow morning?'

'Can you make it lunchtime? I have some meetings in the morning I can't get out of. Things have escalated a bit.'

'The girl in the car?'

'Yes.'

'OK, but I must get a train from Northallerton in the afternoon.'

'I'll give you a lift to the station.'

'Good. I will come to your office first. Goodnight, Alan. Enjoy Zhivago.'

'I will. Goodnight. And thanks.'

Banks turned back to *Doctor Zhivago* and soon found himself drawn into the sweeping love story set against a background of social upheaval, war and revolution. He was sure that Boris Pasternak's novel was nowhere near as romantic as David Lean's film, with its lingering, exquisitely lit close-ups of Julie Christie's eyes, and he vowed to read it soon. But for now the movie version would do.

When the film ended, a few hours and a bottle of wine later, he cried just the way he had the first time he saw it, when he had to hide his tears from Emily Hargreaves. But tonight he had nobody to hide his tears from.

10

The morning meetings had gone as expected, with grumblings all around from the brass about the expense, but in the end both Area Commander Gervaise and ACC Ron McLaughlin, along with Ken Blackstone's supervisor in West Yorkshire, had bowed to the evidence that there was a link between the Adrienne Munro and Sarah Chen cases.

Banks was named SIO, and Blackstone his deputy. Budgets were allocated, manpower assigned and the complexities of a major inquiry team began to take shape. They decided to keep the Eastvale boardroom as their incident room. There didn't seem much point in positioning a mobile unit halfway down the A1. The travel distances were not so great, anyway. Terminals and phones were installed, office manager, document reader, researcher and the other key roles filled, and HOLMES was set in motion. Gerry worked with one of Ken Blackstone's men getting the programme up and running.

About noon, when Banks was finally free to relax for a moment, enjoying a coffee in his office and listening to Murray Perahia's recording of Bach's *French Suites*, a clearly spellbound young PC brought Zelda up to his office. Banks could hardly blame the boy. Zelda was wearing jeans and a black polo-neck jumper under a long navy woollen coat with a fur collar. She was wheeling a suitcase with one hand and carrying a Russian-style fur hat that could have come straight out of a Tolstoy novel, or *Doctor Zhivago*, in the other.

'Ah. Bach,' said Zelda. 'Such a civilised policeman.'

Banks stood up and reached out to shake her hand. She turned it to be kissed, so he kissed it. He noticed how long and tapered her fingers were. A pianist's hands. 'What on earth are you doing with that philistine Ray?' he said.

Zelda laughed and squeezed his hand. 'I can put up with a bit of Led Zeppelin once in a while,' she said, then made a face. 'It's that Captain Beefheart that drives me mad. And that Nico woman. She sounds as if she is singing from beyond the grave.'

Banks laughed. The way she pronounced *Beefheart* indicated the exact amount of scorn she felt. 'The Captain always was one of Ray's favourites,' he said. 'I think he even saw The Magic Band perform live once, back in the day. Never got over it. And as for Nico ... well, what can I say? Sit down, please. Did Ray talk to you? Have you had second thoughts?'

Zelda smiled. 'No second thoughts, despite Raymond's efforts. I'm going to London this afternoon. More surveillance photographs for me. I wanted to see you first so that you can brief me, tell me what you want me to do.'

'Is it always at such short notice?'

'Mostly, yes.'

'Is there anything you want to tell me now that you didn't want to say the other night?'

'No. Why should there be?'

Banks shrugged. 'I just got the impression there's much more to your job than you say, that's all.' And your life, he almost added, but managed to restrain himself.

'There is always more. You must understand that. But there are certain expectations of silence and secrecy, as I know there is in your job, too.'

'I do understand that. I was talking about the element of risk.'

'Oh, that.' She waved a hand dismissively. 'I told you. Mostly I sit in an office and look at photographs or CCTV footage. It is boring, but necessary. I'm no Modesty Blaise, Alan. I cannot run around tracking down the scum who profit from these crimes. But this I *can* do. And I know it gets results.'

'Nobody's denying that,' said Banks who had hardly got over his surprise that Zelda had heard of Modesty Blaise. 'But a man like Keane—'

'I have met many men like Keane.'

'You don't—'

'You'd be surprised how many men there are like Keane. Men for whom human life or happiness means nothing. Men who will take what you love from you in the blink of an eye just because they can. Men of power and money who will steal your dignity and leave you with nothing.'

Banks gave a slight nod. There was something that struck a chord in what she said, but he couldn't quite put his finger on. 'You sound as if you know what you're talking about,' he said. 'Did you lose someone, Zelda?'

She glanced away sharply. 'How could I lose someone? I am an orphan. I had no one to lose. Friends, yes. I lost many friends, and I soon realised it was best not to make friends because they came and went.'

'Then it *was* you, wasn't it? I'm sorry, Zelda.'

'No. I do not want your pity, Alan. But I also do not think I need to tell a man like you all this, tell you what I have suffered, what many others like me have suffered. I think you know a great deal about these things. But even with all you know, you could not even begin to imagine the horror of my life.'

But he could. Imagine it, that is. The beatings, the rapes, the constant fear, the squalor, the sweaty pigs grunting as they came in her, one after the other. But that was all he could do. Imagine it. The only action he could take was to try to stop as many others as he could from doing it. It might be like cleaning the Augean stables, but nobody should have to go through what Zelda had been through. Or Linda. Ever. End of story.

'In all your work since then,' Banks asked, 'have you ever come across the men who hurt you?'

Zelda looked towards the window. 'Some of them, yes,' she said. 'It was long ago. Perhaps many have moved on? Or they are dead. That would be better. Perhaps too much to hope for.' She turned back to face Banks and smiled. 'It's a beautiful day. Cold, but beautiful. The sun is shining. The sky is blue. Do we have to sit in this dreary office to make a plan? Would you like to hear my story, or do you have more important work to do?'

Banks smiled. 'No, not at the moment.' He grabbed his overcoat. 'Come on. Let's go. You can leave the suitcase here.'

Banks and Zelda went out of the station into the market square. Zelda was a couple of inches taller than Banks, and she certainly drew admiring glances as they walked. She fastened her coat loosely and put on the fur hat. 'Like a true Russian,' she said, laughing.

'You're not Russian, are you?'

'My mother's family came from St Petersburg – or Leningrad as it was then – to Odessa after the war. The world war. That was where my mother was born, in nineteen sixty-five. They had survived the siege. Odessa is also where my father met my mother, and later they moved to Moldova for my father's work. He was an engineer. That's where I was born. So yes and no. My father also came from Russia, but he believed his parents migrated from the east. So mine was a very mixed family. It is hard to sort everything out. And I never really got a chance to ask them for their life stories.'

Despite the chill, they bought ice creams at the corner shop and walked along Castle Walk, a tree-lined cinder path that circled Eastvale Castle high above the river valley. Zelda smiled as they passed groups of unruly children in bright orange shell suits and young lovers hand in hand. Banks watched her from the corner of his eye as she occasionally put the cone to her mouth and licked at the scoop of ice cream. It was a gesture both sensual and child-like in its innocence. Which seemed all the more odd coming from a woman who was far from innocent. Or perhaps innocence was more a matter of the heart, or soul, than of things that happened to the body.

The path emerged into the open high above the silver river. It was a good site to choose for a castle, Banks had always thought. High and compact, with a view for miles around. The wooded slope down to the water was steep. It would have been easy to pick off any marauders from the top of the ramparts, pour boiling oil on them or whatever.

They sat on a bench with their backs to the castle walls and enjoyed the view across the river to the opposite bank. The trees were bare, which gave a better view of the fields and rising daleside beyond, but the fields themselves were still bright green with the recent rains and rose in the distance to steep hills with outcrops of grey limestone catching the winter light. Sheep grazed everywhere, and the landscape was criss-crossed with drystone walls. In one of the lower, riverside fields, two sleek and beautiful chestnut mares, backs covered with blankets, nibbled at the grass. Directly below them, the river ran down a series of weirs and rocks, giving the effect of mini rapids, and children stood on the banks and threw stones into the water.

'I cannot believe how much I love it here,' said Zelda. 'It makes me feel like I have come home.'

'To Moldova?' Banks asked, quickly trying to prevent a blob of vanilla ice cream from dropping onto his trousers.

Zelda laughed. 'Moldova? No. I mean home in my heart. But we lived in Dubăsari in Moldova, stuck right between Ukraine and Romania. It is next to Transylvania, where your Dracula comes from.'

'He's supposed to have landed in Whitby,' said Banks.

'Maybe that is why I feel so much at home here. I love Whitby, too. The Magpie. Fish and chips and vampires and goths. Wonderful.' She smiled.

Banks laughed. 'Go on. You were going to tell me your story.'

'I cannot remember much of my childhood because my parents were killed during an uprising in Bendery in nineteen ninety-two, when I was five, and everything was topsy-turvy for a while. I remember my parents spoke Russian as well as Moldavian. Language was always a very political issue in that part of the world. I also speak Russian, some French and German, too. The war came after the break-up of the Soviet Union. But it was not a big war in Moldova, not famous like Serbia and Bosnia. My parents were not political, just ordinary people caught in the crossfire. What do you call it? Collateral damage?'

'Some cynics would call it that.'

'Yes. Collateral damage.'

'And after that?'

'An orphanage. That was my life for next twelve years. But it was a good life. You hear so many stories about what terrible places orphanages are, what cruelties are inflicted on the children there, but not this one. People find it difficult to believe, but the nuns were not cruel. They did not beat us with Bibles and thorns. And they were good teachers. Not only arithmetic and history, but art, music, literature. We had food – not always enough, but food – and we stayed warm. It was a simple life, and they were very strict, but it was also a good life. You understand?'

'Yes, I think so,' said Banks.

'But one day it ended. I had to leave. Everyone has to leave eventually. I had nobody on the outside, and I had hardly got to the end of the street when I was picked up by some men, some very, very bad men. For the next few years things were very difficult for me. How much I cannot say. But I survived. And I escaped in the end. It doesn't matter how. The story has a happy ending. That is what matters. My life is very different now. But I am still involved with the people who hunt these monsters down, the people who saved my life and gave me a new identity. So that is why it is very important for me to do what I can to fight the evil things these gangs do. I owe it to the thousands of other girls caught in their nets.'

'Who do you work for?'

'All I can tell you is that it is an international organisation. Naturally, it has to be. The sex traffic is an international problem. Europol is involved, and many other agencies, including your own National Crime Agency. Of course, I am a mere pawn. I am not a police officer. I have no powers of arrest. Mostly I work in London, in an office, as I told you before, but sometimes they send me to airports or train stations, even to ferry docks, if they think girls and their traffickers are coming in. But I am always hidden away in a special room nobody can see into. And it is rare that I do anything more than look at photographs and videos. My job is intelligence gathering, as I said, helping expand the database. These people move around, pop up all over the place, as you say. They are smart and usually manage to stay at least one step ahead. They are constantly adapting to new and better ways of doing what they do. I just try to put names to faces, perhaps remember when and where I saw them first, then the files are passed on to someone else. There are squads that go out and arrest suspects and try to help the girls, but I never meet them. Sometimes there are meetings or conferences in the Hague, Brussels or Lyon, if something new or big is happening. But not often. It is not a glamorous job.'

'But somebody has to do it, right?'

Zelda finished her ice cream cone. 'Yes. At least for the moment. Nobody knows what will happen after this Brexit.

We may be able to continue, but perhaps not. There is talk of losing funding.'

'There's always talk of losing funding. That's pretty much par for the course with Brexit.'

'Par for the course?'

'The normal thing. Nobody knows.'

Zelda smiled. 'Ah, yes. I see what you mean.' She paused. 'Do you know, I feel guilty because I cannot talk to Raymond about things like this. He is like a child . . . too quick to react, too emotional. If I tell him about my work and the bad things in my life, he treats me like I am made of plastic for days.'

'Porcelain?' suggested Banks.

'Yes. Porcelain.'

'And me? I'm cold?'

'No.' She touched his arm. 'But you are a cop, Alan. You understand. I don't want sympathy. I don't want . . . what do you call it? Cuddling?'

'Cuddling would be nice,' said Banks. 'But I think you mean coddling.'

'Yes. Coddling. Like an egg. I don't need that.'

They admired the view in silence for a while, watching a mother walk by pushing a pram, and an elderly man in a scarf and flat cap walking his Jack Russell. It was quite warm in the sunshine, but a cold wind blew up from the water and rattled the bare branches now and again.

'So, your man Keane?' said Zelda.

Banks turned to face her. 'I wanted to talk to you so that I could try to persuade you to forget about him,' he said.

'But?'

Banks smiled. 'You're very perceptive. Now I'm not so sure. Ray said you're not the type to back down.'

'I did try to tell you the other night, Alan. Besides, I assure you it is not dangerous for me.'

'Danger is always relative, and with someone like Keane you always have to be aware that it's there, or you'll make a mistake and . . . well, like I did.'

'This Keane. He was Annie's boyfriend, am I right?'

'Yes. He used her to keep track of our investigation. He made her feel betrayed, humiliated, a fool. He's very charming on the surface, but if he feels cornered he'll kill or run. Or both.'

'I can imagine how betrayed and used she felt. But were you not . . . not with her at the time?'

'No. We'd split up by then.'

'But she still cares for you.'

'Does she?'

Zelda nodded. 'I think so.'

'Anyway, to cut a long story short, Keane drugged me and set fire to my cottage with me inside it. If it wasn't for Annie and Winsome, I'd be dead.'

'Why did he do that?'

'Because he suspected we were on to him. He was covering his tracks.'

'And he escaped?'

'Yes, he drove over the hills and far away.'

'And now he turns up again in a photograph I have seen?'

'The man he was with—'

'Is a very bad man. Croatian. He was part of the gang that took me.' She gave a little shiver. 'He's a pig.'

'And he hasn't been stopped yet?'

Zelda shrugged. 'He is clever. And lucky. Just as he was in the war. And he knows who to pay. Why should he stop?'

'So what would he be doing with Keane?'

'As I said before, the only thing I can think of is that he would want false documents of some kind. Shipping, bills of lading, passports, even. I don't know.'

'For himself?'

'Or someone else he was trying to smuggle somewhere, or place in a position of influence. They forge work backgrounds, resumés, references and so on, for customs officers, lorry drivers, that sort of thing. And they do not only snatch girls from the street. They are skilled at creating official-sounding fronts to persuade them to leave their homes – marriage and employment agencies, fake modelling agencies, fake film production studios, and fake opportunities for work and study abroad. All these things exist legitimately, so it is often impossible for the girls looking for jobs abroad to separate the fake advertisements from the real ones until it is too late. Nobody checks the authenticity of these advertisements.'

'And the photograph you saw was definitely taken in London?'

'Yes.'

'I'd like to see it.'

Zelda turned away, staring towards the hills again. A blackbird started singing in a nearby tree. 'I'm afraid that might not be possible.'

'The secrecy?'

'Yes. I think my team is very much concerned with making a case against the other man in the photograph. If Keane can lead them to him, all is well and good. But to them I think Keane is just a pawn.'

'Look,' said Banks. 'I want Keane. Not just for personal reasons, not just for what he did to me and to Annie, but because he's a cold-blooded murderer.'

'These men are all cold-blooded murderers.'

'Well, Zelda, you're in Yorkshire now, and you're not entirely surrounded by cold-blooded murderers and rapists all the time any more.'

Zelda laughed. 'There must be some, or you would not have a job.'

'There are some. More than enough. But what I'm saying is that while Keane may not be unique in your world, he is in this one, or at least to some extent.'

Zelda frowned so Banks went on quickly.

'All I need is a lead. An idea of where I might find him. A town, an address, a phone number, whatever. That's all. I don't want to interfere with your work. If you've got an operation going on, I'll even wait until you've done what you need to do before moving in. I don't want to interfere. But I *do* want to find him.'

Zelda paused before answering. 'I will help you if I can,' she said. 'But you have to understand that the other night when we were all talking about how dangerous it was, you might have been worried about danger to me, but that's not what I was thinking of.'

'Oh?'

'No. I was thinking about the danger to you and Annie. And to Raymond.' She paused 'When you – how do you say it – disturb a sleeping bear. It is not only this Keane you have to worry about. He has some very nasty new friends now. Men like the Croatian. If he is valuable to them, they will kill to keep him alive and free.'

'I wouldn't expect anything less of them,' said Banks.

'Believe me, I know what they are capable of.'

'Let's be especially careful, then. Be patient. Wait for the right time. Don't take unnecessary risks.'

Zelda glanced at her watch. 'I must go. My train.'

Banks stood up and held out his hand to take her arm. 'Come on, then. We'll go back and pick up your suitcase and I'll give you a lift to the station.'

'Bugger me, it really *is* him,' said Ronald Hadfield, staggering slightly as the mortuary assistant gently pulled back the sheet. Noticing that Ronald had turned ashen, Annie grabbed his elbow and led him out of the morgue. He eased himself out of her grip, firmly, but politely. 'I'm all right,' he said. 'It's just that I couldn't really believe what I was seeing. I think I had expected it all to be a big mistake. I can't believe the miserable old bastard's dead at last.'

Ronald Hadfield had behaved like a total arse so far, complaining about being dragged all the way back from Tokyo and missing important business meetings, then he had demanded to see the real body instead of a closed-circuit TV image or a photograph, insisting he could handle it. Annie had hoped for a moment that actually seeing his father's corpse for real might suddenly make him more human, but apparently, it was not to be.

'If you need a few minutes to recover,' she said, 'or require counselling—'

'I could do with a fucking drink,' Ronald said

They were certainly a foul-mouthed pair, the Hadfield siblings. Annie wondered if they had got it from their late father Laurence. Still, if Ronald Hadfield wanted to go around effing and blinding, who was she to complain? She'd done it often enough herself when things went tits up. 'We'll go over to the Unicorn,' she said. 'It's never likely to make it into the tourist brochures, but they serve a decent measure.'

The Unicorn was quiet on a Tuesday afternoon, and they found a table far enough away from the bar to give them some privacy. Hadfield seemed uncomfortable in the grimy corner pub, being more at home perhaps in the clubs and bars of Hampstead or the City. He asked for a double brandy, which Annie bought for him, wondering how come she was always the one buying drinks for the filthy rich Hadfields these days, and sticking to Diet Coke herself.

'I suppose you're going to give me the third degree now?' said Hadfield, after a bracing slurp of brandy.

'Just a few questions, if that's OK?'

'You realise what a bloody big mess this will cause, don't you?'

'What?'

'Father's death. He was a very important person, you know. The economies of several small countries depended on him. Not to mention that he was one of the main players in the Brexit think tank.'

That sounded like an oxymoron to Annie. 'No doubt he left a detailed will,' she said.

'Hah! The will, yes. Are we going to have some sort of Agatha Christie reading, the family gathered together around a big table, the solicitor reading out the bequests?'

'We don't do that sort of thing any more.' They never had, as far as Annie knew.

'Just as well. He didn't like me, Father. Do you know that? I could never do anything right in his eyes, never be as good as him. And he doted on my fucked-up junkie slut of a sister. Knowing him, he's left everything to her to fritter away on toy-boys and cocaine. But you can bet it'll be left to me to tidy up his business affairs.'

'No doubt all this will be a big threat to future world order,' Annie said, 'but it's really got nothing to do with what I wanted to talk to you about.'

Hadfield ignored the sarcasm. 'I suppose you think I did it, don't you?'

'Did what?'

'Killed him.'

'As far as we know, your father's death was an accident. There are just a few oddities that require explanation.'

'Like why his body was found on a bloody moor miles from anywhere with no sign of a car to be seen?'

'Something like that,' said Annie.

Hadfield ran his hand through his hair. He was a large, jowly man, though not quite as overweight as his father had been. 'When did it happen?' he asked.

'We don't know for certain, but we think it was sometime last weekend. When did you last speak to him?'

'I can't remember exactly. We speak as little as possible, and then only when we have to. It must have been about a month ago. Young Roderick's birthday. I'll say that for him, he always remembered his grandchildren's birthdays. Can't fault him on that.'

'You're not in business together?'

'Lord, no. It's not a family business, not by any stretch of the imagination. I'm CFO of an international corporation. We just rape the environment. Father was basically a moneylender, though he'd have called himself an investment banker, financier and venture capitalist. As I said, there are small countries that depend on him for their economic stability. Not that he was averse to the occasional arms deal or hiring the odd band of mercenaries if some tinpot dictator got a bit bolshie.'

'Where were you the weekend before last?'

Hadfield smiled a rather nasty smile. 'I was wondering when you'd get around to asking that,' he said. 'As a matter of fact, I was in Geneva. There's an important merger going on, and I had to oversee a number of important meetings. I flew on from there to Tokyo.'

'I suppose there are plenty of people who can verify this?'

'Naturally. Though they wouldn't appreciate being pestered by the police.'

'We'll be gentle with them, if we have to check your alibi.'

'I thought you said Father's death was an accident?'

'It looks like an accident. In my experience, though, it's not that difficult to make murder look like an accident. That's why we need to go over the inconsistencies very carefully. Someone could easily have transported the body up to the moor and dumped it down the gully. But killers usually make a mistake somewhere along the line. It may seem like just a little one, but it's often enough.'

'A proper little fucking Miss Marple, aren't you?'

'And here's me thinking the sight of your father's body would stop you behaving like a complete arse.'

He smiled the nasty smile again. 'Are you supposed to talk like that to the bereaved son? Shouldn't I report you?'

'Do what you fucking well like,' said Annie. 'Just answer my questions first.'

Hadfield smirked and inclined his head 'Yes, ma'am.'

'And don't call me ma'am.'

'You've made your point.'

'Did your father have any enemies?'

'Hundreds, probably. Maybe thousands. He was a very unpleasant human being.'

'Anyone recent? Anything personal? Someone who might want to do away with him?'

'Again, probably hundreds. But if you asked me for their names, I couldn't tell you. I wouldn't put it past an ousted government official or two to put what's left of their life savings together and hire an assassin. Then there's the hundreds of suckers who invested in his crackpot ventures over the years.'

'This is not very helpful,' Annie said.

Hadfield leaned forward and rapped on the table. 'I can't help that. What I'm saying is that my father made enemies quite easily. It's unavoidable when you're in the business he's in. Whether any of them would actually go so far as to kill him, I can't say. Even his enemies usually have some vested interest in his staying alive and thriving. Greed breeds greed, inspector. There's always the hope of more. That's what keeps even the most desperate losers going, and more than willing to throw good money after bad.'

'What about on a more personal level? Did he have any business partners?'

'He had employees, not partners. They depended on him for their livelihoods.'

'Friends, girlfriends?'

'He had a certain circle of people he mixed with. I'm sure you'll find them all listed in his contacts. Mostly politicians, high-ranking police officers, celebrities and so on, though I'm sure you'll also find a sprinkling of locals – perhaps a wealthy farmer or two, if there is such a thing, a few professionals, lawyers, doctors, that sort of thing. People he played golf with. Father could be very charming when he wanted to. He liked to collect people. Mix with the crème de la crème. Especially if he thought they might prove useful down the line. As for his love life, I assume he had one. Father always had his little peccadillos, even when mother was still alive. It's not something I care to contemplate.'

'Poppy said he didn't have anyone, not since your mother died.'

'Maybe she's right.'

Annie had photographed the Pandora treble clef before lodging it with exhibits, and she placed the picture in front of Ronald Hadfield. 'Do you recognise that?' she asked.

Hadfield frowned. 'What is it?'

'A charm from a bracelet.'

He shook his head. 'Afraid not.'

She placed a copy of the photograph Adrienne Munro's parents had given Banks in front of him. 'Ever seen her?'

'No. Is this father's squeeze? If so, I'd say he's done rather well for himself, though she looks a bit young.'

'Her name was Adrienne Munro. She was nineteen. Has your father ever mentioned her?'

'Not to my knowledge. Was?'

'She was found dead around the same time as your father.'

'A suicide pact? Is that what you're suggesting?'

'No. But this charm was found in your father's bathroom at Rivendell.'

'Well, I've never seen it, or her.'

Annie put the photographs away. 'How about your father's relationship with Poppy?'

'You don't mean—'

'I'm not suggesting anything untoward, but if you do have information we're not aware of . . .'

'No, there was nothing like that. I'm certain of it. Father may have been a bastard, but he wasn't into incest. Poppy was the apple of his eye, that's all.'

'And she felt the same way?'

'As far as I know. Definitely a daddy's girl. As far as she's capable of having feelings with that fucked-up brain of hers. The number of times he's forked out to cover up scandals, blackmail, or to put her in rehab. Makes me wish I had shares in The Priory.'

'You mention blackmail.'

'Poppy's indiscretions know no bounds. But in those kinds of situations you'd be looking at Father as the perpetrator of the murder, not the victim. It was always easier to pay them off.'

'You never know where blackmail might lead.'

Hadfield shrugged. 'Well, you're the expert.' He slugged back the rest of his brandy. 'Thanks for the drink. I hope you can claim it on expenses. If that's all, I'd like to get going.'

'Are you sure you should be driving?'

'Certainly not. That's why I have Mark waiting outside. My driver.'

'Are you thinking of going back to Rivendell?'

'No fucking way. I'm going back to Hampstead.'

'Good. The house is a possible crime scene. It's out of bounds. But your father has just died. There must be things to do, things to organise, even though it might be some time before the body is released? You said yourself his death would cause problems.'

'Let Poppy deal with it. Like I said, she'll probably be the one to benefit most.'

'I'm not sure Poppy could organise a piss-up in a brewery.'

Hadfield laughed. 'You're probably quite right about that. But she can certainly afford to hire someone to do it for her. Isn't that what expensive lawyers are for? By the way, where is the little charmer?'

'Been and gone.'

'That's our Poppy. Hope it was a pleasant visit.'

'We may need to talk to you again,' Annie said.

'I'm not that hard to get hold of.' Hadfield reached into his pocket. 'I'll tell you what, just because it's you, here's my mobile number. And don't you dare fucking give it to anyone else.'

Leaving a final nasty smile that faded slowly in the air, like the Cheshire Cat's, Ronald Hadfield left the Unicorn and Annie put the card in her briefcase. Then she went to the bar and asked for a pint of Black Sheep. She had had it up to her back teeth with the bloody Hadfields.

That afternoon, DS Winsome Jackman went to talk to Sarah Chen's housemates in Leeds. They rented a big old house on Clarendon Road, around the back of the university. Set back from the street, it was a grand red-brick building, darkened by years of industrial pollution, complete with gables and bay windows. Trees grew high in the garden, winter sunlight filtering through their bare branches.

Winsome rang the doorbell and a young fair-haired woman, probably about Sarah's age, answered. She didn't seem unduly surprised or distressed when Winsome showed her warrant card, but simply asked her to come in and walked ahead of her to the living room. Winsome could see immediately that the interior of the old house had been refurbished and given a more modern appearance. The students had added their own bits of colour here and there – a reprinted *The Third Man* film poster, a Monet reproduction, a large stereo system and plenty of second-hand or makeshift furniture, from mismatched armchairs to bookcases built of planks and bricks, probably stolen from the nearby building site.

The young woman introduced herself as Fiona, then introduced Winsome to the other two, Fatima and Erik. They were all clearly grieving, but Fiona had the grace to offer Winsome a cup of tea, which she accepted gladly. There was some left in the large pot on the glass table, and Winsome said she'd be quite happy with that. She didn't need milk or sugar.

'I'm sorry about your friend,' she began. 'I don't know if you know, but there was also a student in Eastvale who died recently, and we think the two incidents might be connected. Her name was Adrienne Munro. That's why I'm here.'

'Died or murdered?' said Erik.

'We're not sure,' Winsome answered. 'It looks like suicide, but someone else was definitely involved.'

'Because Sarah was murdered, no doubt about it.'

'I know,' said Winsome. 'I didn't mean to imply any different. But the local police found a slip of paper in Sarah's room with Adrienne's name on it, along with a phone number we can't trace. Do any of you know anything about it?'

They all shook their heads. Fatima had clearly been crying, and she brought out a tissue from the folds of her clothing to pat her eyes.

'The officers compared it with some of Sarah's lecture notes, and the handwriting wasn't hers,' Winsome went on. 'Did any of you write it down? Was it a phone message for her or something?'

'We don't know anything about it,' Fiona said. She was wearing the student uniform of jeans and a chunky sweater with the sleeves pulled down to cover most of her hands. 'We've never heard of Adrienne Munro.'

'I understand that,' said Winsome. 'It was just a possibility. I had to ask. Little things like that can drive you crazy in my job, and when someone comes along later, after you've been banging your head against a brick wall for days, and says, "Oh, I did that. Sorry. Didn't I mention it earlier?" it can make you kind of mad.'

Fiona managed a grim smile and nodded. 'I understand,' she said. 'And I'm sorry we can't help you.'

'Did Sarah have any visitors shortly before she disappeared? Anyone who might perhaps have left the note for her?'

'I don't think so,' said Fatima. 'We don't keep an eye on one another, and we're not always home at the same time, but I don't remember seeing anyone. Fee?'

Fiona shook her head, and Erik did likewise.

'While she was out, perhaps?'

'One of us would have noticed,' Erik said. 'If we're all out, the place is locked up. But our rooms have their own locks, too, so if Sarah went out, she'd make sure she locked her bedroom door. We all would.' He smiled. 'Not that we don't trust one another, of course.'

The others nodded.

'OK,' said Winsome. 'Someone must have given it to her somewhere else. A pub, perhaps, or a coffee shop?'

'That's more likely,' said Fiona.

'Let's move on. Do you know of anyone who might want to harm Sarah?'

'The other policeman asked us that,' said Fatima.

'I'm sure he did, but it always helps to take a fresh look.'

'No,' said Erik. 'Sarah was hardly a saint. She never did her fair share of the dishes or cooking, and the washing machine and dryer were always full of her clothes, but you would forgive her, you know. You couldn't . . . She was so, such . . .' He just hung his head and stopped talking.

'I'm sorry, Erik. Were you and Sarah—'

His head shot up. 'No. We weren't a couple. Why would you assume that? That would be crazy, something like that, with someone you have to share a house with. I liked her. That's all. She was my friend. And now she's gone.'

Winsome held her hand up at the vehemence of his reply. 'OK. I get it.'

'What Erik means,' said Fiona, 'is that Sarah was a special person. She was a bit chaotic, a bit of a free spirit, but you couldn't help but love her.'

'Do any of you know if Sarah had a boyfriend?'

'She didn't,' said Fiona. 'Not for any particular reason. I mean, she could go through boyfriends pretty quickly when she wanted to, but she was between right now.'

'Could there be anyone in her past disturbed enough to want to take revenge on her for being dumped or humiliated?'

'I don't know,' said Fiona. 'But I doubt it. Sarah wasn't the kind of person to humiliate anybody. She was always sensitive to other people's feelings, even if she was splitting up with them. As far as I know, she never had anyone obsessed with her or anything like that. No stalkers or voyeurs or anything. She liked a good time, and she was fun to be around, but she wasn't promiscuous or a tease.'

'Was she exclusively heterosexual?'

'What a strange question,' Fiona said, frowning. 'But yes. I'd say she was.'

'I wouldn't be asking if it wasn't important.'

'This other girl who died, was she gay?'

'Not as far as we know. Who was with Sarah on the Saturday you last saw her?'

'I was,' said Fiona. 'We went in town shopping.'

'And Sarah bought a red dress?'

'Yes. It was lovely. Pricey, too. I asked her where she was going in something like that, but she just widened her eyes in that way she had and said, "Never you mind."'

'And that was the last time you saw her?'

'Yes.'

'Did you travel back here together?'

'No. I was heading off to visit my folks in Manchester. I went to the station and took a train. I left Sarah in the Trinity Centre. I suppose she must have gone home to change and get ready later.'

Winsome looked towards Fatima and Erik.

'We were both away that weekend,' Erik said. 'I was staying with some old mates in Newcastle and Fatima went to her cousin's wedding in Hull.'

'How did Sarah manage financially?' Winsome glanced around the room. 'I mean, this is a nice place, great location. It can't have come cheap.'

'It's two thousand two hundred and twenty quid a month,' said Erik. 'Four bedrooms and five bathrooms. We each pay our share. And no, it's not easy, not with the money they demand for an education. But we manage. There are loans.'

'So you all have student loans?'

The three of them nodded.

'And Sarah?'

'Not this year,' said Fiona. 'She finally got some insurance money for her father's death, and he left her a bit of money in his will, too.'

Winsome made a note to follow up on that. It was interesting that both dead girls had come unexpectedly into money at the start of their second year. She knew that it could take a long time to settle insurance claims and probate estates, so maybe two years after the death wasn't so bad. 'But she had her mother to take care of, didn't she?'

'Her mother's in a home,' said Fatima. 'I think it's NHS.'

'No. She did a deal with the house,' Fiona said. 'Sarah told me. You basically have to sell your house to pay for your care when you're old and sick. But it's a nice home. They don't starve or beat the patients.'

It was a fine recommendation, Winsome thought. Something to bear in mind when the time came. Avoid places where they starve and beat you. 'I get the impression that the four of you were pretty close,' she went on. 'Did you hang out together? Go to gigs, dances, pubs, that sort of thing?'

'Sometimes,' Fiona said.

'I don't drink,' Fatima answered.

'But she *loves* to dance,' Erik said.

Fatima blushed. 'Well, maybe.'

'So you did hang out together?'

'Sure,' said Fiona. 'The student pub, that sort of thing.'

'Clubs?'

'Sometimes. In town.'

'I know what you're going to ask next,' Erik said. 'The other police, they asked the same thing. Do we do drugs? That answer is yes, sometimes we smoke a little marijuana and sometimes take ecstasy, like just about everyone else on campus, but that's all.'

'Not me,' said Fatima.

'OK,' said Erik. 'Fatima's a good girl. So are you going to arrest us?'

Winsome smiled. 'I don't think so. Our problem is, we don't know why the girls were killed, or died. Drugs is one possibility. We know that Adrienne Munro died from sleeping tablets, which her student health centre and her GP say they certainly did not prescribe. But she must have got them from somewhere.'

'Well, not from us,' said Fiona. 'We didn't even know her.'

'I'm not saying she got them from you, merely pointing out that there is already a drug element in this investigation. If either – or both – Adrienne and Sarah were involved with drugs, they could have become exposed to some pretty nasty people.'

'I think we would have known,' said Fiona.

'There was nothing odd or different about Sarah's behaviour lately?'

'No. She was the same as normal. We didn't see quite so much of her, but that's all.'

'Why not?'

'I don't know. We just didn't.'

'But if she didn't have a boyfriend, wouldn't she be around more, hanging out with her friends?'

'I think she went to visit her mother pretty often,' said Fatima. 'It was very upsetting for her.'

'I'm sure it was.' So painful, Winsome thought, that a young woman like Sarah would perhaps do her duty but would hardly wish to spend more of her spare time with a woman she loved who didn't even recognise her. Besides, the staff at the care home didn't appear to have seen that much of her. 'Was there anyone else especially close to her? Any other friends around the place?'

'A couple,' said Fiona.

'And there was Mia,' Fatima added. 'Don't forget Mia.'

Winsome's ears pricked up at the name. 'What about Mia?' she asked.

'They met near the beginning of term,' Fatima said. 'Sarah and Mia. They hung out together for a while. Don't go reading anything into this. It wasn't a lesbian thing or anything. They just . . . you know, found they liked the same music and books and stuff. Just hit it off.'

'And the rest of you?'

'I don't know about the others,' said Fiona, 'but I always found Mia a bit stand-offish.'

'She was weird,' said Erik. 'She didn't really seem to want anything to do with us. Just Sarah.'

Winsome remembered Colin Fairfax, Adrienne Munro's ex-boyfriend, saying that he got a 'bad vibe' from Mia. Surely this had to be the same person? 'But you say Sarah wasn't gay. How do you know?'

'I suggested it one night,' Erik said. 'Just making a joke, like, and Sarah got really pissed off with me.'

'She wasn't gay,' Fiona said. 'Take it from me. But Mia was a bit weird.'

'So they were just friends?' Winsome said. 'What happened?'

'Mia just disappeared.'

Exactly the way Adrienne's Mia did, Winsome thought.

'When?'

'Around the middle of October. Poof. She was gone.'

'Did she drop out?'

'I don't think she was ever in,' said Erik. 'She told us she was studying English, had transferred after doing her first year in Sussex because she wasn't happy down south. But I never saw her with a book in her hand.'

'That doesn't mean anything, idiot,' said Fiona. 'You're studying engineering but I don't see you running around with a spanner in your hand.'

'It's electrical engineering.'

'All right, a spark plug, then.'

Erik laughed and broke the tension. 'A spark plug. The woman's crazy.'

'Back to Mia,' said Winsome. 'Can you describe her for me?'

They thought for a moment, then Fiona said, 'She's about my height – that's five foot six – wavy reddish brown hair, medium length, oval face. Brown eyes, I think.'

'How did she dress?'

Fiona shrugged. 'Just like any student, really. Jeans, denim jacket. I didn't really notice. She didn't dress to show off her body, though. Most of her clothes were fairly loose.'

'She had a great body though,' said Erik. 'You could tell. She certainly had a decent pair of tits.'

'Oh, you. Typical male. Always the breasts.'

Winsome thought she had enough without going further into the ins and outs of Mia's breasts. What she had heard so far matched almost exactly the description given by Colin Fairfax of the Mia who had befriended Adrienne Munro, and under much the same sort of circumstances. As far as Winsome was concerned, they were one and the same. What she needed to do next, she realised, was to get Ray Cabbot, if he was available, to work on a sketch with Colin Fairfax, then perhaps show it to Fiona, Fatima and Erik to check for accuracy, and to get their input.

'Did Mia ever come here, to the house?' she asked.

'Not that I know of,' said Fiona, still scowling at Erik.

'No,' said Fatima. 'None of us hang out here, anyway. It's mostly just for working and sleeping and eating. We go out when we want to see people.'

'OK,' said Winsome, putting away her notebook. She slipped a card from her purse and dropped it on the table. 'If any one of you thinks of anything else, especially anything that might help us find this Mia, then please call me.'

They all nodded.

'And again,' said Winsome as she got up to leave. 'I'm really sorry about your friend. She sounds like a truly special person.'

Winsome saw Fatima's eyes mist up before she turned and headed for the door.

The businessman across the aisle was staring at Zelda. It didn't bother her; it happened a lot. Over time, she had learned to differentiate a lascivious stare from a suspicious one. This man wanted to fuck her. That was all. She gave him a look that told him she knew exactly what he was thinking. He immediately blushed and turned guiltily away, perhaps plagued by a mental image of the wife he had been dreaming of deceiving. Zelda smiled to herself and glanced out of the window. It worked every time. Well, almost.

Zelda enjoyed the train journey to London from Northallerton, just as she had from Penzance. She had always travelled first class and tried to book a single seat so that she wouldn't be bothered by any nuisance neighbours who wanted to talk. Men like the one across the aisle undressed her with their eyes, certainly, and perhaps wished they were sitting next to her, or more, but she found it easy to deal with them. She enjoyed a sandwich and a glass of wine as she travelled, looking out at cooling towers shaped like huge stiff corsets across dark muddy fields. Horses wandered here and there, sheep grazed and cows lay in close groups or munched what little grass there was. Occasionally the sun would reflect on a stretch of water or a car windscreen; a town would flash by, terraced housing, children playing in a schoolyard, church towers or spires, the station with a nameplate they were always travelling too fast to read. She liked to watch the people getting on and off at the different stops, wondered where they were going, what they were going to do, who they were going to meet. She made up stories about them in her mind.

Sometimes, if it was a dull day, or if she simply felt like it, she would read through most of the journey. This time, though, as soon as the train left the north, the weather was good, the sky blue and filled with white fluffy clouds casting swift-moving shadows as they scudded on the wind over the fields, and her attention moved in and out of Kawabata's *Beauty and Sadness*, which she had read several times before. Mostly she didn't think about the tasks that lay ahead of her – the time for that would come soon enough – but luxuriated in being suspended in an eternal now.

Sometimes, though, she couldn't help but think about the past. She hadn't told Ray the half of it, or Banks. She thought perhaps Banks could guess, but even his imagination might fall somewhat short of the full horror. She remembered the street in a suburb of Chişinău, with Soviet-era tenements, the tobacconist's shop, the little bar on the corner where the menfolk gathered to watch football. Until that day her life had been good. It was true that she had no parents, no family – they had all been wiped out in the war – but that was a long time ago, and the orphanage had given her a sense of belonging, had been a good place to grow up, even when the government money ceased to come and they had to make do with what little charity they could get.

Zelda had been very lucky. She had been a good student; she had loved learning. Before most of the children could stumble through a sentence of English, if she could get to them before the nuns caught her, she was reading books by Charles Dickens and Beatrix Potter and Sir Arthur Conan Doyle, and whatever strange English language titles turned up in the boxes people donated. She loved reading in English, and now, so many years later, it was the language she dreamed in, too, though even in her dreams she couldn't always find the right word. Even more than in languages, though, she shone in art. But she was not well versed in the ways of the world and was a very naive, inexperienced girl for someone of her age.

In that one day, when she was eighteen and it was time to leave the orphanage, her whole life changed in a split second. Nobody was throwing her out; they didn't do things like that. Zelda had done very well in all her exams; her teacher had sent out samples of her best work, and she had been accepted into a prestigious art college in Bucharest in neighbouring Romania. She was walking to the train station with her small suitcase of worldly possessions, a few *leu* in her pocket, an introduction to the head of the college and her ticket to Bucharest, feeling a little sad because she had to leave her friends behind, but happy and excited about the future because . . . well, because she was young and fearless, and she had the whole world ahead of her.

Just around the corner, two scruffy, unshaven men lounged against the wall smoking. Zelda had never seen them before, though she had walked the area often with her friends. The nuns had always warned the girls to be careful, especially of the men who frequented the bar. Zelda moved towards the edge of the pavement, stepping down into the road to give the men a wide berth. There was a black car parked just in front of her, and before she could react, the men had taken her by her arms and pushed her into the back. One of them got in beside her, and the other got in the front to drive. The car smelled of tobacco and sweat and Zelda was scared. She tried to scream but the man beside her put his hand over her mouth while the other drove the car away. The hand tasted nasty and she bit it as hard as she could. The man snatched his hand away with a grunt and then punched her hard in the face. Her head swam. She slumped back in her seat. Blood flowed from her nose. The car bumped over cobbles and she was tossed around while the man she had bitten held her down with one hand and sucked his damaged hand, cursing under his breath.

And that was how it all began.

The last thing she saw in the neighbourhood of her childhood was that her small suitcase had fallen to the ground and broken open, spilling her few meagre possessions and articles of clothing over the road surface, along with the scrapbook she had kept so diligently for so long, the well-thumbed copy of *Bleak House* that she had been reading, and the small music box that held all that was left of her mother, a few cheap rings and necklaces. She wore the golden heart with her mother's photo inside, and as she sat there bleeding and crying, she fingered it, as if it was a talisman and would give her strength to endure whatever was to come. But nothing could have given her the strength to endure all that, nothing but the ability she developed to absent herself from her experiences, to be elsewhere, in the world of the imagination, her own fantasy, looking down on her misused and abused body while what happened, happened.

Zelda felt her chest tighten as if her very breath was turning to stone.

'Are you all right, miss?'

She looked up, startled by the voice, and saw the ticket inspector standing over her.

'Are you all right?' he repeated.

Zelda tried to smile. She patted her chest. 'Yes. Yes, thank you. I must have dozed off for a moment. A bad dream.'

'As long as you're all right.'

'Yes. No problem. It's very kind of you.'

The inspector nodded and walked away, glancing back anxiously. The man across the aisle sneaked a quick glance to see what all the fuss was about. Zelda sipped the last of her wine and breathed slowly, melting the stone back to air again. It was talking to Alan that had brought the past so clearly into focus again. She looked out of the window. They were on the edge of a town. The railway lines ran beside a canal, where brightly painted houseboats lay moored along the towpath. On the opposite bank was a pub where some people were sitting outside in their overcoats on wooden benches. Beyond them were a school, a small housing estate, and high on the hill far in the background, over the fields, a stately home. This was England, then. Not Moldova. Not Croatia. Not Romania. Not Belarus. She was safe. She picked up her book and carried on reading.

It was almost the end of another day, and Banks felt no closer to finding out what had happened to Adrienne Munro than he had the moment he first saw her body. Despite his walk with Zelda at lunchtime, he felt restless and cooped up in his

office. He decided to go out and check the second-hand bookshops for a copy of *Doctor Zhivago*, then return and see about
having a quick meeting with his team about where to go next.

When he stepped into the market square it was dark, though
it wasn't yet five o'clock. It started to get dark shortly after three
at this time of year. Shopkeepers took it as a sign to close up
early and go home, and that was what had happened at the first
second-hand bookshop, built into the side of the church. The
market square, usually thriving in late afternoon, was almost
deserted. The charity shop was still open, though, and Banks
walked through to the back where the books were. They had a
pretty good stock of literary classics, including lots of Dickens,
Jane Austen and Henry James. They also had an old Penguin
classics edition of *War and Peace* in one hefty volume, but there
was no sign of the Pasternak novel. Banks bought *War and
Peace*. He had never read it, though every year he had sworn to
himself that this would be the year. He didn't know why he had
put it off so long, as he had really enjoyed *Anna Karenina*.

Luckily, the other second-hand bookshop, down the narrow
street beside the police station, was still open, and even better
still, on its shelves was a paperback copy of the book he was
after in relatively fine condition. It even had a still from the
movie on the cover – showing Julie Christie and Omar Sharif,
of course. He bought it, chatted briefly with the bookseller,
who extolled its merits over a more recent translation, and
headed back to the station, pleased with his success.

He checked his pigeonhole and found nothing but a printed
copy of the budget approved by the ACC that morning. Still
no tox results. If they didn't turn up by tomorrow morning he
would drop by the lab and see if Jazz could hurry things up a
bit.

Gerry was the only one in the squad room. Banks knew that
she had been working on HOLMES most of the day. Annie
was out on the Laurence Hadfield case, and Winsome was in

Leeds liaising with Blackstone's team on the Munro–Chen cases and trying to track down the mysterious phone number. She had had so little success with it so far that Banks was beginning to wonder whether it was a phone number after all. At least she had heard from the bank and told him that Adrienne's recent hefty deposits were all cash, which meant they couldn't be traced.

'Finished with HOLMES?' Banks asked Gerry, leaning back against Winsome's desk.

'For today, sir.'

'It went well?'

Gerry smiled. 'Well enough. Ken's man, Jared, is pretty good. I think we've got everything covered. I've also been doing a bit of digging into Laurence Hadfield's business practices.'

Banks remembered his conversation with Linda on Saturday about Hadfield's business. 'And?'

Gerry swivelled to face him and put the end of her pencil to her lips. 'It's all a bit confusing, sir,' she said. 'Earlier this afternoon, Ronald, the son, gave DI Cabbot to believe that his father was the next worst thing to that character Hugh Laurie played in *The Night Manager.*'

'The worst man in the world?'

'That's right. Gave the impression he brought down governments for profit, sold weapons to the bad guys, had corrupt leaders in his pockets, and so on.'

'But?'

'From what I can gather – mostly from newspaper and magazine and Internet articles, and talking to a few of his close colleagues on the phone, that wasn't the case at all. Hadfield was tough, drove a hard bargain, but he was also a pretty straight businessman. At least for the business he was in, which was high finance, venture capital, emerging markets, that sort of thing.'

'I can't say I understand any of it, myself,' said Banks.

'Me, neither,' said Gerry. 'That's why I had a chat with Cath from the fraud squad. I still don't understand it, but it comes down to the fact that Hadfield was pretty honest and well liked in his world. He didn't have a lot of enemies screaming for him to be hanged, drawn and quartered.'

'So the son exaggerated?'

'Yes.'

'Think he had anything to do with it? Ronald? Was he laying a false trail for us?'

'Possibly.' Gerry chewed the end of her pencil.

'But?'

'I think it was more a matter of bad blood. At least that's the impression I got from DI Cabbot. But somebody I spoke to mentioned that if I wanted to know who was the real crook in the Hadfield family, I should look more closely at Ronald.'

'And you did?'

'Yes. There's nothing proven, no charges brought, but there's a strong suspicion going about that he's been involved in money-laundering.'

'I see,' said Banks. 'So he won't like the attention his father's suspicious death has brought?'

'Not at all.'

'And it would make sense for him to have us think we were searching for some Somalian hit man, or some such mythical killer.'

Gerry smiled. 'Exactly.'

Banks folded his arms. 'Excellent. Good work.'

'Thank you, sir. Shall I keep plugging away?'

Banks glanced at his watch. 'No, not tonight. You deserve a drink. My treat. Besides, Ronald Hadfield's business practices aren't our concern unless they have some connection to his father's death. And after what you've just told me, they probably don't. We'll let the fraud squad deal with him. I think we need to look a bit closer to home. Where's Annie?'

'Gone to see her dad, sir, about working on that sketch of Mia. DS Jackman said Sarah Chen and her housemates knew Mia, too.'

'The sooner we find her, the better. Just you and me, then.'

Gerry got up and reached for her coat from the rack, and as Banks helped her on with it he noticed a photograph on Annie's desk and went over to see what it was.

'What's this?' he asked, holding it up for Gerry.

'Oh, that. It's a photo of a treble clef the CSIs found in Laurence Hadfield's bathroom. Annie had it photographed before she took it down to exhibits. It's in her report, but I haven't had time to enter it into HOLMES yet.'

Banks hadn't read the most recent statements and exhibits reports on the Laurence Hadfield case yet, mostly because he had been distracted by the Sarah Chen case, or by Zelda. 'It's not Poppy's?'

Gerry laughed. 'According to DI Cabbot, sir, she almost had apoplexy at the mere suggestion.'

Banks stared at the photograph.

'It's a charm from a bracelet, sir,' said Gerry. 'Pandora, apparently. Very popular.'

'I've heard of them,' said Banks. But already he felt the thrill of connection, the cogs and wheels in his mind shifting, engaging, grinding out images. Adrienne Munro sitting in the Ford Focus, a charm bracelet loose on her right wrist. Whether it was from Pandora or there had been a missing charm, he couldn't be certain, but it would be easy enough to find out. It was a treble clef, a musical symbol, and that seemed to suit Adrienne, he thought, with her violin and love of classical music.

Then there was the conversation with Colin Fairfax, who had said at one point that he had bought Adrienne a charm for her bracelet. Again, he hadn't said what kind of charm, but that could also be easily checked. If it happened to be the same one, then it linked Hadfield with Adrienne, who was already linked with Sarah Chen through the note in her room and now also through the mysterious Mia. Perhaps this wasn't about drugs, after all.

'Let's postpone that drink for a short while, Gerry,' Banks said. 'Come with me. We've got work to do.'

Zelda loved walking around London in the evening, especially the West End. She loved the lights and the crowds heading for theatres and restaurants, the narrow streets, the noise from the cafés spilling out into the street.

She left her boutique hotel near Seven Dials at seven o'clock to find somewhere to eat in Covent Garden. Though she never worried about it in Yorkshire, she usually dressed down in London to avoid drawing attention to herself, and tonight was no exception. Her clothes were plain and loose-fitting, though not the kind of loose that simmered like a waterfall over her arse as she walked. She wore a padded jacket and a woolly hat to keep warm. No matter what the temperature, though, the streets were always full of people, some of the young girls very scantily dressed. When she had first come here, she had thought they were prostitutes, but Raymond put her right on that score. Though it was a chilly evening, people sat outdoors at café tables smoking, talking and drinking espresso, or stood outside pubs with pints in their hands, laughing at jokes. Sometimes as she walked around the city, Zelda had the eerie feeling that she had seen every face before, that each one was stored in her memory, and she recognised all of them.

Over the past few years, Zelda had become adept at making herself invisible. She hadn't followed many people in her life, but it had been necessary on occasion, and her skill of invisibility had come in very useful. It was more a state of mind than anything physical. She didn't need a disguise, but simple, ordinary clothes in dull colours helped: a brown winter coat, woolly hat, a straightforward gait of someone who knows where she's going but is in no hurry, no signs of a strut or a wiggle.

She loved the anonymity, how she could walk around by herself without being pestered. Every time she went to London, she stayed in a different hotel, a different part of the city – Chelsea, Kensington, Soho, Piccadilly, even Earls Court, Notting Hill or Swiss Cottage. And it seemed there was nothing odd about a woman eating alone in London. At least not in the kinds of restaurants she sought out. She always managed to find some hidden-away treasure, a little backstreet bistro or trattoria of some kind.

Tonight she spotted a tiny French restaurant off Mercer Street which had a few empty tables, and she went inside. A maître d' seated her without even asking whether she had a reservation, and she ordered a carafe of claret and studied the menu. When she had decided on the steak frites, she took out her e-reader and propped it up on the table. She had bought the kind with the origami cover, as it folded over and made a stand for itself, which was perfect for reading while eating alone. She had found that people were even less inclined to disturb her when she was reading.

Zelda always liked to get to London the night before she started working; it was a kind of buffer between the beautiful but remote and isolated world of Beckerby and the depressing reality of her job. It was useful and necessary work, but she couldn't deny that it was often dispiriting, recognising those dreaded faces from her past, from some of the worst times of her life. In this state, tonight, she felt that she floated free of it all, was able to empty her mind of her concerns and concentrate on the words on the screen: Kawabata and the otherworldly Japan.

The waiter brought her meal and poured some more wine for her. She hadn't thought it was the kind of restaurant where the waiters did that, so she guessed he was a gentleman of the old school. That was the thing about these hidden French restaurants, the waiters were almost always elderly men, much the same as at many of the best restaurants in Paris.

As she ate her steak, sipped her wine and looked up at an antique travel poster showing the Eiffel Tower on the wall, she thought of Paris, where she had spent her last year in servitude. Almost anyone she had known the previous few years would have killed for the life of luxury she had led there. But it was still slavery. She was wined and dined by the rich and powerful. Politicians. Bankers. Oligarchs. Gangsters. But she was still expected to lie on her back and please them. And her enforcers were never far away. They made it clear that she was not free to leave the luxury of the high-price call girl's life. Slob and Vitch, she called them. They delivered her to the fancy restaurants and five-star hotels and waited while she did her duty, then they drove her to her flat afterwards. Sometimes they insisted on a piece of the action, too, one after the other, just to put her in her place, before they left her alone for the night. And even then, she knew, they were never far away, always watching.

And Paris was as good as it was ever likely to get.

The only reason she had risen so high in the first place was that someone had seen enough potential in her to know that she was being wasted where she was in the cheap brothels of the Balkans, so he had made an offer for her, which was accepted. She was sold. No more backstreet brothels in Sarajevo or Zagreb, cramped cars off the autobahn or kerbside promenading in Prague. Suddenly, it was all expensive perfumes, fine clothes and top-drawer clientele. But Zelda soon learned that the only difference between these men and the ones she had encountered in backstreet brothels was the quality of their suits. The man who bought her, Darius, once made Zelda watch while his minders kicked a rival pimp to death in an alley in the rain. The message was clear and simple: cross us and this will happen to you. She didn't feel a thing.

No more than she did when she slit Darius's throat less than a year later.

11

'As you all know,' Banks began, standing before the white-boards on Wednesday morning, 'things have changed a lot since our last meeting. First of all, I'd like to welcome the officers from West Yorkshire who have joined us on this inquiry.' Banks paused for a moment while the detectives nodded or waved to make themselves known. 'You've all been allocated your roles and responsibilities, and I know some of you are double-hatting, but none of that should stop you from doing your main job: crime investigator on this team. We don't want any tunnel vision here. All input is welcome. Not just welcome, but expected. And I won't say we have all the technical resources of the various experts and specialists constantly at our fingertips, but the experts are here and available, and they will be working with us. There'll be time for introductions later. What I'd like to start with is a summary of what we've got so far and what we need to know. When we've finished here, there'll be actions and TIES aplenty, so make sure you grab a good spot in the queue or you'll never make it to the Queen's Arms before closing time.'

A polite ripple of laughter went around the room.

Banks turned to the whiteboards, one of which had a number of points listed beside colour photographs of Adrienne Munro, Laurence Hadfield and Sarah Chen. 'On Monday,' he went on, 'DCI Blackstone from the West Yorkshire Homicide and Major Inquiry team brought to my attention the murder of a Leeds University student called Sarah Chen, found dead of serious head wounds in a ruined bothy in open country north of Leeds. The interesting thing about Sarah's murder as far as we're concerned is that she had a slip of paper in her room with Adrienne Munro's name on it. As yet, we can make no other connection between Adrienne and Sarah, except that both were second-year university students, and both were dressed for a party or a night on the town when they were found dead in remote rural locations.

'In a further development, as a result of information from a case DI Cabbot was working on with DC Masterson here in North Yorkshire, a Pandora charm was found by our search team in the bathroom of a house owned by Laurence Hadfield, an international financier who was found dead under mysterious circumstances on Tetchley Moor last week. Adrienne Munro was wearing a Pandora bracelet when her body was found.

'On the instructions of DI Cabbot, the CSIs returned to make a thorough search of Hadfield's drains and found hair samples that match Adrienne Munro's, which would place her even more certainly at Hadfield's house – in his bathroom – recently. I know that a hair match isn't the most reliable form of identification, but it'll have to be enough to be going on with. We'll have DNA on the hair samples soon, I'm assured, as enough of them had follicles attached.

'Pathology indicates that both Laurence Hadfield and Adrienne Munro died within a short time of each other. As yet, we don't know the exact time of Sarah Chen's death, since the post-mortem won't be carried out until this afternoon. Estimates at the scene, though, indicate she had been dead about a week when she was found, which could put her in the same time bracket.

'Last night, DC Masterson and I contacted the Exhibits Officer and checked the bracelet Adrienne had been wearing. We were able to ascertain that there was one charm missing.

We then re-interviewed Colin Fairfax, Adrienne's ex-boyfriend, who told us that he had bought her a Pandora charm for her birthday. It was quite distinctive, and expensive, a treble clef of silver encrusted with cubic zircons.

'So we now have definite links between Sarah and Adrienne, and Adrienne and Laurence Hadfield. Also in the picture somewhere is a surgeon, Anthony Randall, a friend of Hadfield's, who phoned the deceased three times on the day we think Hadfield disappeared. Mr Randall has offered no reasonable explanation for the frequency or content of these calls. The last one, close to eleven thirty in the evening, went through to voicemail, but Randall left no message. We think Hadfield was dead by then. But we still have no idea how he got to Tetchley Moor. When DI Cabbot and DC Masterson arrived at Hadfield's house last Friday, they found his mobile on his study desk. According to his cleaning lady, he would normally not go anywhere without it. This also applies to Adrienne Munro, who left her mobile in her bedsit. Sarah Chen was carrying nothing on her person when her body was found, and there was no mobile in her room, though her housemates say she had one. Is everyone with me so far?'

Most of those present nodded; a few made sounds of assent. Many still looked puzzled.

'Good,' said Banks, 'because it only gets more complicated. Along with Adrienne Munro's name on the slip of paper in Sarah's room, there was what appeared to be a mobile telephone number. It wasn't Adrienne's, and so far it doesn't appear to belong to anyone else. Naturally, we're assuming it's a pay-as-you-go phone, a "burner", as the American cop shows would have it. We have no idea why Adrienne would have a second mobile phone, if indeed she had, as none was found either on her person or in her bedsit. Needless to say, we need more information on this mobile.

'Drugs are certainly a possibility. Both dead girls were known to have been at least casual users, though there is no evidence of hard drug use. Nor do our drugs squads have them on their radar. So if it is drugs, they're relatively new to the scene. I know I said we have no evidence that Adrienne Munro was murdered, but she didn't get into that car by herself, and there was no sign of her possessions at the scene. The phones we do have – Adrienne's and Laurence Hadfield's personal mobiles – have only innocuous numbers, texts and emails on them, as far as we can gather so far. Just friends and family, doctor, dentist and so on, as you'd expect. Hadfield's phone, of course, needs extensive investigation, as it was also used for his business purposes, which could be connected with his death.

'There is also a mysterious presence in all this known simply as "Mia". DS Jackman talked to Sarah Chen's housemates last night and found out that this Mia had befriended Sarah in the student pub close to the beginning of term and then disappeared from the scene completely. The same happened in the Adrienne Munro case. According to the descriptions DS Jackman elicited, we're sure it's the same woman. We have a sketch artist working on this, and we hope to have something ready by end of play today. Any questions?'

A stunned silence greeted Banks's summary of the investigation, but eventually a detective from West Yorkshire shyly raised her arm.

'Yes?' Banks said.

'DC Musgrave, West Yorkshire, sir. Do I understand correctly that the three deaths are linked?'

'We have links between Sarah and Adrienne – the name and phone number – and between Adrienne and Hadfield – the Pandora charm. We have no specific link between Sarah Chen and Laurence Hadfield. We can also link Randall to Hadfield, but not to either of the girls. Yet.'

'Has Laurence Hadfield ever been involved in the drug trade?' someone else asked.

'Not as far as we know,' said Banks. 'I realise there are too many gaps in our knowledge. That's what I want us to work on. We can start by finding out what the phone number meant, what Anthony Randall talked about to Laurence Hadfield and what their relationship was, why Sarah Chen had Adrienne Munro's name. We'd also like to know how the Pandora charm ended up in Hadfield's bathroom.'

'Do we know who wrote the note with the name and phone number?' another West Yorkshire detective asked.

'That's an interesting point,' Banks answered. 'The short answer is no, we don't. But we have checked, and our handwriting expert has determined through comparison that it wasn't written by Adrienne Munro, Laurence Hadfield or Sarah Chen.'

'Mia, perhaps?'

'Possibly.'

'There's been cases of students hooking up with older men for sex and companionship in exchange for money,' said DC Musgrave again. 'For the older men, I mean, the sex . . .'

Banks smiled. 'I think I know what you mean, DC Musgrave. Sugar daddies.'

'Yes, sir.'

'And it's a good point. It's a line of inquiry we're not going to overlook, along with Hadfield's business interests. Both girls were dressed up a bit more than your usual student, even for a Saturday night. And the dresses they were wearing weren't cheap. Adrienne Munro concocted a story about a scholarship to explain her improved financial situation this year, but all the large recent deposits in her bank account were made in cash. Sarah Chen told her housemates she had received an insurance payout on her father's death, along with money left to her in his will. He died over two years ago, so that seems unlikely, but we're checking into it. There may be a very good reason for all this, and if it isn't drug-related, it could involve sex for cash. On the other hand, neither girl had been interfered with in any way, and neither had had sex recently, according to the pathologists, though Sarah Chen's post-mortem might tell a different story. Perhaps they'd been acting as escorts only, something of that nature. Hadfield was a wealthy businessman, so he could no doubt afford a pretty girl or two to hang on his arms if he had clients he wanted to impress, even with a hands-off embargo. Anything else?'

Nobody said anything.

'OK,' said Banks. 'Check in with the incident room as often as you can. We'll be constantly updating HOLMES. Any leads you come across, contact DCI Blackstone or me if you can get hold of us. But use your initiative. Better to get something done and moving than sit around on your arse because I was out of the station at the time. What do they say? "It's better to ask forgiveness than permission." Even from me. Now off you go. Pick up your actions on the way, and let's see some progress before the day's out.'

The offices Zelda worked in occupied two floors of a building on Cambridge Circus. The upper floor consisted of work spaces for the six people, though it was rare that they were all occupied at the same time, and the lower floor was given over entirely to archives and records. The decor was typical institutional drab, coats of jaundiced gloss so dense you could see your reflection on the walls. The heaters never worked properly, and the most modern elements of the space were its security system and computer software.

Through the tall sash windows she could look down on the Circus in all its glory, the crowds massing by crossings, traffic nudging and edging for advantage, horns blaring, the lumbering buses disgorging their hordes, and at the corner of Shaftesbury Avenue and Charing Cross Road, the huge HARRY POTTER poster had been outside the Palace Theatre for as long as she had been working there. It always gave her a thrill to look out, not least because it was the *Circus*, and it was indelibly associated with John le Carré, one of her favourite writers, and George Smiley, one of her favourite fictional characters.

Nobody really knew what anyone else was working on. It wasn't the kind of office where one shared confidences. Perhaps Hawkins, the supervisor, knew, but sometimes Zelda wasn't even too sure about him; Hawkins had his own agenda as well as his own office, glassed off and soundproofed, in a corner of the room. He liked to give the impression that he was an ordinary bloke, despite the public-school education (a very minor public school, he always stressed) and a first in Medieval History at Cambridge. He wore M&S suits rather than Hugo Boss or Paul Smith, and his glasses were always slipping down over his nose, giving the impression that his mind was on some abstruse problem of Byzantine military history, but he didn't miss a trick. He wouldn't have survived in his job as long as he had if he did.

Of course, Zelda's job wasn't entirely the way she had described it to Raymond or Banks, though recognising people from photos and surveillance was certainly a large part of it. The rest she couldn't talk about, partly for reasons of secrecy and partly because it would change their ideas about her. But she had been honest in offering to help as regards Phil Keane, and she thought she could do it with minimum trouble.

'Just going to check something in the archives,' she said to the man she knew only as Teddy at the next desk. He nodded without looking up. She picked up a batch of photographs from her desk to carry with her. There was nothing unusual in visiting the archives. Quite often a new image recalled an old one, and it helped create a new juxtaposition that had to be checked and verified.

If one of Hawkins's beady eyes followed her as she walked past his office, Zelda was aware of it only in passing and never gave it a second thought.

Banks marched through the double doors that linked the police station to the scientific support department and made his way down the corridor to Jazz Singh's office. The department was mostly open plan, and such 'offices' as there were consisted of rows of glassed-in cubicles along the walls. Jazz's was no exception. Banks tapped on the glass and Jazz beckoned him inside. There was hardly enough space for the two of them, but he managed to shoehorn himself into the second chair opposite her. He had to leave the door open in order to do so.

Jazz sat behind a pile of papers, which threatened to obscure her diminutive form if she slouched down in her seat in the slightest. The bookcases that lined three walls were full to overflowing with scientific texts. All around them was a sense of urgent activity, people coming and going, yet a strange hush presided over it all. Voices were muffled, footsteps inaudible.

'One luxury I have managed to acquire since I've been here,' said Jazz with a smile, 'is an electric kettle and a teapot. Fancy a cup of lapsang?'

'Excellent,' said Banks.

The kettle boiled in no time and Jazz poured the water on the leaves and set the pot aside to let it steep. 'I suppose you'll be anxious to know the results?' she said.

'You've compared the hair samples for DNA?'

Jazz shook her head. 'One thing at a time. I'm on it. Tomorrow? OK?'

'OK. But you're not going to disappoint me on the sleeping pills, are you?'

'I do hope not. And I must say, it's a rather interesting and unexpected result.'

'Do tell.'

'Ever heard of methaqualone?'

Banks cast his mind back and found the word caused little reverberations in his memory, but he couldn't quite grasp them. 'I have,' he said, 'but please enlighten me.'

'Someone of your generation might remember it better as Mandrax,' said Jazz.

'Enough of that my generation stuff,' Banks protested. 'As a matter of fact, I do remember Mandrax. It was very popular in the sixties and seventies.'

Jazz nodded. 'It was patented in the US in 1962 and produced in tablet form. Over there it was sold under the brand name Quaalude.'

Banks nodded. 'Ludes,' he said. 'Bowie mentioned them in a song on *Aladdin Sane*. We called them "mandies". There were mandies and moggies, if I remember correctly.'

Jazz raised an eyebrow. 'Yes. Mogadon. A nitrazepam. I see you do know all about sixties drugs, then?'

'Not really, no.'

'Well, Mandrax were marketed primarily as sleeping tablets, but also as sedatives and muscle relaxants. For a time, they were thought to be a sort of wonder drug – controlled anxiety, high-blood pressure and so on. In the early days they were believed to be purely beneficial and non-addictive.'

'They were popular with the hippies,' Banks said.

'Yes. Mandrax soon became a recreational drug and was found to be extremely addictive and dangerous, especially when consumed with alcohol and other drugs. It builds up quite a physical tolerance. You end up needing more for the same effect.'

'People said it enhanced sex.'

'Oh,' said Jazz mischievously. 'And did it?'

'How would I know?'

'You never even tried it?'

'Once.' Banks sighed. 'I fell asleep.'

Jazz laughed. 'Well, I suppose that proves it did what it said on the bottle.'

'Right.' Banks remembered the evening in 1971 or '72 with Emily. One of her flatmates had given her a couple of mandies to try, and she and Banks had taken the plunge. He remembered a wonderful sensation of relaxation and how his senses seemed heightened when he and Emily touched. But beyond that it was a blank. They both awoke some hours later with stiff necks and wove their way up to bed. So much for experimenting with drugs.

'Anyway,' Jazz went on. 'It was discontinued in the eighties and is now mostly manufactured in illegal drug labs around the world. Apparently, it's big in South Africa.'

'What about here?'

'Not so much. I mean, it's not one of the ones you come across regularly. In fact, this is the first time I've encountered it, which is probably why it took me so long to identify it. That and the fact that it's not the only job I have on. Anyway, it's not something you'd normally test for.'

'So would you think it unlikely that Adrienne got it from a doctor? On prescription?'

'I'd think it bloody impossible,' said Jazz. 'As far as I know the only sources are illegal, though there may be one or two corners of the world where it's still manufactured and sold legally, but not in very large quantities, I shouldn't imagine. No doctor in this country would prescribe it.'

'What about dosage?'

'It used to come in three hundred milligram tablets, but that was when it was made legally. Who knows these days? From what Dr Glendenning and I could estimate, Adrienne Munro had around three thousand milligrams in her system.'

'Enough to cause death, then?'

'Not necessarily. That would take somewhere up around eight thousand milligrams. But more than enough to cause coma when mixed with alcohol, which is apparently what happened.'

'The whisky?'

'Yes. And that's basically how she died. The poor girl fell into a coma, and when her system reacted to the poisoning by vomiting, she was beyond waking up, even to save her own life, and she choked.'

Banks sat silently for a moment. Jazz poured the tea and he inhaled the smoky fragrance of the lapsang. She handed him a cup and he took a sip. 'Nice,' he said.

'You need the occasional treat in this job.'

'Any idea where Adrienne might have got hold of this Mandrax?'

'You'll have to check with your drugs squad, but I haven't heard anything about it doing the rounds these days. It's not the new "in" drug or anything like that. As I said, they stopped making it here years ago.'

'So where and how would someone get hold of it?'

'There are illegal labs all over the world – Mexico, Colombia, Belize, Peru. Even Lebanon and South Korea. Oddly enough, some of it is probably produced for fundraising purposes by combatants in the current Syrian Civil War. They do the same with heroin, opium, morphine, amphetamines, cannabis, hashish and other drugs, so why not mandies?'

'That doesn't really help us much, does it?' said Banks. 'Adrienne could have got it from anywhere. No doubt there are people around the campus with enough connections.'

There was also Laurence Hadfield's doctor friend, Anthony Randall.

'Sorry,' said Jazz. 'Don't shoot the messenger.'

Banks smiled. 'No chance. Sorry. Just thinking out loud.'

'But why assume that Adrienne got her hands on it herself? Surely someone could have given it to her?'

'It's true that she wasn't known as a drug-taker, not by anyone. Oh, she took E occasionally, but that's all, according to everyone we've talked to. It seems the whole world does that.'

'Yes, and in my discussions with Dr Glendenning he mentioned that there were no obvious signs of drug use in the post-mortem – other than the Mandrax, of course – and there were none of the tell-tale signs of methaqualone addiction, either – rotten teeth, yellowish hands, gaunt appearance, swollen abdomen. There are other things we couldn't know about, like drowsiness, loss of appetite, unnatural sleeping patterns.'

'Nobody we talked to mentioned any of those things in connection with Adrienne, either.'

'So we can assume it was a one-off, not the result of an addiction.'

'Again it comes back to suicide,' Banks said. 'A bright girl like Adrienne must have known the dangers of what she was doing, consuming that many pills and washing them down with Scotch.'

'Well, then. Either you're right about the suicide, or someone forced her to take the stuff.'

'The doc said there were no signs of forced feeding, like bruising, or a funnel or tube or anything like that.'

'There are other ways of forcing people to do something they don't want,' said Jazz. 'Physical threats, or threats to her family, friends?'

'I take your point. I just don't see what happened as a reliable murder method. If you want to kill someone – especially if you dump the body in such a way that it's found fairly quickly – would you honestly sit there and force her to take pills washed down with whisky? And why would you just happen to have enough mandies on you? Not exactly the easiest of drugs to get hold of, so you've given me to understand.'

'Stranger things have happened,' Jazz said. 'At least it's bloodless. It's quite possible that the killer didn't want to have to deal with the sort of bloodstains you'd get from using a knife or a blunt object. And guns aren't that easy to get hold of.'

'But it screams of premeditation. Say it was an angry boyfriend or someone like that, done in the heat of the moment. Wouldn't he be far more likely to just strangle her if he didn't want to deal with bloodstains, rather than go to all that trouble? And would he even be thinking about blood-stains if he was so angry and out of control?'

'Perhaps it wasn't an angry boyfriend, then,' Jazz suggested. 'Perhaps you're right and it was a cold, premeditated murder. I did come across something in my research that you might also find interesting.'

'What's that?'

'Remember I mentioned earlier that mandies are still popular in South Africa? One of the articles talked of a massive cache of powdered methaqualone disappearing underground there during the last days of the National Party, when apartheid ended.'

'But that was in the early nineties,' said Banks. 'Over twenty years ago.'

'That's right.'

'When you say "massive" . . .?'

'About a ton.'

'Bugger me! Sorry. But a *ton*?'

'I agree. It is rather a lot.'

'Enough that it might still be in use today?'

'Possibly. If it's being kept under the right conditions. Nobody ever found it.'

'So we're after a South African killer?'

'Or someone who visited that part of the world recently.'

Laurence Hadfield, again. The Pandora charm, and now the Mandrax. Banks finished his tea. 'Thanks, Jazz,' he said. 'As usual, you've raised more questions than you've answered, but I'm very grateful.'

12

When Anthony Randall entered the interview room late that Wednesday afternoon, he was wearing a well-tailored grey suit, complete with buttoned waistcoat. He brought with him his solicitor, a hunched, shiny-domed fellow of about his own age, called Brian Liversedge. Annie had never come across him before, and had no idea why Randall should think he needed a lawyer, but she bade Liversedge courteously to sit down.

'You know,' she said to Randall, 'you're not under arrest or being charged with anything. You're not even under caution. You're merely here as a courtesy to help us with our inquiries.'

'Yes,' said Randall. 'I'm well aware of that. All the same, I feel more comfortable with Mr Liversedge present, if that's all right with you.'

'Of course,' said Annie, giving Gerry a sideways glance. Gerry shuffled the papers on the table in front of her. 'Do you mind if we record this interview?' Annie asked.

'I have no objection,' said Randall. He pulled at his trousers before crossing his legs, so the creases would hold, and clasped his hands loosely in his lap.

He seemed perfectly at ease, Annie thought, which made her feel more convinced that he knew something. He ought to be more nervous that they had asked for an official interview at the station after their last chat at his home. She decided not to offer coffee or tea.

After the formalities for the recording, she began, 'When we spoke on Monday, you admitted to calling Laurence Hadfield three times on the Saturday he disappeared. Am I correct?'

'Yes,' answered Randall. 'But your use of the term "admitted" implies that I had been somehow previously withholding this information, or that the omission is in some way blameworthy.'

'Not at all,' said Annie. 'A simple matter of fact.'

'Then yes. I informed you that I had telephoned Larry on Saturday. I had no way of knowing that he had disappeared. I had no reason to think anything was wrong.'

'Yes, you mentioned that before. One of your reasons for calling was to confirm a round of golf for the following day, right?'

'Sunday. Yes.'

'Did you do that?'

'Yes, we did.'

'Which phone call?'

'I'm not sure what you mean.'

'There were three. Remember? 3.59 p.m., 8.02 p.m. and 11.26 p.m.'

'Oh, I see. I honestly don't remember. Probably the first one. Does it matter?'

'We're simply trying to work on the timing here.'

'Then I'm sorry. I don't know for certain, only that it was mentioned.'

'And Mr Hadfield agreed to play.'

'Yes.'

'But he didn't turn up.'

'That right. I've already told you this.'

'Why did you call him at eleven twenty-six, Dr Randall, if you had already arranged to play golf with him the following morning?'

'I don't know. I suppose I had something to tell him.'

'What?'

'I don't recall.'

'You didn't leave a message.'

'No.'

'Why not?'

'I dislike leaving messages.'

'I see. You just wanted to chat?'

'No. There was something I – that's right. Now I remember! I had the time wrong earlier. I had told him we were teeing off at nine-thirty, but it was actually nine o'clock. I didn't want him to be late.'

'So you phoned him back at eleven twenty-six to tell him that?'

'Yes.'

'But when he failed to answer, you didn't leave a message to give him that simple piece of information because you don't like leaving messages?'

'That's right.'

Gerry slid her pad over so Annie could read what she had scribbled on it, though they had agreed on this strategy before the interview began. It helped unnerve a complacent interviewee sometimes. After a moment's thought and a frown, Annie asked, 'What was your first thought when Mr Hadfield didn't answer your eleven twenty-six call?'

'Thought? Nothing really. I mean, he clearly wasn't there so I hung up. Maybe I was a bit annoyed.'

'You weren't worried? You didn't think something might have happened to him?'

'Why would I think that?'

'It was quite late. There could have been a break-in, something like that. He could have been hurt.'

'That may be the way you think, but it never crossed my mind.'

'Surely a few possibilities must have run through your mind?'

'Well, certainly not that he was dead.'

'Was he?'

'What do you mean?'

'Was Laurence Hadfield dead by eleven twenty-six on that Saturday night? You see, that's one of the things we're trying to find out. We don't know for certain exactly when he died.'

'I don't see why you should expect me to know. You're just playing games.' He glanced towards the solicitor. 'Brian, do I have to sit here and answer these stupid and insulting questions?'

'No,' said Liversedge. 'But I'd advise you to be patient a little longer, Tony. I'm sure these ladies will be finished very soon.'

'We'll do our best,' said Annie, smiling. Then she looked back at Randall, who didn't seem quite so complacent. She noticed he was playing with a ring on one of his fingers. 'Any other reason he might not have answered his phone?'

'I suppose he might have been asleep,' said Randall.

'But surely he would have taken his mobile up to the bedroom with him? A businessman like Mr Hadfield would hardly want to be too far away from it, would he?'

'I wouldn't know about Larry's sleeping habits. I suppose he might have done. But maybe he took a sleeping pill or . . .' Randall stopped. His expression said he would take back his last words if he could, but he couldn't. Instead, Annie sat there silently and let him blunder on. 'I'm sorry,' he said. 'I know the poor girl you found in the car is said to have died of an overdose of sleeping pills. That was insensitive of me. But this whole thing is ridiculous.'

'Was Mr Hadfield in the habit of taking sleeping pills?' Anne asked, as casually as she could. They hadn't found any during their search of Hadfield's house.

'I think he did on occasion. He mentioned he had trouble sleeping, mostly because he was often travelling from one time zone to another, so he took a pill from time to time.'

'Did you prescribe any sleeping pills for Laurence Hadfield?'

'Good Lord, no. That would hardly have been appropriate. I probably told him to be careful with them. I don't trust the things myself. I assume he would have got them from his GP.'

'Mandrax?'

'What?'

'Mandrax. Methaqualone.'

'Yes, I know what Mandrax are. I just haven't heard the term for a long time. I very much doubt that was what he took. They've been banned here for years.'

Gerry passed her pad over again. Annie looked at her and nodded. 'Almost done, Mr Randall,' said Annie. 'Just a few more questions.'

Randall grunted.

'Have you ever heard of a girl called Adrienne Munro?'

Randall frowned. 'Munro. No. Hang on, isn't that the ... you know, the girl you mentioned earlier?'

'Yes,' said Annie. 'The one who was found dead in an abandoned car.'

'Mandrax?'

'I didn't say that, sir, and you'd be ill-advised to tell anyone I did.' Annie had known she was flying a bit close to the wind mentioning Mandrax, but she had to see if she could get a reaction out of him. He was a doctor, after all, and he might have had access. The last thing she, or Banks, wanted was for that to become public knowledge.

Randall smirked. 'Well, to answer your question, no, I didn't know the dead girl.'

'You never met her?'

'Not that I know of.'

'And your friend, Mr Hadfield?'

'If he had, he never told me.'

'And Sarah? Sarah Chen?'

'No.'

Did he hesitate, Annie asked herself, just for a second? 'Did Mr Hadfield ever mention her?'

'Not that I recall.'

'How about a girl called Mia?'

'I'm sure I would remember.' Randall turned towards Liversedge.

'She's the only one left alive,' said Annie.

'I don't see the relevance of that remark,' said Randall.

'Just an observation,' said Annie. 'If she had anything to do with whatever's been going on, three people are dead while you and Mia are still alive.'

Randall glared at her.

'I think that's about it, don't you?' said the solicitor. 'We've been very patient, but you've obviously wandered into territory that means nothing to my client.' They both stood up.

'Maybe the question is,' Annie said slowly, 'would *your* name mean anything to *her*? Maybe she'll be able to tell us what's been going on when we find her?'

Still glaring, Randall followed Liversedge out of the interview room. Gerry dropped her pencil and Annie exhaled. 'He's lying,' she said. 'The slimy bastard. He's lying.'

The archives on the floor below were always a few degrees colder than the office upstairs. Mrs Pryce, a large woman of indeterminate age, sat as she usually did, hunched over her desk in her ill-fitting grey cardigan, big glasses enlarging her eyes as she looked up from the computer screen.

'Ah, Miss Zelda,' she said. 'And what can we do for you today?'

'Nothing to trouble yourself about,' said Zelda, waving the

folder of photographs. 'I just need to go over some of my last month's filings.'

'You know where they are.' Mrs Pryce went back to her spreadsheet, or her game of Candy Crush, for all Zelda knew.

The archive was a large area divided into rows of shelving, much like a library, with filing cabinets of index cards against the walls. Eventually everything was digitised, of course, but the originals remained there, everything in its place, until a file was closed. The place smelled of old photo processing fluids from before digital days, and burnt coffee from the pot Mrs Pryce kept on the boil all day, every day.

The archive was divided into sections according to processor, so it was easy for her to go over to her own section and locate the file. Rather than taking the folder back to the front desk, near where Mrs Pryce worked, Zelda thought it more prudent to do what she had to do right where she was, in the stacks.

It didn't take her long to locate the photograph, one of a series taken by a field agent who had been following the man in the photo with Keane, the one she hadn't told Banks about. His name was Petar Tadić, a Croatian thug, and his story began with war crimes, involvement in massacres, ethnic cleansing and systematic rape, then progressed to trafficking in young women for the sex trade, and eventually rising to the dizzy heights of serving in the private army of a Russian oligarch-cum-gangster called Zhigunov Tsezar Pavlovich, or 'Ziggy' for short.

As Zelda knew all too well, Tadić was a cruel and violent man who liked to torture his victims, especially the women, before dispatching them to the hereafter or sending them off to work in his string of brothels. Zelda had had him in her sights for a while, but he could wait. For the moment, it was Keane who interested her. He was handsome, looked intelligent, well mannered, cultured even. She wondered exactly what his role was in the trafficking world. Who did he work for? Zhigunov Tsezar Pavlovich? And what was he doing with a clod like Tadić? Zelda had to assume that it was something to do with documents or provenance, as that seemed to be his area of specialty. But it wouldn't do to forget that, according to Banks, he was a stone killer, too.

The two of them made quite a pair, Tadić and Keane, and not only because of the physical contrast – Tadić small and barrel-chested with a shiny bald head and a snake tattoo running down his neck. She wished she could have been a fly on the wall during that conversation. The field agent hadn't recorded them speaking, or if he had, Hawkins had decided that what they were talking about was on a need-to-know basis, and he didn't think Zelda needed to know. That happened often enough. He was suspicious of her, not quite convinced, she could tell, as men like him always were about women who had suffered in the way she had. Well, they would both have to live with that.

She found the folder she was looking for easily enough and flipped through the images, picking the best one. It was unlikely that anyone would be checking, but she still decided it wouldn't be safe to take the original. Instead, she rested it on an empty space in the shelf, took out her mobile and snapped a couple of images, making sure that Tadić wasn't included.

She had just put her phone back in her pocket and was about to return the photograph to its rightful place when she sensed a presence behind her. She turned quickly and saw that Hawkins was standing at the end of the stack, watching her. She hadn't heard him enter the archive, and she didn't know how much he had seen.

'Zelda,' he said, walking towards her. 'What is it? Anything I should know about?'

Flustered, Zelda tried to shove the photo back among the

others as she talked, but she didn't have time. 'No. Just something I wanted to look up, that's all.'

'Can I help?' he asked, coming close enough to see what she was holding. 'Ah, our friend Tadić and the mystery man.'

'Yes.'

'Decided you recognise him after all?'

'No. I just wanted to check and make sure.'

Hawkins frowned. 'It's not like you to be mistaken,' he said. 'Is something wrong?'

'No, of course not.'

'Did you recognise him?'

'No. Still a blank.'

Hawkins studied the photo, shrugged and said, 'Well, you can't win them all, can you?' Then he headed off to the filing cabinets.

It was just a coincidence, Zelda told herself, but why was her heart still thudding and her hands shaking as she stuffed the photographs back in their folder?

It was another late finish for the core team, and when Banks suggested a drink in the Queen's Arms at about half past seven, nobody objected. The pub was quiet that Wednesday evening, and the four of them found a table easily enough. Cyril had finished serving food but offered to serve up sandwiches for anyone one who wanted them – which was everyone. The plate duly arrived on the table, a mixture of prawn, ham and cheese and salad, and turned out to be just enough to take the edge off their hunger. Only Banks and Annie were drinking pints of Timothy Taylor; Gerry and Winsome stuck to diet tonic. Cyril's playlist seemed to centre around 1966 tonight, like the Jon Savage book on that year in music Banks had just read. Sir Douglas Quintet were doing 'She's About a Mover'.

'Randall's lying,' Annie repeated. 'No doubt about it.'

'The question is,' said Banks, 'what do we do about it?'

'For a start, guv,' said Gerry. 'I could do a full work-up on his background. Find out if there's any dirt. You never know with doctors. They're pretty good at closing ranks and keeping things quiet when it suits them, but if I could find a chink to get through . . .'

'Do your best, Gerry.'

'And let's not forget Mia,' Winsome added.

'Ah, yes,' Banks said. 'The mysterious Mia. Can I have another look at that sketch, Annie?'

'Sure.' Annie fumbled in her briefcase and handed a sheet of stiff paper over to Banks. Ray had got together with Neela Mitchell and Colin Fairfax in the student coffee shop and had managed to turn out what they said was a fair likeness of Mia. The plan was to test it against Sarah Chen's housemates – Fiona, Erik and Fatima – and then show it around the student areas of Leeds and Eastvale to try and locate Mia. Someone might remember her, even know where she lived. Although it would probably be a quicker route, Banks didn't want her image all over the papers or on TV because that could scare her off, and she might well disappear into the shadows, if she hadn't done so already. But she had no reason to do so at the moment, Banks thought, as she could have no idea they were trying to find her, or that they had linked her with both Adrienne and Sarah.

Despite Ray's grumbling and complaining that the way things were going, his next big show would be called 'The Collected Police Sketches of Raymond Cabbot' and might not do his reputation a lot of good, he had turned out what appeared to be a finely detailed likeness. Now all that remained was to test it against reality.

'We can talk to the girls' friends again, too,' suggested Gerry. 'Adrienne's and Sarah's. See if any of them remember seeing or hearing of Anthony Randall.'

'OK,' said Banks. 'It's a good start. Try to find some dirt on the doc and track down Mia. Is there anything more we can do with that phone number next to Adrienne's name Ken Blackstone found in Sarah's room?'

Gerry shook her head. 'I've been trying to chase it down on and off ever since we got it. There's no mobile active with that number, so it's history by now. Certainly turned off, perhaps minus its battery, and sim card most likely destroyed if it was incriminating in any way.'

'I'm thinking that the way the slip of paper read, it was a contact number for Adrienne, but it wasn't her everyday number, and we also know that Adrienne had left her regular mobile in her bedsit, and there was nothing of interest on it.'

'That's true,' said Winsome.

'So what does it mean?'

'That Adrienne had a second mobile?' Annie suggested. 'A burner? Like you said at the meeting.'

'I do hate that word, "burner",' said Banks. 'It sounds so Americanised.'

Annie shrugged. 'Sorry if it offends your linguistic sensibilities. I can't think of another one.'

Banks gave her a look. 'What's wrong with pay-as-you-go? Or disposable? Throwaway?' He picked up a prawn sandwich and took a bite. Sir Douglas Quintet had finished now, replaced by Count Five's 'Psychotic Reaction'. Banks noticed that Cyril had subtly turned down the volume. 'Let's say we're right about the throwaway phone,' he said. 'Why would Adrienne need a different phone from the one she normally used?'

'Secrecy?' said Annie.

'About what?'

'We don't know. You mentioned drugs before.'

'What *did* you find out about the number, Gerry?' Banks asked.

Gerry sipped her diet tonic and consulted her notes. 'It was part of a batch of cheap pay-as-you-go mobiles – not smart-phones, by the way, so no Internet capabilities or Wi-Fi, just phone and text – and I managed to discover that they were sent to Argos in Leeds. The city centre branch on The Headrow. I got a keen young employee there to track down a few more details for me, but the most I could find out was that it was sold on the ninth of October, along with nine others and as many five-quid top-up vouchers.'

'Sold to?'

'No idea, guv. It was a cash sale. But the same person bought the lot.'

'Damn. Someone was being careful, then.'

'It's an unusual number of phones to buy, and not so long ago,' said Gerry, 'so I asked my Argos pal to ask around in the store and see if anyone remembered the customer. The person who made the transaction said she thought she remembered it was a woman, but they were so busy she couldn't be certain. One of DCI Blackstone's team showed her the pictures of Adrienne and Sarah, but she couldn't be sure it was either of them.'

'OK,' said Banks. 'Good work, Gerry. We have a date in early October and most likely a female purchaser, possibly Adrienne or Sarah, though our witness can't say for certain.'

'Sarah was the one who lived in Leeds,' said Annie.

'But why would Sarah Chen buy ten pay-as-you-go mobiles, including one for Adrienne Munro?'

'Why would anybody?' Annie said. 'I'm just thinking out loud. Adrienne could have gone to Leeds and bought it for herself.'

'But it's one of ten phones bought at the same time, by the same person.'

Annie shrugged. 'All we know is that there was a piece of paper in Sarah's room with Adrienne's name and a phone number on it that corresponds to one of ten bought, possibly by a woman, at the Leeds city centre Argos. Hardly conclusive evidence of anything.'

Banks turned to Gerry. 'Do we have the numbers of the other phones bought from the same batch at the same time?'

'Yes,' said Gerry. 'And I've checked. No activity on any of them. It's a dead end.'

'Double damn. Someone's being bloody smart.'

'Look at the timing in terms of what we have so far,' said Winsome.

'Go on,' Banks urged her.

'The phones were bought on the ninth of October. That's just a couple of weeks or so after the university year began. It's also around the time the mysterious Mia disappeared from the scene. HOLMES threw that up.'

'Are you suggesting that Mia bought these phones?' Banks said.

'I'm only pointing out a correlation,' said Winsome. 'But it's possible, isn't it? If she was running some kind of drug courier or sex service. It's the kind of thing they do. Let's not forget that Hadfield left his phone at home when he disappeared. Maybe he had a second mobile, too? Maybe ten people did, and when the shit hit the fan somebody rounded them all up and got rid of them.'

'My head's spinning,' said Banks. 'I need another pint.'

'My shout,' said Annie, and headed for the bar. The place had filled up a bit, couples sitting close together, a group of tourists from the nearby B&B, the usual locals standing at the bar. Bob Lind sang about an 'Elusive Butterfly', and Banks thought he knew what the man was singing about.

'Mind if I take the last one?' said Winsome, referring to the sandwiches.

No one objected. Annie came back with the drinks. 'Where were we?' she asked.

'Still searching for answers,' Banks said.

'Right. By the way, one thing I forgot to mention. It's prob-ably not important, but the solicitor who accompanied Randall, Brian Liversedge . . .'

'What about him?'

'He's on Hadfield's contact list, too.'

'Hardly surprising, is it? It seems as if Laurence Hadfield knew all the local bigwigs and more. Doctors, lawyers . . .'

'And he's not in the crime business, Liversedge. He's a family law man.'

'He was only there for show, anyway,' said Gerry.

'Yes,' said Annie. 'But why?'

'They're obviously thick as thieves,' said Banks. He glanced at Gerry. 'Perhaps we'd better do a bit of digging into Hadfield's other contacts, starting with Brian Liversedge. In the meantime, let's have a look into the connections we already have here. Maybe something will fly out and slap us across the face. Gerry, you've got the most recent HOLMES printout on the links between the people in the two cases, right?'

'Yes, guv. Right here.'

'Can you go through it for us, slowly?'

'Of course. It works best on this diagram.' Gerry laid a sheet of paper on the table, scribbled with circles and arrows pointing back and forth. 'What's missing?'

They all examined the diagram for a few moments, then Gerry told them. 'There's no connection between Anthony Randall and any of the women.'

'Yet Adrienne had been at Hadfield's house. Most likely on or close to the day they both died.'

'And both Adrienne and Sarah were in their best party clothes,' Annie added. She turned to Gerry. 'And we think Randall was lying about not knowing the girls, don't we? And he phoned Hadfield three times on that Saturday.'

'That's a lot of "ands",' said Banks.

'And if Randall was part of it, he'd have a pay-as-you-go, too,' Gerry said. 'So why didn't he use it to call Hadfield?'

'Why would he?' said Annie. 'Hadfield was a mate. He'd be used to calling him on his regular mobile. He wouldn't think of using the burner for that.'

'Fair enough.' Gerry nodded and added dotted lines in pencil between Randall and all three women. 'Quite a tight little coven, isn't it, when you look at it like that?' she said.

'And don't forget the mandies,' Banks said. 'No matter what Randall told you, he's a doctor. If anyone could get hold of them, it was probably him.'

'But Hadfield had the South African connection,' said Gerry. 'Adele Balter mentioned that he visited Cape Town just a few weeks before his death. And mandies are still more prevalent there than anywhere else. I think it's a lot more likely that he picked them up from a friendly doctor or client on his trips over there.'

'So they're all connected, and three of the five are dead,' said Banks. 'Short of finding Mia, which we need to do as soon as we possibly can, I think we've got to put more pressure on Randall. He definitely knows more than he's saying. But how do we do that?'

'Could you get Ken Blackstone to put someone on him?' Annie asked.

'I certainly think we can get Ken's team to help us on this. After all, we're officially together in this investigation. I'll talk to him tomorrow, see if I can do something about it.' Banks paused. 'Winsome? Something on your mind.'

'Oh, what? Yes, guv,' said Winsome. 'I was just thinking.'

'It's encouraged.'

'Well, I know we've been thinking about drugs, and I know I've been one of the prime movers in that direction, but what if it's not? What if it's something else?'

Banks nodded. 'Sex. We've all thought of that angle, too.'

'Yes,' said Winsome. 'What if that was the case? And what if it was organised?'

'Go on,' said Banks.

'Well, I doubt the students and the old blokes who want to get them into bed move in the same circles, so what do you do if you're a rich old geezer and you want to meet a student? Put an ad in the papers or a card in a phone box? I don't think so.'

'An escort service?' suggested Annie. 'There are plenty of sugar daddy sites online.'

'Something like that,' Winsome said, 'only not perhaps on so grand a scale. Say you want a more specialised service, something more select than an Internet dating site. And say you want to be more discreet about it, you don't want to leave an electronic trail. This Mia only ever appeared around the universities at the beginning of term, didn't she, in the case of both Adrienne Munro and Sarah Chen?'

'That's right,' said Annie.

'What if she was recruiting? Or filling orders?'

'For Hadfield?'

'And others. Remember, someone bought ten burners from Argos.'

'What's in it for Mia?'

'Money, same as for Adrienne and Sarah. Finder's fee. She wouldn't do it for nothing. An introduction service. Private, reliable. Remember, both girls were a lot more flush this term, and they lied about why. I've checked into Sarah's insurance and inheritance situation, by the way, and there's nothing there. She got a small insurance payment shortly after her father died, but that was it.'

'And where does Randall fit in?'

'Sarah Chen.' Winsome held her hand up. 'All right. I know we've got no evidence. I know all that. But . . . I don't know . . . call it a hunch . . .'

'Symmetry,' said Gerry.

'Pardon?' Winsome said.

Gerry tapped the diagram. 'Symmetry,' she said again. 'It completes the diagram, Randall being involved with one of the girls. And if Adrienne was at Hadfield's place . . . Maybe they had something already arranged, a get together of some sort, a party, or maybe they were arranging something?'

'Let's also not forget,' Banks added, 'that Randall is a doctor. Doctors can have all kinds of uses, especially in situations where something goes wrong and people need to keep quiet.'

'Between eight o'clock and eleven?' Annie said.

'If Adrienne took an overdose of Mandrax, for whatever reason, wherever she got them, and if she was at Hadfield's house, his bathroom, say, where she lost a charm from her bracelet, even in the bath, as Dr Glendenning mentioned she had been in contact with water . . . Well, he'd hardly want the whole world to know, would he? What better than a friendly medic to sort things out? Phone a friend. Especially one who was also involved in the same sort of dodgy business with the girls as he was. That way Randall could be guaranteed not to talk.'

'And Sarah?' asked Annie. 'Where exactly does she fit in?'

'I don't know,' said Banks. 'I don't profess to have it all worked out. We know she had that slip of paper with Adrienne's name and throwaway number on. At least we assume that's what it was. Maybe Sarah was with Randall? Maybe she saw too much?'

'And Randall *didn't* save the day,' said Annie.

'Exactly.' Gerry brought another sheet of paper from her briefcase. Banks could see it was a map with markings in red pen. 'I didn't think much of it until Winsome just spoke out,' she said, 'but if you look at the map you can see two things.' She pointed to the lines on the sheet. 'In the first place, the Tetchley Moor parking area is just beside the direct road between Hadfield's house and Belderfell Pass.'

They all looked, then moved on to the next line. 'And,' said Banks, 'the bothy where Sarah Chen's body was found is directly on the route south between Hadfield's house and

Bramhope, where Randall lives, which is just along Otley Road from Hyde Park, where Sarah lived.'

They all paused to let the ideas sink in. Banks finished his beer and noticed that Manfred Mann were doing 'Pretty Flamingo'. 'We'd better not get too carried away,' he said. 'Most of this is still pure speculation.'

'Isn't that what our job is most of the time, anyway, guv?' said Winsome.

'I'm not disagreeing. Just saying that we can't go to the CPS with what we've got. Or even to Chief Superintendent Gervaise. We need evidence. We've got to keep moving along the lines we've already established – more pressure on Randall and finding Mia. We can conduct more interviews with Sarah's and Adrienne's friends. Show them Ray's sketch. See if anyone else talked with Mia. See if anyone can place Randall with Sarah Chen. I don't think that whatever happened that day was in any way planned, so if Hadfield and Adrienne and Randall and Sarah were connected in some way, they'd have no reason to avoid going out, maybe to fancy restaurants.'

'Except if they wanted to keep their relationships secret.'

'I doubt they'd shout it from the rooftops,' said Banks, 'but as far as they were concerned, they didn't think they were doing anything wrong. But I don't think it would go down well with Randall's medical council.'

'Well, we have a few more glimmers now, don't we, guv,' said Winsome.

Banks smiled. 'We do, indeed.'

'And while we're speculating,' said Annie, 'there's something else we might care to consider.'

'What's that?' asked Banks.

'If we're right, and if Mia was recruiting or grooming young students for predators like Hadfield and Randall, and maybe even Liversedge, for all we know, then how did Hadfield and Randall get her to do that? Where did they find her? She was a bridge between the two groups, the men who wanted to pay for a young girl's company, and the girls who needed the money for their education. She was the match-maker who put student with old codger. What if it was Mia who bought the phones and handed them out? What if she was the one who got rid of them after whatever happened that Saturday? Shut down the network, so to speak. That way all communication between her, the men and the girls would be restricted to burners.' She gave Banks a sarcastic look. 'Sorry.'

Banks smiled. 'And where are the phones now?'

'If it was Mia who collected them and got rid of them after everything went pear-shaped,' said Annie, 'they could be anywhere now. If I were her, I'd put them in a bag full of rocks and chuck them in a river or reservoir.'

'Good point,' said Banks. 'But we can't drag all the reser-voirs and rivers in Yorkshire, even the one near Hadfield's.'

'We don't have to if we find Mia,' said Gerry.

'So we're back to that,' said Banks. 'We're going round in circles here.'

'No we're not,' said Gerry sharply. 'Sorry, guv. But I just had a thought. If what DI Cabbot says is right about Mia being the one who brought the men and the girls together, then she needed access to both. It was easy enough for her to hang about student pubs and chat with the girls. And when you think about it, second-year students would be feeling the pinch. They'd be a bit more desperate, having found out how tough it was to get through the first year financially. Lord knows, I might not have said no to a sugar daddy myself in my second year.' She reddened. 'No. I take that back. But do you see my point?'

'I do,' said Banks. 'And it makes a lot of sense. Mia obvi-ously looked enough like a student to blend in at the student hangouts.'

'Yes,' said Gerry. 'But what about the men? How did she make contact with Hadfield, Randall, maybe Liversedge, and the others? How did she get access to them? What did they have in common? They wouldn't normally move in the same circles. I'm thinking a posh local pub where she worked behind the bar, perhaps? Or an upmarket shop where they bought their cigars or brandy or whatever? Got chatting, got the measure of them, found out they were lonely and randy, said maybe she could help?'

'I like your first idea best,' said Annie. 'It'd need to be a place where people could be casual, relax, chat, with the barriers down. A posh pub would be ideal.'

'Or a club,' said Banks.

It was late, and everyone else had gone home, but Annie went back to the station and sat alone in the dimly lit squad room listening to the sounds from deep in the building. A laugh. A voice raised. The clanking of the heat pipes. A drunk complaining loudly about being arrested. This business about Keane reappearing had got her on edge, no doubt about it. Perhaps Banks was the one he had tried to kill, but she was the one he had deceived, used, humiliated and betrayed. Over the past few years she had often dreamed of revenge until, like everything else, it had ceased to trouble her day-to-day mind to a large extent, though it still occupied her dreams and those moments when, for whatever reason, her guard was lowered.

She sighed and picked up the phone. It was hard to know what would be the best time to phone Poppy Hadfield. Morning was obviously out, as she was definitely a nightbird, but there was no telling how smashed she would be now, at eleven o'clock. Annie decided to risk it anyway.

Poppy answered on the fourth ring. 'Yeah, this is Poppy Hadfield, honey, what do you want?'

'It's DI Cabbot here. Annie.'

'Annie! I was going to ring you, but I lost . . . you know . . . that thing you gave me.'

'My number?'

'That's it.'

She was at least partially out of it. Better move fast. 'Poppy, do you know anything about Mandrax?'

'Mandies? Ludes? Not my thing, honey. Now Mad Dog, Mad Dog used to lo-o-o-o-ove his mandies. Crazy bastard would pop a couple and want to fuck all night.'

'Where did he get them? I thought they'd been discontinued years ago.'

'Yeah, they were. But this was Mad Dog, honey. He could get whatever kind of drugs he wanted to. God, I do miss the bastard sometimes. Why are you asking me about mandies, anyway?'

'Remember that girl I was telling you about? Adrienne?'

'The one who died? Yeah.'

'Well she died because of an overdose of methaqualone.'

'Poor chick.'

'And we don't know where she got it from.'

'And you thought I could help?'

Annie heard the sound of a cigarette being lit, smoke breathed in and out. 'Something like that,' she said.

'Cool. That you think I would know, I mean. But it's not my scene.'

'You like Valium, don't you?'

'Like it? No way? It's just to take the edge off. Anyway, it's a different thing entirely.'

'Edge off what?'

'You know. Life.'

'So you know nothing about Mandrax, Quaaludes?'

'Nah.'

'You didn't supply them to your father?'

'The old man?' She cackled over the line. 'Was the old man doing ludes? Well, fuck me.'

'We don't know,' said Annie. 'I'm asking you.'

'Nah. Besides, I'm not a dealer. People give me the stuff. That's how it usually works.'

'OK,' said Annie. 'Just thought I'd check. You doing all right?'

'So-so,' said Poppy. 'I'm just, you know, chilling right now. Ronald called earlier. Wanted me to handle the details of Daddy's estate. He seemed pissed off you had him go all the way up to Yorkshire.'

'Yes. He didn't seem very happy at the time.'

'He's a charmer, isn't he?'

'Sure is. Why did you want to call me?'

'Call you?'

'Yes, you said you wanted to, but you lost my number.'

'Oh, that. Yeah, I remember. It's, like, nothing really. Just that you asked me to tell you if I remembered anything odd, and there was this one time I was up at Rivendell for a visit about a month ago, and Daddy's phone went off, only it wasn't his phone.'

'What do you mean, Poppy?'

'Well, you know all those different sounds they make, right?'

'Ringtones?'

'That's the things. His always sounded like church bells. But this was like a tikitikitiki sound, a cricket or something.'

'Couldn't he have changed it?'

'Why would he do that?'

'Just for the sake of it. People do. That's why there are so many different ringtones.'

'Whatever. But no.'

'How do you know?'

'Because I *saw* the phone, too. It wasn't anything like his. He's always got the latest most expensive iPhone or Samsung or whatever, but this was one of those really old types, like just a phone. Probably didn't even get email.'

'Do you know what kind it was?'

'Nah. Just that it wasn't his.'

'Who was ringing?'

'I don't know. He went away to have his conversation. Excused himself. Seemed a bit embarrassed.'

'Why would he be like that?'

'It was a woman.'

'How do you know.'

'I heard her voice. At first, when she said his name. Just over the line. I could tell it was a woman's voice even though I couldn't hear what she said.'

'You didn't catch her name?'

Annie heard a buzzing in the background. 'No. Sorry. Look, gotta go, sweetie. Someone's at the door. Party time! Catch you later.'

And the line went dead.

Banks's head was still spinning when he got home that evening, and he was keen to forget the whole wretched business for the rest of the night. Over the years, he had found that it often helped to stand back and clear his mind, let the unconscious do its work. It sounded like gobbledygook, and he had never awoken the following morning with the solution glaringly obvious to him, but there did come a point when overthinking only complicated the issues.

His recipe for escape was much the same as his recipe for mulling over a puzzle. Music and wine. Sometimes a movie or television and wine worked better if he wanted to let his mind roam freely over a tough problem. There was something about watching TV that numbed a part of the brain and let the thinking bit do its work almost unhindered by having to pay attention. Of course, Banks wasn't thinking about Bergman or Kurosawa here, not even David Lean, but something more like a mindless action film – Bond or Bourne – or a silly comedy – old Norman Wisdom or a *Carry On*. But it was escape from thought he wanted tonight, not working on a problem, so it would have to be wine and music.

The wine was easy. All he had left on his rack was a bottle of Languedoc he'd bought on sale at M&S the previous week. He opened it, poured a generous glass, and went into the conservatory. Music was a little more difficult than wine, and in the end he chose one of his favourite oldies: Debussy's *Orchestral Music* by Haitink and the Royal Concertgebouw. He turned up the volume, then settled back and let 'Prélude à l'après midi d'un faune' work its magic.

It did. Soon he was drifting far away from Adrienne Munro, Sarah Chen, Laurence Hadfield and Anthony Randall, passing through thoughts and images of Emily Hargreaves, his parents, his ex-wife Sandra, his son away touring in America, Tracy, pursuing her academic career in Newcastle, and of all the choices and accidents that had brought him here, to this place at this time. Alone.

He had nothing to complain about; he knew that. He had chosen his path, and on the whole it had worked out well for him. He was good at his job, had been a reasonably good, though too frequently absent, father, a not-so-good husband, and hopeless at sustaining, or even igniting, relationships since his marriage had fallen apart. But that was just life, wasn't it? If Sandra hadn't left him, he would never have been romantically involved with Annie, Sophia or Oriana. And no matter how much grief those relationships had caused him in the end, he wouldn't have done without any of them.

On the other hand, if he had remained with Emily in London, if she hadn't chucked him, perhaps she would have persuaded him to forego the police for some other path, and who knew where that would have led him? But then neither Brian nor Tracy would have been born, and that didn't bear thinking about. Even if it wasn't all for the best in the best of all possible worlds, it would have to do, and there was no point indulging in these speculative pasts and futures. He didn't feel sad, just lonely sometimes. But it was true that much of the time he enjoyed being alone. Like now.

He thought of Ray and Zelda and their new lease of life. Old Ray couldn't believe his luck. Even that old goat Picasso hadn't done as well as he had in the female department. And after everything Zelda had been through, to be loved so much and to have the freedom to live a creative and fulfilling life had to be good for her. Banks wondered if she wanted children. That would be a bit of a problem with the prospective father being already over seventy. But who could say? Ray might live to be ninety or a hundred and see his children grow up.

Banks refilled his wine glass and put on a recent disc called *Voyages,* various settings of Baudelaire's poems by such composers as Debussy, Duparc and Fauré, sung beautifully by Mary Bevan. Banks had talked with Linda Palmer about Baudelaire at one of their sessions, and he had bought Anthony Mortimer's dual-text translation so he could follow along with the words. His school French wasn't good enough, and besides, no matter how clearly the singer enunciated, it was hard to translate from simply hearing the poems sung in French.

He had set his mobile down on the table beside him, just in case anything came up, and no sooner had 'L'invitation au voyage' begun than it rang. Curious, he picked it up and felt his chest tighten when he saw the picture of Phil Keane downloading. It was him, no doubt about it, accompanied by a simple message:

'Best I could do. For now.

XX

Z'

Keane's hair was a little longer and refreshed by applications of Grecian Formula, by the looks of it. But it was him, all right, and it seemed very much as if he was standing on the embankment somewhere near Tower Bridge talking to someone out of the picture.

As Banks studied Keane's familiar face, he thought again of that near fatal evening in his cottage, at least what he could remember of it. The taste of the whisky – which had put him off Laphroaig for years – the sudden drowsiness, the distant smell of smoke, crackling sounds, then voices, cool air, darkness. And as he looked again at the face of the man who had caused all that, he felt a desire for revenge burn inside him. If he did find Keane, if this picture led him to the man, then he didn't know whether he could trust himself not to cross the line.

He texted a thank you back to Zelda, refilled his glass and listened to Mary Bevan sing 'Chant d'Automne'.

13

The following afternoon, a mizzling Thursday, Banks sat in his office reading through witness statements, HOLMES printouts, interviews and forensic reports, trying once again to make sense of recent events. There had been plenty of activity, it seemed, but very little progress.

The one interesting titbit that HOLMES had thrown up was that the amounts of the cash deposits into Adrienne Munro's bank account matched withdrawals from one of Laurence Hadfield's chequing accounts. It was another confirmation that the two were linked, and that Hadfield was probably paying for the pleasure of Adrienne's company. It was sad, he felt, that she had been brought so low. Everyone said she was a shy, bright, hard-working young woman with a desire to eradicate poverty and make the world a better place. It was easy to be cynical about the naivety of the young, but without it nothing would ever change very much. And there she was, cavorting with an old man like Laurence Hadfield. Banks thought of Zelda, who had no choice in the men who had used her and abused her.

Banks got up, stretched and looked out through his rain-spattered window down on the cobbled market square. The festive lights were on in the square, the market cross lit up. It reminded him he would have to do his Christmas shopping soon. He wasn't sure what he was going to do over the holiday period this year, but spending Christmas alone at Newhope Cottage with a plentiful supply of food and wine didn't seem like a bad option. Unless Tracy or Brian turned up, which would be even better.

The rest of the team had headed off on their assigned tasks, which mostly involved showing Ray's sketch of 'Mia' around the pubs, cafés and coffee houses of Eastvale College. A few members of Ken Blackstone's team were doing the same thing in Leeds.

Banks had already heard from Winsome, who had quickly discovered that no one resembling Mia had ever worked behind the bar at Hadfield's golf club. Gerry, who had remained in the squad room along with Annie, researching Anthony Randall, had not managed to dig up any serious dirt on the doctor. He hadn't been struck off, not even close, though there had been a minor incident some years ago in which a young female intern had made a complaint of sexual harassment against him. Apparently, the charges had been investigated and dropped, the doctor completely exonerated, which was hardly likely to happen today, Banks thought. But it was something, and he had asked Gerry to follow up, to try to find the complainant and get the details.

Annie also told Banks about a phone conversation she had had the previous night with Poppy Hadfield, the upshot of which was that Laurence Hadfield had more than one mobile phone, though only one was ever found at Rivendell.

Before Banks got back to his desk, there was a soft knock at his door and Jazz Singh walked in carrying a slim folder.

'Come bearing good tidings?' Banks asked, offering her a seat.

Jazz sat down. 'I suppose you could say that.'

'Do tell.'

'I've finished the DNA comparison between the hair found in Laurence Hadfield's bath drain and Adrienne Munro's, and the short version is, it's a match.'

Banks leaned back, trying to put this new piece of the puzzle in its correct place. 'Short version?' he said.

Jazz waved her hand. 'Just technical stuff, that's all. We were lucky to get enough hairs with follicles to make the comparison. As you know, comparing hairs themselves is hit and miss at best.'

'I know,' said Banks. 'And likely to get thrown out as evidence in any trial.'

Jazz nodded. 'But this is solid. I won't bore you with the numbers, it's all in the report, but take it from me, one way or another, some of Adrienne Munro's hair found its way down Laurence Hadfield's plughole.'

'Could she have died there?'

'She could. Or maybe she just had a bath there. On the whole, I'd go for the former.'

'Is it possible she drowned, or *was* drowned?'

Jazz shook her head. 'No. I thought that myself at first so I went over the post-mortem report again in detail. First of all, there are no signs of bruising on her body, which you would almost certainly find if someone had held her head under water.'

'And second?'

'No water in the lungs. Which she would definitely have had if she *had* been drowned.'

'So we can stick with our original cause of death?'

'I think so.' Jazz paused. 'There was something else in that bag full of gunk the CSIs brought me, and on further analysis it turned out to be a small amount of Adrienne Munro's vomit.'

'You mean—'

'Yes, she was sick in the bath.'

'And she died of asphyxiation due to inhaling her own vomit while unconscious, so . . .'

'So, she very likely died there.'

'Thanks, Jazz,' Banks said. 'That's brilliant.'

And it was, but it didn't solve the case, he realised. If there was a case to solve. Both Adrienne Munro and Laurence Hadfield were dead, so even if Hadfield *had* been responsible for Adrienne's death, there was nothing to be done about it now. Randall, on the other hand, was still alive and well. And Mia.

'With a bit more time, I should be able to find traces of methaqualone in the vomit, too,' Jazz went on. 'If there are any, that is. It's a small sample. That would probably clinch it as far as the CPS are concerned.'

'Anything else?'

Jazz stood up. 'Isn't that enough for you? Jeez, I don't know. You give the man gold and he wants diamonds for icing. No, there isn't anything else. As I said, just the numbers and technical details. I'll get back to you on the methaqualone as soon as I can.'

'I appreciate that, Jazz. Thanks.'

'Just doing my job.'

After she left, Banks leaned back in his chair and wondered what had happened at Hadfield's house that night. When Adrienne had died in his bathtub, had he called Randall to try and resuscitate her sometime between eight and eleven that evening? If he had, he must have used another mobile as there was no record of a call *to* Randall on the phone they'd found in his study. In the circumstances, that was probably exactly what he would have done. And if Hadfield had another phone, a pay-as-you-go, it had definitely disappeared. Clearly, Randall hadn't succeeded in the resuscitation, so had they then disposed of Adrienne's body together? But what could have persuaded Randall, with his career at stake, to help even a friend like Laurence Hadfield dispose of a body? Did Hadfield have something on him?

And then what happened? How had Hadfield ended up dead on Tetchley Moor? Had he gone there with Randall for some reason, and had Randall pushed him into the gully? Again, if so, why? A falling out of some sort, obviously, but over what? Every development in this case seemed to raise a dozen more questions or objections. There were no signs of foul play on Hadfield's body, though both Dr Burns and Dr Glendenning did say that it was possible he had been pushed into the gully. A gentle shove was all it would have taken, and that wouldn't have left any marks. So had Randall taken him to the abandoned Ford Focus first to dump Adrienne, then killed him on the way back? And what role did Sarah Chen have in all this? Why was she killed, and by whom? Then there was Mia.

The phone rang and interrupted his chain of thought. It was Ken Blackstone calling from Leeds. 'Ah, Ken,' Banks said. 'I was going to call you about putting someone on watch at Anthony Randall's place.'

'Already done,' said Blackstone. 'I've got someone here who met Mia. I think you'd better come down and hear her story for yourself. Can you get away?'

'I can make it in about forty-five minutes to an hour. I'll bring Annie with me. OK?'

Banks could hear muffled voices on the end of the line, then Blackstone came back on the line. 'No problem,' he said. 'Apparently, we're quite happy to wait as long as there's another drink in it. We're in the Original Oak. Headingley.'

Banks and Annie made it to the Original Oak in fifty-two minutes, Creedence Clearwater Revival's greatest hits on the stereo speeding them on their way. He pulled up in a side street near the pub just as 'Up Around the Bend' was finishing. Annie gave him a look of relief when the music stopped.

'What's up? You don't like Creedence?' he said.

'I'd rather have a bit of Barry Manilow or Neil Diamond, to be honest.'

'I give up,' said Banks.

Annie grinned. 'Maybe on the way back.'

They walked into the busy pub and found Ken Blackstone with DC Sharon Musgrave, who had been showing the likeness of Mia around the student haunts, sitting in a corner with a young woman, who seemed to be happily tucking into a plateful of fish and chips, a half-finished pint of what looked like lager beside it.

Blackstone shrugged as if to say it was only a minor bribe, and Banks and Annie sat down. 'Leila didn't want to go to the station, but she was happy enough to wait here and have a bite to eat,' he said. 'We didn't see any reason to disagree, as she's done nothing wrong.'

Banks nodded and turned to Leila. She was an attractive young woman with short dark hair and pale skin, marred only by a nose ring and another ring by the side of her right eye. She was wearing a soft tan kidskin jacket over her T-shirt, and the regulation distressed jeans. Banks sometimes thought they must be issued on entrance to all institutions of further education.

'Sorry to keep you waiting,' Banks said. 'But I suppose DCI Blackstone has already told you it's important.'

'It's OK,' said Leila. 'There are worse places to wait. I can't tell you any more than I told her, though.' She gestured towards DC Musgrave.

'It's very important that we find this Mia as soon as possible,' said Banks.

'Like I said, I'll do my best.'

'Can you tell me what happened, how you met?'

Leila sighed and put her knife and fork down. Conversations rose and fell around them, but Banks fixed his attention on her words.

'We met here,' she said. 'Not this room, in the beer garden. It was a fine day near the beginning of term.'

'Not so long ago, then?'

'Couple of months or so.'

'Was it your first time here?'

'No. I'm a second-year student. It's my local. I live down on Bainbrigge Road.'

'So you're here quite a lot?'

'Quite a lot, yeah.'

'And you'd never seen her before?'

'No.'

'What did she tell you?'

'She said she was an English student from Bristol, but she'd got fed up of it down there and transferred. She'd heard Leeds was a good place.'

'Did you ever see her around campus?' Annie asked.

'No. But I'm in psychology. Our departments aren't exactly close.'

'How about the student pub, the coffee shops?'

Leila just shook her head.

'So you got talking,' Banks said. 'What happened then?'

'Nothing, really. I mean we talked about music, and stand up. Discovered we both like stand up. We had a few drinks. Maybe a few too many in my case, truth be told.'

'Was there anything unusual about your conversation?'

'Not really. Just . . .' She gave a shake of her head. 'I could have been misreading her, but at one point I thought she was telling me I could make a lot of money if I wanted.'

'Did she tell you how?'

'Just that she knew people, men, who would happily pay to be seen with me. I mean, she didn't make it sound like prostitution or anything, but I sort of took it that way.'

'How did you react?' Annie asked.

'I told her I wasn't interested in men.'

'And then?'

'She backed off, but . . .'

'What did you talk about next?'

'I can't remember it all.' She gestured towards Blackstone and DC Musgrave. 'Like I told them, I was a bit pissed by then. Only the long and short of it is I went home with her and we spent the night together. I'm a lesbian.'

She said it proudly and defiantly, as if expecting some sort of shocked reaction.

'So she took you to her home?' Banks said.

'Yes. I . . . I mean, I share a house with a couple of other students. There's never enough privacy. Mia has her own place.'

'Good,' said Banks. 'So you know where she lives.'

Leila bit her lower lip. 'I should, I know. I can remember the street but I'm not exactly sure about the house. Like I said, we'd had a few drinks. I mean, it's not something I do every night, get picked up by a strange woman in a pub.'

'I don't suppose it is,' said Banks. 'Did you see her again?'

Leila looked angry and took a long pull on her lager before answering. 'No,' she spat. 'She gave me a phone number, and I called her the next day. It was . . . I mean, I liked her. I thought we really hit it off. We'd had a good time, and I thought maybe, you know, maybe she just cared about me a little bit, maybe there might be a relationship or something.'

'But?'

'She never answered. Not then, not ever. It was like she could see who it was calling and just pressed the red button on me.' She shook her head slowly. 'I don't know why. It wasn't meant to be a one-night stand. I don't do one-night stands.'

'It was nothing to do with you,' said Banks. 'It's my guess she had other things that required her attention. It was just bad timing.' But this was the one mistake Mia had made, the careless moment he had been waiting for, and it had occurred at a time when all was going well for her, and when whatever happened later to Adrienne and Sarah was still part of an unimaginable future. Mia let her guard down with Leila, let her feelings and her desires run away with her, with no reason whatsoever to believe that her lapse would come back to haunt her. But it had. 'Did you ever try to find her?'

Leila seemed embarrassed by the question. Finally, she said, 'I went back a couple of times, hung around the street, hoping to see her.'

'Did you?'

'No. I felt like a fool. I mean, we'd only spent the one night together. What did I expect?'

'You didn't think of knocking on a few doors, asking after her?'

'I thought of it, but when it came to it, I didn't dare. I mean, maybe if I'd seen her in the street I might have plucked up courage to talk to her, but if she thought I'd been tracking her down, stalking her, or whatever . . .' She let her voice trail off.

'I understand,' said Banks. 'You still have the phone number?'

Leila nodded towards Blackstone and DC Musgrave. 'I gave it to them.'

'They're working on it at the station,' said Blackstone. 'Shouldn't take long.'

'Pay-as-you-go?'

'They don't think so.'

'Excellent.' Banks guessed that Mia would have given Leila her real phone number, not one of the throwaways she used for business. He looked back at Leila, who seemed saddened by reliving her night of dashed hopes. 'Can you show us the street, at least?' he asked.

Leila nodded.

There was no sense in them all going, so Banks and Annie drove off with Leila while Blackstone and DC Musgrave returned to their headquarters at Elland Road.

Following Leila's directions, Banks headed back towards the university and turned left off Headingley Lane before they reached Hyde Park, into an area of grand old houses. The street that Leila eventually pointed out was less grand than some of the others, but nonetheless impressive, all walled stone mansions with gables and turrets.

'Pretty much all of these houses are divided into flats,' Leila said. 'I remember thinking it was a bit upmarket for a student, but, well, by then, I wasn't all that much interested in how she managed to pay for it. I just remember it was nice, the furnishings and all. And big.'

'But you can't remember which one it was?'

'They all look the same from the outside, and the streetlights are widely spaced and not very bright. It was dark and Mia was driving. Maybe she shouldn't have been, but it wasn't that far. We were talking, then she'd pulled into a drive. I didn't notice which one.'

'Do you remember the car?'

Leila shook her head. 'I really wasn't paying attention to the car.'

'What about when you left the following morning?'

'I walked home. My head was spinning a bit, and I had a bit of a hangover. I wasn't really paying attention to my environment. I mean, despite the headache and all, I was feeling pretty good. It had been a long time, you know, since I met someone. I was sure I'd see her again. I mean, I'd no reason to try and memorise where she lived. I thought she'd ring me.'

As they stood at the end of the street and looked at the two rows of similar houses facing one another, Banks knew it wouldn't take them long to find Mia's, even if they had to resort to knocking on doors. But before they could make a move, Banks's mobile went off. It was Blackstone with the address. The phone number was registered to a Mariela Carney. Number 36, Flat 5.

'She didn't even use her real name with me,' said Leila
bleakly, after glancing at the screen.

Banks turned to her. 'Leila, you've been really helpful,' he
said. 'And I'm sorry the memories have caused you pain. But
you don't have to stay. We may need to talk to you again, but
DI Cabbot can take you back to the Oak now, if you like?'

Leila shook her head. 'No,' she said. 'I'd like to walk, if that's
all right.'

'Of course it is,' said Annie.

Leila gave them her address then walked off down the
street, shoulders slumped.

Banks could feel the excitement rising as he and Annie
approached the house. There was no list of names, just door-
bells marked with numbers, but as it happened, they didn't
have to ring Mariela's, as the front door was on the latch.

Banks and Annie walked up the next well-carpeted flight of
stairs and stood on the landing, listening. Banks thought he
could hear faint music coming from inside the flat. He knocked
and waited, Annie standing to one side. Slowly, the door
opened a few inches on its chain. The face he saw in the gap
resembled the one in the drawing, except that her hair was a
little longer. Gone was the spiky shaggy student style people
had described.

'Yes?' she said.

Banks showed his warrant card and said, 'Police.'

Her door shut. For a moment Banks didn't know whether
she was going to lock it and try to escape through the window,
but she was only taking it off the chain. Eventually, she opened
it wide and invited them both inside.

14

Mariela Carney's living room was as spacious as a ballroom, well furnished and dimly lit by strategically placed shaded lamps. Mariela – or Mia, as she insisted they call her – seemed to have an eye for antiques, Banks noticed, as she busied herself making them tea: gilt-framed watercolours on the walls, a glass-fronted cabinet filled with vintage porcelain figurines, an ornate mirror, a fine-looking walnut escritoire – but the sofa and armchairs arranged around the low wooden table were contemporary in design, as was the bookcase filled with an interesting selection of literary classics and biographies. Piano music played softly from speakers Banks couldn't pinpoint. Chopin, he thought.

Mia was, as everyone had said, a very attractive young woman with auburn tresses falling to her shoulders, olive skin and expensive clothes – a silky aubergine blouse and light blue designer jeans that showed off her shapely figure without a hint of vulgarity. He noticed the whiteness of her teeth contrasted with her loam-coloured eyes. She wore little make-up. She didn't need to. Her skin was naturally smooth and flawless, her lips the right shade of coral. In a way, she reminded Banks of a young Joan Baez. She had clearly dressed down for her appearances in the university pubs and student bars, but even then she hadn't seemed able to hide her natural beauty. Ray's sketch was a good likeness, though the real thing was a far more classy version. She set the tray down on the table and smiled at Annie. The teapot and cups were Royal

Doulton. Here was a woman who clearly liked the good things in life. *Poise* was the word that came to Banks's mind as he watched her move.

'Isn't this what they always do on TV?' she said. 'Make tea when police come to call?'

'That's one thing they get right,' said Banks. 'Thanks. It's most welcome.'

'My pleasure.'

As they settled down around the table, Annie took out her notebook and set her phone to record.

'Do you mind?' Banks asked, indicating the mobile.

Mia shrugged. Her silk top shimmered in the shaded light. 'Not at all. I've got nothing to hide.'

'You do understand that we're only here to talk to you, that you're not under arrest or charged with anything?'

'I've done nothing wrong,' Mia said. 'I'll answer your questions as best I can.' She rested her hands on the table, wrapping one around her tea as if she needed its warmth. She had thin wrists and pianist's fingers, Banks noticed. She wasn't wearing a watch but a loose gold chain instead hung around her left wrist.

'Why didn't you come forward?' Banks asked.

'About what?'

'The suspicious deaths of Adrienne Munro and Laurence Hadfield and the murder of Sarah Chen. Your name's come up quite a lot.'

'Why would I come forward? I know nothing about them. I didn't mean to be elusive, I assure you.' As she spoke, she smiled, a teasing, flirtatious gesture. Banks sensed Annie bristle beside him. She hated it when women flirted with him. Or perhaps it was the way he always rose to the bait that annoyed her.

'But you don't deny that you knew Adrienne, Laurence and Sarah?' he went on.

'No, of course I don't. Though perhaps it might be more true to say we were acquainted. I didn't really *know* them.'

'Then you surely must have known we'd be looking for any information we could find about them?'

'In that case, I apologise for not realising and coming forward sooner. But I didn't think I'd be able to help you then, and I don't think I can now.'

'Let us be the judge of that. Sometimes people aren't always aware that they know something that could be vital to our investigations.'

'I can see how that might happen.'

'How did you come to know Adrienne and Sarah?'

'I suppose you could say they were clients of mine.'

'In what sense?'

'I introduced them to men.'

'Laurence Hadfield and Anthony Randall?'

'Yes.'

'So Adrienne became Laurence Hadfield's mistress?'

'I wouldn't put it quite that way. A companion, perhaps.'

'And Sarah Chen and Anthony Randall?'

'The same.'

'Are there others?'

'Yes.'

'Why did you do that?'

'It's my living. I run an escort service. A rather specialised one, perhaps, but an escort service, nonetheless.' She paused and leaned forward. 'It's what I do, bring people together. You could call me a matchmaker.'

'Or a pimp,' said Annie.

Mia raised an eyebrow and gave her a withering glance. 'That's not very nice at all. I agreed to talk to you voluntarily, without need of a solicitor, or so I thought, and you start insulting me.' She looked to Banks. 'Do I need a solicitor?'

'Mr Liversedge?'

Mia snorted and leaned back in her chair, cradling her tea. 'I think I could do better than him.'

'Come off it, Mia, you must have known what those men were after,' said Annie.

'All men are after the same thing as far I'm concerned, my dear. But that's beside the point. How could I know what would develop between two people I brought together? I simply made the introductions.'

'Did the transactions you brokered involve sex?'

'If they did, those were decisions agreed to by both parties later, consensually, at their own instigation. Not by me. And without my knowledge.'

'How did you know Laurence Hadfield and Anthony Randall?' Banks asked.

'I meet a lot of men like them.'

'Where?'

'Here and there. Certain clubs they frequent, a couple of posh pubs. Places I've worked from time to time. Company dos.' She gave another teasing smile. 'I scrub up quite nicely, you know. I also have quite an attractive body, too, which, believe me, gets me into plenty of places where I can meet wealthy men. I could be a grid girl, or a darts girl, or one of those girls at the Presidents Club dinner.' As she spoke, Banks took in her beautiful skin, full lips and dark brown eyes, as well as the hint of cleavage her blouse allowed. He couldn't argue with her self-assessment.

'So you work as an escort?'

'That's not a word I would use. It has very negative connotations.'

'But do you?'

'I'm twenty-five years old, but I know I look younger. I was a student myself a few years ago. I know what it's like trying to scrape by on a mere pittance. I went out with an older man. He was a very nice and a very cultured man, not at all like those spotty lecherous boys who hang around the student pubs. Just lonely. He paid for my company, took me places – the opera, art galleries, theatre, even to Paris for the weekend once. I met some of his friends and colleagues. That's how I know there are plenty of men like Laurence Hadfield and Anthony Randall who are more than happy to pay a good deal of money to have the pleasure of an intelligent young woman's company and conversation. If they decided to make it a sexual relationship too, that's their business. They both seemed like decent men as far as I was concerned, certainly not men who would force themselves on a girl, though I wasn't always too sure about Randall. Anyway, as I said, I don't think I can tell you anything you don't know. And I've done nothing to break the law.'

Banks smiled. 'Except practise matchmaking without a licence?'

Mia smiled back. 'Guilty as charged. But I just make the introductions. I don't think that's illegal, is it? What do you call someone who does that? A lobbyist? A facilitator?'

'Whatever fancy terms you come up with, I still know what I call it,' said Annie.

'There you go again. Nasty. Judgemental. You must have a big chip on your shoulder, you know.'

'Let's move on to Adrienne and Sarah,' Banks said quickly.

Mia shifted in her chair and pouted at him. 'Let's.'

'Where did you meet the girls?'

'I met Adrienne in the bar at Eastvale College and Sarah in the University of Leeds pub.'

'You were pretending to be a student?'

'I don't remember ever doing that. I may have said I was an English student, but that's true. I left after my second year and haven't graduated, so I suppose I'm still technically an English student.' She smiled again. 'At the very least, I *am* English.'

'Any plans to finish your course?'

'Not in the near future.'

'So what did you say to Adrienne and Sarah to get them interested in your proposition?'

'I talked to them, found them both intelligent, articulate and presentable, so I told them I knew of a way they could make some extra money. Both were depressed about debts and fees.'

'By sleeping with older men like Hadfield and Randall?' said Annie.

'By spending time with rich and influential – and lonely – men like Hadfield and Randall. How they spent it was up to them. Perhaps by attending parties and charming important guests, if they wished, though both Laurence Hadfield and Tony Randall were more secretive, wanted their relationships to remain private. I suppose Randall was worried about his ethics committees and whatever, and with Hadfield it was his family, the son and daughter.'

'Did they go with only one man each?'

'Yes, of course, as far as I know. That was the plan. I told Adrienne, Sarah and the others that I'd done it myself, and it had worked for me. It was all pretty harmless.'

'Except both girls are dead,' Banks said.

Mia looked down at her tapered fingers. For the first time, Banks thought he saw a hint of genuine emotion show through her slick, glib mask. 'Yes. That's sad. They were both nice girls. But it was nothing to do with me. I generally consider myself a good judge of character, but you know as well as I do that in certain extreme situations, you can't always predict how things are going to turn out. People do desperate things.'

'Is that what happened with Adrienne and Sarah?'

'I don't know what happened, but you said it yourself: both girls are dead.'

'Do you know what Mandrax is?' Annie asked.

Mariela frowned. 'Never heard of it.'

'Methaqualone? Quaaludes?'

'Quaaludes? Downers of some sort, aren't they? Why? I don't take drugs.'

'It's what Adrienne Munro died of. Do you know where she got them from?'

'How would I know that?'

'Your friend Anthony Randall?' Annie suggested.

'Randall isn't my friend, and I have never discussed anything remotely like that with him.'

'Did he supply the drugs to Laurence Hadfield and Adrienne Munro? Did something go wrong? Was he involved in Adrienne's death?'

'Well, something obviously went wrong somewhere, but I doubt that Tony Randall had anything to do with supplying drugs. Don't forget, he isn't your typical NHS GP; he's a world-renowned cardiothoracic consultant and surgeon, as he never tires of telling people.'

'Can't these rich and powerful men just have any woman they want?' Banks asked.

'Ah. If only it were as simple as that. But not these days. No. Besides, that only works with a certain type of woman. Girls like Adrienne, Sarah and the others are different – rare, natural beauties. Innocent, even. Yes, they need money – what student doesn't – but they're not gold-diggers, and they're also bright as well as beautiful.'

'Has Randall been in touch with you since last week?'

'No. Why should he be?'

'Well, you're the only two left.'

Mia started playing with her gold chain. 'What do you mean?'

'We've managed to come up with links between you, Adrienne, Sarah, Laurence Hadfield and Anthony Randall. Three of them are dead, leaving you and Randall.'

'But why would he want to get in touch with me?'

'I don't know,' said Banks. 'That's why I'm asking. Unfinished business? Maybe you've got something on him, saw something you shouldn't have. Something like that.'

'Stop it. You're making me nervous.'

'OK, let's move on. What can you offer that one of those online dating sites or escort agencies can't?'

'Personal service. Discretion. No internet footprints.'

'Bright, attractive young girls for conversation,' said Annie. 'And for sex. Are these men you set the girls up with married?'

Mia sighed. 'Hadfield and Randall, no. Some of them, maybe. I don't ask. How they make their domestic arrangements is none of my concern.'

'Do you give them special phones?'

'They want privacy, so I give them dedicated phones. All part of the service. Only used to contact one another, or me.'

'What's in it for you?' Annie went on. 'What are your motives?'

'Oh, I do well enough, thank you very much. As for my motives, you wouldn't understand, but as I said before, I did it myself when I was a student, and I found it beat working behind the bar in the Original Oak or some similar pub, being pestered and groped by the managers and customers all bloody night.' She dismissed Annie with a flick of her head and turned to Banks. 'Not that it matters or anything, but I'm curious. How did you find me?'

'You were pretty careful to cover your tracks, weren't you?' said Banks.

'I value my privacy.'

'You were careless. You gave out your real phone number.'

Mia looked away. 'Leila,' she whispered. Then she went over to her cocktail cabinet and poured herself a large Courvoisier.

Banks didn't confirm or deny it.

Mia sat down with her drink. 'I knew I shouldn't have done it,' she went on. 'But she was so . . . you've met her, I assume?'

Again, Banks said nothing.

'Of course. You can't say anything. I get it. It's all right. I'm not angry. I'm not going after her or anything.' She shook her head slowly. 'It was just bad timing, that's all. I could have fallen for Leila in a big way, but I just couldn't afford to get involved with anyone emotionally at that time. It hurt to cut her off like that.'

Not as much as it hurt her, Banks felt like saying, but kept quiet. At least he now knew that Mia had used her real name with Leila. Perhaps that would be some compensation. 'So what happened with Adrienne and Sarah? Were you emotionally involved with either of them, too? Were you looking at Leila as a replacement?'

'God, no!' said Mia. 'No matter what you think of me, I'm not promiscuous and I'm not a heartless bitch. Leila just sort of came out of the blue when I least expected it. Knocked me for six. And I don't know what happened to Adrienne and Sarah. I didn't see them again after the introductions. They were on their own.'

'Didn't you talk to them from time to time?'

'Once or twice. Just to see how they were doing.'

'And?'

'They said they were doing fine.'

'But three people are dead, Mia. So what do you think went wrong? What's your guess?'

'As good as yours. Or maybe not, given that you're the detective.'

'Don't you feel guilty about what happened?'

'I feel terrible about what happened to Adrienne and Sarah. They were lovely girls, and they didn't deserve to die. But they did. I don't know how, and I don't know why.'

'You had no idea why Adrienne Munro would take her own life?'

Mia shook her head. 'None at all. As I said, I consider myself a pretty good judge of character, and I never saw Adrienne as a potential overdose, whether by intent or by accident.'

'Do you think it was an accident?'

'I don't know. I assume you have more information on the subject than I do.'

Banks studied her for a few moments. The mask was firmly in place again, and he realised he wasn't going to get anything more out of her. He glanced at Annie, who nodded and put away her notebook and phone.

'Don't feel too bad, Superintendent,' Mia said as she showed them to the door. 'It's not as if I'm getting away with murder. I really didn't kill anyone.'

Hawkins had been behaving strangely ever since he caught Zelda in the archive. She would notice him watching her through his office window and frowning at her as he talked on his phone. He also turned up with alarming frequency at her desk asking about some petty matter or another. It wasn't like him, and it worried her that she might have set off an alarm bell by her actions. Did he know that she had taken a copy of the photograph? Was it obvious from her behaviour?

Five o'clock, rush hour in London in the rain. Not that every hour wasn't rush hour in London, but things did gather a bit of momentum around five. Looking down from the office window Zelda noticed an undulating sea of umbrellas, rain bouncing from their taut convex covers. Lights from Old Compton Street and the HARRY POTTER sign lit up the darkness and reflected in puddles by the roadside. A string of buses lumbered along Charing Cross Road, splashing pedestrians who jumped back as if they'd been scalded and waved impotent fists at the culprits. Shaftesbury Avenue was jammed up with traffic at the Circus and hordes of people stood at every traffic light waiting to cross. The occasional impatient soul made a dash for it, only to be startled by the blast of a car horn, which somehow managed to sound angry, though Zelda knew the sound was intrinsically neutral.

There were people everywhere. People under umbrellas. People going bareheaded or wearing rain hats or hoods. People heading home from work. People heading to the West End for a night out. People trudging towards Oxford Street to do their Christmas shopping. The lights were already strung up over the streets. And despite the rain, Zelda also noticed the occasional knot of tourists, Japanese or Korean, perhaps, standing patiently by a building while a guide lectured them on its importance. Naturally, the Palace Theatre was a big draw. Perhaps they were fortunate enough to have tickets.

It was almost time to go back to her hotel. She would have a long shower and then go out to find a restaurant in a neglected backstreet, perhaps Italian tonight. After dinner, she would go back to her room and read, phone Ray, then sleep. Tomorrow afternoon she was heading back home until they called her again.

Hawkins left a little earlier than usual – most nights he was still there when Zelda left – and almost without thinking, she grabbed her raincoat and hat and hurried off after him. When she got down to the street, she realised she had probably set herself an impossible task, even though she had followed people often enough before. But she spotted his distinctive striped umbrella, and found that if she kept her focus on that, ignoring all the rest, she could follow its progress through the crowds. She stayed well behind him, always the best way if you were the only one doing the following, keeping her eyes fixed on the umbrella as he crossed Charing Cross Road and walked down Old Compton Street into Soho.

Hawkins turned into Dean Street, which was fortunately busy with early revellers and the sort of people who seem to spend their days and nights hanging out in Italian coffee shops. She noticed Hawkins lower his umbrella just before he turned into the doorway of a fashionable café. She crossed the road and went into a pub from where she thought she could keep an eye on the café entrance without being seen.

Of course, Hawkins might merge into the slipstream of passers-by without her noticing when he came out, but that was a risk she had to take. She bought herself a vodka and tonic and wedged herself into the corner that gave her the best view. She unbuttoned her coat but kept it on, along with her hat, and nobody paid any attention to her. The rain continued, blurring the view from the window, and only a few hardy souls ventured to stand outside and smoke. She thought she would be able to see Hawkins when he came out, though, even through the rain-spattered window.

'I think I believe her,' Banks said to Annie over a pint and lamb vindaloo at one of the many Indian restaurants in Headingley. It was a bright noisy place, full of students dining cheaply on aloo gobi, chapattis and lager. 'What about you?'

'I don't think she killed anyone,' agreed Annie, 'if that's what you're saying, but I don't think she's telling us the full story.'

'No,' said Banks. 'It was the same with Randall, too. Though in Mia's case, I think there was a lot of sugar-coating about what she does, and she's very defensive. Maybe Hadfield and Randall did like a good argument about Brexit with young girls, but I'll bet a pound to a penny they liked a good fuck even more.'

Annie nodded. 'We could probably do her for pimping.'

'You were a bit sharp with her,' Banks said. 'Did she strike a nerve?'

'Just strategy,' said Annie, dipping a piece of her naan in the sauce. 'I was trying to get a rise out of her, that's all. I don't suppose you noticed her flirting with you.'

'Of course I did,' said Banks. 'That can be as useful as getting a rise out of someone on occasion. Besides, it's an occupational hazard.'

Annie smiled. 'That's your story and you're sticking to it?'

Banks laughed. He chewed on a piece of fatty lamb which he thought was far more likely to be mutton. Despite the lights and the conversation, the sitar music was unobtrusive enough, and the waiter only appeared when you needed him, if then.

'Those two are all we have left,' said Banks. 'If we don't find out what happened that night from Mia Carney or Anthony Randall, we may never find out at all.'

'Do you think they were involved, the two of them?'

'Romantically? I doubt it very much. We know that Mia's inclinations are towards women. Though I suppose she might be bi. Either way, I don't really see Randall as her type, money or no.'

'I meant criminally.'

'It's possible. The one covering for the other? There could be blackmail involved, too. Certainly the kind of business Mia is in invites it. We think Randall is lying, but we can't prove it, or place him with Sarah Chen. Mia may know something about that. Maybe we should go over his house with a fine-tooth comb, see if we can find any evidence of Sarah's having been there? He's smart enough to clean up, but even the smartest people often miss something. I know Ken's forensics people are still working on trying to coax evidence out of stuff they collected at the bothy. We should be able to get a search warrant for Randall's property.'

'What about the others?' Annie asked. 'Mia said Adrienne and Sarah weren't the only girls she fixed up with sugar daddies.'

'I imagine we can get some more names out of her if we try hard enough, but I'm not sure it'll give us much help in solving this mystery. The solicitor, Liversedge, was on Hadfield's contacts list, and there are plenty of others, but that doesn't mean Mia serviced them all. Besides, even if she did, they've probably got nothing to do with our case, or cases. We're not on some moral crusade.'

Annie pushed her plate to one side and looked at her watch. 'Should we be heading home soon?'

'I think so,' he said. 'Let's have a coffee first.'

They chatted over their coffees for a while, mostly about Zelda, Ray and Keane, and Banks showed Annie the photo Zelda had sent him. Then they walked out on to the road, which was busy with traffic heading out of town, double-decker buses carrying city workers home to Weetwood and Lawnswood, or even as far as Bramhope, Pool and Otley. It was still early evening, dry, and the pavements were crowded with groups of students heading from pub to pub.

As they were heading towards Banks's car, parked in a side street nearby, his mobile rang. It was Blackstone calling from Elland Road.

'Just heard from our man,' he said. 'Randall's on the move.'

'Is he following?'

'Yes. Are you still around?'

'We're still in Headingley,' Banks said. 'We'll stay put until you have some idea of his destination.'

'He's heading your way,' Blackstone said. 'Driving down Otley Road towards Headingley.'

It was about an hour later and still raining when Zelda spotted Hawkins come out of the café opposite. He was with some-one, and they were saying goodnight, shaking hands. She couldn't get a good look at the other man as he had his back turned to her. She snapped a couple of discreet shots through the window with her phone before she dashed off the rest of her second vodka and tonic, fastened up her coat and walked towards the door.

That was when she noticed someone else join the two men. A woman this time. Zelda stayed in the shadow of the pub doorway. From what she could tell through the rain and the layers of clothing, the woman was young and attractive. After shaking Hawkins's hand, she turned to the other man and the moment he half-turned towards her, Zelda could see from his profile that it was Keane. She snapped a couple more photos, keeping her phone in her hand at hip level and just hoping she had it pointed the right way.

The woman linked her arm in Keane's and they set off towards Oxford Street. Hawkins headed in the other direction, towards Shaftesbury Avenue.

Coloured neons reflected on the pavements. Zelda kept her head down and her hands in her pockets and went after Keane and the woman as they continued along Dean Street past the Pizza Express and Pierre Victoire opposite the building site. There were still plenty of people around, despite the rain, mostly coming and going from the Tesco Metro. It didn't matter if Keane saw her – as far as she knew, he didn't know who she was – but she hung back because it wouldn't do to let them know that someone – anyone – was following them.

Then she was dazzled by the bright lights of Oxford Street, their usual brilliance augmented by the seasonal display. The pavements were crowded with tourists and shoppers. Keane and the woman turned left and walked along slowly, huddled together, stopping now and then to glance in shop windows and exchange a few words. Zelda cursed to herself. They were going bloody shopping.

She had hoped she might be able to follow them on the tube to Keane's current home, or at least the woman's, but God only knew how long they would be, or where they would go next. She trailed along for a while, then they turned left at Oxford Circus down Regent Street, still checking out the shop windows, and before she knew it, they jumped into a taxi. She probably had more than enough time to flag one down herself, but the thought of having to tell the driver to 'follow that cab' just didn't sit right. He probably wouldn't do it, anyway; surely that only happened in movies?

She realised as the taxi edged its way into the Regent Street traffic and merged into a whole fleet of London taxis that she had more than enough to think about, and now that she knew there was a link between Hawkins and Keane, and that Keane apparently had a girlfriend here in London, it ought to be enough for Banks to go on.

Besides, she was tired out, soaked through and fed up. It was time to head back to her hotel for that long hot shower.

15

Banks and Annie soon found themselves back in the tree-lined lane of stone mansions at an intersection about a hundred yards from Mia's flat. A light breeze had sprung up, and the high bare branches trembled against the moonlit sky, casting shadows everywhere. Dry leaves skittered across the pavement and rough road surface. The air smelled of woodsmoke and wet dogs.

Blackstone and DC Musgrave were standing with DC Collier, who had been tasked with watching Randall's house.

'What happened?' Banks asked.

'Randall went into Mia Carney's building, sir,' said DC Collier.

'How did he know where she lived?' Annie asked.

'She brought Randall and Sarah Chen together. Who knows? Maybe she invited them all over to a soirée.'

'Makes as much sense as anything in this case,' said Blackstone. 'Besides, it doesn't really matter at the moment, does it? The question is, what do we do about it?'

'Did Mia let him in?' Banks asked DC Collier.

'Hard to tell, sir. The front door was open, so he didn't need to ring the bell. After that . . . I don't know. Should I have gone after him?'

'No, lad,' said Blackstone patting DC Collier's arm. 'You did the right thing. We'll take it from here.' He looked at Banks. 'So what's the plan?'

'Why don't Annie and I go see what's happening? Confront them. Unless you'd—'

'No,' said Blackstone. 'Too many cooks. Besides, it was your case from the start, and you've talked to her before. You're familiar with the terrain. DCs Collier and Musgrave and I will take positions at the front and back exits, in case we're needed.'

'Thanks, Ken,' said Banks. 'Let's hope you won't be.'

'Me, too. Good luck.'

Banks and Annie walked along the lane towards the large house. It looked sinister against the night sky, with its gothic gables and turrets, roof slates reflecting a hint of moonlight. Banks could see the lights on in Mia's flat and one on the ground floor. Her living room was large enough to have two windows facing the street, and both were dimly lit, with the curtains open, just as they had been when Banks and Annie had visited earlier. Banks could see the edges of some of the paintings on the walls.

'What do you think?' Annie asked.

'Not sure. If they're in it together, they could be hatching some sort of escape plan, or some way of covering one another.'

'Or if Randall thinks Mia is a liability . . . Remember, we planted the idea.'

'Yes. I've thought of that, too.'

'Perhaps we'd better just go up and ask them?'

'Right,' said Banks.

They moved closer to the house. The front door was still on the latch. Banks and Annie made little sound as they climbed slowly up to the second floor. Pausing before Mia's door, Banks strained to hear the sounds of conversation, or argument, but the room appeared to be silent, not even a distant hint of a Chopin nocturne.

Banks tapped on the door and said, 'Mia?'

No answer.

He held his breath, Annie beside him. Banks tried the handle. Locked.

He knocked again, harder this time. Still no answer. For a moment, he wondered if DC Collier could be wrong. He said he'd followed Randall from Bramhope and seen him enter the building, but he hadn't seen him enter Mia's flat. Maybe he was somewhere else in the house? Maybe he was visiting another tenant? Then he realised that his reasoning was simply a delaying tactic, that Randall knowing someone else in the same house as Mia would be beyond coincidence. Whether they were hatching a plot together or one of them was in danger, it was time to intervene.

Banks took a few steps back, lifted his leg and snap-kicked the door. It took him two kicks to get it open, then he and Annie hurried inside, where they saw Randall putting something in his bag beside the sofa. Mia was nowhere to be seen.

'Thank God you're here,' said Randall.

'Where is she?' Banks asked, moving forward.

Then he saw her.

Mia lay on the sofa, her eyes closed, her clothing dishevelled, top torn open.

'Move away, doctor,' said Banks, shoving Randall back. He bent over Mia. Her skin was cold and clammy, and she was hardly breathing. 'Annie, call an ambulance. Tell them we need paramedics fast.'

'I found her like this,' said Randall. 'I think she must have taken something. I was trying to resuscitate her when you burst in.'

'What were you putting back in your bag when we walked in?' Banks went on. 'What have you given her, you bastard?'

'Nothing. She was like this when I found her. She must have taken an overdose.'

'You're lying. Show me.' Banks snatched the bag from him and upturned it so its contents fell all over the glass coffee table.

'You can't do that. I'm a doctor. That's—'

But Banks was already going through the contents of the bag, and one of the first things he found was a used syringe. 'Are you in the habit of leaving sharps in your bag like this?' he asked.

'I . . . You startled me . . .'

'What did you shoot her up with?'

'I told you. Nothing. I was trying to help her.'

Banks grabbed Randall by the throat and bent him backwards over the sofa. He could hear Annie talking to emergency services on the telephone.

'Stop it. My back. You'll break my back.'

'I can find it, whatever you used. I'm sure there'll be an empty phial somewhere among this lot. But you can save me a lot of time. It's over now, Randall. You've nothing more to gain.'

'All right. All right! Let me go.'

Banks let go. Randall stood up, rubbed his back then straightened his clothes. 'Morphine,' he said.

'How much?'

'A hundred and fifty milligrams.'

'Jesus Christ.'

'I've still got emergency on the line,' said Annie. 'The infirmary's not far away.'

'Tell them we've got a morphine overdose, that she's hardly breathing. Tell them to inform A&E. And get this bastard out of here.' He pushed Randall towards Annie.

Annie gave the message over the phone, then cuffed Randall and half dragged him towards the stairs. Banks bent over Mia again. He felt for a pulse first in her neck and then on her wrist, but he couldn't feel anything. Cursing his lack of first-aid knowledge, he could think of only one thing to do, and that was to keep her breathing at all costs. Gently, he tilted her head back and began mouth-to-mouth.

He didn't know how long he'd been doing it before he heard the sirens, then the sound of heavy, fast-moving footsteps on the stairs. A hand touched his shoulder, and a calm voice said, 'Move aside, sir. We'll take over now.'

Banks flopped back in an armchair and put his head in his hands. 'I think it's too late,' he said. 'I think she's dead.'

But Mia wasn't dead. Not quite. Banks, Annie and Blackstone paced the waiting area while the doctors gathered around her. Fortunately, Annie had been able to tell the hospital over the phone what the problem was, and that it had happened recently. Opioid overdoses weren't exactly out of the ordinary in a big city like Leeds. Though both paramedics and A&E were prepared, the doctors looked serious as they rushed Mia into the depths of the building on a gurney, and they wouldn't even deign to answer any of Banks's questions about her chances.

'I hate these places,' said Banks.

'Who doesn't?' said Annie.

'They always make me wish I still smoked.'

'Ironic, that, isn't it?' said Blackstone. 'This is probably exactly where you'd end up if you still smoked.'

'Very funny.'

Blackstone's phone purred. 'Yes?'

Banks heard him grunt 'OK' a few times. Finally, he turned and said, 'Collier and Musgrave got Randall to Elland Road. They've got him waiting in an interview room. Unfortunately, he's insisting on having a solicitor present. I told them to let him sit and sweat it out for a while.'

'Liversedge again?'

'Aye,' said Blackstone.

'I don't think he'll be a problem, do you?'

'Doubt it.'

They found a coffee machine, fed it some coins, then sat down with their drinks. The coffee lacked flavour, but it didn't

really seem to matter. It wasn't a busy night, not like a weekend, but there was a fair bit of bleeding and moaning around
the place before one of the doctors came back. She looked
about twelve years old and tired beyond belief. Even the steth-
oscope around her neck looked weary. 'We've done what we
can to make her comfortable and slow down the absorption,'
she said. 'Naloxone to reverse the effects of morphine first,
then activated charcoal to make sure her system doesn't
absorb any more. It was a large dose for someone as small as
her, and for someone who isn't used to opioids. But we're not
out of the woods yet. Not by a long chalk. There's still a long
way to go. Her breathing's really shallow. We'll have to intu-
bate her. Who gave her mouth-to-mouth?'

'I did,' said Banks.

'You probably saved her life.'

'Will she make it?' Banks asked.

'It all depends on how much damage was already done,'
said the doctor. 'Opioid overdoses can be tricky things. They
can cause brain damage, for a start, or coma. We'll have to do
an EKG and monitor her vital signs. Luckily, we know the
exact dose she was given from the phial and syringe we found
in the bag you brought. That was good thinking. And if you'd
been maybe even ten minutes later . . . All I can tell you is that
we'll know more in the morning. My colleagues are still with
her. Don't worry, she's in good hands.'

'We'll be putting a man outside her room,' said Banks. 'That
OK?'

'She won't have a room for a while yet, not while she's being
treated by the team, but if you tell your man to ask for me,
that's Dr Elaine Logan, then I'll make sure he's in the right
place when we send her up to intensive care.' She paused and
frowned. 'There was also a blow to the back of her head.
Nothing serious, but probably enough to stun her and give
her a slight concussion. Did somebody do this to her? Is she

in danger from anyone? Is there something more we should know about?'

'There's nothing to worry about,' said Banks. 'Yes, someone did this to her, but he's in custody.'

Dr Logan started to turn away, gave another low wattage smile and said, 'Just let me know if he escapes, then. OK?'

Anthony Randall had been stewing in an interview room for over two hours before Banks and Blackstone got around to talking to him while Annie watched from the next room through the two-way mirror. Liversedge made the usual noises about abuse of upstanding members of the public. Banks and Blackstone ignored him and focused their attention on Randall. As the building was fairly new, the interview room didn't have the same atmosphere or smell as the ones at Eastvale. It could almost have been a doctor's waiting room.

'It must be your lucky day, Tony,' said Banks. 'You got a Detective Superintendent and a DCI interviewing you. I doubt that's happened since Dick's day, if it ever did happen. Hope it makes you feel important.'

Randall scowled. 'I want to go home.'

'Don't we all?' said Banks, as Blackstone set up the video and recording equipment. 'But I'm afraid it's going to be a long night. That's unless you want to confess right up front?'

'Confess to what? I haven't done anything wrong.'

Banks sighed and turned to Blackstone. 'Like I said, Ken. Long night.'

Blackstone nodded.

'You can't interview my client without a break for any longer than—'

'We know his rights, Mr Liversedge. If you'd keep your interruptions to a minimum we'll get through this a lot faster, and then we'll be able to move on to your part in all this.'

'I don't know what you're talking about.'

'Oh, I think you do. No matter. It'll dawn on you eventually if you pay attention. You ready, Mr Randall?'

Randall nodded without looking at them. Blackstone turned on the machines and went through the formalities of the caution. Their advantage with Randall, Banks realised, was that he wasn't a habitual criminal. He hadn't been through this sort of process before, hadn't become inured to it. He'd never been in jail, and the odds were that the thought terrified him, as it did most people. That might make him lie to avoid prison at all costs, but it might also make him hope that, somehow, if he could explain himself, they would understand and come to realise that he wasn't the sort of person who belonged in a jail cell. Or so Banks hoped. It had happened before, and it beat the usual 'No comment' interviews you got from hardened criminals. But he wouldn't let himself forget that Randall was intelligent and shrewd. And, in all likelihood, a murderer.

'Funny you didn't ask how Mia was doing,' Banks said.

Randall shrugged. 'I did my best to help her.'

'Bollocks,' said Banks. 'To get rid of her, more like. You've already admitted you gave her a shot of morphine. According to the doctor at the hospital, she'd been hit on the back of the head before being injected. Did you really believe you could get away with it?'

'I told you. I found her like that. I was trying to help her.'

'Is that why you ripped her blouse open?'

'Don't you understand, man? She was hardly breathing, and the heartbeat was dangerously slow. Her heart's right here.' He banged the centre of his chest.

'Sounds hollow to me,' said Banks.

Liversedge gave him a stern look but said nothing.

'How were you going to arrange things? Make it appear as if she injected herself and hit her head on the side of the table when she fell?'

'That's what must have happened.'

'You do realise, don't you, Mr Randall,' said Ken Blackstone, 'that our forensic team will be carefully studying the scene and the clothing you were wearing when you were brought here. There'll be traces.'

'Well, of course there will,' said Randall. 'I was trying to save the poor girl's life.'

'What were you doing in Mariela Carney's flat?' Banks asked.

'I just went to talk to her.'

'A woman you told us you'd never met before, never heard of?' said Banks. 'Whom you suddenly went to visit after thinking over our previous little chat with you? Lucky for her you didn't know we'd already found her.'

'I don't know what you mean.'

'I think you do, Mr Randall,' said Banks. 'Mia Carney was the only person left linking you to Sarah Chen. And don't try to tell us you don't know who *she* was. Think carefully about what you say.'

'All right, so I knew Sarah Chen. I lied about that. I didn't want to get involved. She was over the age of consent. We were both adults. Nobody was forced into anything. I know my rights. It wasn't illegal.'

'You paid for her company.'

'So what? I never made her do anything she didn't want to do.'

'Gave you a thrill to have a pretty young woman in your bed, did it? Made you feel young again? Vibrant? Virile?'

'Say what you like. It doesn't mean I killed her.'

'What happened that night in the bothy, Tony?' Banks asked. 'What made you smash Sarah over the head with a rock?'

'You're talking rubbish.'

'But you were with her, weren't you?'

'I didn't see her that night. Obviously, she went out with some other bloke. Tramp like that, you can hardly expect her to stick with just one man. Perhaps he was the maniac you should be after.'

'Any idea who he might be?'

'Me? No.'

'That's because he doesn't exist. Come off it, Tony. Once more, I'd suggest you stop lying and tell us the truth. Our CSI teams and scientific support are very good indeed. There'll be evidence to connect you with the scene in Mia's flat, and we'll find it. There'll be evidence in the bothy to connect you with Sarah's murder, and we'll find that, too. It may take a while, but we'll find it. We may have to take that bothy apart stone by stone but, by God, we'll do it. Perhaps you had a good reason for what you did? Was it self-defence? Was she blackmailing you? I don't think your Medical Ethics Committee would have been too thrilled to hear about what you were up to, would it? Come on, tell the truth.'

Randall folded his arms. 'I don't have to say anything.'

'No, you don't. But you heard DCI Blackstone issue the warning. Anything you don't say now but rely on later in court will go against you.'

'What makes you think I'll end up in court?'

'Mia Carney.'

'Is she . . . I mean . . . ?'

'Whether Mia lives or dies, the scientific evidence won't lie, nor will Annie or me. It'll be your fingerprints we find on the syringe and phial, not Mia's. You didn't have time to arrange the scene the way you wanted it to look. We'll be taking a sample from you, too, for DNA testing.'

'And if I refuse?'

'Well, that's your prerogative. We'll get it, anyway, one way or another. But it sounds better to a jury if you give it voluntarily.'

'Are you saying that if I've got nothing to hide, then I have no reason not to submit an intimate sample?'

'That's about it. But you don't have to get *too* intimate. Saliva will do.'

'But what if I just happen to value my privacy? What if I don't want to end up in some police database?'

'Again, I can't imagine why it would bother you if you haven't done anything illegal, and don't intend to. Besides, all samples are destroyed if you're not convicted of anything. Come on, we're already searching your house.'

Randall jerked forward from his chair. 'You're doing what?'

'Searching your house. Calm down. It's quite legal. We have a warrant.' Banks glanced at his watch. 'The lads should be giving it a good going over right at this very moment.'

Randall half stood and spread his palms on the table. 'You've no right! Do you hear me? You've no right. I'm an upstanding pillar of the community. Tell them, Brian.'

Liversedge just swallowed and turned pale.

'Oh, spare me the theatrics,' said Banks. 'You're a lecherous, murderous bastard. No doubt you expected something like this, so I imagine you've tidied up pretty well at home. Got rid of the clothing and shoes stained with Sarah's blood. Right? Use the washing machine, did you? Well, as I said, our experts are very good, and if it's there, even in minute quantities, they'll find it.'

Randall raked his fingers through his curly grey hair. 'I've admitted to knowing Sarah. She's been at my house on occasion. No doubt she might have had her period, or a nosebleed or something, while she was there, which would explain any traces of blood your experts might find.'

'Why did you phone Laurence Hadfield three times a week ago last Saturday, around the time Adrienne Munro, Sarah Chen and Hadfield himself died?'

'I told you. To arrange a round of golf for the following day.'

'Did Laurence Hadfield call you before eight o'clock to tell you Adrienne Munro had taken an overdose of Mandrax in his bathroom? Did he ask you to come over and see if there was anything you could do? Did you take Sarah with you and ring him on the way? What happened then?'

'This is ridiculous.'

'Why did you call back at half past eleven? Did you want to find out how things were, whether he'd got rid of the body?'

'Don't be absurd.'

'Or did you want to tell him that you'd killed Sarah and needed *his* help? Does Mia know what happened that night? Is that why you tried to kill her?'

'I was trying to save her. Can't you understand?'

'My client is tired, Superintendent,' said Liversedge. 'I suggest we take a short break now, perhaps some refreshments?'

Banks drummed his fingers on the table. He was tired, too. And he didn't feel they would get any further with Randall tonight. Perhaps a night in the cells would change his perspective.

'OK,' Banks said. 'Interview suspended at eleven thirty-five.'

Blackstone turned off the video and audio. Without looking at Randall or Liversedge, Banks said to him, 'Ken, will you arrange for Mr Randall to be taken to the custody suite. I hear they're quite nice and modern. Have him fingerprinted and take saliva samples for DNA analysis.' He glanced quickly at Randall, who was turning pale. 'Only if he consents, of course. Oh, and give the poor bugger a cup of tea and a digestive biscuit. Two sugars, I'd say.'

It was beyond late when Banks got home, and most of the lights were out in Helmthorpe when he drove through the village on his way up the hill to Gratly. Despite the lateness of the hour and the prospect of another busy day tomorrow, he was glad to be back at Newhope Cottage for the night and not in some hotel. Tired as he was, he felt too wired and on edge to go straight to bed. He'd been listening to *The Doors Live at the Isle of Wight* to help him stay awake on the drive home, and Jim Morrison's dark lyric wanderings still haunted his imagination, but once in his conservatory with a glass of wine, he felt like some jazz, so he put on Miles and Coltrane live in Stockholm, from 1960, and settled back in his chair.

It had been an exhausting day, both physically and emotionally, and Banks was feeling his age. His bones ached, mostly from standing out in the damp chilly weather, and the evening's vindaloo sat uneasily in his stomach. He was relying on Zantac more and more these days, and he realised he might have to think about changing his diet. He would talk to his doctor about it on his next visit; then he remembered he hadn't scheduled a visit in a couple of years. He was probably off the list now.

Which led to thoughts of Anthony Randall. There was no doubt in Banks's mind that Randall had tried to kill Mia Carney that evening, and he could only hope the attempt hadn't succeeded. Randall must have thought that Mia had known something incriminatory about his relationship with Sarah Chen in order to attempt her murder. He wanted a clean slate. Only Randall's arrogance could have led him to believe that he would get away with it, even if Banks and Annie hadn't arrived on the scene and caught him red-handed.

He thought about Mia and tried to fathom his complex and contradictory feelings towards her. In the end, he decided that he felt the way he did because of Zelda, who had had no choice about the way she had to live and the way she had been mistreated. Mia had groomed and exploited girls for the pleasure of men, for money, and two of them had died. But the girls had a choice. And Mia had seemed to care about them. A prostitute with a heart of gold? He doubted it. Both she and the girls were probably well paid. It was definitely prostitution, after a fashion, but Adrienne and Sarah hadn't been raped and exploited by unscrupulous pimps. And although Annie had done it, he nevertheless felt equally guilty that they had planted the idea in Randall's mind that Mia could be a liability. The moral conundrums of it all were too much for him to handle so late after such a day. He gulped down some wine and let a Coltrane solo carry him away.

Tying Randall to the attempted murder of Mia Carney would be easy now, but it might be a bit harder to nail him for the murder of Sarah Chen, unless Mia survived and really had something to tell them. They would certainly be able to link Randall and Sarah, and would no doubt find evidence of her presence at his house, in his bed, but whether their evidence would carry enough weight for a murder charge was another matter. The CSIs and scientific support were working as hard as they could. They had already found the stone they thought was used to kill Sarah, part of a pile in the corner, sheltered inside the bothy, so spared to some degree from the elements. Scientific support had found blood and a partial fingerprint on it. If the blood was matched with Sarah's and the print with Randall, they would be on more solid ground, though they doubted there would be enough points of comparison on the prints to use in court. The pathologist at Sarah's post-mortem earlier that day had also found traces of skin under her nails, which could be a match with Randall's, if he had killed her. Apparently, Sarah had put up quite a fight.

As 'So What?' morphed into 'On Green Dolphin Street', Banks replenished his drink.

Just before bed, he called the hospital. It was very late, he knew, but they never slept, did they? It took him a long time to persuade the nurse who answered the phone to let him speak with one of the doctors on the Mia Carney team, but in the end he was in luck, and he was put through to Dr Elaine Logan.

She sounded as exhausted as he felt. 'How's the patient?' he asked.

'She's still unconscious,' said Dr Logan. 'We think we've managed to control the morphine, and we've got her on a respirator, but her heart rate is still too slow for my liking, and it appears she suffered from a slight arrhythmia. Nothing to worry about normally, but in these circumstances ... She's being closely monitored. I've asked to be informed of any changes in her condition. I still wouldn't expect any news until tomorrow, though.'

'Thank you,' said Banks. 'It sounds as if you should try to get some sleep, doctor.'

Banks heard a cross between a laugh and a yawn. 'That would be nice. Not yet for a while, though, I don't think. Is that John Coltrane and Miles Davis I hear in the background?'

Banks was stunned into silence for a moment. Out of the mouths of babes ... 'Well, yes, as a matter of fact, it is. Stockholm, 1960.'

'Ah, that one. Thought so.'

'You know Miles and Coltrane?'

He heard her laugh again. 'Don't sound so surprised. My grandparents loved jazz. I picked it up from them. Goodnight, Superintendent Banks. Sweet dreams.'

Some hope of that, Banks thought. *Grandparents*, indeed. Then before she hung up, he heard the sound of an alarm and an urgent voice over the PA system in the background. 'Must run,' said Dr Logan.

'Is that Mia?' Banks asked, but the line had gone dead.

*   *   *

Banks lay tossing and turning in his bed, but sleep just wouldn't come. He found some Beethoven cello sonatas played by Jacqueline Du Pré on his old iPod and put in his earbuds, but even the music didn't help. His mind kept jump-cutting through the events of the evening juxtaposed with wild dreams about what had happened in the bothy and at Hadfield's house. Eventually he gave up and went downstairs to make a cup of tea and sit in the conservatory. It was almost four in the morning, dark and cold, and it wouldn't be daylight for hours yet. This had always been his worst time of the night, when all his faculties were at their lowest ebb and the silky tendrils of depression started to slink in and twist around his thoughts and memories, wrapping them in darkness. Again and again his mind went back to the alarm and the urgent voice over the PA. Was it Mia? Was she dead? Had he and Annie brought it on her?

He considered his options. He could remain as he was, he could phone the hospital again, or he could reach for a bottle of whisky. In the end, he decided on none of these, but quickly got dressed, went out to his car and set off back to Leeds.

There was very little traffic on the roads. Even the A1 was quiet except for a few long-haul lorries and delivery vans. He passed a couple of patrol cars lurking in lay-bys, the officers either grabbing forty winks or hoping to trap some unfortunate speeder.

The city was asleep, as much as cities ever sleep. Lights came on in windows here and there as people got up early to get ready for work; vans dropped off the morning papers, and the bundles landed with a thud outside darkened newsagents; street sweepers moved at a snail's pace along the edge of a major road. There were even a few pedestrians about, some of them clearly winding their ways back home after a long night on the town. Banks heard a couple of distant sirens, too, before he entered the city centre and found a parking spot in the street near Leeds General Infirmary.

It looked as if he had arrived just after a car crash, as the A&E was swarming with firefighters and harrowed doctors and nurses, and a bloody body was being rushed in on a stretcher. Banks bypassed the chaos and followed the signs to intensive care. The hospital was already a hive of activity, despite the early hour, and he wondered how anyone ever got any sleep. At the nurses' station he asked for Dr Logan, but no one knew where she was. Someone suggested that she might have gone home. When he enquired after Mariela Carney, the nurse he was talking to became suspicious and asked him why he wanted to know. Banks apologised for not introducing himself immediately and brought out his warrant card. The nurse examined it closely, then asked him to follow her.

A uniformed constable sat outside the room. The poor kid looked so tired he might slip down to the floor at any moment. Banks showed his card again, and the PC did his best to sit to attention. Banks told him to relax.

'The doctor's in with her now,' the PC said.

Gingerly, Banks opened the door. The lights were dim, but he could see Mia's dark halo of hair against the white sheets, and Dr Elaine Logan checking the monitors and making notes on a clipboard.

She turned when he entered. 'You,' was all she said.

'Is it OK to be in here?' Banks whispered.

'I don't suppose you can do any harm,' Dr Logan said. She rubbed her eyes. 'And there's no need to whisper. She can't hear you, anyway.'

Banks sat beside the bed. 'Is she OK?' he asked.

'I'd hardly say that, but she's improving,' said the doctor. 'She gave us all a scare earlier.'

'Was that when we were on the phone?'

'Yes. She suffered a myocardial infarction.'

'A heart attack?'

'Yes. Lack of oxygen to the heart muscle, coupled with her existing arrhythmia. Luckily she was here and – well, you heard – we were able to treat her immediately, before any serious damage was done. There may be some moderate damage to the heart, but for the moment she's resting comfortably. Naturally, she's receiving oxygen, and her breathing is still assisted. But what on earth are you doing here?'

'I couldn't sleep,' said Banks.

'I hope you've not come to me for sleeping pills.'

'Wouldn't think of it. No, I just wanted to . . . you know . . . I was worried.'

'About your witness?'

'It's not just that.'

'You have feelings for her?'

'It's not . . . For Christ's sake, she's a young woman. I've got a daughter not much older than her.'

Dr Logan put her hand on Banks's arm. 'Why don't you sit with her for a while? It's all right. Don't worry. She's hooked up to all the monitors she needs, and the slightest change in her will have us all running up here as fast as we can.'

'Thanks, doctor. If that's OK.'

'I wouldn't say it otherwise. I'll let your man on the door know you'll be here for a while. I have a feeling he's been secretly yearning to go outside for a smoke.'

Banks smiled. 'Let him go, then. But ask him to bring me back a big strong black coffee, or I'll have him on the carpet.'

'You're a hard taskmaster, I can tell.'

Dr Logan left Banks alone in the room with Mia. He was aware of the slow, steady rhythm of her breathing, the beeping from the machines, the slow drip of an IV, the various tubes attached to her body. He could also hear, but only just, occasional sounds from outside: someone walking past, the clatter of a tray, a patient calling out for painkillers. The constable, smelling of smoke, came in with coffee and disappeared again.

And so the hours passed. There was a clock above the door, and Banks mostly just sat and watched Mia breathing as he listened to the second hand make its rounds minute after slow minute.

Mia opened her eyes at seven minutes past eight. It may have been a trick of the light, but Banks thought he saw, as her lids slowly lifted, a swirling mass of dark red fire deep in her eyes, as if she were returning from some distant circle of the inferno.

16

It wasn't until after the weekend when Banks was finally allowed back to talk to Mia in Leeds General Infirmary, three days spent on paperwork and catching up with as much rest as possible. According to Dr Elaine Logan, they had carried out various tests on Mia, and though they intended to keep her under observation for a while yet, she was regarded as fit for visitors.

Anthony Randall had spent the weekend in a cell, there being no courts in session to hear a bail application. He had appeared in front of the judge on Monday and been turned down. Though the doctor was apparently of good standing in the community, Banks's account of Randall's visit to Mia Carney's flat and what he and Annie had witnessed there gave the judge pause for thought, and bail was denied.

The forensic evidence against Randall in the Sarah Chen case helped, too. Only that morning had Banks got the results from Ken of the tests on the bloodstained stone they had found in the bothy: Sarah Chen's blood and a possible match with Anthony Randall's fingerprints. Far more damning was the DNA match between the skin under Sarah's fingernails and Randall. So the good doctor was enjoying a little holiday at Her Majesty's pleasure. And the rest of the forensic evidence was mounting up. Circumstantial, most of it, according to their CPS rep, but shaping up well.

Mia was propped up in her bed when Banks entered with a bunch of grapes and a small bouquet of flowers. She still had the transparent oxygen tube running under her nose, but most of the other tubing was gone, and she was breathing by herself again. The heart monitor still beeped a steady rhythm, and the clock's second hand still ticked, reminding Banks of the hours he had spent sitting by her bed. She raised her eyebrows and smiled. 'What a picture.'

He gave her the grapes and arranged the flowers in an empty vase on her bedside table. 'Brightens the place up a bit,' he said.

She touched her hair, which was plastered to her skull. Her eyes were sunken and dark circled, her olive skin a little more pallid. 'I'm sorry. I must look such a mess,' she said.

'Don't worry about it. How are you?'

'I'm feeling a lot better, thanks. Except for the dreams. I'm having terrible nightmares.'

Banks remembered her eyes opening when she came out of the morphine haze, the fires he saw blazing in there. Was she remembering what she saw on the other side?

'Anyway, to be honest, I'm a bit bored being stuck here, but they say they want to keep me in for a while to do some more tests. They gave me a room of my own. Was that your doing?'

Banks shook his head. 'No influence when it comes to the NHS. It's just easier to isolate you this way, lessen any risk to the other patients.'

'Charming.'

'Not that there's any risk to you. Randall is in custody.'

Mia closed her eyes and breathed deeply. When she opened them again she gave Banks a direct look and said, 'I understand you kissed me?'

Banks felt himself redden. 'I gave you mouth-to-mouth, if that's what you mean.'

'The kiss of life,' she whispered, and turned her head away. 'Thank you.'

Banks shifted uncomfortably in his chair.

'I suppose you want to know everything?' Mia went on.

'It would help. If you can manage it. You really should have told the truth sooner, then we might have avoided all this.'

'Oh, you sound just like my father.'

At least it's not her *grandfather*, Banks thought. 'Do you mind if I bring my DC in to take notes?' he asked. Annie was busy with the forensics team so he had brought Gerry Masterson. She deserved a road trip, and besides, in his experience she was one of the most competent note-takers they had.

'No.'

Banks opened the door and beckoned to Gerry, who was waiting outside. When she came in, Mia looked her up and down and gave an approving smile. 'Nice hair,' she said.

'Don't even think it,' Banks said. 'We pay our DCs very well. They don't need to moonlight for you, thanks very much.'

'Spoilsport,' said Mia.

Gerry made herself as comfortable and unobtrusive as possible in a corner chair and readied her notebook. 'I don't know, sir,' she said. 'You don't pay *that* much.' She set her phone down to record the conversation. Mia wasn't under arrest, merely 'helping with inquiries' but even so, this would avoid having to go over it all again at the station when she was released from hospital, and it might help with the case against Randall.

'Could you get me some water first?' Mia asked. 'It's in the cabinet under the flowers.'

Banks took out a bottle of spring water and looked for a glass.

'It's all right,' Mia said, taking the bottle from him and unscrewing the cap. 'I don't need a straw.' And she proceeded to glug down half the bottle. 'And in case you're worried, there's a bedpan in the toilet.'

'It's good to see you haven't lost your sense of humour.'

'Who said I'm joking? Where do you want me to start?'

'With the other night,' said Banks. 'Randall. What happened?'

'I heard someone knocking at my door. The front door must have been on the latch. I've told the bloke in 1A about it, but he takes no notice. Anyway, I wasn't expecting anyone, and when I answered it I saw it was Randall. I remembered what you'd said about us being the only ones left, but he pushed his way in.'

'You didn't have the chain on?'

Mia shook her head. 'No. Not since you left.'

'How did Randall know where you lived?'

'I'd given him my address ages ago, when he hooked up with Sarah. Just in case of emergencies. It's all part of the service. Anyway, Randall was in a bit of a state.'

'What did he do?'

'At first he was just ranting on about his reputation and how his association with me could ruin it. I told him I didn't consider him to be associated with me, but that only made him worse. He grabbed my blouse and it tore. Then he grabbed my breast. To tell the truth, I didn't know whether he wanted to rape me or murder me. I'm not sure he knew, himself.'

'He wanted you out of the way,' said Banks. 'He didn't know we'd found you, but with you around there was always the risk of the full story coming out. Unless there's more to it. Unless you were a witness. *Were* you a witness?'

Mia shook her head. 'To poor Sarah's murder? No. But he did it. I know he did it.'

'Tell us what happened next.'

'Things get very hazy. I turned away, and he hit me with something. I think I passed out. I felt a sharp pain in my arm, but I couldn't do anything about it. Then I felt like I was float-ing. I had the most wonderful sense of well-being until ...' She put her hand to her throat. 'I suddenly couldn't breathe, then I couldn't even move. I was just so limp. Then I suppose you came in. My knight in shining armour. And you kissed me.'

Gerry gave Banks a questioning glance and pulled a face.

'I gave her mouth-to-mouth resuscitation, DC Masterson,' said Banks. 'It's text book.'

Mia looked at Gerry and laughed. 'Get him. But he was. Really. Your boss was my knight in shining armour. And Annie, of course. His gallant page.' She paused and eased herself back into the bed as if the laughter had tired her. 'After that it's all vague, just the hospital, machines, tubes down my throat, in my arms, up my whatever, and needles. Elaine – that's Dr Logan – says it was touch and go.'

'Anthony Randall injected you with a high dose of morphine, which can cause you to stop breathing, and he tried to tell us that it had happened before he arrived, that you had done it to yourself and he was trying to save your life. Now can you tell us about what really happened on Saturday night two weeks ago?'

Mia drank some more water. 'It started out as just an ordinary day,' she said. 'Like all the rest. But I suppose I already knew it might turn into something different. Nothing like what it did become, but . . . just . . . difficult.'

'How did you know?'

Mia took a deep breath. 'As you know, I supply all my clients, the girls and the men, with dedicated mobiles. Burners, if you like. So the couples could communicate with one another as they wished, and with me, without anyone else knowing. You wouldn't believe how many erring husbands, or boyfriends, get caught out by their mobiles.'

'Both Sarah and Adrienne had left their own mobiles at home,' said Banks. 'That seemed odd, an indication there was something wrong.'

Mia nodded. 'I advised them to take only the burners when they were meeting,' she said. 'It's easy to make mistakes, get mixed up. Better to be safe than sorry.'

'What happened to those phones?' Banks asked.

'I'll tell you about that later. Another aspect of my role was to reassure the girls that I would always be there for them if they needed me. That they didn't have to put up with anything they didn't want. I know that sounds strange, given the nature of their relationships, but some men . . . well, let's just say they don't like to stop at what we might consider natural or normal relations. If the girls had any problems, they knew they could come to me. The men, too, but their problems would be of a different kind, and to be honest, they never had any complaints. I'm not saying I could always help, and looking back I think I let Adrienne down badly.'

'How?'

'You have to understand that Adrienne and Sarah were very different personalities. Sarah was outgoing, a bit brazen, up for anything, scared of nothing. Adrienne was shy, more reserved and pretty conservative sexually. They were both incredibly sexy, but for different reasons. There was an innocence about Adrienne and a sort of earthy *joie de vivre* about Sarah.' Mia drank more water. 'As you know, Laurence Hadfield and Anthony Randall were mates. Apparently, they went out for dinner together once with the girls, some swank restaurant in Manchester. Well, Adrienne caught Randall's eye – he was always a bit of a sadist, I thought, and despoiling innocence would probably be right up his street – and Hadfield developed an itch for eastern promise.'

'Let me get this straight,' said Banks. 'Both girls were sleeping with their partners, right? Having sex with them?'

'Yes. But, as I said, Adrienne had this aura of innocence. As a good deal of sex has to do with fantasy, Randall could *imagine* himself despoiling her innocence. I'm not saying he was into rape or S&M or anything, except in his fantasies.'

Banks glanced at Gerry to see how she was doing. She gave him a nod, which let him know she was keeping up fine. And no doubt understanding it. 'Go on,' he said to Mia.

'Randall and Hadfield came up with the idea of a sort of girlfriend-swapping scenario. But first they wanted to watch the girls frolic by themselves for a while, just to get their juices going, you might say. Adrienne rang me when Hadfield was putting pressure on her to get involved with this foursome scheme, and it made her nervous.'

'And your role was?'

Mia looked away. 'I'm ashamed to say that I talked her into it. I'm not proud of myself, but Adrienne lacked confidence. She was a true natural beauty, but it was a hard job talking her into having a sugar daddy in the first place. It was the money that did it, really. The poor kid was broke and she wanted to finish her studies. She also wanted to go off to Africa or somewhere and see wildlife, help the starving people. Adrienne was a humanitarian. She felt she was sacrificing something, her innocence, whatever, for her ideals. I grasped that when I first tried to persuade her to try the life, and I thought if I had succeeded there, I could succeed with this other thing. All she needed was a gentle nudge in the right direction. After all, what did it amount to? A roll in the hay with Sarah wouldn't have been so bad, then she just had to fuck Randall. Well, I could think of many better things, like having a root canal, but there you go. And there was a nice bonus in it for everyone. But Adrienne was already feeling bad about what she was doing. You know, being Hadfield's sugar baby. Just how bad I didn't quite realise. She just ... It wasn't her ... Nobody forced her. She forced herself, and it damaged her.' Mia shook her head. 'I should have seen that coming, done something about it. Do you know, I think she died of shame.'

'Did you have feelings for Adrienne, Mia?'

'I ... I ...'

'Be honest. We're not here to judge you.'

Mia was silent for a while, chewing on her lower lip. Finally, she nodded. 'I liked her, yes. Maybe more. But it couldn't be more. I can't have feelings for the girls I recruit. Or the men. I'm bi, but Adrienne wasn't. Looking back, I shouldn't have tried to persuade her. I should have just told her to forget the whole thing. In fact, I shouldn't even have convinced her to go with Hadfield in the first place.'

'Easy to say with twenty-twenty hindsight.'

'Well, given what happened . . . I mean . . . I just told her to take a couple of pills to relax, you know, like when you go to the dentist's sometimes.'

'What pills?'

'I gave her two Valium. I have them on prescription.'

'From Randall?'

'God, no. I wouldn't go to him for an ingrown toenail. Besides, like I said, he's not a GP.'

'Just two Valium?'

'Yes. I honestly don't do drugs. Nor do my girls, at least not if I can help it. I try to be very careful about that. Sometimes, though, with the kind of thing they were planning, you just need something to take you out of yourself.'

'What did she do with them?'

'Took them, I suppose. The next time I saw her she was dead. But it can't have been because of two Valium.'

'Back up a bit, Mia.'

Mia sniffled, and Banks passed her a tissue. 'Look at me,' she said. 'Behaving like a silly little girl.'

'It's OK. Take your time.'

'I persuaded her to go through with it. That's all there is to it. I persuaded her, and she ended up dead. I also gave Sarah Adrienne's number so they could talk it through and feel more comfortable together. Like I said, Sarah was so much more confident than Adrienne. It was all set to take place at Laurence Hadfield's house on that Saturday night.'

'What time?'

'I don't know the exact time. Evening.'

'So what went wrong?'

'I got a call from Hadfield at about nine. He said something had gone terribly wrong and I had to get over to his place right away. He wouldn't tell me what it was, not even over the burner. Naturally, I was worried something had happened to Adrienne or Sarah, so I headed out there.'

'And what did you find?'

'Randall and Sarah were there with Hadfield. I didn't see Adrienne. Sarah was in hysterics, saying we had to call the police and an ambulance, and Randall and Hadfield were telling her not to be a fool, it was too late for that. I asked what had happened, and Hadfield told me Adrienne had taken some of his pills from the bathroom cabinet and must have had a bad reaction. Mandrax. He has trouble sleeping and he gets them from a doctor he knows in Cape Town. Adrienne also had a bottle of whisky with her. She never usually drank much. She was probably trying to psych herself up for the show.'

'Where was she?'

'Upstairs. In the big bathroom. Apparently, she'd been there a long time, too long, and both Randall and Hadfield were getting impatient, so they sent Sarah up to talk to her. It was Sarah who found her body. Hadfield told me Adrienne had been edgy all evening and had even told him she wasn't sure she could go through with it.'

'Are you sure he didn't offer her the pills and booze to make her comply, the way you offered her Valium?'

'No, I'm not sure. I wasn't there earlier. But what does it matter? They're both dead. All I knew was that she'd taken them.'

'What happened next?'

'I tried to calm Sarah down, but I couldn't. There was no way. She was in a hell of a state. In the end, Randall took her out to the car and they drove off. I'm sure her carrying on must have sent him over the edge, and he killed her, but I can't prove it. I wish I could.'

In all likelihood, Mia was right, Banks thought. When they got to the bothy off the country lane, Randall had had enough of Sarah's hysterics and threats of calling the police, so he let her out of the car. She ran off, he went after her, then they argued some more and he killed her. Annie had mentioned seeing evidence of his quick temper in her and Gerry's first interview with him.

'Don't worry about that,' Banks said. 'We'll make sure Randall pays for what he did. He's got more than the Medical Ethics Committee to deal with now. Why didn't he try to help Adrienne? He is a doctor, after all.'

'He did,' Mia said. 'Before I got there. He said he'd been up and checked, but he was positive she was dead, and there was nothing anyone could do about it.'

'So what was your role?'

'Cleaner-upper, basically. Someone had to take charge. They were all in shock. After Randall and Sarah had gone, I got Laurence to sit down with a glass of whisky and went up to the bathroom.' Her breath seemed to catch in her throat. She put her hand to her chest.

'All right?' Banks said. Mia nodded. 'Take a few deep breaths. Can you go on, or do you want me to fetch the doctor?'

Mia took some deep breaths then nodded again. 'No. I'm OK. It was just so awful.'

'Can you tell us what you found in the bathroom?'

'Adrienne was lying in a bath full of water. It was lukewarm by then. There was a bottle smashed on the floor and a smell of whisky. God, I hate the smell of whisky.'

Banks remembered Keane and the Laphroaig. 'I can understand that,' he said.

'It was clear even to me that Adrienne was dead. Her skin was almost white, her eyes were open. I took a shaving mirror from the washstand and held it to her lips. Nothing. There was a little trickle of vomit from the corner of her mouth, down to her chest.'

'What did you do next?'

'I went back down to Laurence and asked him what he wanted to do. He said we had to move her, get her out of his house. He seemed fairly calm about it, but I could tell there was going to be no arguing with him.'

'So you went along?'

Mia nodded. 'I got a large bin bag from him and cleaned up the bathroom, all the glass, and washed off the whisky. Then I drained the tub and Laurence helped me get Adrienne out onto a plastic sheet. After that, I washed out the tub and picked up her clothes and stuff where she'd left it on the chair. I dried her off as best I could. We dressed her downstairs. It wasn't easy, but she hadn't . . . you know, her body wasn't stiff or anything, so we got it done. Put her clothes and her bracelet back on.'

'It was missing a charm,' said Banks.

'Oh. I didn't notice that. It must have come off when she took it off to get in the bath.'

'Go on.'

'I put all her other stuff in the bin bag. And the burners. It was a bit of a nasty night out, fog mostly, but it wasn't impossible. Laurence said we should bury her somewhere, but I said we should just take her into the country and put her somewhere she'd be found before too long. That it would be cruel to bury her and have no one know where she was or what had happened to her. He was worried there'd be evidence linking him to her death, but I persuaded him that the bath would have washed everything away, and it would look like a suicide anyway, which he said he thought it was, and in the end he agreed we'd leave her somewhere more open.'

Banks nodded. 'It did look like a suicide, except we figured out pretty quickly that she didn't die in the car. No sign of the whisky, for a start and, of course, we wondered how she had got there.'

'I admit we weren't exactly thinking too clearly. I just wanted her to be found. I mean, I knew you wouldn't just assume it was her car, that you'd check and find the owner, but I thought you might accept that she'd just taken an overdose and wandered into the wilderness to die.'

'People don't really do that in real life, Mia.'

'Maybe I've got too much imagination. Anyway, we were just driving around, and I saw that car on Belderfell with the POLICE AWARE sign. I'd seen them before and I knew it could be a few days before anyone got around to it. I'd like to say I was struck with the irony of it, but I wasn't. I wasn't in a mood for irony at all. We got her into the driver's seat of the car – we were both wearing gloves – then we set off back.'

'What about Hadfield?'

Mia rubbed her eyes. 'Laurence was in a really bad state when it was done. I think it just hit him all at once, you know, how real it was. Before that I think he'd been living off nervous energy, but when it was done and the body was gone, he started to get restless. He said he wanted to be sick, and we were near Tetchley Moor, so I pulled into the car park there and he got out. Then he said he needed some air, to think things over, and he headed out onto the moor.'

'Were you worried that he might decide he needed to get rid of you?

Mia glanced sharply at Banks. 'No. Never. We were accomplices by then, in whatever we'd done. I couldn't incriminate him without incriminating myself. We'd agreed to hush everything up. I had the bin bag full of Adrienne's stuff – her handbag, the burner phone, Hadfield's too, the towel we'd used to dry her off, the smashed whisky bottle – everything that could be incriminating.'

'What did you do with it?'

'I took out the sim cards so I could destroy them, then I put a couple of heavy rocks in the bin bag and dumped it in that reservoir near Laurence's house. Then I picked up the other burners over the next few days. I'd bought them all at once, you see, and I was paranoid that you might be able to trace them. I know I wasn't thinking clearly, but I went around everyone and got them new ones, from different shops, a place in Huddersfield, another in Bradford, and so on. Maybe I've got too much imagination, but I've seen TV programmes where the police work magic with mobile phones, so I wanted to leave no traces of the original batch.'

'What about Randall's and Sarah Chen's phones?'

'I assume Randall must have got rid of them himself. He may be a bastard, but he's not stupid. I didn't see or hear from either him or Sarah again after they left that night. Not until . . . you know.'

'We got as far as Argos,' said Banks, 'so your imagination probably served you well. What happened to Hadfield?'

'I waited and waited and I thought I heard something, a cry or something, from the moor, so I got out and went up after him. It was hard to see up there in the mist, and I was worried I'd trip over some roots and twist my ankle or something. But before I'd got far, I saw him. Laurence. He was lying at the bottom of a gully, about twenty feet down. It was a pretty clear view, and I had my phone light with me. I could tell right away that he was dead. His neck was at an odd angle, there was a lot of blood on the ground, and he wasn't moving. I called his name but got no answer. I couldn't figure out a way to get down there.'

'You didn't think to call an ambulance?'

'That would have meant questions. Just what we were trying to avoid. It was too late, anyway.'

'What questions were you trying to avoid? Remember, there was only you left now. You and Randall.'

'I didn't know about Sarah. Not then. How could I? I got no answer when I tried to call them to tell them to destroy their phones. I just assume Randall did it, anyway.'

'When did you find out about Sarah?'

'Not until the body was found and it was in the papers.'

'Randall didn't tell you?'

'No. Why would he?'

'He didn't ask for your help?'

'Obviously not.'

'Weren't you worried about Sarah, though, before her body was found?'

'Maybe a bit, when I couldn't get through to her, but I assumed she'd just got rid of her burner phone, as I wanted. It made sense for us to keep apart for a while, till things blew over.'

Banks sighed. 'Oh, dear. You ought to know that things like that never blow over.'

'Well, what would you have done?'

'So you left Laurence Hadfield for dead in the gully. Then what?'

'He *was* dead.' Mia seemed to sulk for a moment, then she said: 'I went back to his house to make sure everything was in order. Wiped any surfaces I thought I'd touched. Checked the bathroom again, checked for anything of Adrienne's that might still be there, clothes in the wardrobe and so on. Found nothing, so I left. I just dumped the bin bag in the water and went home. I was bloody exhausted by then.'

'I'll bet you were. And Adrienne was sitting dead in the broken-down car, Laurence Hadfield was lying at the bottom of the gully with a broken neck, and you'd no idea what had happened to Randall and Sarah?'

'That's right. I'm not proud of myself, but I didn't see what else I could have done at the time.'

Banks shook his head slowly. 'There were dozens of things you could have done, Mia, *should* have done, and none of them were what you actually did.'

'What will happen to me? Will I go to jail?'

'Honestly? I don't know. That depends on the Crown Prosecution Service.'

'But I didn't hurt anyone. I didn't kill anyone. You have to believe me.' Her voice took on a pleading tone.

'I know,' said Banks. Though he didn't. He didn't know whether Mia had sneaked up behind Laurence Hadfield on Tetchley Moor and given him a little shove. He would like to think she hadn't done, but he realised that he might never know for certain. As things stood, both Laurence Hadfield and Adrienne Munro had died by misadventure, and only Sarah Chen had been murdered.

'Anyway,' Mia said, turning her head to one side. 'I'm tired. And I could use that bedpan now.'

Banks would hardly have called the night out at the Queen's Arms a celebration, but it was tradition to mark the successful conclusion of a case. The whole Eastvale crew was there, such as it was – Annie, Gerry, Winsome, a few of the uniforms, Jazz Singh, Stefan Nowak, Vic Manson and several CSIs – along with Ken Blackstone, DCs Collier and Musgrave and a few other members of his team. Despite the jokes and laughter, such occasions always held a residual sadness for Banks, who couldn't help but think of, in this case, Adrienne Munro, Sarah Chen and Laurence Hadfield. In a way, the events of that fateful Saturday had been like the perfect storm. Things didn't need to have happened that way, but they had.

'Penny for them?' It was Annie plonking a pint in front of him on the table and sitting down beside him.

'What? Oh, just the usual, you know.'

Annie nodded and clinked glasses. 'To the fallen.'

'To the fallen.'

'So apart from Randall, nobody killed anybody else?'

'So it would appear.'

'What about Mia Carney? Will she do time?'

'I don't know,' said Banks. 'She'll have to face some charges, but I've talked to Diane from the CPS, and they'll probably strike some sort of bargain, after everything she's been through. She might avoid prison. I suppose they could charge her with interfering with a dead body, wasting police time, perverting the course of justice, tampering with evidence, maybe even pimping and Lord knows what else, if they wanted to make an example of her, but . . .'

'But what?'

'Well, she might have suspected that Randall killed Sarah, but wasn't involved. She's not an accessory to murder. And she should have called an ambulance for Laurence Hadfield. I know it sounds trite, but I think she's learned her lesson. Or *a* lesson.'

'Ever the optimist.'

Banks laughed. 'It's not often I get called that.'

'Don't fancy her, do you?'

'Don't be daft.'

'Methinks the man doth protest too much.'

'I like her spirit, that's all. There's something refreshing about her. But I don't like what she does. Anyway, I think she's found someone else. The last time I went to visit her I saw Leila heading in while I was on my way out. She was carrying a bunch of flowers.'

'Lucky Mia.'

'Especially after the way she treated Leila. Still, it takes all sorts.'

Annie clinked glasses again. 'Spoken like a true wise man.'

'You pissed already?'

'Getting there.'

'How's Ray?'

'Haven't seen him for a while.'

'Nothing wrong, is there?'

'No. I just haven't seen him.'

Winsome wandered over and started talking to Annie. Banks drifted back to his thoughts. The conversations drowned out most of the music, but he could pick out 'The Maigret Theme' among the general hubbub. Cyril's little joke. Though not, apparently. It had disappointed him slightly to find out from one of the temporary barmaids that it was an Internet radio channel and not hand-crafted sixties playlists that Cyril broadcast in the pub. Even so, the music was as good, wherever it came from. One of the Leeds DCs knocked over a pint and everyone cheered. Except Cyril.

'Keep it down, lads, keep it down,' he said. And most of those present took note.

Annie turned back to Banks. 'What do you think about Zelda's picture, then? Keane?' she asked.

'It's him, without a doubt.'

'Yes. But what do we do about it?'

'Haven't had time to think yet,' said Banks. 'Let's have lunch next week and talk about it.'

'Fine with me. The sooner we get the bastard, the better. By the way, have you heard from Zelda?'

'Not since she sent the picture.'

'Maybe you should introduce her to Mia?'

'Now that would be an interesting conversation.'

'Or not.'

Annie went over to join one of the Leeds detectives she'd had her eye on for a while.

Banks turned to Winsome. 'Is it true?' he asked.

'Is what true, guv?'

'That you're going to have a baby.'

'Who told you that?'

Banks put his finger to the side of his nose. 'I'm a detective, you know.'

Winsome laughed. 'Between you and me, yes. I'm *so* excited. But I don't want the whole station to know yet. It's early days.'

'My lips are sealed. Congratulations.' Banks raised his glass. 'Cheers.'

Winsome clinked with her diet tonic. 'I'll confess I'm a bit scared, too.'

'That's not unreasonable. I was just thinking I'll be down another officer soon. There'll only be me, Annie and Gerry left. Some Homicide and Major Crimes Unit.'

'I'll be around for a while yet, guv, don't you worry, and I'm sure HR will do something about finding a replacement for Doug.'

Banks got up and circulated among the crowd, offering congratulations here and there. At the bar, he bought another couple of pints and took one over to Annie, deep in conversation with her Leeds detective, then leaned back against the bar to survey the scene. They had already scared off most of the locals and tourists, so they practically had the place to themselves. Cyril was used to it, so he wasn't going to complain unless someone broke another glass. Banks looked out of one of the clear panes in the window across from the bar. The Christmas lights twinkled outside in the market square, and there were a few people standing outside around the pubs and restaurants enjoying the festive spirit, despite the drizzle and the winter chill.

He thought of Mia Carney and how foolish she had been. Had she really learned her lesson? Does anyone, ever? Wouldn't she be back at the same game again as soon as she recovered her health? He had to admit that he didn't know the answers, only that he didn't believe jail would do her a great deal of good. She had almost died, after all, and Randall's assault had left her with permanent, if not fatal, cardiac damage. And he wished her good luck with Leila.

Then he thought of Adrienne Munro, whom he had never known, who was so desperate for money to get through her studies and save the world from famine that she had prostituted herself. He assumed that he would never really know whether she had deliberately taken that overdose of Mandrax or simply tried to sedate herself enough to be able to handle what lay ahead that night, and drastically miscalculated. It was easy to do, according to Dr Glendenning, even if you knew something about drugs, which Adrienne didn't. There were still so many unknowns in the case, and they were likely to remain unknown. The one certainty was that Sarah Chen had been murdered, and Anthony Randall was going down for it. The skin under Sarah's fingernails had nailed him, along with the minute traces of her blood the CSIs had found in his drains.

Gene Pitney had just started singing 'Town Without Pity' when Banks saw the door swing open. Zelda stood there for a moment, framed in the doorway with a serious expression on her face, wearing her long winter coat and fur hat. She scanned the room, and when her eyes lit on Banks, she started walking towards him.

ACKNOWLEDGEMENTS

As usual, I have plenty of people to thank for helping me get this book ready for the road, starting with my wife Sheila Halladay, who read the first draft and sent me back to the word-processor with many valuable suggestions. At Hodder & Stoughton, I would like to thank my editor Carolyn Mays and her assistant Madeleine Woodfield, along with the rest of the gang: Jamie Hodder-Williams, Lucy Hale, Kerry Hood and Justine Taylor. At McClelland and Stewart, my thanks go to Kelly Joseph, Erin Kelly, Martha Leonard and Jared Bland, and at William Morrow, to Emily Krump and Julia Elliot. Also thanks to agents Dominick Abel, David Grossman and Rosie and Jessica Buckman. I would also like to thank the overseas editors and translators who have stuck with me over the years. Needless to say, there are many others who contribute, including proof-readers, sales reps, booksellers and librarians, and I would like to thank all those people, too. Last, but far from least, thanks also to you, dear reader.